HARMLESS

A Pier 70 Novel
NICOLE EDWARDS

BECAUSE NAUGHTY CAN BE OH SO NICE®
NE
LTD

By Nicole Edwards

The Alluring Indulgence Series
Kaleb
Zane
Travis
Holidays with the Walker Brothers
Ethan
Braydon
Sawyer
Brendon

The Austin Arrows Series
Rush
Kaufman

The Bad Boys of Sports Series
Bad Reputation
Bad Business

The Caine Cousins Series
Hard to Hold
Hard to Handle

The Club Destiny Series
Conviction
Temptation
Addicted
Seduction
Infatuation
Captivated
Devotion
Perception
Entrusted
Adored
Distraction

The Coyote Ridge Series
Curtis
Jared

The Dead Heat Ranch Series
Boots Optional
Betting on Grace
Overnight Love

Harmless

Pier 70, 4

NICOLE EDWARDS

Nicole Edwards Limited
PO Box 806
Hutto, Texas 78634
www.NicoleEdwardsLimited.com

Harmless – A Pier 70 Novel is a work of fiction. Names, characters, businesses, places, events and incidents either are the products of the author's imagination or used in a fictitious manner. Any resemblance to actual persons, living or dead, or actual events is purely coincidental.

Cover Image: © Wander Aguiar | wanderbookclub.com
Models: Jacob Cooley and Grant Foreman
Ebook Image: © magenta10 | 123rf.com (formatting image - 14284060)

Cover Design: © Nicole Edwards Limited
Editing: Blue Otter Editing | BlueOtterEditing.com

ISBN (ebook): 978-1-939786-78-4
ISBN (print): 978-1-939786-77-7

Gay Romance
Mature Audience

Dedication

Chancy Powley

For the endless amount of time you spend on the phone with me. Namely, those times you text and say "Hey, can I call you real quick?" and it turns out to be a 3 hour phone call. Those are my favorite. So, thank you.

Prologue

Fourteen months ago
August

"CAN I BUY you another drink?"

Roan Gregory hoped he wasn't sporting his *who me* look when he cast a quick glance up and to the left, startled by the offer from…

Well. Okay.

Not what he'd expected.

Standing before him was the sexy guy who'd been checking Roan out since he walked in the door. Discreetly, sure. But Roan's attention had been unfocused at best. He'd noticed. And yes, this was the same guy Roan had fought hard not to sneak a peek at for the past hour.

The guy was totally his type back when he'd had a type. At least in the physical sense.

Blond hair, blue eyes, long and lean, with the perfect balance of muscles tossed in.

But that was the key. Roan didn't have a type anymore. He was more interested in ignoring men for the duration.

Sexy Guy nodded toward the empty beer bottle in front of Roan. "Another?"

As though the guy wasn't possibly talking to him, Roan continued to stare. Only this time, he was captivated by the seductive smirk on Sexy Guy's smooth lips. *Nice* lips. Full, *perfect* ... lips.

Obliterating the thought from his sex-starved brain, Roan dropped his gaze down to his beer. Yep, definitely empty. He must've drained it when he'd been lost in his own damn thoughts. Unfortunately—no matter what his *little* head was telling him—he wasn't interested in company, sexy or otherwise, so he wanted Sexy Guy to go sit back down at the table by the wall where he'd come from.

"I'm good." Shaking his head, Roan avoided the man's eyes, hoping he would take the hint.

"I figured if you're gonna drown your sorrows, probably should do it right."

If Sexy Guy only knew.

Lifting his gaze once more, Roan met the determined steel-blue eyes still studying him. He bit back a retort. Didn't the guy understand that he wanted to be alone? Seriously, what did he need to do? Hold up a sign that said, PERSONAL PITY PARTY, NO COMPANY WANTED?

What the...?

Clearly Roan needed to improve his turn-down skills. Sexy Guy surely mistook his *I'm good* for *sure, sit down and join me* because, of course, Sexy Guy was now sitting at his table. And he hadn't bothered to ask.

"I promise, I'm harmless." To reiterate his point, Sexy Guy held up his hands in surrender.

Big hands. Nice hands. *Perfect* hands.

Son of a bitch.

Now that Roan thought about it, the guy didn't look harmless. He looked like ... well, hell, he looked like temptation.

Good thing he'd cut temptation from his diet long ago.

Leaning back, Roan tried to appear casual, not wanting to show that he was taken aback by the guy's forwardness. He also didn't want the incredibly handsome blond to see that Roan was discreetly attempting to check him out. Mainly, the way that snug charcoal-gray T-shirt stretched across his impressive chest and the way the corded muscles in his neck shifted inconspicuously when he lifted his arm.

How discreet he was actually being was anyone's guess since there was only about three feet between them.

Not only was he at least an eleven, Sexy Guy also looked familiar. Eerily so. Only Roan couldn't place him.

Roan shrugged off the thought and continued to stare the guy down.

For the past half hour, Roan had been nursing a beer while pretending to watch the baseball game playing on the television closest to him. He wasn't really paying attention at all because his brain was inundated with how shitty he'd allowed his life to become. In fact, he'd been paying so little attention he *had* noticed that the handsome man now sitting across from him had been staring his way every so often.

After the guy signaled the waitress for two more beers, he turned back to Roan.

Bold move considering Roan had already told him he wasn't interested. Or that had been his meaning anyway.

"Colton Seguine," Sexy Guy said smoothly as he held out his hand.

Roan detected an accent, but he couldn't quite place it. Canadian, maybe?

"Not interested," Roan grumbled, ignoring the introduction, hoping the guy would get it through his thick skull that Roan wasn't...

Wait.

Did he say...?

The name registered and Roan's gaze slammed directly into the big guy.

Wavy blond hair, a thin scar running through one of his thick eyebrows, pale blue eyes with the perfect balance of gray running through them, a slightly crooked nose, and a jaw that looked as though it had been carved from stone, not to mention sharp cheekbones and those lips...

Holy shit.

The harmless temptation sitting across from him was none other than a fucking hockey player.

Harmless. *Right.*

"You're Colton Seguine," Roan muttered, feeling stupid.

The guy's lopsided smirk transformed his face from sexy to ... hot as fuck. "That's what they tell me, but everyone calls me Seg. Unfortunately, I don't recognize you, so..."

Roan held out his hand seeing that Seg's was resting on the table as though waiting for this moment. "Roan Gregory."

"Nice to meet you, Roan Gregory."

Yes, it was.

Seg's hand was strong, his grip firm. And holy fuck. This was Colton Seguine. Seg.

Roan briefly forgot all of his problems as he stared at the defenseman for the Austin Arrows hockey team. He knew the man was big—he'd read his stats a few dozen times—but up close and personal, he was ginormous. Six foot four, two-twenty, if Roan remembered correctly.

The waitress interrupted their staring contest when she delivered their beers, and for a few seconds, Roan was caught up in those smoky blue eyes, unable to look away.

It no longer mattered that he'd been wallowing in self-pity, trying to get over the fact that nearly four months ago he'd professed his love for his best friend. He no longer felt the chest-constricting pain that had engulfed him as soon as he realized Cam had fallen in love with someone and they were incredibly happy. The pain hadn't come from the fact that Cam and Gannon were happy. As far as he was concerned, that was a good thing. It came from the fact that Roan had been insecure enough to think he would lose his friendship with the most important person in his life.

Only right now, the fact that he'd blurted out that he loved his best friend seemed unimportant—not to mention, completely untrue.

Nope. None of it mattered because his brain was misfiring; the only thing he could think about was sex. Sex with this incredibly sexy hockey player. Dirty, rough, highly-erotic sex.

And wasn't that a kick in the nuts? Roan wasn't the sort to succumb to insta-lust. It usually took him some time to warm up to a guy. A hell of a lot longer than a brief introduction anyway.

Roan took a long pull on his beer, breaking the eye contact.

This was insane.

Why the hell would this guy even be over here? It wasn't like he was...

Nah. No way was this guy gay.

Plus, if he was—which he wasn't—there was no way Seg would know Roan was gay. Seriously. How would he know? They weren't in a gay bar. And it wasn't like Roan was wearing his *I'm out and proud* T-shirt today.

The thought had Roan staring at Seg thoughtfully.

Did he know Roan was gay? Was it something he broadcasted without realizing it?

After glancing around the room cautiously, Seg leaned in and lowered his voice. "What do you say after this beer, I take you back to my place and we have a drink there?"

Okay, so maybe along with some finely tuned gaydar, Seg was gay.

Not openly, obviously, since Roan distinctly remembered a recent article about Seg and some model chick he'd been dating as of late. Yes, in case there was any confusion, Roan was a fan of the Austin Arrows. *Huge* fan.

Maybe Seg was bisexual?

Roan let that thought roll around for a few seconds. He didn't do bisexual. He had absolutely no intention of being with some guy who would wake up the next morning, crying and whining because he was so fucking confused about his life. Pussy or dick, it wasn't that hard to figure out which you preferred.

Not to mention, Roan didn't need that shit on top of everything else he was dealing with.

Leaning closer, mirroring Seg's posture, Roan shook his head. "I'm pretty sure"—he tilted his head toward the waitress—"*she's* more your type."

Seg leaned even closer. "I'm pretty sure ... you're dead wrong."

Roan sat up straight, taking another pull on his beer as he studied this man.

Here was a guy Roan had watched play for years. A guy who was as masculine as they came. A guy who was now sitting here, in this sports bar, coming on to him.

He was coming on to him, right? Roan had been out of the game a long time; maybe he was imagining it.

He instantly thought about Cam. About how Roan had damn near fucked up their friendship because of his momentary lapse in judgement. His stupid freak out had nearly cost him the most important person in his life.

Then he thought about his sister and her fucking drug problem.

And his father, who was beside himself on how to help her.

His stepmother, who had threatened to leave his father if they didn't find a way to get Cassie some help.

A fucking mess was what his life had been reduced to.

No way should Roan add fucking a hockey player to that long list of screwed-up bullshit.

Clearly Seg sensed Roan was considering the idea. "One night. No strings."

Nope, no mistaking *that* come-on.

Roan considered it.

No-strings sex. Was there even such a thing?

Roan adjusted his position, trying not to give the idea the merit it deserved, but unable to help himself.

A one-night stand with a hot hockey player.

Who could really say no to that? More importantly, who *would*?

His world was crumbling down around him, and this guy was offering him an opportunity to forget about it for a little while. An opportunity he'd be stupid to pass up.

"One night?" Roan confirmed.

Seg nodded.

"Tomorrow we pretend this never happened?"

Another nod.

Downing what was left of his beer, Roan reached for his wallet, pulled out a couple of twenties, and slapped them on the table before getting to his feet.

"I'll follow you," he told Seg.

The grin on Seg's face made Roan's dick jump to life.

Oh, yeah. This was definitely a good decision.

COLTON SEGUINE—NICKNAMED Seg during his early years playing hockey—would likely have a million regrets come tomorrow, but right now, as he pulled up to his house, he couldn't think of one.

Well, other than he hoped like hell no one had noticed him coming on to the hot guy who'd looked as though he needed something to focus on other than his personal problems.

Right. Because *that* was why Seg had come on to him.

It had been a first for him.

Coming on to a guy in a public place.

A guy he hadn't even been sure was gay. It'd been a huge risk, but there'd been something about the man that had called to him. Seg had spent the better part of an hour trying to ignore the desire to talk to him, but in the end, he hadn't been able to resist.

He'd known from the second he got up from his table to approach him that his actions could potentially change the course of the rest of his life. Yet he'd done it anyway.

Looked as though the risk had paid off.

In his rearview mirror, he saw the big blue Chevrolet pulling in behind him and the hot-as-fuck guy sitting behind the wheel.

Nope. No regrets.

Not yet.

From the instant he'd set his sights on Roan Gregory—with his dark honey-gold hair, matching golden eyes, and conventionally handsome face—back at the sports bar, Seg had been intrigued. Like, sneak-off-to-the-bathroom-and-get-this-crazy-lust-out-of-our-system intrigued. Enough that Seg had spent an hour watching Roan before he got the nerve up to talk to him. That in itself wasn't an easy feat considering he wasn't looking to make his interest known. Not to anyone other than Roan Gregory, that was.

Pretending not to be interested took finesse. Seg had long ago mastered it.

Although he knew the risks of giving in to his sexual desires, Seg hadn't been able to resist. There was something dark and intriguing about this guy. Something that made him want to peel back the brooding outer layer to the sexy guy underneath.

It'd helped that they hadn't been at Seg's usual hangout. Had they been at the Penalty Box, Seg wouldn't have been able to approach him at all because someone he knew would've seen him.

He chalked it up to right place, right time.

And now they were at Seg's house.

Better place, perfect time.

After climbing out of his Range Rover, Seg walked around to meet Roan between the vehicles. He was shocked that Roan had followed him. During the ten-minute drive back to his house, he'd expected Roan to veer off and disappear. But he hadn't, which meant one night, no strings sounded as good to Roan as it did to him.

Seg led the way up the wide concrete stairs to his front door. He typed in the code to unlock the deadbolt, then turned the knob and waited for Roan to precede him, all while managing to pretend this was a normal, everyday thing for him. Truth was, he'd never picked up a guy in a bar before. In fact, he'd only been with two men in his life, and both of those instances had been after far too many drinks—for both parties involved—and with very few memories of the actual events.

For some strange reason, Seg wanted memories of tonight. He wanted to be able to think back on them for as long as they'd last. Maybe he was simply getting older and tired of the same old bullshit. Or—a much more likely answer—he was tired of being someone he wasn't.

The steady beep of the alarm system had Seg moving to the keypad by the door. He quickly punched in the code to disarm the system. He turned back to find Roan's gaze scanning the room.

Seg eyed Roan as he took everything in. The man's short hair was in chaotic disarray, as though he'd run his fingers through it a dozen times. Which Seg knew he had because he'd watched him. He'd had no clue what was on the guy's mind, but whatever it was had to be weighing heavily on him because he'd seemed distraught.

Hence the reason Seg had so boldly invited himself to Roan's table.

And now, here, Roan looked somewhat less stressed, as well as incredibly casual in his navy blue polo pulled snug across a nice upper body and dark jeans that hugged a very impressive ass.

What did this guy do for a living?

Wait. That didn't matter. This was a one-time thing. No personal shit to ruin that.

Seg didn't need to know if the guy was married, separated, recovering from a bad breakup. He didn't need to know where Roan lived or worked, if he spent a lot of time with his friends or got along with his parents. He knew the guy was old enough to drink, wasn't wearing a wedding band, and that he was sexy as fuck. Plus, he seemed fairly adamant that this thing between them fizzle out in just a few hours.

Yeppers, they were going to have fun tonight.

"How about a beer?" Seg suggested, sensing the tension in Roan.

Yeah, this was a hookup. No doubt about that. He wasn't even going to pretend otherwise. Based on Roan's reaction, he didn't mind a one-night stand, which was exactly how Seg wanted it to be.

And he knew he'd made the right choice when Roan had recognized him yet still managed to keep his cool. Oftentimes, when he had conversations with men—straight, gay, whatever—Seg would be inundated with hockey chitchat by this point, and he wasn't really looking to talk.

Tall, golden, and brooding was just his cup of tea.

Speaking of tea…

Before he could turn toward the kitchen, Roan ambled over to him and came to a stop less than a foot away. He was a few inches shorter and probably a good thirty pounds lighter, which Seg liked immensely. Although he got an intensely alpha vibe from Roan, Seg knew he'd have the upper hand here. For all of ten seconds, those golden eyes searched Seg's face, and he waited to hear what Roan would come up with.

Had he changed his mind? Was he going to start talking hockey?

"I no longer want a drink," Roan muttered, and Seg felt a hint of insecurity right then.

As he was gearing up to suggest something else—grapes, cheese, ice cream … fuck, anything—Seg kept his eyes on Roan. He couldn't figure out what he wanted to say, but that didn't matter for long, because the next thing he knew, Roan's lips were on his and they were…

Damn.

Warm, smooth, firm.

Roan smelled like sin and tasted like beer and man and erotic promises. A combination that had Seg's dick throbbing incessantly, desperate for attention.

Mouth to mouth had never been this fucking good. There wasn't an ounce of hesitation in the kiss, but Seg knew just how much to give to ensure Roan didn't mistakenly believe he was in charge. Before that could happen, Seg gripped Roan's head, spearing his hair with his fingers and then spinning them both around. Using his full body weight, Seg pushed Roan against the door. Hard.

Their dicks ground together, although the only friction came from the denim that separated them. Seg wanted to get closer. He wanted to feel this man's skin beneath his palms. He wanted to run his hands over every hard plane, every sharp angle, and kiss every inch of him, then sink deep and…

Goddamn, it had been so fucking long. Too long. This man was like chocolate, a treat Seg had no choice but to keep himself from craving too damn much. He wasn't one to give in to temptation, because he knew the repercussions.

"I don't bottom," Roan grumbled against Seg's lips.

Seg managed to pull back enough to look into Roan's eyes. "If you're gonna be with me you do."

Expecting a full rebuttal, Seg didn't move. He waited patiently while Roan's eyes locked with his before dropping once again to Seg's mouth. He was fairly certain there was a battle brewing there. When Roan's eyes met his once again, it appeared as though Roan had settled it.

"Fuck it," Roan whispered, then crushed his lips to Seg's once more.

Good answer.

The kiss went nuclear.

Seg would've been content to stand here in his lavish foyer and fuck this incredibly sexy man against the wall, but he had other things in mind. It'd been so long since he'd given in to these urges. He needed a little more than a quick fuck.

But not too much more.

He managed to walk them toward his bedroom, their lips still locked together, hands fumbling. By the time they reached their destination, they'd relieved one another of their shirts, and Seg was already working on Roan's jeans while Roan kicked off his shoes.

Breaking the kiss, Seg ran his lips over Roan's stubble-lined jaw, working his way lower, pushing his jeans down as he went. The guy smelled good. Like the outdoors and … something musky. It was intoxicating. He kissed his way down the hard plane of Roan's sun-bronzed chest, over the gentle ripples of his abs, trailing the thin line of hair that led downward until he was on his knees before him.

Staring up into those golden-brown eyes, he waited to see if Roan would say something.

He didn't.

Seg took that as permission to continue.

It only took a moment to free Roan's dick from his jeans, and when he did, Seg took a deep breath, stroking the thick, velvety length in his fist while he ran his tongue over the swollen head.

He could count on one finger the number of times he'd done this. Not once during his previous encounters with men had he dared to take a cock into his mouth, yet he was salivating with the need to do so now.

Roan hissed, his fingers digging into Seg's hair, holding him in place. Seg didn't mind the rough treatment. In fact, he preferred it.

"Put my dick in your mouth. All the way," Roan groaned, the demand in his tone not to be mistaken.

Seg slid his lips over the smooth head, then sucked Roan into his mouth. The warm flesh slid over his tongue, forcing his jaw wider as Roan's dick filled the space completely.

Another hiss escaped Roan, along with a tightening of his grip as he pulled Seg toward him. Giving the man what he needed, Seg took every inch of Roan's thick cock, all the way to the back of his throat.

"Fuck, that's nice," Roan mumbled, holding Seg still as he began pumping his hips.

Their eyes locked momentarily and Seg wondered if Roan knew this was a first for him.

Seg allowed Roan to use his mouth, to fuck his face. He held on to Roan's hips, dug his fingertips into his glutes, and took every inch as deep as he could, gagging a few times before Roan would pull out. He couldn't even remember the last time he'd been with a man. It'd been so damn long, and now that he was here, tasting, touching, devouring, he wasn't sure how he'd managed to hold back his urges all this time.

You're in the closet, dumb ass.

Well, there was that.

No way could he risk his teammates finding out that he preferred to be with men. That would just be awkward, and he loved his job too damn much to risk being ousted because he was gay.

There was a stigma associated with gay professional athletes, and Seg wasn't interested in fighting that uphill battle. Instead, he pretended to be straight, going out with women, even sleeping with a couple here and there to ease some of the frustration and appease all the curious people, although it never worked. He was never sated. Pussy just didn't do it for him.

When Roan urged him to get up with a tug on his hair, Seg got to his feet and slammed his mouth over Roan's. A few minutes of fumbling ensued while they rid themselves of their remaining clothing. Shoes were kicked off, jeans and underwear discarded, socks followed.

And then they were both naked. Hot skin against hot skin.

Seg shoved Roan onto the bed, then reached for a condom and the lube in the table beside his bed. Good thing he preferred a slick palm when he jacked off, or they would've been shit out of luck.

Without a word, Seg gloved his dick, greased up, and then crawled on the mattress just as Roan was turning over onto his stomach.

A frisson of disappointment shot through him. He'd wanted to look at the man while he was buried deep in his ass, but this would work, too.

"Fast and dirty? That what you want?"

"That's *all* I want," Roan confirmed.

Okay then.

Without romance or finesse, Seg guided his dick to Roan's ass and slowly sank inside.

He didn't offer foreplay, didn't tease with his fingers, simply pushed himself inside, allowing the tight ring of muscle to grip him and pull him in deep. Still, he went slow, not wanting to hurt Roan. The man had informed him he didn't bottom, yet here he was. Seg felt an overwhelming responsibility to make this good for Roan.

The heat of Roan's body was like a furnace, engulfing him, sending electrical sparks firing beneath his skin.

So good.

Too good.

Son of a bitch.

Had it been like this before? Seg didn't remember, but he seriously doubted it. Shit, he seriously doubted anything had ever felt as fucking good as being lodged inside this man's ass.

Roan's head tilted back and Seg reached around him, cupping his neck without applying any pressure while he kissed Roan's cheek, his ear, his jaw.

"Hurt?"

Roan shook his head.

"Want me to fuck you hard?"

Roan nodded.

Seg pulled his hips back and slammed home, burying himself to the hilt inside Roan's tight ass. He groaned from the pure bliss that consumed his entire body. The hair on his arms stood on end as the sensations exploded through him. Fucking felt amazing.

While Roan jerked himself, Seg pounded into him, enjoying the way Roan's body strangled his dick, the way Roan pushed back against him, taking all of him. Their grunts and groans echoed in the room, spurring Seg on.

When he knew he was close, he turned Roan's head so he could claim his mouth. It was an awkward angle, but Roan didn't resist, their tongues dueling while Seg continued to thrust deep and hard.

Roan jerked his mouth away, a tortured moan escaping him. "Fuck, yes... Don't stop... Fuck... Don't you dare fucking stop."

Seg continued drilling him hard until Roan cried out as he climaxed. Only then did he give in, letting himself go right over the edge with him.

After a few seconds, Seg pulled out and dropped to his side, placing his hand on Roan's back.

"That was pretty damn good," he said, keeping his tone neutral, his lungs fighting for air.

"Not bad."

Seg chuckled. "Want to try it again? We've still got the rest of the night."

Roan rolled over and glanced at Seg. For a second, he thought the man was going to tell him he had to bolt. Instead, Roan sighed. "Yeah. A beer would be good. Then I could probably go for round two."

If Seg had his way, they wouldn't be stopping with round two.

One

Friday, October 14th

ROAN KNEW HE shouldn't have come. And not only because he risked running into the one man he'd been doing his best to forget about completely.

Sure, that was a concern—more so since Cam informed him they'd get a chance to meet the team after the game—but he was more concerned that he'd left his sister at home alone this afternoon and something had felt off.

Seriously off.

In fact, he'd been worried enough that during the third period of the game, he'd snuck out to the concourse and called her, but she hadn't answered, and now he was having to go meet the team with his friends. On a normal day, this would've been a dream come true. Today, not so much.

Good God, a year and a half ago, Roan would've shit monkeys if someone asked him to go meet the Austin Arrows. Unfortunately, a lot of shit had gone down since then. He'd had an unforgettable one-night stand with one of the players and... Well, there was too much other stuff to think about right now. So much that Roan's entire world was flipped upside down and sideways. No way was this night going to end well.

For one, by going to the locker room, he risked coming face-to-face with Seg. A man he'd promised himself he would never think about again. Not the way he found himself thinking about him anyway. There were a million reasons keeping a safe distance from the famous defenseman was imperative. One, the guy was definitely in the closet, and it wasn't a secret that Roan had no interest in being some guy's closet play toy. Remarkable sex or not.

And two, Roan needed to check on his sister. He was worried and there was this strange buzzing in his head. It was like a warning that he needed to get home. Although he hadn't talked to her, Cassie had texted him a couple of hours ago.

She'd been in pure bitch form, of course.

I wish you'd leave me alone. I'm fine. I don't need you checking up on me. In fact, why don't you find someone else to bother tonight because I'm not in the mood to deal with your shit.

Roan had fought the urge to shoot off a message telling her exactly how he felt. That particular text was actually one of the nicer ones he'd received from her. Most of them told him he was an asshole, that all the bad shit that had ever happened to her was his fault. Somehow he always managed to bite his tongue and not give her a piece of his mind. Ever since her drug problem had become *his* problem, Roan hadn't been dealing with it well.

So, he had given himself a few minutes to calm down, then shot a quick text back, letting Cassie know he'd be home as soon as the game was over. Before he could even get the phone back in his pocket, another text had come through: *Fuck you, Roan. I hate you, and I wish you'd leave me the fuck alone.*

Yep, pure bitch mode seemed to be her only setting these days.

Following behind Cam and Gannon as they led the way to the locker room, Roan did his best to disappear into the background. He wasn't going to ruin anyone's night by insisting they head out now, but he didn't have to be all gung ho about it either. He slowed his steps, trying to let Teague and Hudson go in front of him. Even though it meant he would not get to personally meet any of the players, Roan did not need to be the guy at the front.

Teague's head pivoted as he looked at Roan, confusion forming a wrinkle in his forehead. "Going somewhere? Looks to me like you're trying to hide from someone."

Not in the mood to deal with anyone's shit, Roan mumbled, "Shut the hell up."

Of course, that went right over Teague's head. "Not all that fun to get your balls busted, huh?"

Roan bit his lower lip to keep from saying anything. Okay, fine. He probably deserved that. He had personally busted Teague's balls—figuratively, of course—on more than one occasion.

"Guys," Phoenix Pierce—the owner of the Austin Arrows—prompted, "I'm sure he doesn't need an introduction, but this is Spencer Kaufman, the Arrows captain."

While Roan lingered behind them, he watched as Cam shook Spencer's hand, his eyes wide, his jaw nearly on the floor. It almost made Roan laugh. Almost.

"And that over there is Kingston Rush, the man in the net."

Roan glanced over to see the Arrows goalie talking to a reporter, but he didn't get to watch for long because they were on the move again, following Phoenix toward another group of guys. He didn't pay much attention as Phoenix rattled off names. Roan already knew who the players were. He'd been a fan for a long damn time.

"And this right here is the man of the night," Phoenix noted with pride in his voice. "Colton Seguine, defense. Seg, these are some friends of mine. They own the marina out on Lake Buchanan."

Shit.

Shit, shit, shit.

Roan let his gaze slide to the concrete floor, hoping to become invisible.

Unfortunately, that didn't work, because he felt those cool blue eyes land on him, and he couldn't resist looking up and meeting them head on.

Don't let him talk to me. Don't let him talk to me.

For a brief moment, he had to wonder whether Seg even remembered him. It was possible that the man had so many one-night stands that he couldn't keep track. Unfortunately, Roan didn't have that luxury. And since Seg had been his last one-night stand, which meant he'd also been the last man Roan had been with, it wasn't quite so easy for him to forget. Still, in the past year, Roan had never once seen an article or story tying Seg with another man. Women, definitely. Which meant Seg was still guarding his secret. And Roan reminded himself again that the sex might've been the best he'd ever had, but it wasn't good enough for him to spend the rest of his life hiding out, so a repeat was definitely out of the question.

He was tired of people being ashamed of him. Hell, his own mother had walked out on them when Roan was sixteen. The homophobic bitch had claimed he was cursed and wanted nothing to do with the devil's work, so she packed a suitcase and abandoned them all. From that moment on, Roan had vowed that he would never be embarrassed by who he was. Not for the woman who'd given birth to him, and certainly not for a guy whose bed he'd occupied for only a few hours.

The thought made him snort and he felt more eyes turn his way.

Looking up, he met Cam's concerned stare.

"We done here?" Okay, so he sounded like a dick, but Roan really needed to get away from Seg. The man was not good for his health.

As it was, he'd enjoyed many sessions with his own hand by remembering that one night. It didn't make pretending it never happened any easier when that delicious temptation was standing only a few feet away. Even disheveled and sweaty from the game, he was hot.

Phoenix cleared his throat as though he sensed Roan's tension. "Again, thanks for coming out tonight. Tickets for the games are yours whenever you want them. I've gotta go catch up with my husband and wife. I'm sure they're looking for me."

As those words processed, Roan glared at Seg. Here was a man who was too afraid to come out of the closet, yet the owner of his freaking team was bisexual and in a long-term, committed relationship with a woman *and* a man.

Roan turned away from the others and started for the parking lot. He'd done his part. Night was officially over.

"Hey!"

Or not.

Shit. That voice... He still heard that deep baritone in his fucking dreams.

Pretending he hadn't heard him, Roan continued walking, stopping only when a big hand landed on his shoulder. He dropped his head in resignation. He was not going to get out of here without facing this man.

"How's it going? Roan, right?" Seg asked, sounding as though he was catching up with an old friend.

Roan pivoted to face him, cocking an eyebrow and hoping to hide his surprise at being approached like this. Here. In front of all these people.

What was Seg doing? He should've just let Roan walk away and they could've pretended not to know each other. The handshake was the clincher though. Acquaintances coming face-to-face again.

"Fine. You?" Did he sound as casual? He hoped so.

Roan took a quick look around to see who was watching. They all were, damn it.

"You were great tonight," Roan said, trying not to meet Seg's eyes.

"Yeah. Thanks. Hey, the guys go over to the Penalty Box on nights we win." Seg glanced over at Cam and Gannon, then back to Roan. "It's not too far from here. Maybe you and your friends can stop by. Hang out. Have a beer to celebrate. It would be great to catch up."

"Sorry. Can't. I've gotta get home. Need to check on…" Roan shook his head. He didn't need to explain himself to this man.

"All right. Cool, man." Seg seemed to be studying him. "Good to see you."

"Yeah. You, too." Roan didn't want to sound like such a prick, but it hadn't been all that easy putting Seg in his past the first time around. He didn't trust himself around him, and he damn sure didn't have the time or patience to deal with this. He had more than enough on his plate, and a one-night stand repeat sounded just about perfect to him right now.

However, it wouldn't sound good tomorrow.

Maybe he was imagining it, but Roan thought he saw a glimpse of hurt in Seg's eyes. He tried to remember what he could've said to put that look there, but he couldn't come up with anything. They'd both agreed to one night. The next morning, Roan had bolted before Seg even opened his eyes, which had seemed like the right thing to do. He hadn't expected to encounter the guy again. And he certainly hadn't anticipated the man approaching him.

Roan glanced over and noticed everyone was still watching them.

Ahh. Maybe that was what Seg was worried about. That Roan had leaked his secret.

"Later, man." He purposely tried to sound "straight" enough for Seg to get his drift.

As he held Seg's gaze, Roan realized it would've been so easy to head over to whatever bar Seg had mentioned, pretend to be friends with Seg for a little while, then sneak away, go back to Seg's house, and let him fuck the daylights out of him one more time.

Yeah. Stupid idea.

"Why don't you give me your number," Seg suggested. "Maybe y'all can come hang out sometime."

Roan knew if he turned Seg down, the others would start asking questions. They would want to know why Roan didn't jump at the chance to hang out with the Arrows players.

Instead of telling him no, Roan sighed, then fished a card out of his wallet. He kept a few for the marina on him. He was simply going to pass it over, but Seg produced a Sharpie marker out of thin air, and he had no choice but to write his number on it. That was what Seg wanted, apparently.

If Seg only knew all the stuff Roan was dealing with, he'd probably put his hands up in surrender and run—not walk—away. He damn sure wouldn't be considering a repeat, and based on the heat Roan saw in Seg's eyes, he was definitely considering it.

After jotting down his cell phone number—he would kick himself later for that one—Roan passed over the card and the marker. Then, rather than wait for Seg to say anything more, he turned and walked away. He didn't even wait for Cam and Gannon. They would catch up to him eventually.

DAMN, HE LOOKED good.

Seg watched Roan until the man disappeared out of sight. He had to fight the ridiculous urge to follow him, to chase him down just so he could talk to the guy for a little while. However, he knew that would be insane. Namely because he couldn't show his interest.

Not here anyway.

He'd already taken too much of a risk as it was. There were too many eyes on them, and although Seg had played it off as seeing an old friend, he didn't want these guys getting any ideas.

He had to figure he'd pulled it off considering the incinerating look Roan had given him when Seg pretended to hardly remember him. Oh, Roan didn't have to worry about that. Seg remembered him. In fact, he recalled every little detail about the man.

Squaring his shoulders, Seg turned back to Roan's friends. "Great to meet you guys. The invite to the Penalty Box stands if anyone's interested."

For a second, he thought they might take him up on it, but then they each started rumbling off things they had to do. Seg boldly met the blue eyes of the biggest guy, holding his stare for a moment. He could see a million questions in the man's eyes. Seg didn't miss the fact that the guy was holding hands with the skinnier guy with glasses standing beside him. Clearly they were open and out, and if Seg had to guess, this guy was trying to imagine Seg and Roan together.

"Cool," he said, starting back down the hall. "Have a good night."

Shit. He'd been stupid to approach Roan in the first place, but the instant he'd seen him, he couldn't help himself. He usually had more self-control than that. Especially since his entire career could go down the drain if he was outed. He could practically picture the looks on his teammates' faces. And opposing teams… Yeah, no thank you.

No guy was worth that hassle.

Of course, that thought triggered the memory of that one night he'd spent with Roan. The one night he desperately wanted a repeat of because there was absolutely no way it could've been as good as his memories claimed it was.

"Great to meet you," the big guy said.

"Y'all played awesome tonight," the guy with glasses stated.

Seg offered a curt chin nod as his only response to Roan's friends. He tried to pretend those weren't curious glances he got, but unfortunately, he knew they were. And that meant Seg was going to have to find some chick to bang in order to counter any of the fucking rumors that would likely start because he hadn't been able to hide his surprise when he saw Roan.

He tried to tell himself that the only thing he wanted to do was talk to Roan. To ensure Roan hadn't mentioned their encounter to anyone, maybe to find a little closure because he'd spent far too much time thinking about the man over the past year. Unfortunately, he had never managed to get Roan's phone number or address. Why would he? It'd been a one-nighter.

Seg fingered the card in his hand. But he had Roan's phone number now.

"Shit." He pivoted on his heel and headed back to the locker room. He needed to spend some time on the bike before he called it a night. If he didn't, his muscles would lock up and he'd be hating life.

Forty minutes later, as he walked to his SUV parked in the players' lot, Seg pulled up his contacts and added Roan's information in his phone. Then he hit the button to send a text. Once inside the Range Rover, he started the engine and then took a moment to shoot off a message.

It was great to see you tonight. Wondered if maybe you'd like to get together. Hang out. Talk. Maybe you could stop by my house for a drink sometime.

There. That sounded hetero enough.

He hit send.

Seg didn't expect a response, but he needed to make the effort. No matter how hard he tried, he couldn't stop thinking about Roan. For months on end, he had thought about the man. Fourteen months, to be exact. To the point of distraction even. The fact that he'd stressed over being outed could've very well been the underlying reason for Seg's shitty end to the season last year. The team was going through some major changes right now thanks to the way they'd handled things, but until Seg had some assurance from Roan, he wasn't sure how far past it he'd be able to go.

Or so he told himself.

The fact that no one had looked at him sideways since then should've been enough confirmation. He seriously doubted Roan had said anything. If he had, someone would've called him on it. Even the guys Roan was with tonight seemed none the wiser.

Still, he worried.

It hadn't been until the morning after, when Seg had woken up to an empty bed, that he'd started sweating it. He and Roan hadn't done a whole hell of a lot of talking that night. In fact, before he'd drifted off, Seg had made a mental note to talk to Roan the next morning. Make sure he wasn't going to say something and to let him know that if he did, he'd deny the accusation.

Dropping the phone into the cup holder, Seg shifted into drive and started out of the parking lot, memories of that one night with Roan flashing in his mind.

"Fuck, yes," Seg hissed. "You've got a fantastic mouth."

Seg sat naked on the kitchen counter, holding tight to Roan's hair as the man deep-throated him like a pro. So much for grabbing snacks from the refrigerator. He much preferred this interesting turn of events.

"Mmmm..." Roan hummed, making electrical sparks shoot straight to Seg's balls.

As good as the blow job felt, he wasn't ready to come again. Not yet.

"We need food," Seg mumbled, tugging on Roan's hair.

"I've got what I'm hungry for," Roan countered.

Using a little more force, Seg managed to pull Roan back. He quickly hopped off the counter, jerking Roan into him and kissing him hard.

God, he could get used to this. Never had he been this consumed by lust before. His entire body seemed to vibrate with it.

"I say we eat," Seg suggested. "Then we shower."

Roan leaned in closer, nibbling Seg's ear. "I agree. Then I say you let me eat your ass."

Fuck. Seg's ass clenched at the thought. No one had ever done that to him before. And vice versa.

Roan's gaze stroked across Seg's face, and he wondered if Roan had figured him out yet.

Seg grinned. "And then I get to fuck you again. This time while you're looking at me."

Something passed in Roan's eyes, but Seg didn't know what it was. He chose to ignore it because it didn't matter.

He slipped out from between Roan and the counter and made his way to the refrigerator. There was plenty of food to choose from. The housekeeper had made sure to stock his favorites, even prepared him a few meals he would simply have to heat up. Seg wasn't big on cooking for one and he'd started boycotting fast food long ago. Eating alone at a restaurant wasn't high on his to-do list either, so he'd learned to stock up on stuff that was easy to put together.

Roan reached around him and grabbed a beer while Seg pulled out what he needed for sandwiches. He was starving, and if he intended to go at this all night—which he did—they both needed to replenish.

Half an hour later, Seg had fumbled his way to the shower with Roan practically wrapped around him. They'd made quick work of the food, but his hunger was still burning hot. Only this time, he wanted to devour this man.

They managed to soap up and rinse off, although Seg wasn't sure how that happened when they were basically glued together at the mouth. Kissing Roan was unbelievably good. Not once had Seg ever felt anything like this. The notable differences being the rough scrape of Roan's stubble against his cheek, the firm, callused fingers stroking over his skin…

It was as though Roan had found a knob that turned his lust up to scalding. No matter how much he touched and tasted, Seg couldn't get enough.

"Turn around," Roan demanded.

Seg turned around, planting his hands on the tiled wall.

"Spread your legs," Roan instructed, his lips trailing down Seg's back.

His legs spread on their own.

Closing his eyes, Seg focused on the heat of Roan's mouth as it moved down his spine, over his ass, then down the crack. Roan's hands were firm as they caressed his sides, easing their way downward.

"Fuck," he moaned when Roan pulled his ass cheeks apart, his tongue searching, teasing.

His lungs locked up as Roan's breath caressed sensitive skin. Seg's heart pounded, his body tensing, coiling tighter and tighter until...

"Oh, fuck."

Seg hadn't known what to expect, but the instant Roan's tongue speared his asshole, he damn near lost his balance.

He couldn't help himself, he began rocking against the intrusion. It felt good. Too good. He'd never allowed anyone to play with him like this. For him, sex was usually more about the means to an end, with the end being him coming as hard and as fast as he could.

With Roan ... Seg wanted more. He wanted to experience everything he'd denied himself over the years. He wanted to find a way to sate these urges and get this out of his system. He couldn't be with a man. Not in the long term, but this would work.

Roan's tongue disappeared and his hands roamed back up Seg's back. He was tempted to turn around, but Roan wouldn't let him, his palm flattening between Seg's shoulder blades.

"I want to feel you," Roan whispered against his ear. "Let me feel you, Seg. Let me slide my cock deep into your ass and feel you."

Goddamn. His ass clenched again.

But dammit, he couldn't. He'd never...

Seg shook his head. "Can't."

"Can't? Or won't?" Roan didn't sound pleased.

His brain was telling him to turn around, but his body wouldn't move.

"Ever let a man fuck you?"

Seg shook his head.

"It doesn't make you any less gay because you're the top." Roan's tone sounded both amused and disappointed. "Let me, Seg. Let me be the first man to take your virgin ass."

Although he knew he shouldn't, Seg wanted that so badly.

Never had he been tempted to give in, but with Roan, he found himself nodding.

Roan's lips continued to work over his back while Seg remained stone still, his forehead pressed to the tile, the warm water raining down on them. He heard the rustle from the condom, heard the click from the bottle of lubrication. It was going to happen. He was going to let Roan fuck him.

And Roan would be his first and probably his last.

"You ready?" Roan asked, his voice rough.

Seg nodded again.

"I'm gonna use my fingers first."

"Ahh, shit," Seg groaned as one finger pushed inside him. Slowly, gently. His body acclimated to the intrusion, chills racing down his arms as the sensations intensified.

"Okay?"

Seg nodded.

Roan added another finger, stretching him. Seg groaned, closing his eyes as he let the pleasure take over.

A strangled groan escaped him when Roan pushed in three fingers.

"Relax."

Easier said than done, but Seg did his best.

He didn't move, trying to enjoy it, trying to ignore the bite of pain that accompanied it. He was overwhelmed with sensation when suddenly—"Oh, fuck... Oh, fuck ... Roan..."

"You like that? That's your prostate. Feels good, huh?"

Good? That was an understatement. What he felt was something beyond good, bordering more on unreal.

Roan's fingers continued to penetrate him, fucking into him slow and easy. If the man wasn't careful, Seg was going to come long before Roan had the chance to fuck him.

"Still good?"

Shit. It felt so damn good it was a wonder Seg hadn't gone off like a rocket. He'd come precariously close though.

"Want more?" Roan inquired, his fingers retreating.

"Yeah," Seg breathed. So fucking much more. "Want to feel you."

Seg tensed when Roan aligned his cock, pushing against the tight ring of muscle.

"Relax," Roan whispered. "You've seriously never done this before?"

Seg shook his head.

"I'll be gentle, I promise."

Roan pressed in gradually while Seg took deep, slow breaths.

"Push back against me," Roan ordered.

He did. The pain was intense, but it quickly morphed into pleasure. And every time Roan's cock brushed against his prostate, Seg saw stars.

"That's it," Roan urged, his fingers digging into the flesh of Seg's hips. "So fucking tight."

Seg let himself get lost in the sensation as Roan rocked into him over and over. Roan didn't fuck him hard or fast. He simply filled him. In. Out. In. Out.

When Roan's arm circled him, his fingers wrapping around Seg's cock, he jerked, his body on the verge of explosion.

"Come for me," Roan said gruffly. "Come for me while I come in your ass."

Yep. That was all it took.

Seg pulled his SUV into the garage and hit the button to close the door. He should've gone out with the team tonight, but he couldn't bring himself to do it. Not after seeing Roan. He needed to get his shit together and figure this out. No way could he keep going on like this.

At the time, giving in to Roan for one night had seemed harmless. Unfortunately, thanks to the fact the man made him want things he knew he shouldn't want, it turned out to be anything but.

Two

"YOU WANT US to come inside with you?" Cam Strickland-Burgess asked Roan as he steered the car down the narrow road lined with duplexes.

"No. I'm good."

Funny. Cam didn't think Roan sounded good. Not good at all.

"You sure?"

"I'm sure. I'm not a kid, Cam. I can take care of myself." Roan's tone was a little harder this time, and Cam knew he had to stop pushing him.

But damn it to hell. It'd taken an act of congress to get Roan to agree to go to the game tonight. And then after... If Cam didn't know better, he would've sworn Roan had no interest in meeting the Austin Arrows players.

"All right." Cam stopped at a stop sign. Took a right. "So, how do you know Seg? Seguine?"

"I..."

Cam peered at Roan in the rearview mirror, waiting, watching. For months, Cam had gotten the impression that Roan was hiding something. At the very least, he knew Roan had lied to him a time or two. About what, he hadn't figured out yet.

"I met him at a bar once."

"A bar?"

"Yeah. One of my trips into Austin."

Feasible.

Cam chuckled, focusing on the road. "And you didn't think to mention it? Like, hey, Cam, guess who I met today?"

When Cam checked the rearview mirror again, he noticed Roan was looking out the window. "Must've slipped my mind."

Right. There was more to that story, Cam knew. But again, he had learned that pushing Roan only made the man close up more.

Cam pulled the car to a stop in front of the duplex Roan lived in with his youngest sister, Cassie. It had been her place before Roan moved in to help her out with bills. Cam knew she couldn't keep up with the rent most months because he suspected she was spending whatever money she did have on her drug addiction. Based on the way the house looked, there wasn't anything left over for upkeep. Not that Roan was hurting for money. The marina was doing great, and Cam knew his friend had more than enough to get by.

"Thanks for the ride. See you tomorrow." Roan didn't look back as he hopped out of the car, shut the door, and took off toward the house.

Gannon squeezed Cam's hand, as though reminding him that he needed to get them home. Without wasting another second, Cam put his foot on the gas and drove down to the other end of the street. He hated leaving Roan like this. However, every attempt he'd made to talk to his best friend had resulted in Roan shutting him out more, usually picking a fight to ensure there was distance between them.

When they were two streets over, Cam glanced over at his husband. "Is it just me or does something seem really off with him?"

Gannon's dark eyes peered over at him in the dim light of the dashboard. "I assume you mean tonight."

Cam frowned.

"Babe, he's seemed off for a long time," Gannon said. "Ever since you and I got together."

Yes. Roan had initially had a problem with Cam and Gannon getting together. But they'd worked through that. Roan had even been the best man at their wedding. Surely he wasn't still worked up about that.

"Okay, sure. He hasn't been himself for a while, you're right," Cam acknowledged. "I know he's having a hard time dealing with Cassie. But tonight, it was really weird. For some reason, I don't think we should've left him alone."

This time Gannon was frowning. "He's not alone, Cam. He's got his sister living there with him."

Cam glared over at Gannon. "And we all know how well they get along."

"Like oil and water, yes," Gannon stated.

"Exactly. Did you hear him a minute ago?" Cam questioned, although it was rhetorical because Gannon had been in the car. He had to have heard. "He accused me of treating him like a child. It's always something with him. It's like he tries to pick a fight whenever I get too close."

Cam stopped the car before leaving Roan's neighborhood, turning to look at his husband more fully.

"I haven't been the greatest friend to him lately. I don't get to spend much time with him. Since he moved in with Cassie, he won't let me come over. For whatever reason, he's stopped coming over to our place. And he's missed so much work. I know something's bothering him, but I can't get him to talk about it."

"And you think tonight's gonna be different?" Gannon asked.

Cam shrugged. He didn't know. But he could confront Roan about it, at least. If he simply barged into his house, no way could Roan blow him off the way he had all this time. No matter how annoying he'd been lately, Roan never backed down. He didn't want to talk. He didn't want to hang out. He didn't want to do anything but go to work and go home. It was as though his sister had taken over his life and he had to spend all his time taking care of her. But for fuck's sake, the woman was almost thirty years old. She didn't need Roan holding her hand.

Cam knew Roan needed a friend.

"We're going back," Cam said.

"I thought you'd say that." Gannon smiled. "I go where you go."

Cam nodded, then pulled a U-ie, heading back to Roan's house.

The place was nothing more than a rundown POS that was in desperate need of a new roof and some grass in the front yard. According to Roan, it was where Cassie lived, and since he'd practically forced her to let him live with her, he couldn't be picky.

"I'm not even gonna knock," Cam said as they sidestepped the cracked walkway on their way up to Roan's front door.

Music blasted from one of the other duplexes, a baby's loud wail sounded from nearby, and Cam was fairly certain he smelled pot.

"Hopefully he's dressed," Cam muttered, keeping his eye on his surroundings. He already detested this place and he'd been here all of a minute. How the hell could Roan live in this filth?

"Hopefully his sister's dressed," Gannon noted, sounding as though the idea of seeing her naked was far worse than the idea of seeing Roan naked.

"I doubt she's even home." Knowing Cassie, she was out somewhere getting high. It was all she ever did. Roan spent all of his time saving her from herself. Or trying to anyway. Cam wondered when the man was going to realize she had to be held responsible for her own actions. Him coming to her rescue every damn time was only enabling her.

"Someone needs to take care of that baby," Gannon said absently.

Cam took a deep breath as he put his hand on the doorknob. He turned it slowly and yes! It was unlocked.

The next thing Cam knew, he and Gannon were opening Roan's front door, stepping inside and…

The music sounded even louder in here. As did the baby crying. How thin were the walls? Seriously.

And damn. What was that smell?

The house was completely dark except for a dim light from the kitchen. It wasn't enough to light up the room, but enough that Cam could see someone over by the couch. On the floor.

"Roan?" Cam fumbled blindly on the wall with his hand. Surely there was a light in here. When he found the switch, he hit it and the room lit up, casting a dingy yellow glow across the cheap furniture and ratty carpet.

And that was when Cam saw them.

"Oh, shit," Gannon yelled, shoving Cam forward. "Fuck."

It took a minute for it to register for Cam. He saw Roan and…

"Oh, my God!" Cam bolted across the room, dropping to his knees beside Roan, who was holding his sister, the woman lying motionless on the floor between the cheap brass coffee table littered with cigarette butts and the secondhand couch with what looked to be fast-food wrappers decorating it. "What happened?"

Oh, damn. The smell was so much worse over here.

Cassie's bleached-blond hair was matted and tangled. Her T-shirt was hanging off her bony shoulder, and her shorts looked as though they hadn't been washed in days. Her skin was paler than usual, and there was something caked on her lips.

Was that foam?

Oh, God. Oh, God. Oh, God.

"Shit!" Cam yelled at Gannon. "Call 9-1-1. Damn it. I left my phone in the car."

"It's too late," Roan said softly. "Call the police, but it's not an emergency."

Cam pressed two fingers to Cassie's neck, trying to find a pulse because surely this wasn't happening. No pulse, but he hadn't really expected one. It only reaffirmed what he feared.

Shit.

Leaning down, he pressed his ear close to her mouth. She wasn't breathing.

Sitting back on his heels, Cam looked at Roan, then back to Cassie. She looked to be asleep, but he knew better. She wasn't sleeping. She was dead. And from the looks of it, she'd been that way for probably a couple of hours.

In the background, Cam heard Gannon rattling off the address, but Roan was right, there was no point. The EMTs didn't have to hurry, because there was nothing they could do for her. The syringe she had used, the needle still piercing her vein, hung from her arm where a strip of yellowed rubber was stretched tight.

Cam knew that Roan had feared this for too long. And just as he'd predicted, Cassie had succumbed to the drug. She had overdosed, and he didn't think she'd done it on purpose. This was likely a nightly ritual for her and this one time...

Unfortunately, one time was all it took.

Holy shit.

"They're on their way," Gannon said, his voice panicky.

"She's dead," Cam said, as though saying it would make it truly register.

"I knew something was wrong," Roan muttered, his voice strained. "I should've been here."

"Man, you can't—" Cam stopped talking. "Seriously, is your neighbor going to take care of that baby? It's been crying since we walked up."

Roan looked up at Cam, and it was as though someone flipped on the light switch in his head. "Oh, my God! Oh, shit!"

Cam stared after Roan as he shot to his feet and practically sprinted down a narrow hallway. Cam looked over at Gannon briefly, but his husband looked as confused as he felt.

"I'll wait for the police," Gannon said. "I think you should probably go check on him."

Yeah.

Someone probably should.

ROAN THREW OPEN the bedroom door and smacked the light switch on the wall.

Relief slammed into him, damn near taking him to his knees when he saw Liam in his crib. Sure, the baby was screaming bloody murder, but at least he was safe where he was.

Pulling in a calming breath, Roan reached for the little boy, lifting him into his arms and murmuring softly as he held him close to his chest.

Aww, damn. He was soaked clean through. The outfit Roan had dressed him in before going to the game was drenched.

"It's okay, baby boy. I'm so, *so* sorry. Shh ... shh ... shh. God, it's gonna be all right. I swear to you."

Roan ignored the pee soaking through his shirt, doing his best to soothe the tiny little boy he clutched in his arms.

"Liam, I'm here now. I've got you."

It only took a few seconds for Liam to quiet, his screams turning to choked sobs as he fought to catch his breath. God only knew how long Liam had been lying there, screaming at the top of his lungs. The duplex that shared a wall with Cassie's was empty, so no one had been there to hear him. Roan probably would've heard him if he hadn't been shocked to the roots of his hair at finding his sister laid out on the living room floor, her body cold...

Cassie was dead.

A shiver trickled down his spine as his brain processed everything that'd taken place in the last few minutes.

"I've got you," Roan whispered to Liam as the reality of it all sank in. Liam's mother was dead. "I promise. I'm here. I'm not going anywhere."

Roan turned to the door, finding Cam standing there staring at him. His eyes were wide, his jaw damn near unhinged.

"Uh... Holy ... sh—"

This was what Roan had been trying to avoid by keeping his friends away. Not because he necessarily wanted to take on the task of raising his sister's son on his own, but because it was all too much to handle and he was trying to deal with it.

The house was a disgusting mess. It didn't matter that Roan cleaned it morning and night, it was as though Cassie purposely messed it up. Roan hadn't wanted anyone to see the place, certainly not his friends.

And no one should've had to come in to find Cassie's lifeless body on the floor, proof that she hadn't tried to stay on the straight and narrow dangling from her arm.

"Is that…?" Cam seemed at a loss for words, his eyes wide, eyebrows scraping his hairline.

"My sister's son?" Roan nodded. "Yeah. His name's Liam."

Cam took a step closer. "He's tiny. How old is he?"

"One month, yesterday."

"Cam? Roan?" Gannon's calm, smooth voice floated into the room from somewhere down the hallway. "The police are here."

Roan looked at Cam. "I know I have a lot of explaining to do, but…"

Cam shook his head. "I'll talk to the police. Tell them what I can."

"I need to change him," Roan whispered, looking down at the sweet little boy cradled in his arms. He was trying to fight the tears, hating that this precious boy was going to go through life without his mother. Roan's own mother hadn't died, but he'd lived his life as though she had.

"Sure thing. I'll … uh… Yeah."

Roan turned to the changing table and placed Liam squarely in the center, then went to work removing the wet clothes and changing his soggy diaper as quickly and efficiently as he could. God knew he'd had enough practice over the last four weeks.

When he was finished, he dumped the soiled diaper in the pail, picked Liam up, and cradled him against his shoulder, keeping his hand across Liam's back, his fingers keeping his head secure. He took a second to peer around the room. Everything was new. The crib, changing table, dresser. Roan had purchased every piece of furniture, every stitch of clothing, the diapers, wipes, powder, baby bath. All of it.

Every single thing Liam had, Roan had bought for him. And not begrudgingly either. He'd bought it because he wanted to ensure Liam had what he needed.

"What're we gonna do, baby boy?" he whispered as he headed toward the kitchen.

A quick peek at the counter proved what he'd feared. Cassie hadn't fed him tonight. Every day Roan filled the bottles with water and placed them on the counter so Cassie would have them. The only thing she had to do was add formula. Roan even kept the can beside the bottles with a Post-It note advising how much formula for her to use. By providing the bottles, it allowed Roan to keep track of what she'd done and what she hadn't. For the most part, his sister had tried. More accurately, she had *wanted* to try.

She really had.

She hadn't been the greatest mom. No one could dispute that. More than half the time, Roan was the one who got up with Liam in the middle of the night because she refused to get out of bed. In the beginning, Cassie had seemed willing to give the mothering thing a shot. A week in and Roan realized he would have to do more than simply monitor her. She started relying more and more on him to take care of Liam, and Roan had done what was natural. He'd taken care of the little boy knowing his sister wouldn't.

Roan fought the tears that were threatening as he pulled the lid off the formula can and got to work getting Liam's bottle ready. The little boy wouldn't be quiet for long.

Gannon appeared in the kitchen. "They'd like to talk to you." Gannon nodded toward Liam. "May I?"

Clearly Cam had given Gannon a heads-up, because he didn't seem at all surprised to see an infant in Roan's arms.

Roan knew he needed to deal with this, but he hated letting go of Liam. If he could, he would hold the boy forever, right there against his heart, keeping him safe and protected from the world. In just the few short weeks of his life, he'd had to endure so much. More than he should have.

"Sure," Roan said, reluctantly passing Liam over.

"He's tiny," Gannon said softly, his eyes warm as they roamed over Liam's small form. "So tiny."

Yeah. He was.

Gannon took him, gently cradling his head and situating him so he could handle the bottle.

"I'll sit here," Gannon told him, glancing over at the table.

"Okay."

Roan shook the bottle to mix the formula and water, then made sure the nipple was working. After handing it off to Gannon, he swallowed hard and steeled himself for dealing with the police.

Someone—likely Gannon—had kindly draped a sheet over Cassie's body. Roan kept his attention on the man standing in the doorway, otherwise, his knees would likely give out on him and he'd be in a heap on the floor.

"Detective Wayne Simpson," the man greeted him, all business.

Roan nodded, waiting for the questions.

"You're"—the detective peered at his notepad—"Cassie's brother? Roan?"

"Roan Gregory, yes," he confirmed.

He quickly gave the man the story of how he'd come home to find her lifeless on the floor, the syringe still dangling from her arm. He answered questions as best he could. Yes, Cassie was a drug addict. Yes, she had been trying to get clean. No, he didn't know where she got the drugs from. Yes, the little boy was her son, but Roan had guardianship. Yes, he had the papers to prove it. No, he did not intend to stay here in this house. Yes, he would be the one arranging the funeral.

Cam remained right by his side, handling as many of the questions as the detective allowed. He steered Roan out of the way when someone—he didn't even know who—wheeled Cassie's body out of the house.

It all took less than an hour, and by the time things calmed down, Roan felt numb.

It was too late to save Cassie. *He* was too late.

He rubbed his fist over his heart. The damn thing ached. A physical pain he didn't much care for.

"She overdosed," Roan mumbled. "Just like I knew she would." He took a deep breath, tried to hold back the tears, but he couldn't stop them this time. "God*dammit*, Cassie."

Staring into space, Roan recalled the last conversation they'd had before her hateful texts. It'd been right before he left for the game.

"Are you sure you don't mind me going?" Roan asked for the third time.

Cassie peered up from the television long enough to roll her eyes. "I'm quite capable of taking care of myself."

It wasn't her he was worried about.

"And Liam," she added belatedly. "We'll be fine."

"I just bathed him. He's got clean clothes and a dry diaper. He'll be ready to eat in an hour. Can you handle that?" Roan knew his tone was harder than he'd meant it to be, but it was difficult for him to trust Cassie to do what she said she'd do.

"I'm his mother, Roan. I think I know when my kid wants to eat."

He bit back a retort. "The game starts at seven. I'll be home around ten. Ten thirty at the latest."

Cassie waved him off, her attention once again on the television.

He should've gone through the house with a fine-toothed comb and thrown out any drugs she might've had. But he'd believed she'd stopped.

Or rather, he'd wanted to believe.

More importantly, he should've stayed home.

His chest expanded and heat encompassed his sinuses as the tears came in a rush.

The next thing he knew, Cam's arms were around him and Roan was crying like a baby. He hated that he couldn't hold it together. Cam had been close to Roan's sister growing up and he probably felt the same sharp stab of pain that Roan felt.

"I need to call my dad," Roan noted, pulling back and wiping his eyes.

"I'll call him, Roan." Cam's voice was strong and steady. He was taking charge and Roan appreciated it. "I think you and the baby should come stay with us tonight."

Roan nodded, a tear dripping off his cheek and onto his hand. Just this morning, he had given Cassie shit because she was being obnoxious and not in a good way. For the past five months, Roan had been living with her, sleeping on her couch, invading her space, attempting to force her to quit the drugs. Ever since she found out she was pregnant. He had tried to be there for her. Tried to help her through it. They'd fought every damn day over the same shit. She didn't want him there; he didn't want to be there. She hated him, he hated her more. It was a vicious cycle and though most of what he'd said wasn't true, she had simply pushed him to his limits.

Rehabs had accepted her only to let her go because she refused treatment, becoming belligerent and disturbing the other patients. She hadn't wanted help.

Not from him. Not from their father. Not from anyone.

And look where that left her.

Dead at twenty-nine. She wouldn't even see her next birthday, only three weeks away.

His father and his stepmother were going to be devastated. And his sister Eva, too.

Or hell, maybe they wouldn't. Not a one of them had lifted a finger to help Cassie. Not for months. At first, his stepmother had tried to help, but Lydia had grown tired of the effort it took to deal with Cassie. And that left Roan. He'd had no choice but to stick his nose where it didn't belong because he hadn't wanted...

This.

"Roan," Cam said softly. "Let's go pack some of Liam's things."

Cam's firm grip registered on his arm and Roan managed to take a step. Then another. He was having a hard time processing all of the emotions. He was furious with Cassie for refusing help. She had insisted that she could do this on her own. Now that she had Liam, she had something to live for. Or so she'd told him.

He was heartbroken that he hadn't been able to stop her. But worse than that, he was riddled with guilt. But he couldn't deny the relief he felt. He knew he shouldn't because it was selfish, but he had spent so long trying to help her, getting verbally abused—sometimes even physically abused—because of it. Cassie hadn't been herself; the drugs had turned her into someone none of them recognized.

But now she was at peace. She wasn't fighting the addiction any longer.

HARMLESS

When Cam's arms came around him again, Roan fought to keep it all in. He tried to break free of Cam's hold, but he couldn't, so he gave in and let his best friend reassure him that they would get through this.

Three

SEG WAS SITTING on his couch, channel-surfing when he heard his phone buzz. He leaned over and grabbed it off the table, wishing like hell it was Roan responding to his text by calling to say yes, he would like to meet for a beer. Only that was wishful thinking and Seg knew that it wouldn't be him. His luck had been all used up on the ice tonight.

He glanced at the screen.

Nope. Not Roan.

Mom.

She always called after a game and he'd been waiting for her.

"Hey, Ma."

"Did you see that game tonight?" she asked excitedly. "It was beautiful! Absolutely beautiful!"

"I saw it," he assured her, chuckling. "I was there."

"I know you were, honey. And it was incredible. Marjorie's jealous, let me tell you. She's so proud of you, she wants a hockey son of her own." His mother giggled. "She came over to watch it with me. I was jumping up and down, yelling like a crazy woman. I even spilled the popcorn. I thought she was going to need oxygen she was so shocked. You'd think she would be used to it by now."

Seg knew his mother. She was extremely animated when it wasn't related to hockey, and when it was... He imagined Marjorie, his mother's best friend, was beside herself. That's how Debra Seguine worked. She was overly proud of him—which made him pretty damn lucky.

"I don't know if Marj'll be coming around again for more games." She sounded somewhat relieved, which made him laugh. Considering Marjorie had sat through plenty already, he seriously doubted that was the case.

"I take it that was the plan?"

"Of course not." Her laugh was husky and sweet, and only a little mischievous.

"Ma, you're bad."

"Don't I know it, honey. I got that from your father. Rest his soul. So, next game is on Monday, right?"

"Yes, ma'am. At home again. Then we're on the road."

"I'll be rooting for you! You looked amazing out there, by the way. And don't think I missed that assist. Best play ever."

Her praise always made his heart swell. "Thanks, Ma."

"So, how are things going otherwise? You know, your life off the ice?"

There were so many things he wanted to tell his mom. *There's this guy I met and I think I might actually be focused on something other than hockey. However, I only got to spend one night with him and that was more than a year ago, but I still can't stop thinking about him. I saw him again tonight, and I want to hop in my truck and chase him down just so I can look at him, hear his voice.* Of course, he couldn't tell her that. He couldn't tell *anyone* that. "Good. Now that the season's underway, we'll be busy."

"That's a good thing, right? But you've got to have time to date those supermodels. Are you still seeing that one girl?"

Seg knew his mother didn't really care. She was asking to be nice. He'd told her long ago that his hockey career was the only thing that mattered. He'd also warned her not to believe everything she read or saw on television.

"Not seeing anyone right now," he said because it was true. "She was just a friend, Ma."

"That's what you always say. You're not getting any younger, Seggy."

His cheeks heated at the nickname. While his friends and the rest of his family called him Seg, his mother had insisted on making the nickname "cute."

"Last I checked, twenty-seven wasn't exactly old," he told her.

"Maybe not. But one of these days, you'll wake up to find that you're sixty."

"I'm sure I'll be happy at sixty."

"I'm sure you will." She chuckled. "I can take a hint. I won't keep you. Had to make sure I told you how amazing you were tonight."

"You always say that."

"And you always are," she said, sounding somewhat indignant.

"Thanks, Ma. I love you."

"Love you too, Seggy. Talk to you later."

Half an hour later, Seg was in bed, watching the highlights from all the games of the night. He should've been asleep or even out at the bar, but he wasn't. He was sitting there on his bed, trying not to think about that one incredible night with Roan. All the things they'd done right here on his bed.

"Not tired yet?" Roan mumbled when Seg moved closer.

"Not even close." Shit. *At this point, Seg wasn't sure he would ever sleep again. After what Roan had done to him in the shower... He'd be thinking about that for a long damn time.*

"What're you thinkin' then? Round three?"

"Fuck yes," Seg whispered, pressing his mouth to Roan's as he moved over him. *"Right now."*

Roan rolled onto his back, kissed him with such urgency, and Seg took that as agreement.

"Lift your legs up," Seg instructed. *"To your chest."*

"Condom," Roan muttered.

"Already on." While Roan had dozed beside him, Seg had kept his eyes on him, slowly stroking himself until he was hard.

Roan lifted his knees up, opening himself to Seg. After kissing Roan once more, deep and hard this time, he lifted up onto his knees, pressing his hands against the backs of Roan's thighs.

He slid his lubed cock against Roan's puckered hole, then used one hand to guide himself home. The heat of Roan's ass strangled his dick as he pushed inside. Seg met Roan's gaze, holding it while he rocked forward, going deeper, then pulling back. He continued the motion, inching in a little more each time. When he bottomed out, he retreated, then slammed home.

"Hard," Roan insisted. *"Use me. Fuck me hard."*

Damn. Why was that sexy as fuck?

Unable to resist, Seg pulled back, then slammed in again. He watched Roan's face, captivated by the way his eyes rolled back, his mouth hung open.

"Oh, yeah... Faster."

Seg drove his hips forward again and again.

"Harder."

He gave Roan what he asked for.

Roan opened his eyes and met Seg's gaze. "Deeper."

Goddamn. If Roan kept that up, Seg was going to come again. Fuck.

He pounded Roan's ass harder, faster, deeper, keeping his hands on the backs of Roan's thighs, trying his best not to hurt him.

"So good. Fuck me... Yes ... just like that."

Roan groaned with every punishing thrust, and Seg never looked away from his face. He wasn't sure what was happening here. This was supposed to be one night, but fuck if he didn't already want a replay. Shit. He wanted to spend the rest of the week fucking Roan until he could get his fill.

He briefly wondered what Roan would think if he made the suggestion.

Seg hated that he never got the chance to ask Roan. That night, after he'd come harder than he ever had in his life, they'd both drifted off to sleep. When Seg woke the next morning, it'd been in an empty bed. Roan hadn't left a note, and Seg had known he would never see him again.

It was stupid that he wanted another go at it. He should've been relieved that Roan had never said anything to anyone. Or at least he didn't think he had. It should've made him happy to know that he didn't have to worry about being outed. As it was, he'd spent the last year avoiding sexual relationships at all costs.

Oh, he had made sure to be photographed with women, but only women he considered friends. The ones who didn't want anything from him. Not his dick. Not his money. Not his fame.

It had been one hell of a year. Lonely as fuck. And all he'd done was think about Roan. Wishing like hell he didn't live in a world where he had to pretend to be someone he wasn't.

BY THE TIME Roan got Liam back to sleep, this time in Cam and Gannon's guest room, where they'd set up the portable crib, he was emotionally drained. Although Cam had broken the devastating news to Roan's father, he'd had to do his share of explaining when his father insisted on talking to him.

It'd been clear to everyone what had killed Cassie. Not only because of the needle that had been hanging from her arm either. Based on her skinny, malnourished body, it was also evident that this wasn't a one-time thing, despite the fact his sister had promised him she wasn't using.

Roan had believed her for the most part. Since she'd stopped going out, he'd thought she'd given up the drugs. He should've known. He should've realized that she'd started again. Perhaps he would have if he hadn't been so busy taking care of Liam.

Admittedly, he'd turned a blind eye, not wanting to know for sure. It had been easier than dealing with her shit. Although his father had asked for details, he hadn't seemed all that interested. In fact, now that Roan thought about it, he'd seem more interested in how Liam was than the fact that his own daughter was dead.

She was in a better place now. That's what Eva and Lydia had said when they'd learned the news. His sister and stepmother had been upset, but Roan was sure he'd heard a hint of relief in their tear-laced voices.

Yes. Relief.

That horrible guilt grabbed hold of him again, and Roan had to sit down. He hated himself for feeling that Cassie really was in a better place, but he couldn't help it. She had been spiraling out of control... He had tried to pretend that she was getting better, but he'd known that wasn't true. It was the very reason he had put his entire life on hold. He had needed to make sure that Liam was taken care of. Of course, Cassie saw that as interference, and they'd been butting heads for so long that he felt as though a weight had been lifted from his shoulders.

For fuck's sake. He was not supposed to be thinking like that.

Strangely enough, his father and stepmother were more worried about Liam, but not in the way Roan would've expected. He'd detected a hint of concern from Lydia that Liam was now being raised by a gay man. It stood out to him because neither his father nor his stepmother had ever seemed concerned with him being gay.

Roan could do nothing but assure them that he would be taking care of him. He and Cassie had agreed that if something happened to her, Roan would raise Liam. She had been adamant that their father not take Liam. That relationship had long ago deteriorated, so Roan understood where she was coming from.

When Cassie asked if he'd be Liam's legal guardian, Roan probably should've protested some, forced her to take responsibility, to be a mother. According to her, it was to protect him so the state couldn't take him. Cassie had been aware of her issues, even if she'd had no desire to change.

It had been the only rational thing Cassie had come up with in years. So, Roan hadn't argued, but then again, he'd practically been raising Liam since the day he was born.

When his father tried to insist that Roan bring Liam to their house, he'd refused. At one point, he had even raised his voice. No way was he taking Liam anywhere. Not right now. It was bad enough that he'd had to take the baby away from the home he was familiar with, but Roan refused to stay in that shithole even one minute longer.

A light knock sounded on the bedroom door, and Roan pushed to his feet, checking on Liam one more time. He grabbed the baby monitor and turned it on, then went to the door.

"Hey," Cam said softly. "How's he doin'?"

"He's asleep," Roan told him as he pulled the door closed.

"You wanna talk?"

Not really, but Roan knew that Cam and Gannon deserved some answers. They were opening their home to him—albeit temporarily—and he felt they should know what was going on.

Roan followed Cam into the kitchen. Gannon was sitting at the table with three mugs.

"Decaf," Gannon said, nodding to one of the cups.

"Thanks."

His legs seemed to go out from under him as he took a seat. He was exhausted, but he ignored it. That was what he'd been doing for so long now.

Before Roan could say anything, Cam spoke up. "I need to apologize."

Roan met his eyes, but he couldn't hide his frown. Apologize? For what?

Cam glanced at Gannon quickly, then back to Roan. "I know I haven't been a good friend for … a while now." His head tilted in the direction of the bedrooms. "I didn't even know… I should have known. I should've offered to help you. It's clear you didn't trust me enough to tell me—"

"That's not true," Roan argued, his tone reflecting his guilt. "This didn't have anything to do with trust." It really hadn't.

Cam didn't seem convinced. "I know that since I met Gannon, I've been a little … preoccupied. You deserved better than that from me."

Roan cleared his throat. Although he'd known Cam was taking the guilt on himself all these months, believing he was the reason Roan was keeping his distance, Roan hadn't bothered to correct him.

"This isn't on you." He watched Cam, then briefly glanced at Gannon. "Or you. This is all my doing. Cassie's been…" God, how did he say it? "She's been fucked up for a long time. I didn't want to deal with it, but someone had to. I knew she needed me, even if she hated me."

"She didn't hate you," Cam debated.

Roan laughed without mirth. "Oh, she hated me. With a passion that rivaled all." That was the truth. Cassie had hated everyone, but especially him since he refused to leave her alone. "She wasn't nice, and I didn't want anyone to have to deal with that shit. It was hard enough for me."

"But she made you Liam's legal guardian," Gannon noted, a question in his eyes.

"She did. But I think that was because she didn't want the state to take him. Plus, she couldn't financially support him." Nor had she made an effort to try.

"Do you know who the father is?" Cam questioned.

"No. Cassie had no idea." Roan hated this story, but he couldn't keep it quiet any longer. "She'd been having sex for money. That was how she would get her next fix. She said it could've been any number of guys." He glanced at the table. "Honestly, I think Liam's better off without whoever it is. I figure Liam's father is a dealer or something."

"Is Liam doing okay?" Gannon asked. "I assume he had some issues at birth."

Roan nodded, sliding his fingers down the coffee mug. "Yeah. He did. But he's a fighter. She found out she was pregnant when she was five months along."

"That explains where you've been all these months," Cam noted, his tone harder than before.

"Someone had to try to help her get clean," Roan told him. "Since my father and Lydia refused to help before she got pregnant, she made me swear not to tell them."

"They didn't know?" Cam looked appalled.

"They never saw her. Not once did they stop by to visit and they rarely called." That wasn't unusual though. His father and stepmother lived in their own little world.

"So you found out she was pregnant and then what? Did she quit using?"

"No. It was a battle for a long time. She wouldn't stop using, wouldn't stop drinking. We fought *all* the time. Especially after I moved in with her. I knew someone had to keep an eye on her though. Finally..." Roan looked up at Cam. "I thought I'd gotten through to her. She cleaned herself up for a while, or so she said. I suspected she had relapsed a couple of times, but I gave her a pass." Like an idiot. "I thought she was back on the straight and narrow. I thought that was why she was being such a bitch."

It had all been a lie. Cassie had never stopped using; she'd merely hidden it from him.

He didn't want to go into details about Liam being born addicted to drugs. He'd been damn near murderous when he found out Liam had to be weaned off the drugs because Cassie had been feeding them to him throughout the pregnancy. It had been a horrific point in Roan's life, watching that baby hooked to IVs while they pumped him full of something to mimic the toxic shit she'd been injecting into herself.

It was at that point Roan had told Cassie that he hated her. Hated her for what she'd done to Liam.

"I wish you would've said something," Cam said, his voice low. "I know I should've tried to talk to you, but…"

Roan held Cam's gaze. "I didn't want anyone to have to endure Cassie's wrath. And let me tell you, she was ferocious."

She'd been brutal most of the time. Not that Roan had been much nicer to her.

"What do you need us to help with?" Gannon offered.

Roan shrugged. He hadn't had time to think about any of that yet. "I'm gonna need some time off," he told them.

"Absolutely. We'll make sure it's all covered," Cam assured him. "And we're here to help, too. I'm sure it won't require much effort to learn how to change a diaper and prepare a bottle. Gannon's working from home a lot more these days." Cam offered a small smile. "You know, for the days you need a break."

"Milly's gonna go apeshit," Gannon said, grinning. "You won't be able to hold her back with a stick. So, you might as well agree to let her help, too."

Roan smiled as he looked at his friends. Cam had always been there for him. Even when he'd thought he wasn't, he had been. And Gannon… Despite Roan trying to sabotage Cam and Gannon's relationship in the beginning, the man didn't seem to hold a grudge. Roan was the one who'd managed to alienate himself from everyone. He knew he had to rely on them now. No way could he get through this by himself.

"Thanks for that."

"And we're not gonna let you push us away again," Cam stated, his eyes reflecting the seriousness of his statement. "You never should've done it in the first place."

Roan nodded. He knew that. Would he change what he'd done if he could? No, probably not. But Cam didn't need to know that.

"When are you gonna tell Dare and Teague?" Cam inquired.

"I don't know. I'll have to do it soon, I guess."

"They'll want to help you, you know."

Yep, he knew.

All this time, he'd been wishing he had their help, but he'd known how nasty Cassie could get, and he hadn't wanted any of them enduring her wrath. Instead, he had isolated himself, making sure that he was there for his sister. And when Liam was born, Roan had done everything he could, but he'd found he stopped helping Cassie because he was more focused on taking care of Liam.

Not that he minded. In fact, in four short weeks, he'd fallen absolutely head over heels for the kid. So much so, that half the time he'd wished that Cassie wasn't even there so he could raise the baby himself.

Now it looked as though he got his wish.

And that load of guilt nearly took his breath away.

CAM WAITED UNTIL he and Gannon got into bed before he asked the one question he hadn't been able to ask Roan tonight.

"Did you see what happened between Roan and Seg?"

"Who's Seg?" Gannon looked sincerely confused.

"The defenseman for the Arrows. Colton Seguine. The one who was talking to Roan when we went to meet the team?"

That seemed to clear the fog from Gannon's eyes. "I saw them talking. Seemed completely innocent. Plus, Roan said they'd met at a bar, right?"

Cam shrugged, leaning back on the pillows. "That's what he said, sure. But something was up with those two."

"*Up?*"

"I'm wondering if they had a thing."

"Why would you think that?" Gannon rolled closer, putting one leg over Cam's legs, his arm across Cam's chest.

"I don't know. Roan looked ready to run when he was talking to him."

"And that's unusual how?"

"I don't know. They clearly knew each other, but it seemed more intense than just a quick *hi, how are ya* at a sports bar. I find it funny that Roan never mentioned the fact that he was friends with a fucking hockey player."

"By friends, you mean…?"

He shrugged again. Cam didn't know what he meant. "I'm not sure, but I haven't seen Roan act like that before. It was … weird, I guess. I don't even know how to explain it. But I saw it."

"Really?" Gannon pulled back to look at Cam. "In all the years you've known him, Roan's never greeted another man casually?" Gannon laughed.

"There wasn't anything casual about that."

"Looked casual to me."

"They were hiding something." Cam wanted to know what it was, too. "Roan has never been the type of guy to date much. At least not that I've seen. I know he's had some casual encounters, but he's never brought anyone around."

"So what you're saying is you really don't know what this guy is to Roan. If anything at all."

"That's what I'm saying." He didn't know. However, he got the sneaking suspicion that there was *something* going on between the two of them. Or perhaps it had in the past. Cam had watched Seguine. He didn't know the man, but he'd seen something on his face.

"You should ask Roan about him."

Yeah. Maybe. After everything settled, he might.

"Is that guy gay?" Gannon questioned.

"No idea."

"I thought you were a hockey fanatic."

"I am. But I'm interested in the game, not the love lives of the players."

"You're telling me that you never had a crush on one of those guys?" Gannon moved closer, his breath warm against Cam's neck.

"I didn't say that."

"And to think, you married a gamer nerd with glasses," Gannon teased, his lips gliding over Cam's neck.

"That I did. A sexy"—Cam tilted his head a little— "gamer nerd … oh, hell yes…"

"With glasses," Gannon added.

"Yes, with glasses. God, I love those damn glasses." Okay, and now he sounded winded and he wasn't even moving. Then again, Gannon did that to him. Even after the hell they'd gone through the past few hours, the man could still make him crazy with want.

And like every other night, Cam was going to allow Gannon to take his mind off the crazy shit taking place in the world. Even if just for a little while.

Four

Three days later...

ROAN WAS EXHAUSTED.

Liam had been unusually fussy for the past few days. He often wondered if the little boy realized his mother was gone. Or maybe he sensed all the mourning that was taking place. Then again, he might've picked up on the tension, because there was certainly an overabundance of that.

They had buried Cassie this morning, which had been far less stressful than Roan had originally anticipated. At least until they'd arrived at the funeral home. With so much help, putting it together had taken little effort. Cam and Gannon, Dare and his fiancé, Noah, Teague and Hudson, and even Milly and AJ had been front and center, helping him through it all without so much as a single question.

Well, no questions *after* he'd shocked the shit out of everyone and introduced them to Liam. Rather than wait, Roan had gone to the marina the morning after they'd found Cassie. Figuring it was easier to rip the Band-Aid right off rather than drag it out, Roan had asked Cam to ensure Dare and Teague—the other partners in the marina—as well as Hudson, their mechanic, would be there.

Cam had delivered not only them but he'd managed to snag Noah, telling Roan that this was a family and if one of them was there for him, they all were.

Dare had pretended to have a heart attack, but he'd also been insistent that Liam call him My Favorite Uncle. Teague, who was doing so much better these days after his suicide attempt several months back, had kept a safe distance from the baby, but Roan could tell the guy had absolutely no experience with kids.

Big, bad Hudson Ballard—Teague's other half—had wanted to instantly teach Liam how to fix a boat and had actually gotten into a silent argument—full-on jerky sign language included—with Noah about it. Noah, of course, insisted that Liam was going to grow up to be a firefighter.

Roan had felt so much relief that they'd accepted him and Liam, that they forgave him for being so secretive without so much as an accusing glare, he'd had to slip into Cam's small office and fight off the tears he'd been overwhelmed by for the past few days.

Liam's introduction to the vibrant and chipper Milly—Gannon's administrative assistant/best friend—hadn't come until this morning when she'd surprised him by showing up at Cam's place before the funeral. When she offered to keep Liam, Roan found that he couldn't refuse. Partly because Milly *told* him that he couldn't refuse.

Because Roan knew his father and stepmother were not happy that Roan was Liam's legal guardian, he had agreed, hoping to limit the drama at the funeral. It had worked, and now Daniel and Lydia were sitting in Cam's living room, oohing and ahhing over their grandson while Roan let them spend time with him.

"Eva head back to Ohio already?" Cam asked, his voice low enough not to carry into the living room.

"Yeah." His sister Eva had been at the funeral and the gravesite, but she was back on a plane to Ohio, where her husband and two kids were waiting for her safe return.

"Where were the husband and kids?" Cam leaned against the counter, arms crossed over his chest.

Roan cocked one eyebrow. "She said they didn't need to be subjected to this."

Cam grunted. Clearly he felt the same way Roan did. Eva was Cassie's sister. Her family should've been there to support her and the rest of the family. Since Roan knew that Eva and Cassie had never been close, he sort of understood. He didn't particularly like it, but he got it.

Cam turned, placing his hands on the counter, his gaze following Roan's. "You cool?"

Roan nodded. As cool as he could be. Right now, he was fighting the urge to snatch Liam up and clutch him close to his chest to ensure no one tried to take him away. These were Liam's grandparents, for chrissakes. It wasn't like they would do anything to hurt Liam on purpose, and they all knew that taking the little boy from Roan right now wouldn't be in anyone's best interest.

"You should go in there."

Yeah. Roan had been hoping to avoid that. He knew Lydia wanted to talk about Liam, and Roan would do pretty much anything to avoid that.

"Suck it up, buttercup," Cam said, his tone teasing before sobering quickly. "We're right here. You don't have to fight this battle alone."

Knowing Cam was behind him on this, Roan forced his feet to carry him into the living room.

"Roan," Lydia prompted as soon as he appeared in front of her. She glanced down at Liam. "We were wondering what your intentions were for Liam."

"Intentions?" Roan wasn't catching on.

"Where will you be living? Who will you be living with?" Her eyes flicked up to him briefly. "That sort of thing."

"Uh…" Roan's hands fisted at his sides. "I'm looking for a place right now."

Lydia lifted her head, her back straightening slightly. "Do you think it's wise to raise Liam in a gay household?"

Well. She'd come right out with that one, hadn't she?

Roan glanced between his father and stepmother. It was evident Daniel was trying to avoid the conversation altogether.

"I didn't realize it was a problem."

"It's just…" Lydia glanced over at Daniel. "We believe it's important that children grow up with a mother and a father."

Hmm. Funny how Lydia continued to say "we," yet Roan grew up in a house with a single father for part of his life.

"So is this a concern because I'm gay? I'm confused."

Lydia squirmed. "I'm not saying it's … wrong necessarily. But it's not natural, Roan." She still wouldn't meet his gaze. "A child should have a mother and a father."

Okay, so clearly she didn't have the balls to say what she really meant. Her reference to "we" meant she was hiding behind his father, and the fact that she wouldn't look at him meant she wasn't all that confident in her defense.

At least that was how Roan saw it.

Roan believed that every child should grow up with loving parents—mom and dad, dad and dad, mom and mom, single mom, single dad, grandparents, it didn't fucking matter. As long as the child was the most important thing, as long as they loved the child unconditionally, who really gave a shit about the sex of the parents or whether there were two parents in the household? But he couldn't tell Lydia any of that. Arguing with her would only make things worse.

"Considering I'm single, I don't see how that'll be a problem."

And it wasn't a problem.

Not that he was worried about it. He had one priority. Liam. Nothing and no one else mattered.

Wanting to avoid any more of this bullshit, Roan turned toward the kitchen, catching Cam's attention in the process.

He went right for the refrigerator, yanking it open and staring at the contents. He saw none of it, but the cool air did wonders for his overheated skin.

"You good?" Cam asked, passing him in the kitchen.

"Yeah." Roan closed the refrigerator and turned to watch his father and stepmother. He half expected them to tuck Liam under their arm like a football and make a run for it.

"Gannon and I are gonna run to the store. You need anything?"

Roan shook his head. He turned to look at Cam. "We'll be outta your hair soon, I promise."

Cam looked shocked and maybe a little irritated. "Y'all aren't in our hair. Gannon and I like having you here. I understand if you want your own place, but don't think that we're put out."

"I was thinking about getting an apartment, but I think it's best if I buy a house. Get Liam settled permanently. Put down roots, you know? I don't like the idea of having to move him too many times."

"Roan, you're gonna be a great father. Liam's extremely lucky to have you."

Roan swallowed hard. He wasn't sure why he needed to hear those words, but he had. One minute Liam had been his nephew, the next he'd was his son. Then again, from the moment that he first laid eyes on him, Roan had known that Liam would become the most important thing in his life. He had never expected to have children of his own. Sure, he'd hoped that one day he might have the opportunity, if and when...

Since thirty-four was just around the corner, Roan was starting to think there was more if and less when.

Regardless, he'd never gotten his hopes up.

"Thanks," he said softly.

Liam started crying in the living room and Roan decided to help out the grandparents. By help, he meant send them on their way.

After the stress of the day, Roan finally managed to get Liam down around seven. He knew he'd be back up around nine for a bottle, but at least Roan would get a chance to grab some dinner while the house was quiet.

When he made it into the kitchen, he found Gannon pulling something out of the oven.

"Perfect timing." Gannon smiled at him over his shoulder. "I made lasagna. I'd hoped to time it right. Hungry?"

"Starving," Roan admitted.

"Damn, it smells good in here," Cam said, coming into the kitchen. "Want a beer?"

"Nah. Tea's fine." Roan grabbed plates and silverware while Gannon put the food on the table and Cam got the drinks.

It seemed as though it was going to be a quiet dinner with Roan being the third wheel, but he should've known that Cam wouldn't be able to hold out for long.

"So, tell me more about Colton Seguine."

Roan knew he didn't mask his reaction to the request before Cam noticed. But the inquiry caught him off guard, and he stopped eating, fork halfway to his mouth.

"Okay, let me be a little more specific," Cam stated. "I could tell that y'all are more than just friends who *met in a bar.*" Cam used air quotes and everything. "How good of friends are you?"

God, Roan wished they could talk about anything else. He'd spent so long isolating himself, holding back from his friends, it was as though he'd ingested truth serum and he couldn't lie. He wanted to. Definitely. But he hated not being honest.

"I met him awhile back." That didn't seem to satisfy Cam, because he continued to stare at him expectantly. "What?"

"You met him and yet you never introduced me?"

Roan knew that Cam was a huge fan. Knew that he would've been beside himself to meet any of the Arrows players.

"I couldn't," he admitted before filling his mouth with food.

"Ahh."

Roan tried to say, "Ahh, what?" but his mouth was too full. It came out sounding garbled.

Cam chuckled. "So it was one of *those* relationships."

It took a minute, but Roan managed to swallow, then chased the lasagna with iced tea before answering. "There was no relationship."

"No?"

Roan shook his head. "It was one night. Nothing more."

"Oh." Cam sounded disappointed.

Gannon picked up his glass, and Roan waited for him to speak. He could see the man's question in his eyes. "So you were seeing him?"

"No. I *saw* him. One. Night. I haven't talked to him since."

It was Cam's turn again. "One night? You had a smoking-hot"—Cam glanced sheepishly at Gannon, then back to Roan—"hockey player in your bed for one night and you just let it go at that."

"Not my bed. His," Roan clarified. "I met him at a bar, went home with him, end of story."

"So what was it like?"

Roan cocked an eyebrow. He'd never been the type to kiss and tell. Not even with his best friend. And quite frankly, Cam had never been the type to ask for details. Roan damn sure wasn't going to start sharing his personal life, especially not with Cam and his husband. But something passed over Cam's face, and Roan knew he was trying to get around to what he really wanted to ask.

So Roan waited.

They ate in silence for another minute or two and sure enough, Cam didn't disappoint.

"Was there a possibility of this going further? Or were you … uh … hiding from him too?"

Roan dropped his fork, pinning Cam with a glare. "I'm sorry, all right? Yes, I pushed you away, okay? I didn't want you to have to deal with her. She wasn't … Cassie. The drugs had turned her into someone else entirely."

Cam set his fork down. "I'm not talking about me," he clarified, his voice eerily calm despite Roan's outburst. "I'm as much to blame as you are, Roan. I should've been there for you. I should've pushed my way into your life, refusing to let you shut me out. But if there was something with this guy…"

"There wasn't, okay? Nothing worth talking about, anyway." And that was the truth. The night they'd spent together... Well, it had been off the charts, sure. But sex was sex. It didn't matter that Roan had never felt as connected to anyone in his entire life as he had with Seg that night. They had agreed to one night. Roan only did what he'd promised.

"He came to the marina looking for you today," Cam stated.

Roan's eyes widened.

Cam nodded, as though answering Roan's unspoken question. "Dare was there. Told him that you were taking some personal time."

"How did he...?" Roan stared at Cam, unable to finish the sentence.

"Know where you worked?" Gannon chuckled. "I'm pretty sure it was on the card you gave him."

"Shit."

"No," Cam countered. "Not shit. This guy's into you, man. He came looking for you. That's not a *shit* moment."

Roan shook his head in disbelief. "Probably only so he could get me to guarantee I'll never tell anyone he's into dudes."

"Closeted, huh?" Gannon asked.

"He's so far in he can't even see the door," Roan stated, hoping they didn't hear the disappointment in his tone.

"But if he wasn't, you'd be interested?"

Roan didn't answer that. "Dare didn't tell him about...?" He peered down the hall.

"No. Of course not." Cam looked at Gannon briefly, then back to Roan. "Seg said he'd like to talk to you. Asked Dare to give you his number."

"I can't talk to him," Roan admitted.

"Sure you can."

Roan shook his head. "I can't." He got to his feet, suddenly no longer hungry. "I've got to focus all my attention on Liam right now. I can't… I don't have time to deal with that."

Shit. He knew he was letting Cam and Gannon both see his true feelings, but he was a little shaken by the knowledge that Seg had come to see him. It had been hard enough for him to ignore the text Seg had sent the other night, but he'd managed. For Liam.

Although a spark of hope flared somewhere deep inside him, Roan knew he had to tamp it down. He didn't have time for this. Not for dealing with Seg or the unexpected and ill-timed feelings he'd managed to brush under the rug.

Hell, it was all he could do right now to keep going through the motions.

SOMETIMES SEG WISHED they had more games on the road. Especially on nights like tonight when he could do little more than drink beer at the Penalty Box and wish like hell Roan would show up out of the blue. He knew it wasn't going to happen, yet he still sat at the table with a half dozen of his teammates, pretending to be celebrating last night's win.

Truth was, Seg would've preferred to stay home tonight. After his trip out to the marina today—in which he'd hoped to find Roan—he'd been filled with disappointment. According to the guy he'd talked to in the small office, Roan was taking some time off for personal reasons.

Knowing he couldn't look too interested, Seg had played it off, pretending he'd been in the area and wanted to stop by. Since the guy had been the one who had taken them out on the boat when Arrows management had attempted some sort of team-building exercise last summer, they chatted about the possibility of doing that again. The conversation had gone on far too long, but Seg had hoped it put the guy's mind at ease, not leading him to believe that Seg was seeking out Roan for romantic reasons. Then again, he was pretty sure the guy in the office thought he was full of shit, but what could he do?

"What's up, Seg?" Spencer Kaufman asked, bumping Seg's shoulder as he passed by.

Seg didn't bother to respond. It was simply Spencer's way of checking in.

"Gorgeous, I think you might wanna go talk to my buddy over there," Mattias Valeri—their first line right winger—said to one of the puck bunnies who had snuggled up around the table.

Seg damn sure wasn't interested. A year and a half ago, he would've made a big production about some cute chick wanting to hop up on his lap and take a ride. That had been before Roan had blown his mind and made him seriously question what it was he really wanted.

"Chelsea," the little blonde said by way of introduction, coming around to stand beside him.

Casting a glare at Mattias, Seg pushed back from the table and let the woman perch on his leg.

"How old are you, doll?" he asked, both to make small talk and to ensure he wasn't about to make the world's worst mistake ever.

"Twenty-two," she said sweetly.

Twenty-two, his ass. She was nineteen if she was a day.

"You know what, sweetheart, I gotta hit the head. Keep my seat warm?"

She gifted him with a radiant smile, turning her attention to something being said across the table, as though in the past thirty seconds, she'd been pulled into the inner sanctum of the hockey underworld.

Christ Almighty.

Without feeling an ounce of guilt, Seg walked right out the front door and into the night.

It wasn't until he got home that he pulled out his cell phone. Rather than send a text to Roan, he decided to give the man a call. He was gearing up for what he wanted to say on Roan's voice mail when the rumbled, "Hello?" surprised him.

"Hey," Seg greeted, feeling a little tongue-tied all of a sudden.

"Hey."

"Got a minute?"

"Not really, no."

Seg smiled. "Then why'd you answer?"

"No fucking clue," Roan said with a snort of derision. "None whatsoever."

Seg liked Roan's honesty, even if it made him bristle a little.

"I heard you stopped by the marina today."

"Yeah. Wanted to talk," Seg explained.

"I won't be around much for a while. Did you need something?"

Seg swallowed, debating on how he wanted to do this. He could go with the truth, or he could use the same lame excuses he'd used for too long now, making up some bullshit that would likely get him no closer to seeing Roan again.

"Look," Roan began before Seg could get a word out, "I know you're worried that I might say something. I swear to you, what happened between us will stay between us. I don't have some crazy vendetta. I'm not looking to hurt your career, so you don't have to worry about that. It's been what? A year?"

"Fourteen months," Seg blurted.

What the fuck? Desperate much?

"Okay." Roan sounded surprised. "It's been fourteen months. I haven't said anything yet. I'm not gonna say anything now."

"I know that. That's not…" Fuck. Why was this so damn hard?

They said silence was golden. On a phone call, silence was a bitch. Seg's shoulders knotted the longer it went on.

"Okay. I'll just come out with it," he finally told Roan. "I want to see you. That's all I know to say. I've spent too damn long thinking about … that night. I just… Goddammit. Why is this so fucking hard?"

Roan sighed on the other end of the phone, and Seg realized he'd said all of that out loud.

"Can I see you again?" Seg asked. "I can come to your place."

"No."

Okay, that was a quick answer. The way Roan said it sounded more as though he didn't want Seg at his place and less like he was opposed to seeing Seg again period.

"I mean, I don't have a place right now," Roan continued. "I'm staying with friends."

"Then you can come to my place. Remember the way?"

"No, I can't."

Disappointment stabbed his gut.

"Look, Seg, I've got a lot going on right now. I really don't have time for … anything."

"I'll make you dinner," he offered.

Another sigh from Roan and Seg realized he sounded desperate.

"Tell me this," he told Roan, "do you even remember that night?"

There was silence for several seconds. Seg was starting to think Roan wasn't going to answer when, finally, Roan cleared his throat.

Seg held his breath.

"Yeah," Roan confirmed. "I remember it. Maybe a little too well."

Seg lowered himself to the couch, his legs unable to hold him up any longer. Neither of them said anything for what felt like an eternity.

Unfortunately, Roan was the first to speak. "Look. I really do have a lot going on in my life right now. I don't have time for—"

"Dinner?" Seg interrupted.

"Hell, I don't have time to eat most of the time, no."

Seg realized Roan was serious. "Something wrong?"

"My ... uh ... damn it." Roan cleared his throat again. "My sister died a few days ago."

"Oh, fuck, man. I'm sorry."

"Thanks."

"Was she sick?" Seg was craving even the smallest detail about Roan's life. For some stupid-ass reason, he wanted to know something about him other than he was the best fucking lay he'd ever had in his life.

"Yeah. You could say that."

To his dismay, Roan didn't elaborate, so Seg left it at that. "I really would like to see you again. I don't want to be a burden or anything. But maybe you could call me, you know, when you've got a few minutes to spare." Damn, he sounded desperate, but he couldn't help it. This man had him twisted up in knots.

"Yeah."

By his tone, Seg knew Roan wasn't promising anything. But he'd already said too much, made himself look too vulnerable. That was something he'd never done before and he didn't know what it was about Roan. He seemed to be his Kryptonite or something.

"I'll talk to you later," Seg told him.

"Yeah. Okay."

And with that, the call ended, and still, Seg felt no better than he had before the call.

Five

Almost two months later
December 10th

"WHAT DO YOU think, Liam?" Roan asked his son—yep, that was exactly how he was thinking of him these days—as Roan carried Liam into the new nursery he'd set up that very day. In their very own house.

"I think it suits you well, little man."

It hadn't taken much time at all for Roan to find a house. Granted, he'd had the help of his friends, and thanks to an eager-to-sell couple who needed to close in as few days as possible, Roan had managed to get it all handled in just under a month. The three weeks after he'd signed the papers, Roan had spent most of his time with either a hammer or a paintbrush in hand, working to make the new-to-them house their own.

Liam helped, of course. Roan had shown him paint samples, which had gone over really well. Apparently, Liam wasn't picky. So they went with a blue-gray on the walls in Liam's bedroom. That, combined with the white furniture and the new white ceiling fan, made the perfect room for a three-month-old.

Aside from slapping a few coats of paint on the walls, Roan had redone the floors, laying down hardwood and having carpet installed in the bedrooms. There was still a lot to do, but Roan was satisfied with the progress.

"One of these days, we've gotta work on my room," Roan told him as he carried the boy into the kitchen.

Liam's face scrunched up in that way that said he was ten seconds away from a nuclear meltdown, complete with an ear-splitting cry that would let the man on the moon know that he was hungry.

"Yep, I'm readin' your mind, kiddo. Got the bottle all ready to go."

While Roan bounced Liam gently in his arms, he got himself situated, then set about feeding him using only one arm while he carried a load of laundry to his bedroom.

It was almost eerie how much his life had changed in two months. Then again, it had been changing for a while now. Ever since he up and moved out of the small apartment above the marina office and into Cassie's less-than-desirable duplex, Roan had been living pretty much out of a gym bag. Now, he had twenty-five hundred square feet and a kid.

Life was good.

Okay, maybe not *good* good. But it was better than it had been. If only Roan could stop thinking about Seg. It was getting easier every day since he hadn't heard from the man since the night of that last phone call. The one that had freaked Roan out completely. While Seg had been admitting that he wanted to see him, Roan had been tempted to tell him that there was no way this could possibly go anywhere because he was now a single dad. How on earth would that work into a hockey player's schedule?

Not to mention, he seriously doubted Seg was looking for something serious. Now that he was a father, Roan couldn't fathom having casual encounters. What sort of role model would he be if he let his son see that type of behavior from him?

And that was exactly how Roan viewed everything these days. From Liam's point of view. He peered down at the drowsy baby in his arms. "I want to give you the best life possible," he whispered. "In order to do that, I have to keep my focus right where it is. On you. Not on handsome hockey players."

Anytime he thought about Seg, he reminded himself of what the outcome would be. If anything, Roan figured Seg was looking for a replay of that night. Sure, Roan wasn't above hoping for that as well. Seriously, his brain could easily be overruled by his libido from time to time. But those were simply fantasies. Nothing more.

"Seriously," Roan mumbled, more to himself than to Liam. "If I even wanted a replay, I would have to find a babysitter, hop in my truck, drive the half hour to Austin, another ten to Seg's place…" Roan pressed his lips to Liam's forehead. "By then, I'd be ready to run back home to you. It won't work."

While Roan separated the laundry, he glanced down at the baby still cradled in his arm. As usual, Liam had fallen asleep. Taking a break, he lifted Liam to his shoulder, patted his back gently until he'd earned himself a huge burp, then took the sleeping kid back to his crib. With monitor in hand, he headed back to the laundry. Before he could start folding towels, his phone rang.

His stomach instantly bottomed out, the same way it had every time the phone had rung since the night Seg had called. And just like every time since, it wasn't the hockey player on the other end.

"Hey, Cam."

"Hey, bro. Gannon was sitting here wondering—"

In the background, Roan heard Gannon grumbling, "Don't tell him a story. *You're* the one who was wondering."

"You were, too," Cam told Gannon, then turned his attention back to Roan. "Sorry. So, *I* was wondering if maybe Liam could come over for a sleepover."

"Tonight?"

"Sure. It's Saturday night, right? That's a good night for you to go out, maybe grab a beer, call up a hockey player…"

Roan snorted. "Ain't happenin', man."

"Oh, come on. I want to spend time with Liam. Y'all have been gone for two days, and it's too quiet around here."

"I'm seriously doubting that," Roan countered. "You never shut up, so I'm not sure how that's even possible."

Cam laughed. "It's still early. No game tonight. And I happen to have it on good authority that the Arrows are not on the road."

Roan shook his head, but strange thing was, he was seriously considering this. He could take Liam over to Cam and Gannon's, then head into Austin.

Or … maybe he could call Seg up, see if he wanted to grab dinner.

Maybe he'd want to stop by.

No.

This was a stupid idea.

Hadn't he just been telling himself that this new way of thinking was the only way of thinking? He couldn't do casual sleepovers with hot hockey players ever again.

"I just got Liam down," he told Cam. "I don't think tonight's a good night."

"Okay, fine. I tried. But the offer's open anytime. We'd love to chill with Liam for a while, if, you know, you ever need a break."

"I'll keep that in mind."

"You do that. Talk to you later."

"Later." Roan hung up the phone and dropped it on the bed, but he continued to stare at it.

Forcing himself to finish the laundry, he put it all away, then made a quick stop by Liam's room to check on him. Surprisingly, Liam had been sleeping for close to six hours a night, which was a blessing. If only Roan would go to sleep when Liam did...

"I'm gonna do it," he told himself when he returned to his bedroom to find the phone sitting on his bed. "I'm gonna call him."

He'd been battling himself for so long. And now, with Cam pushing him, Roan couldn't help but think about Seg all day and all night. Even if it went nowhere, why did Roan have to be lonely all the time? Sure, he had Liam, and the time he spent with the boy was more than he could've ever hoped for. Plus, Liam was only three months old. He was young enough that Roan could sow a few wild oats and he'd be none the wiser. That way, when Liam was older, Roan would be content to be alone.

Right now, the loneliness was almost too much to bear. However, this was a different kind of loneliness. A void that would be there until Roan decided to do something about it.

"It's time to do something about it."

SEG HAD BEEN in bed for all of five minutes when his phone rang. He glanced over at the screen. A smile instantly formed on his face and his stomach dropped.

He hit the talk button. "Hey."

"Hey," Roan said softly.

"What's up?"

"I don't know."

Seg settled back against the pillows, pretending it wasn't weird that he was stoked at the fact Roan had called him. Nearly two months had passed, and Seg had given up on ever hearing from Roan again. "You doing okay?"

"Yeah. Tired, I guess."

Seg could hear it in Roan's voice. He sounded exhausted. "You been working a lot?"

"No, actually. I've taken some time off. I ... uh ... just bought a house. Moved in a couple of days ago."

"Well, that's got to be stressful. No wonder you sound dead on your feet."

There was silence for a moment and Seg stared at the muted television. For two guys who'd spent only one night together, it seemed as though they were having a regular conversation.

"I am. Though, technically, I'm not on my feet right now."

"Where are you?"

There was a brief pause before Roan said, "In my bed."

Something in the way he said it had Seg swallowing hard.

"What are you doin'?" Roan inquired.

"Just sitting here. Watching TV." Seg smiled. "In bed."

"Really? On a Saturday night?"

Seg chuckled. "I'm not much of a partier, despite what you might hear. I spend a lot of time at home. During the season, we're on the road so much, when we're at home, that's where I want to be. My place. You know?"

"Makes sense, I guess."

"What about you? It's Saturday night. Why aren't you out?" Seg asked.

"Not big on the party scene either."

"No?"

"Nah. I'm too old for that shit."

Seg realized he had no idea how old Roan was. "And that would make you...?"

A rough chuckle sounded in his ear. "Thirty-three. Soon to be thirty-four."

"Ah." Seg grinned. "That *is* old."

"Yeah?"

This time Roan laughed. A real laugh. One that made Seg feel lighter, but he had no idea why that was.

"You're what? Twenty-seven?" Roan teased.

"Soon to be twenty-eight," Seg corrected.

"Six years... Nah. It won't be long until you're in need of a walker."

Okay, Seg really liked this side of Roan. The lighthearted side. It was a part of him Seg hadn't had the chance to see yet.

"Yeah, well. When I need a walker, we'll get you one of those hov-around carts."

Neither of them said anything when the laughter died down. Seg wanted to say so many things, but he'd spent the better part of two months chastising himself for coming on too strong with Roan. Since Roan had called him, he would let him lead the conversation this time.

"I ... uh... I really don't know why I called," Roan said. "I don't mean that in a bad way. I just wanted... Shit."

"What?" Seg asked. He wanted Roan to finish that sentence. "You just wanted what?"

"I don't know."

"Sure you do," he urged.

"I wanted to hear your voice, I guess."

Okay, so it was a damn good thing Seg was sitting down. "Come over."

"I can't."

"Let me come over there."

"I can't do that either."

Again, Seg noticed a hint of disappointment in Roan's tone. There was something the man wasn't telling him. Hell, there were a million things he wasn't telling him.

Why was he so adamant? Was there something wrong with his new place?

Oh, fuck. Was he married?

Damn it. That had never occurred to him before now. It made total sense, even when it didn't.

Rather than call him on it, Seg said, "Okay. I get it." He wouldn't push.

"No, you don't."

"Sure. We can talk. On the phone."

This time the silence stretched for a few too many seconds, and Seg figured Roan was going to let him go. He didn't want him to, but he wasn't going to do all the chasing here. As it was, he had no fucking clue what he wanted from Roan; he only knew he wanted to see him again. One night hadn't been enough.

"Can I tell you something?" Roan asked.

"Anything."

"Never mind."

"Come on," Seg said, keeping his tone light. "You can tell me anything. What?"

When Roan spoke again, his voice was lower, gruffer. "I want to do more than talk."

Instant boner. Seg's dick roared to life as though Roan had said, "I want to fuck you up against the wall." However, Seg pretended to misunderstand. "You mean like dinner?"

"No."

Okay. "Tell me."

"I shouldn't be doing this. *We* shouldn't be doing this."

"What?" Seg wanted Roan to say it.

"Shit. I'm sorry, Seg. I—"

"Don't apologize," Seg interrupted, keeping his tone gentle. "Take a breath. No one's forcing you to do anything. Why don't I let you go? And tomorrow, you can call me again. And the next day. I like hearing your voice, too." It was the truth.

"Right."

"I'm serious, Roan." Seg swallowed hard. "Sure, I'd like to get you naked and under me again. I'd jump on that in a second, trust me. But this is good, too."

Roan laughed, clearly not believing him. "You're right. I should go."

"Just promise me one thing," Seg added before Roan could hang up.

"What's that?"

"That you'll call me again. Whenever you're ready to talk some more." *Or do other things.* He obviously wasn't going to say that part aloud.

"I will," Roan confirmed. "Later."

Seg didn't even get the chance to say good-bye before Roan had hung up. But that was okay. Roan would call him again, of that he was certain.

Reaching beneath the blankets, Seg stroked his erection, his mind wandering to that night with Roan.

Damn, that'd been the hottest fucking night of his life. He still remembered everything Roan had done, the way his mouth felt on him, his hands.

Gripping his cock, he firmly stroked, his breaths coming faster, the pleasure taking over. What he wouldn't give to be with Roan right now. To have the man's lips wrapped around the head of his cock.

Seg pushed the blankets down, watching as his fist moved up and down his shaft, his thumb swiping the bead of pre-cum pooling on the tip. This was exactly what happened whenever he thought about Roan. He wanted one more night with him.

No, that wasn't true. He wanted many more nights with him.

"Oh, fuck," he whispered, his eyes darting to the TV, then back to his dick. "Roan ... I fucking need you."

Closing his eyes, Seg gave himself over to his release, his heart pounding, his chest heaving as he came down from that temporary high. Damn. He wished he could've spent more time talking to Roan, getting to know him. They didn't have to simply have sex. Seg would be content with more. Did Roan think like that? About him?

What he wasn't sure of was how this would play out. More importantly, he wasn't sure whether it even could.

But he damn sure wanted to see where it went. Even if it was only temporary.

It seemed Seg had spent his entire life chasing happiness that he never could get in his grasp. No matter how hard he tried, how many women he dated, he'd never once come close to feeling this strange euphoria he felt when he simply talked to Roan on the phone.

There was something about Roan that was different. Something other than the fact that he was a man. Seg knew that was more about his own hidden desires than anything else, but he wanted to see this through.

Mainly because he got the feeling it was the only way he'd ever know how to be happy in every sense of the word.

Six

ROAN ROLLED OVER, grabbing for his pillow to pull it over his head.

What the hell was that noise and why wouldn't it stop?

He reached out to hit his alarm clock, wanting the damn thing to shut up, but then the sound registered. It wasn't his alarm he was trying to ignore, that was Liam crying.

"Shit."

He bounded out of bed and made a beeline for the kitchen, popping the lid off the formula and grabbing one of the water-filled bottles. Liam was eating more these days. According to the doctor, he was gaining weight nicely, which was a relief considering how tiny he'd been when he was born. He dumped the appropriate number of scoops, screwed on the lid, and started shaking as he went to Liam's room.

It only took him three minutes to get the baby changed and settled with his late-night snack while Roan relaxed in the rocking chair he'd picked up last week.

God, he was tired. It felt like he'd been awake for a year, and he knew he'd gone to bed not long after he got off the phone with Seg. In fact, he'd forced himself to go to sleep, hoping he could forget the man who seemed to be flooding his thoughts these days.

Good news was he hadn't been dreaming about Seg. Bad news, he'd been dreaming about Cassie. About the day they'd found out she was pregnant.

Closing his eyes while he rocked Liam gently, Roan let the dream bring back the reality of that day.

His phone was ringing and he knew it wasn't time to get up. Hell, it felt like he'd only been asleep for a few minutes. Peeking through one eye, he peered at the clock on the bedside table. One twenty-seven a.m.

What the hell? He had *only been asleep for a few minutes. About twenty, in fact.*

Thankfully, his phone stopped ringing and he rolled again, only to come up short when the damn thing started the high-pitched shrill thing. Then he remembered, that was the ringtone he'd assigned to his sister Cassie. It was a mind-numbing reminder of how she was wreaking so much fucking havoc on his world.

"Yeah?" he grumbled into the phone, turning his head to the side.

"Roan, I'm at the hospital. I need you to get over here now."

Roan bolted upright in bed. "What's wrong?" he asked even as he snagged his jeans from the floor where he'd dropped them.

"You just need to come up here. I came in with a backache and... Roan, if you give a fuck about me at all, just get your lazy fucking ass up here."

Yep, that was Cassie. The sweet little sister he'd once known had been long ago consumed by the raging bitch drug addict who he now found himself trying to take care of.

"What hospital, Cassie?" he bit out, swiping his wallet off the dresser and tucking it into his pocket.

"Brackenridge."

Roan stopped short. "What?" Brackenridge was in Austin. A good forty minutes away. Why the fuck was...? "Goddammit, Cassie."

"Fuck you, too, Roan. I didn't ask for this shit."

He ground his molars together to keep from saying things he would later regret. His only mission in life right now was to survive. He'd made it this far, doing his best to take care of Cassie and keep her from... Keep her from what, he didn't know anymore. No matter how fucking hard he tried to keep her off drugs, she refused his help and did as she damn well pleased anyway. But, he was the only one in his family who was trying to help her. She'd burned her last bridge with their father, their stepmother was more than upset by all of it, and of course, Eva believed that Cassie could quit if she wanted to.

"I'm on my way," he ground out.

Roan was tempted to call Cam and let him know what was going on, but the last thing he wanted to do was drag his friends into this shit. He'd managed by no small feat to keep them all out of it. To them it looked as though he was being the loner asshole he'd somehow managed to turn into recently—in no small part thanks to his sister. He wanted more than anything to confide in them, to get some help before he found himself too far under to dig himself out. Only they didn't deserve the mountains of shit Cassie would rain down on them.

He knew there was only one fucking reason Cassie was at the hospital. Especially one in downtown Austin.

Vicodin.

The girl was looking for painkillers. She'd concocted this screwed-up scheme where she would walk into emergency rooms and complain of severe back pain. He didn't even know what bullshit she fed the doctors, but every damn time, she seemed to score. Of course, she'd played Roan for a while, and he had filled the prescriptions for her, not making the connection. Then she'd done the same to their father until finally Roan caught on. Where she was getting the money to fill them now, he didn't want to know.

After wrangling on a T-shirt, then pulling a ball cap on, Roan yanked on shoes and headed out to his truck. He estimated it would take a good half hour to get there with no traffic on a Tuesday morning. Which, unfortunately, would give him more than enough time to work up a good fucking mad.

He only hoped he didn't lose his shit this time. Cassie knew exactly what buttons to push to get him dangerously close.

Forty-seven minutes later, after parking in a nearby garage and walking into the hospital, Roan was escorted back to one of the small, glass-enclosed rooms, where he could see Cassie sitting up in the bed.

She looked like hell. In the past year and a half, she'd dropped a significant amount of weight. Rather than buy clothes that fit her emaciated body, she continued to wear oversized T-shirts and shorts day in and day out.

"Hey," he greeted when he stepped into the room.

HARMLESS

As soon as she saw him, Cassie rolled her eyes. Roan knew she hated him. She'd made that abundantly clear on more than one occasion. She didn't want him interfering in her life, so she did her damnedest to guilt trip him over every little thing. Her favorite was to let him know that he was a shitty brother because he'd been the one to cause their lunatic of a mother to turn tail and run because of Roan's sexual orientation. According to Cassie, if he would just be normal and appreciate pussy, they wouldn't have grown up without a mom.

The girl was ruthless.

Yet Roan still loved his little sister. He hated to see what the drugs had done to her. Hated who she'd become because of them. More than once, he'd considered telling her to figure her shit out on her own, that he was done. However, he'd never had the balls to come out and say it. It was bad enough that their sister, Eva, had written Cassie off. Eva had said that she did not want Cassie anywhere near her family, and by moving to Ohio, she'd made a point to ensure she never could be.

"What's going on?" he asked, glancing at the machines she was hooked up to.

"I came in because of my back problems. I'm in a lot of pain. I was hoping they could figure out what's wrong with me."

He knew the bullshit was simply because there were nurses around. She didn't have back pain.

"How'd you get here?"

"Cab."

Roan didn't buy it for a minute. "How'd you pay the cab driver?"

"Fuck you, Roan."

More than likely, some fuckup she hung out with had dumped her at the hospital. Hell, the type of people she hung around with probably would've dumped her a couple of blocks away and told her to walk. But Cassie never bothered to tell him the truth. Roan heard every single lie for what it was.

"I knew I needed help. No one seems to know what's wrong, but it hurts. I hurt all the time." Cassie was laying it on thick because there was a nurse currently reviewing one of the machines by the head of the bed.

"They did some x-rays and some other tests," Cassie continued. "I thought they'd let me go with some meds by now, but then they asked if I had any family who could come up here to be with me."

Roan frowned. That definitely didn't sound like status quo for this situation. Glancing at the nurse, he saw that she was trying to make eye contact with him. When she nodded toward the glass door, he told Cassie he'd be right back and followed the older woman into the hall.

"Are you Cassie's brother?"

Roan nodded.

"Your sister came in here earlier complaining of back pain. We've seen her in here before, a couple of years ago, for the same thing." She peered back at the door. "It's evident from her condition that…"

Roan didn't say anything, not sure what the woman was getting at.

"We believe your sister's addicted to prescription pain pills."

Among other things, Roan thought. "And you had her call me here, why?"

"The doctor would like to speak with you. I'm going to page her and let her know you're here."

Now he felt like he was under scrutiny. "So, I'm here for a reason? Something other than my sister's an addict and because she doesn't want help, there's little anyone can or will do to help us out? Because if the good doc wants to have a chat to let me know that my family should probably stage an intervention and get her some help, she can save her breath. I've heard it a million times. And we've done it twice that many times."

The woman's eyes softened, and Roan hoped she no longer thought his sister was living on the streets, strung out and ignored by her family. A lot of people assumed that, but it wasn't the truth. Shit. Roan was practically paying her bills to ensure she had a place to live. The only thing more he could actually do would be to move in with her.

Heaven help him. He did not want to do that. Ever.

"Let me page the doctor. You really are going to want to hear what she has to say."

Great.

He glanced over at the room where Cassie was still sitting, and he had to wonder what could possibly be bad enough that the doctor would call a family member down in the middle of the night. He understood if they wanted someone to pick her up, but this didn't seem as though he'd been summoned as her personal taxi.

Knowing he wasn't going to get out of this conversation with the doctor, Roan nodded at the nurse, then turned to go back in with his sister.

Might as well get this over with.

An hour and fifteen minutes later, Roan wished he'd never been woken up.

"She's what?" He couldn't believe what he was hearing.

While trying to avoid an all-out brawl with Cassie, Roan had been patiently waiting for the doctor to stop by. The nurse had informed him that she would be there as soon as she could. At four o'clock in the fucking morning, Roan wasn't sure what was keeping the woman away so long, but he'd been doing his best imitation of a good guy and drawing on every ounce of patience he possessed.

Only now, his patience had dissipated when the doctor told him that his twenty-nine-year-old, heroin-addicted sister was pregnant.

Fucking pregnant.

He peered over at her. Cassie had managed to fall into a fitful sleep after her last tantrum.

"We need to do an ultrasound to see how far along she is, but by my estimation, she's probably in her fourth month. Maybe further along if the baby's small."

"What does that mean?"

"It means she needs to get help. If she plans for this baby to live, she can't continue on … the way that she is. As it is, she told us there was no way she could be pregnant, which is the only reason X-rays were done. She's going to have to see a specialist who can measure the baby and follow its progress until birth."

X-rays? They had exposed the baby to radiation?

"Holy fuck. How can she be pregnant? How does she not *know?*" Roan wasn't sure why he was asking the doctor these questions.

"A lot of women show very few signs of pregnancy early on. If she isn't expecting it, she may not see the signs. She's not showing. It's still early yet. She's small, so it's possible she won't show for another month even. Maybe longer. Because of the drugs, it's possible the baby isn't developing appropriately, which means—"

"That makes no sense. A woman can't be pregnant and not know it."

The doctor gave him a look that asked him how he happened to know this since he definitely was swinging a penis between his legs. And okay, fine. Maybe Roan didn't know that for sure, but seriously. This was Cassie. How did she not know?

"Roan," the doctor began, her voice still calm, still gentle, "it's obvious she has a problem. A very serious problem."

Roan pulled off his hat and brushed his hands through his hair. "I know that."

"Do you know when the last time she used was?"

He shook his head. If he had to guess, it was only a couple of hours ago.

The woman sounded even more sympathetic when she said, "It's important that she understand that everything she puts in her body is hurting this baby."

He nodded. What the hell was he supposed to do about this? Was he supposed to move in with her? Hover over her? Make her do the right thing?

Shit.

Unfortunately, he really didn't see any other way.

Liam jerked in his arms, startling himself. Putting the empty bottle down, Roan shifted him to his shoulder and patted his back. Several minutes later, when Liam was once again dry and full, Roan put him back in the crib and headed for the kitchen. He cleaned out the bottle and set it in the dish drainer to dry.

He needed to sleep, but the stress was getting to him. He knew that was the reason he continued to dream about Cassie. While he wanted to call Seg, to hear his voice again, he knew he needed to stop that nonsense before he did something stupid. He had enough on his plate right now. If there was any hope that he could live a stress-free life, he needed to figure out how this worked for him and Liam. That meant he didn't have time to work anyone else into the equation.

No matter how much he wished he had someone to lean on right now.

Seven

"HELL NO. I'M serious," Locke stated adamantly. "If there was some chick I wanted ... like, *really* wanted ... I'd make sure she knew it."

Seg stared at their backup goalie. At twenty-three, Josh Locke wasn't much different than the rest of them had been at that age. Hotshots in the NHL, they'd all thought they knew every damn thing. Locke was no exception.

"What if it wasn't that simple?" Patrick Benne questioned, clearly playing devil's advocate on this particular topic.

Benne was a newcomer to the team this year. He'd seamlessly transitioned right into the thick of it, too. Everyone liked to give him shit—something about cowboys and Canadian ranches—but the guy had no problem dishing it right back out, which made everyone like him. They were a close-knit group, even if they harassed each other ruthlessly. Right now, Benne was their star on the ice—a left winger who was proving to be one of their strongest forwards.

"How could it not be that simple?" Locke countered. "I want her. I let her know. Simple."

"What if she's married?"

"That's stupid," Locke said, frowning. "I don't want a married chick."

"You say that now," Benne continued. "Say she's super-hot, super-smart, and her husband's a dick."

"Married's married, dude," Locke said, lifting his beer to his lips. "Not interested."

"Okay, say she's got a kid," Benne pushed. "Not married, but she's got a kid."

"Hell yeah," Mattias Valeri chimed in. "Look at Kaufman's sister. Single mom. Fucking smoking-hot."

All eyes moved to Mattias. Seg peered around, praying like hell that Kaufman wasn't within ear shot. The guy wouldn't hesitate to take Mattias to the ground for saying that about his sister. Worse than that, Seg hoped Kingston hadn't overheard either. Hell, it was obvious the goalie was all sorts of hung up on the woman. Mt. Rushmore would likely pummel the guy for looking at her.

"Kids don't scare me," Locke said, although he had that same not interested look in his eye.

"Does that go for everyone else?" Benne questioned. "You'd do a chick with a kid?"

For whatever reason, Benne looked right at him. Seg lifted his beer, opting for a nonverbal *no comment* on that one. It wasn't the kid thing he had an issue with. It was the chick thing. At the moment, he was so caught up in his thoughts of Roan, Seg wasn't even sure a woman could make his dick hard again.

Which scared the shit out of him.

It wasn't a secret that Seg had been one of the biggest players on the team. Hell, he remembered a few occasions when he'd had more than one woman in his bed at a time. Sure, it generally involved copious amounts of alcohol. But he'd been looking for something to scratch that particular itch. The problem had been that he hadn't known what that itch even was.

Until Roan.

What freaked him out the most was that the one night he'd spent with Roan had sated him in ways he'd never imagined. And yeah, it had left him wanting more.

With Roan.

Seg had battled those desires for as long as possible. He'd simply been hoping that the next woman in his bed would be the one who made him feel whole, complete. That never happened. And now he knew why.

He was gay.

Not bisexual, not bi-curious. He was gay with a capital G.

And he could admit it to himself. However, it was a secret he would have to keep to himself for as long as he hoped to play in the NHL. He could only imagine how freaked his teammates would be if they ever found out.

Damn. Seg remembered a few years ago when a football player came out publicly. He couldn't remember who it was, which likely meant the guy had faded from the limelight, sidelined indefinitely, never to be heard from again.

That was the way shit worked in professional sports.

Thankfully, there weren't many men in his past who could come forward with that sort of accusation. The two that could were from so long ago, and those nights were nothing more than fuzzy memories obliterated mostly by all the alcohol. Hell, Seg hardly remembered them; surely his partners at the time didn't either.

Except Roan.

Seg remembered every single minute of that night.

And he knew Roan did, too.

Damn it. He wanted to see the man.

As it was, it had been five days since he'd heard from Roan, and every time his phone chirped, he lost a year off his life. Roan had promised to call him again. The anticipation was going to be the death of him.

"No issue with kids," Mattias noted. "But that's tricky. Can't simply throw some MILF a bang, you know? Not cool."

"Sure you can," Benne stated. "Nothing to say that sex means commitment. What? You think they don't have needs, too?"

Seg knew this conversation could go on for hours. There were times these guys got into arguments over the stupidest shit. Of course, he'd been known to chime in quite often. But not tonight. They'd already been at the Penalty Box for two hours, and he was ready to call it a night. They had the entire weekend off before they headed out of town on Monday morning for their next game.

If he left now, he could scrounge up dinner and veg on the couch while watching … something … for the next few hours. Yep, that was what he would do.

"I think I'm going to head out," he told the others before pushing to his feet. If he left soon, he could miss the influx of puck bunnies that would likely flood the place in the very near future.

"Cool. See ya, Seg."

"Later, Seg."

He made a quick trip to the bar to close out his tab before getting in his Range Rover and heading home. He'd been in his house all of five minutes when his cell phone rang.

A quick glance at his screen and Seg felt a jolt in his chest. If Roan kept this up, there was a chance that Seg wasn't going to live to see thirty.

"Hey," he greeted as he headed to the refrigerator to see what he could make for dinner. "You called."

There wasn't a response, so Seg immediately thought he'd lost the connection. Sometimes he didn't get calls inside the house. He glanced at the screen. Nope, not disconnected. It was still counting the seconds. He put the phone back to his ear. "Roan? You there?"

A sigh was the only response, but Seg knew he was going to say something.

"That dinner invitation still open?"

It was a good thing he didn't have a beer in his hand because he would've been cleaning glass up off the floor. "Uh … yeah … it's still open," he assured Roan.

"Can I come over?"

Seg swallowed hard, then counted to ten, not wanting to sound too eager. "Sure. When?"

"Right now," Roan stated.

Seg was about to tell him that he'd see him soon, but the doorbell rang.

"That's me," Roan said. "I'm standing on your front porch. I'm gonna hang up now."

The call disconnected, but Seg kept the phone to his ear as he wandered back to the foyer and stared at his front door. Holy shit. He felt his heart slam against his ribs. It pounded harder than when he ran a ten-minute mile during warmups. He had to remind himself to breathe. Not to mention, he had to tell himself he'd look like a little bitch if he went to the door all eager and excited. That wasn't cool.

But shit.

Roan Gregory was at his front door.

Holy fuck.

ROAN DIDN'T KNOW what the hell he was doing standing on Colton Seguine's front porch, but here he was. He'd gone into work for a few hours today, bringing Liam with him because they were both tired of being cooped up in the house. It had been one of those days when nothing anyone did or said could keep Liam from screaming like a banshee. Roan figured he could pass on the good cheer at the marina, share some of the love with Dare and Cam.

It was true, Dare had a way with kids. The guy was a damn miracle worker in the way he made a face and all the fussiness seemed to fade away. Liam was under the guy's spell, that was for sure. Unfortunately, Dare didn't have that same magic when it came to Roan's mood, and he'd been strung tight. Even when the others had Liam cooing and grinning, Roan hadn't been able to let go of the tension in his shoulders.

Apparently, everyone noticed, because they gave him a wide berth. Luckily, for the sake of Roan's sanity, Cam had offered to take Liam for the night. This time, Roan hadn't been able to refuse. So, after work they had gone home, and Roan had packed up everything Liam would need and plenty of stuff he probably wouldn't. By the time he was heading over to Cam's, Liam was once again in rare form. Only then, Roan felt bad leaving him, and he'd told his friend as much. Cam had rolled his eyes and practically thrown Roan out, telling him they *wanted* to spend the evening doting on the baby and that he should go find something interesting to do.

"Go see a movie," Cam had suggested.

"Yes," Gannon had agreed. "But have dinner first. Dinner, then a movie."

Cam had then added, "And while you're at it, find some hot guy to do those things with."

And that was how Roan ended up on Seg's porch, staring at the front door, wondering why the man wasn't opening it.

Shit. What if Seg had someone over? What if he didn't want Roan to come inside?

Damn it. He hadn't thought about that. Hell, he hadn't thought about anything except jumping in his truck and hightailing it to Austin as fast as he could.

The door slowly opened, and Roan held his breath.

Damn.

The guy looked as good as he remembered. Better even. He was wearing a white T-shirt that stretched across his chest, dark jeans that showed off his powerful legs. Yum. And his eyes... Those sparkling blue-gray eyes twinkled with what he hoped was approval.

Seg stared at him for a minute; still, Roan didn't breathe. Much. Only through his nose. Silently.

"Come in," Seg finally said, pulling the door open wider and stepping out of the way.

All the memories from that one night he'd been here came flooding back. How he'd followed Seg from the bar, how he'd argued with himself over whether he would stay or go. How he'd refused the beer and been hell-bent on getting Seg naked.

But that was a different time.

"I should've called first," Roan told him as he stepped inside. "You know, before I just showed up at your door." Roan turned to face Seg. "I didn't mean to interrupt. If you have company or—" Roan stopped talking when he realized Seg was still staring at him, slowly moving closer.

The heat he saw in those brilliant blue eyes had his hands clenching into fists. He had to hold himself back. If he looked nervous, Seg obviously didn't notice, because he took another step closer, their eyes still locked together. It was as though time stood still while this crazy sexual energy swirled around them, gaining intensity with every passing second.

Seg stopped when they were face-to-face.

Oh, fuck. The guy smelled so damn good. Too good.

Without touching him in any way, Seg tilted his head and leaned in. Roan wondered if he expected him to pull back. He sure as hell hoped not, because the only thing he could do was let himself be kissed. And when Seg's tongue thrust into his mouth, Roan grabbed him, jerking him closer, backing up until he slammed into the wall. And still, their mouths remained fused together.

"Fuck," Seg mumbled, his arms coming around him. "Goddamn, Roan. Do you know how fucking long I've wanted to do that again?"

Oh, Roan knew, but he didn't speak. He couldn't. He pulled Seg's mouth back down to his while Seg started yanking Roan's shirt up. Roan was ready and willing, but when he pulled back to help him out, Seg was the one who stopped.

"Shit." He sounded breathless. "We can't do this." Seg chuckled. "Not yet anyway."

They definitely could, but again, Roan didn't speak. Hell, he wasn't sure he'd be able to find his voice.

"Dinner. That's why you came here."

Roan grinned. "Right. Dinner."

Food was the absolute last thing on his mind right now.

Seg's eyebrows lowered slightly. "Unless that's code for something?"

"No," Roan admitted, taking a deep breath and trying to get himself under control. "It's not. Dinner's good."

"Okay. Well, this was kind of short notice so..." Seg glanced at the kitchen, then back at Roan. "Pizza okay? It'll take about half an hour to get here."

"Pizza's perfect."

Roan certainly didn't mind waiting.

And who knew what they could do in half an hour.

Eight

SEG WAS GLAD he'd managed not to maul Roan in his foyer. It had been a close call there for a minute. From the second he laid eyes on the man, he'd wanted nothing more than to strip them both and slide into the warmth of Roan's body, clinging to him, taking everything the man was willing to give him.

The only thing that had stopped him was fear. Fear that tomorrow would come and Roan would be gone and it would be another year before he managed to bump into him again, by sheer luck.

No, Seg didn't want that.

He wanted more than that.

And the only way to make that happen was to put the brakes on. For a little while, at least.

By the time the pizza had arrived, they'd been settled on the couches in his living room and managed small talk. Roan had asked about the season, Seg had told him preseason had been shit, but the season was off to a good start. Seg's contract had been renewed, and he would likely be with the Arrows until he retired. Not a bad thing. The team was better this year than last. Management was making some changes, focusing on the issues they'd seen last year.

They'd continued to talk about the marina where Roan worked while they ate pizza at the breakfast bar. Turned out, Roan was one of the owners of the marina. They were more than a decade in and he loved it. When Seg had attempted to ask about Roan's sister, he'd shrugged off the subject.

Seg knew he wasn't going to get much more out of Roan tonight. At least in the way of conversation.

"Want to go for a swim?" Seg offered.

"A little cold for that, no?" Roan was watching him closely.

"It's heated. Up to you."

Roan moved to the sliding glass doors in the breakfast nook, peering out. Seg tried to keep a safe distance between them. He didn't want to spook Roan, didn't want the man to decide he needed to go. He'd picked up hints of nervousness on Roan's part. Not just tonight but on the phone when they'd talked the other night as well. Seg didn't want to send him running.

Rather than wait for Roan to say something, Seg moved over to him, then flipped the lock on the door and opened it. "Come on."

The lights on the patio were off, but the ones in the pool were on, darkening the water with a deeper blue hue. Without waiting for Roan, Seg kicked off his shoes, pulled off his shirt, slipped out of his socks before pushing his jeans and boxer briefs down. He walked right over to the water and waded in, turning to see Roan watching him.

"It's warm, I promise."

"Yeah," Roan mumbled. "I think the water temperature's the least of my worries right now."

Seg let the warm water settle around him while he watched the fantasy play out right in front of him. Roan stripping down on the patio. It was as though he was gauging every move he made as he made it. Several minutes later, he was joining Seg in the water.

"Since you work at a marina, are you on the water a lot?" Seg asked, trying to keep the conversation going.

"On it, not in it," Roan said, moving his arms beneath the water.

"You have an issue with water?"

Roan shook his head, his attention on Seg. He liked that about Roan. The man always seemed to be watching him, as though he wasn't quite sure how he'd gotten here.

"You own a boat?"

"The marina does."

Okay, so this wasn't going far. Roan inched closer, his hair slicked back, eyes dark. "I don't wanna talk anymore, Seg."

Well, there you go.

Taking that as his cue, Seg moved closer. He stood to his full height, looking down at Roan momentarily before pulling him into his arms.

"We don't have condoms," Roan said, his eyes heavy-lidded as he breathed against Seg's mouth.

"Not having sex," Seg said. "Not yet."

Right now, he just wanted to kiss this man, to touch him, to hold him. What it was about Roan Gregory that made him want things he'd never wanted before, Seg wasn't sure. But there was something.

Seg pulled them out to deeper water so that he could stand and still be submerged. Roan moved with him, their lips brushing, hands roaming.

"Kiss me, Roan," Seg insisted.

Roan didn't hesitate, leaning in closer, his chest sliding against Seg's. While Roan's tongue tangled with his, Seg put his arms around Roan, pulling him even closer. Sensations he'd remembered from that one night so long ago plowed into him. He hadn't been with anyone since that night—man or woman—and this ... this was the reason why.

"Too long," Seg whispered against Roan's mouth. "It's been too long.

Roan pulled back, staring at him. Their eyes locked, and Seg was captivated for a moment, completely caught off guard by the feelings that warred inside him. He was scared shitless that he would say something he shouldn't. Something incredibly ridiculous like *I love you.* No way did he love this man, yet what he was feeling was so foreign to him. Being in Roan's arms again ... it was like coming home.

But his thoughts scattered when Roan wrapped his hand around Seg's cock, stroking him slowly, their dicks sliding together.

"Oh, fuck." Seg let his head fall back against the edge of the pool. "Don't stop doing that."

Roan's mouth was on his jaw, his neck. He was kissing and licking while he fisted their cocks together, driving Seg damn near out of his mind. When Roan's lips wandered to his ear, Seg's heart beat twice as hard. He remembered the way Roan took charge, the way he demanded things from Seg that he'd never thought he could give.

"I want to feel you in my mouth," Roan whispered. "Right now."

Seg opened his eyes to meet Roan's gaze. He was serious.

"Get out of the pool, Seg," Roan instructed, his tone ringing with amusement.

Okay, yes. Getting out of the pool would make that particular task much easier. Safer too. Sure.

Turning, Seg planted his hands on the outside edge and shoved himself up and out of the pool. He dropped to his ass, turning so that he was facing Roan, who was still in the water. Roan came to stand between his legs, staring up at him while he once again wrapped his fingers around Seg's dick.

The air was brisk, but his body was heating itself, thanks to the man standing before him. When Roan's mouth descended, the air temperature no longer fazed him. The only thing he could focus on was the glorious sensation of Roan's raspy tongue along his shaft.

This was too damn good to be true. Seg sat there, stunned as he watched Roan lick him like a fucking ice cream cone. His tongue trailed up his length, then back down. He didn't rush, simply savored him, making Seg sweat even with the chill in the air.

"I'm not gonna make you come yet," Roan said.

Seg nodded, not sure what he was supposed to say to that. Roan's mouth felt so fucking perfect as he took him to the root.

"Son of a bitch," he rumbled. "Fuck, Roan... That feels good."

"I know," Roan said with a smirk. "And it's gonna feel a hell of a lot better."

Yeah. Seg wasn't sure how that was possible, but he sure as hell wasn't going to argue.

ROAN KNEW SEG was trying to take this slow. Of course, if he had his way, he would spend the rest of the night driving the man absolutely out of his fucking mind. For one, Seg was hotter than hell when his eyes glistened with heat like they were right now. The man was hanging on the razor-sharp edge, obliterated by pleasure, and it was empowering to know that Roan was the one pushing him closer and closer.

He continued to work Seg's dick with his hand and mouth, never rushing. He was enjoying the fuck out of this and he knew Seg was, too. It wasn't until Seg wrapped his hand over Roan's, forcing him to stop stroking him, that he knew the man was close to his limit. Not wanting to finish him off yet, Roan released his cock, then tugged on his hand, urging him back into the water.

With a splash, Seg joined him, then jerked him closer, fusing their lips together. Once again, Seg was in complete control. Roan didn't mind that as much as he'd thought he would. Ever since their one-nighter, Roan had known that he was powerless when it came to this demanding hockey player. Never in his life had he allowed another man to have that much control over him. At the time, he'd figured it was a one-and-done type deal, he might as well experiment.

Turned out, he'd thought about that night more than any other sexual encounter he'd ever had. Part of him wanted to see if Seg still had that power over him now or if it had just been that one time.

"Let's move this to my bedroom," Seg suggested. "So many things I want to do to you. Can't do them here."

While Seg spoke, he was moving them toward the stairs, and Roan let him lead. He wanted whatever he could get from Seg. At least for tonight. Tomorrow was a different story. He'd promised himself that tonight was a one-time thing. Like last time. It would have to be enough to tide him over for a while. A long while.

Roan had too much going on in his life to invite Seg into it. No way would this be a permanent thing, and he wasn't about to bring a man into his life who wouldn't be there for Liam in the long run. But this ... one night of incredible sex with a man he couldn't stop thinking about ... this would be enough.

It would have to be.

Once they were out of the pool, Roan allowed Seg to lead him into the house and to the bedroom. He was shivering by the time they made it, but Seg fixed that by flipping on the shower and pulling him beneath the heat of the spray.

Seg never stopped kissing him and Roan never let him stop. He wanted this. Wanted all of this.

He could've remained steadfast if it wasn't for Seg fisting his cock roughly, stroking him until he damn near saw stars. At that point, he pulled back, trying to draw air into his lungs. When he did, Seg spun him around so that he was facing the shower wall.

"Need to be inside you," Seg growled against his ear as he tore open the condom he'd snatched on their way to the bathroom.

Roan picked up where Seg left off, stroking himself while Seg suited up, then grabbed a bottle of lube. He briefly wondered if it was the same lube that had been in here last time. Fourteen months ago. No, wait. Sixteen now.

Sixteen months since he'd last had sex. A long fucking time to go without, that was for sure.

"Slow," Roan warned when Seg pressed the head of his dick against Roan's asshole. "Been a while."

"Me, too," Seg whispered against his ear. "Not since you."

Roan's dick jerked as those words registered. Was Seg for real? Had he honestly not had sex since…? He wasn't sure he believed it, but those words worked for him. Leaning closer to the wall, Roan spread his legs wider, allowing Seg to push in deep.

"Oh, God, yes," Roan hissed, his cheek pressed against the cool tile.

"Feel good?" Seg's voice sounded strained, as though he was trying to hold back.

"Fuck yes. Deeper… Go deeper."

Seg pushed in deeper, pulled out slowly, in deep again. Heaven. This was fucking heaven.

"Roan…" Seg groaned. "So tight. Fuck … not going to last…"

"Fuck me," Roan urged, pushing back against Seg. "Fuck me hard. Come in my ass."

Roan had to grip the tiled ledge as Seg began pounding his ass, slamming into him deep and hard. He didn't even need to touch his dick; within seconds, the overwhelming sensations drove him right over the edge.

"Coming…" Roan choked out.

"Oh, fuck. Me, too," Seg rasped. "God, me, too."

And just like last time, Seg made Roan see stars as he came. Hard.

Nine

PERHAPS IT WAS due to the stress he'd endured waiting for this moment. Or maybe it was because of everything else going on. Whatever it was, Seg could hardly keep his eyes open when he'd dragged Roan out of the shower, dried them both, then tumbled into bed.

That was six hours ago.

Now, as he lay there watching Roan sleep, he wanted to stay like this forever.

Yes, he was an idiot. Yes, he was stupid. This wasn't a relationship, and probably not the beginning of one either. But damn it, having Roan here… Seg hadn't felt this at peace in a long time. Maybe not ever.

He must've made some sort of noise, because Roan shifted, then his eyes slowly opened. He blinked once, then met Seg's gaze.

"Hey," Seg said, smiling.

Roan turned, looking as though he was trying to find the clock.

"It's only five," he told him. "Still early."

"Shit." Roan moved, but before he could get out of the bed, Seg pulled him back down.

"Don't go yet," he said softly, pressing his lips to Roan's shoulder, then moving closer. "Not yet."

"I need to," Roan said, but he didn't attempt to get up again.

Seg kissed him, trying to inhale him, not ready to let him go. He had a feeling that once Roan was out of his bed, he would never be back.

To his relief, Roan's hands came around him, sliding up and down his back as they moved closer. Seg gave in to the kisses, let himself get lost in Roan for a little while. Before he knew what happened, he was on his back, Roan kneeling between his legs.

"Remember last time?" Roan asked, his voice husky from sleep.

Seg nodded. He didn't know which part Roan was referring to, but since he remembered every single minute, every glorious detail, it wasn't like he was lying.

"Good," Roan brushed his lips against Seg's. "This time it's my turn."

Lying there, Seg watched Roan grab a condom and lube. Within seconds he was sheathed with the latex, and that was when Seg realized which moment Roan was referring to.

"Knees to your chest," Roan ordered, his voice, as well as his eyes, full of heat.

Hesitantly, Seg pulled his legs up, exposing himself to Roan.

He sucked in air when Roan reached down, grazing Seg's balls with his fingers. He moved lower, teasing his ass, then pushing one finger inside.

"Oh, God," Seg whispered. "That... Damn, that feels good."

"You missed this, huh?"

Seg nodded, unable to tell Roan just how much.

While he moaned and writhed, Roan fingered his ass. Slowly at first, then deeper, faster.

"Need you..." Seg cried out. "Need you inside me. Now!"

Roan shifted, aligned their bodies, and bless heaven and earth, he pushed in deep. As he'd done that first time, Roan went slow, filling Seg completely before retreating.

"Open your eyes," Roan insisted. "Look at me."

Seg forced his eyelids open. He hadn't even realized he'd closed them. He peered into those golden eyes staring back at him. Oh, how he wished this were real. He wished that Roan wasn't here for only sex, but… "Oh, God, yes."

Roan managed to brush his prostate, over and over.

"Roan." Seg meant that as a warning, but it sounded more like a plea. "Fuck."

"That's what I'm doing," Roan muttered, leaning down so their mouths were touching. "I'm fucking you. Just the way you want me to."

He had no fucking idea.

"Tell me," Roan urged. "Tell me how much you need to be fucked."

"Yes," he ground out. "I need it."

"You need me to fuck you hard. To possess you." Roan nipped his lower lip. "Tell me, Colton."

Oh, dear God. No one called him that. No one ever used his name. To hear it on Roan's lips… It was almost too much.

"Say it," Roan demanded.

"Yes. Goddammit, yes!" Seg tried to pull Roan closer, wanting to feel him deeper. "I want you to fuck me. Hard."

"Hold your legs. I'm gonna nail you to this mattress," Roan growled.

Oh, fuck. Seg reached up and pulled his legs closer to his chest, his breaths slamming into his lungs as roughly as Roan began pounding into him.

"Fuck," Roan hissed. "Oh, fuck, Colton. So damn tight. I'm … not gonna last… Fuck."

Seg didn't want him to last. He wanted Roan to come.

With a wild roar, Seg let go, his dick jerking, spurting on his chest while Roan watched. Seg saw the heat flare, heard his rough inhale seconds before he rammed into him once more, coming with a stream of curse words Seg had never expected to come out of his mouth.

※ ※ ※ ※ ※ ※

"I'M ON MY way," Roan told Cam's voice mail. "Fuck."

He couldn't believe he'd spent the entire night at Seg's.

No, he could believe it. Last night had been ... fucking phenomenal. To the point Roan hadn't wanted to leave.

And now he felt like the world's worst father.

It didn't matter that Cam hadn't called him. That from the lack of messages, Roan could only assume Liam was completely fine and there was nothing for him to worry about. It didn't matter that Liam was completely safe, and Roan trusted Cam and Gannon with his life. Roan still felt like shit because he had allowed a night of exquisite sex to make him forget all of his priorities.

Worse ... part of him wanted to go back to Seg's. To crawl back into bed with him. To tell the man all of his secrets. Roan was tempted to tell Seg about Liam, to ask him if he'd ever wanted kids.

Only he wouldn't do that because he knew the answer. Seg would look at him as though he'd lost his mind. The guy was a hockey player. He spent most of his time on the road. No way would he want to be tied down.

Which meant it was in Roan's best interest to let last night be the end of it. That was what he'd promised himself when he'd gone over there.

"Yeah," he said to his eyes in the rearview mirror. "How'd that work out for you *last* year?"

Shit.

Roan was so screwed.

He was thinking long term with a guy who would never come out of the closet because it would hurt his career. No, Seg had never told him that exactly, and he probably wouldn't, but Roan could tell. And Roan lived his life out and proud. The way he wanted to live it. No way was he going to even entertain the notion of being with someone who would hide him away.

Nope.

No fucking way.

So why had he shown up on Seg's doorstep last night? That was the question of the hour.

Seriously. Roan hadn't had sex in more than a year. It wasn't like he wasn't going to survive without it.

Except sometimes—ever since he'd seen Seg at the arena—he felt like he might not.

And last night, Seg had given him what he needed, and Roan had returned the favor. Roan knew he was the first and only to top Seg. He'd known it the first time around. And if what Seg said was true and he hadn't had sex since then, it was still true.

"Damn it," he growled at his dick, which was coming to life.

Roan needed to stop thinking about him.

Last night was fantastic. It was also in the past, where it needed to stay. Roan had to get to Cam's, pick up Liam, and do what he'd promised his sister he would do. Take care of Liam. That was the only thing he should be focused on. Definitely not some closeted hockey player who would be happy to throw him a bone from time to time but would never be able to provide anything more than that.

No, Roan definitely didn't see Seg hooking up with a single dad. No way. That would probably scare the guy to death.

"Okay, good," Roan mumbled to himself. "Next time Seg calls, I won't answer. That's the easiest thing to do. I'll put him out of my mind. If I don't hear his voice, it'll be easy."

Yeah, right.

Even *he* didn't believe that shit.

Didn't mean he wasn't going to take his own advice though. All in all, it really was the best thing for everyone.

Ten

Three and a half weeks later
January 5th

"FUCK!" SEG ROARED, gripping his stick, tempted to break the fucking thing over his knee. The only reason he didn't was because that shit would get him in some serious fucking trouble.

Plus, it would hurt like fuck and he was already dealing with what was, quite possibly, a broken finger.

Rather than make matters worse, Seg exhaled roughly, skated to the sin bin, then planted his ass on the bench and grabbed a water bottle.

He was going to have to get his shit together. The ice was no place for him to be losing it. Coach wouldn't give a shit that he was stoking this fucking flame of anger that had been burning inside him since the day he'd tried to call Roan only to get his voice mail. Three fucking weeks ago. Coach wouldn't care that Seg had left at least five messages since then and not once—not *one fucking time*—had Roan returned his call or texted him back.

Sure, Seg had made plenty of excuses for Roan. After all, it had been the holidays. He'd figured Roan was busy celebrating Christmas and New Year's with his family. That was the reason he hadn't called him back.

Right.

Because there hadn't been seventeen other fucking days within that time frame when Roan could dial the goddamn phone.

Fuck.

It was exactly as he'd feared. Roan hadn't been interested in anything more than one night. A goddamn meaningless hookup. And though Seg had agreed to that the first time around, he damn sure hadn't signed up for it the second. If he'd known...

Fuck that. Seg knew that if he'd known he would never see or hear from Roan again, he still would've let him come inside. He wanted Roan with a passion that rivaled anything he'd ever known. Even now as he fumed after that bullshit penalty he'd received.

Glancing up at the clock, he saw there were only thirty-five seconds left on the two minutes he'd been relegated to the box.

Grabbing the bottle again, he squirted water in his mouth, swallowed, then put it back. By the time the clock was at the ten-second mark, he was on his feet, waiting for the door to open. It wasn't that he was looking forward to the ass reaming he was going to get from Coach, but sitting here thinking about Roan wasn't going to change a damn thing.

He knew—just like with everything else he'd wanted in his life—if he really wanted Roan, he had to make it happen. He couldn't sit around with his thumb up his ass and wait for shit to happen.

The door opened and Seg shot out onto the ice, heading for the bench as the Arrows crossed the blue line. Someone else would go out there this shift while he sat and fumed a little longer.

That was the way it worked.

"THAT WAS A good game," Cam said, although he didn't sound quite so upbeat.

"Yeah, if by good you mean shitty," Roan offered, following Cam down the row of seats to the aisle.

"Yeah, they lost, but still."

"Still nothin'," Roan argued. "They looked like shit. Something's off with them."

"They look better than last season," Cam countered.

"Agree. But they aren't meshing out there. It's like their timing is off."

This was the same conversation—although it went either way—that he and Cam had after most Arrows games. Didn't matter if they were watching at home or if they'd come to the arena. They hadn't been able to go to many games this season, so when Cam called and offered to take him while Gannon and Milly babysat, Roan had been hard-pressed not to say yes.

Once they made it up the steps to the concourse, Roan fell into step beside Cam. He glanced up to realize they weren't walking toward the doors they'd come in from the parking lot.

"Where're you goin'?" he asked, feeling suddenly nervous.

"Phoenix told me to stop by after the game. Said he had something for us."

Roan narrowed his eyes. "Well, I'll wait for you outside."

"Bullshit," Cam snapped. "No way are you gonna miss seeing the players again."

"Yeah, I am," he confirmed, making sure Cam heard the unwavering tone.

Cam kept walking, but for some stupid reason, Roan didn't stop and turn around. He continued to follow Cam. Maybe if he was quiet, he could disappear into the background and no one would know he was there.

Right. Because that had worked so well last time.

As they reached the area that led to the locker rooms, Cam slowed, his eyes scanning the crowd.

"Who're you lookin' for?"

"Mia," Cam stated. "Phoenix and Tarik's wife. Phoenix said she'd be here to take us back."

"She's short, man," Roan said matter-of-factly. "You're not gonna see her with all these people around."

"Cam!"

Cam turned and cocked a brow at Roan, clearly telling him that he couldn't possibly be more wrong.

"Hey," Mia greeted with a smile. "You remember my husband Tarik?"

Behind Mia was her husband Tarik Marx. Roan had learned long ago, when you saw Phoenix, you generally saw Tarik, too. Apparently, the bodyguard/spokesman for the Austin Arrows was interchangeable when it came to which body he was guarding. It looked as though he was here for Mia's protection tonight.

"Nice to see you again," Cam said. "This is Roan Gregory. One of the marina owners and my closest friend."

Mia shook Roan's hand, then Tarik extended his. "Nice to meet you," Roan said.

"Well, come on," Mia said excitedly. "Phoenix put together some stuff that he thought you guys might like."

"Stuff?" Roan glanced over at Cam.

Cam shrugged.

"You know, jerseys, pucks, sticks. Bunch of autographed stuff." Mia shot them a grin over her shoulder. "He's more than impressed by what Gannon's doing."

Cam nodded, but Roan simply stood there staring. When he didn't inch forward, Cam looked at him.

"Gannon's working with the children's home. His company's running a contest, and the kids are getting hands-on experience in developing video games. He thought it'd be cool to throw some hockey gear into the mix. He came up with the idea after they did a charitable event at Christmas."

Roan had heard about Gannon's company partnering with some local place, and he knew there were kids involved, but he hadn't paid much attention past that. Gannon had always been involved with the community, especially when it came to kids.

"The Austin Arrows Foundation is thrilled to be contributing," Mia continued, leading the way. "He said they had such a great time last year. Right now, he thinks the team needs something to take their minds off the game. Some sort of team builder, so he's working to get them over to the home."

Roan also knew about the Austin Arrows Foundation and all the charities they worked with, but he didn't ask questions. He was secretly hoping they'd be able to slip out without anyone else seeing them. With all the commotion and people moving around, there was a possibility.

"He wants to get them over there ASAP," Mia said, still walking. "He wants to get it on the calendar now. He gets antsy at this point in the year and he starts forgetting some things. He told me this was far too important to let slip by."

Roan could understand that. With their current standings, the Arrows were well on their way to making it to the playoffs; however, they didn't have much room for error, so they had to stay focused. With the new year well underway and the trade deadline coming up, it was easy to get caught up in other things. If they wanted it, they really did need to get on another hot streak. And soon.

Mia stopped in front of the doors to what appeared to be an office. Across the hall was the Arrows locker room. Or part of one. A set of double doors was open and there were players wandering about, reporters with microphones rumbling question after question.

"Roan?"

Fuck.

Roan's spine went instantly straight when he heard Seg's voice. Knowing he couldn't be rude, he managed to pivot around to face him. His smile wasn't nearly as forced as he'd been planning. Seeing Seg was … better than good. In an effort to appear friendly, he offered a hand. "Hey. Good to see you again."

Seg glared down at his hand, then met his eyes again. Rather than shaking his hand, Seg held up what appeared to be a bandaged finger. Roan instantly wondered if he was all right, but he didn't ask questions. He sensed that Seg wasn't in the mood to answer them.

"Yeah," Seg said curtly. "Good to see you again."

Roan had no idea what to think, except damn, the man looked good. He'd already changed out of his pads and skates, wearing an Arrows cap and a dark gray T-shirt stretched across his chest. He clearly wasn't ready to leave, hence the lack of a suit. Roan knew the players left the arena in a suit.

"I need to talk to you for a second," Seg said, surprising him. "Alone."

Okay then. Roan turned back to see Cam staring at him. If he didn't know better, he'd think there was a rueful smile on the man's lips.

Rather than stand there and look like a dumb ass, Roan followed Seg down the hallway and closer to an exit door.

When they were out of earshot of the others standing around, Seg stopped but made sure his back was to the people down the hall.

"I tried to call you," Seg said. Although his voice was pitched low, there was a distinct ring to it.

Roan could tell he was pissed and he was working pretty damn hard to hide it.

"I know," he replied, trying to sound nonchalant. As though he didn't give a shit that a previous hookup had tried to get in touch with him. Truth was, in every spare minute he had, he'd thought of nothing except for Seg.

"I'm coming by tomorrow," Seg stated. It wasn't a question; it was a flat-out statement. Almost like a threat. "I want to talk to you."

"Can't do that," Roan told him, desperately trying to avoid his gaze.

"Tough shit."

Roan met Seg's eyes, holding them. He made sure Seg saw every ounce of defiance that had built up in him. No one was going to talk to him like that.

"I don't want to see you," he lied.

"Bullshit." Seg's voice dropped another octave. "But if that's your stance, so be it. I'm still coming by so we can talk."

Roan shook his head.

"It's nonnegotiable, Roan."

Roan took a step closer, getting right up in his face. "You want to play rough? You think you can threaten me? There's a room full of people behind you who would be over the fucking moon to know a few things about you."

Seg never moved; his gaze never wavered. "You want to threaten to out me? Fine. That doesn't change a goddamn thing. You want to ruin my career? Have at it. That doesn't mean I don't have a few things to say to you."

Shit. That threat didn't work the way he'd hoped. It wasn't like Roan would ever out the man anyway. That was his fear showing. Fear that Seg would find out things about him that he didn't like, and Roan preferred that didn't happen. He wanted his memories with the guy to remain untainted by anger or disappointment.

"See," Roan grumbled, "that's the reason I don't answer your calls, Seg." Roan peered behind Seg to ensure no one was listening. "I'm not gonna sign on to be anyone's dirty little secret. Not now, not ever. You want to keep parading around with women so the tabloids will pick that shit up, that's your business. But I'm not the man who will sit back and watch."

That time his words did seem to surprise Seg.

And even though it was only a partial truth, Roan knew that was the excuse he was going to have to stick with.

Eleven

ALTHOUGH IT SOUNDED like a legitimate reason for Roan to keep his distance, Seg didn't buy it for a second.

Oh, sure. Maybe the guy wanted to live out and proud. Seg got that vibe from Roan. He got that vibe from all of Roan's friends as well. They didn't hide. They didn't give a shit about what anyone thought of them. That was great and fine.

Unfortunately, it wasn't that easy for everyone. Especially not for Seg.

Still, he wasn't going to let it stop him.

"I'm still coming by," he insisted. No way was he going to let Roan slip through his fingers one more time.

"Not an option," Roan hissed. "I'm done, Seg. No more."

With that, Roan brushed past him, bumping Seg's shoulder as he did. It took everything in him not to put his fist through the wall. Considering it was made of concrete blocks, that would've been a tragic thing. Instead, Seg remained where he was, fuming. When he finally got some of his anger under control, he turned around to see Roan's friend coming out of the office, carrying an armful of stuff. Seg watched Roan, who looked disinterested in anything that was going on.

Before the two of them turned to leave, Roan glanced once more down at Seg, and he held his stare. Seg was going to Roan's place. Even if it meant he was going to piss Roan off. He deserved the chance to say something. And then, if Roan didn't want to have anything to do with him. Fine. He'd go about his business.

Maybe if Roan would make it a little less clear that he wanted him, Seg might be able to buy his bullshit. But he'd seen it in Roan's eyes. He'd seen the heat that flashed there. Roan wanted him. Whatever Roan was running from, Seg didn't think it was entirely his fault.

He finished in the locker room, spending the required ten minutes on the bike, followed by a few calisthenics, then on to the showers. By the time he was dressed in his suit, the reporters had dwindled and the guys were leaving.

Seg grabbed his bag and headed out to the parking lot.

It had taken a little effort, but Seg had Roan's address. He knew where the man lived, but he hadn't had the guts to go see him yet. He considered waiting until tomorrow, going to the marina instead. But that was Roan's place of business, and Seg had no intention of causing the guy any problems. He merely wanted a chance to say how he felt.

"See you at practice tomorrow, Seg," Kaufman called out as he headed down the hall.

"Yeah."

He should probably go home and get some sleep so he wasn't dead on his feet tomorrow, but he'd had enough. No more running from what he wanted. If the world found out about him, so be it.

His phone rang as soon as he got in the Range Rover. He hit the Bluetooth button to engage the call.

"Hey, Ma," he greeted, trying to be cheerful but failing.

"You okay, Seggy? How's your hand?"

He sometimes wondered how his mother noticed everything.

"It's good," he assured her. Yeah, his middle finger on his right hand was broken, but the trainer had wrapped it, which was the best he could do. Being that he was left-handed, it wouldn't be nearly as difficult to deal with as it could've been.

"Is it broken?"

"Yeah, but it's good, Ma. Promise."

"I was thinking I'd come down and stay for a couple of weeks at the end of January. I didn't get to see you enough at Christmas."

"I'd like that," he told her, and it was true. Although he'd managed to get home for two days at Christmas, he hadn't seen her since late October when they'd had games in Ontario and Calgary. Seg always made a point to visit her when they were in Canada, and he always looked forward to the times she came to visit him.

"Good. Okay, then. If you need to talk, you know my phone number."

Seg didn't say anything for a minute. He wanted to talk to her now, but he wasn't sure what he could say.

"Seggy? Are you really okay?"

"No, Ma. I'm not," he admitted, still sitting in his SUV in the arena parking lot.

"Want to talk about it?"

"Not really." It was the truth. He'd rather talk about anything else.

"Does it have to do with that woman you were seeing?"

Seg sighed. "No, Ma. I told you, the women I've dated … they're only friends."

"I get the feeling that's true," she said, her voice soft, understanding.

He wondered if she knew.

"But there is someone?" she probed.

"There is," he admitted.

More silence followed, and Seg desperately wanted to get the courage to tell his mother, but he couldn't seem to find the words.

"Seggy, do me a favor."

"Sure."

"Breathe." Her voice was soft, soothing, the same way it'd been his entire life. "Stop for a moment and simply breathe. The choices that you need to make aren't as difficult as you think. I've never been prouder of you in my life. You deserve happiness in every aspect of your life. And if your next decision is what makes you happy, honey, then I say go for it. Do what's right for you, because you're the only person who can make that choice. I'm here if you want to talk."

Seg felt his chest constrict. His mother had always been his rock. Her support was steadfast, unwavering, and that was something that had never changed throughout his life. "Thanks, Ma."

"I love you, Seggy."

"Love you, too."

When his mother disconnected, Seg sat in the parking lot and considered her words. He could do this. He *would* do this. Nothing was going to change until he decided to make that change.

And he was ready.

More than ready.

AFTER PICKING UP Liam from Cam's, Roan went straight home. He took the time to bathe his son, watching the little boy grin and coo in the warm water. Liam was picky when it came to baths. Sometimes he loved them, others not so much. Tonight was a good night, though, and now his son was clean, fed, and sleeping soundly in his bed.

Roan knew he should probably get some sleep, too, but he was too keyed up to close his eyes. He couldn't stop thinking about Seg's threat to come by. No way could the man just show up. Seg had no idea where Roan lived, but he still worried.

Not because he didn't want Seg to show up on his doorstep and insist that Roan stop hiding either. It would probably be the best thing that ever happened to him. Sure, Seg would probably turn right back around and run out the door when he saw the baby swing in the living room or the package of diapers sitting on the kitchen table. Roan knew Seg didn't have a clue what he was getting himself into, but in the same regard, Roan was tired of hiding.

He'd spent a year and a half hiding from everyone. It started when he'd mistakenly informed his best friend he was in love with him. Then he spent months trying to protect Cassie from herself, and during all that time, he'd alienated himself. For his entire life, he'd thrived on his friendships. He wasn't a loner, didn't do well being alone. And though he had Liam, the loneliness was still there, still gnawing at him.

Roan stopped pacing when the knock on his front door sounded.

Without looking, he knew exactly who was out there. How he'd found him was anyone's guess. Why he'd come tonight instead of tomorrow like he'd said…

Shit. Shit. Shit.

Roan couldn't move. Fuck, he couldn't even breathe. For a second, he considered hiding all the baby stuff, but he thought better of it. If Seg wanted to fight this out, he could, but he had to do it knowing all the facts. This was Roan's life now and he didn't want to change it. Not for anyone.

Going to the door, he smoothed down his shirt, then reached for the knob, taking a deep breath in the process.

The sexiest man alive was standing on his front porch, wearing a black suit, crisp white shirt with the button open at his neck. No tie for Seg, but that didn't surprise Roan. Still, he looked good enough to eat.

"How'd you find out where I lived?" he asked, not bothering to step back out of the way.

Seg simply stood there, staring at him.

Roan's breath lodged in his throat.

"You don't have to let me in," Seg finally said. "But I've got some things to say to you. I'll do it out here if you'd like."

Feeling slightly put out, Roan nodded. Seg's threats didn't bother him.

A hint of disappointment flashed in Seg's eyes, and Roan felt like a shithead, but he didn't relent.

"I don't know why you're running from me," Seg began. "Maybe I'm delusional, but I can't help but think that what happened between us—twice—doesn't usually happen. Not for me anyway."

Roan waited, biting his tongue to keep from agreeing.

"I turned twenty-eight six weeks ago, Roan. Not once in all my life have I ever met someone who has taken up so much of my headspace. Not. Once." Seg sighed. "I can't stop thinking about you. Fuck, at this point, I can't sleep for thinking about you. If you don't want me, don't want to see where this might go, fine. But I need you to say it. And I need you to make me believe it, because dammit, I feel something between us."

The fact that the man could make him melt with a few words only pissed him off. Seg was destroying his resolve, and Roan had to be strong. "You're in the closet, Seg. How the hell do you even know what you feel? You're hiding."

"Maybe I am, but I'm not the only one. It sure seems like you're doing some hiding of your own."

"You don't know the first fucking thing about me," he countered, hating that Seg was right. Roan *was* hiding. He'd been doing it for a long damn time now, at the expense of his own happiness.

"You're right, I don't. But not because I don't want to know you. You simply have to let me in."

"And then what?" Roan asked, his anger rising. "We're gonna fuck like rabbits and then you're gonna disappear with the next supermodel to come your way? Is that how it works? I'm gonna fuck you in the dark of night while some woman gets to parade around on your arm and smile for the camera? I don't live in the dark, Seg. And I damn sure don't plan to."

"Is that really what this is about?" Seg's mouth thinned, his eyes narrowing.

Roan couldn't answer because he knew that it wasn't. Not really.

"Do you want me to find a reporter and tell him I'm fucking a guy? That no matter how hard I try, I can't stop thinking about you? Tell him that a year and a half ago, my life changed in a matter of hours? That my priorities got screwed up at that point? That my career became the least of my fucking worries?" Seg frowned. "Or do I tell him that the same guy showed up on my doorstep and spent the night in my bed and I woke up realizing that my entire life has been a fucking lie? That I'm tired of living it that way? Is that what you want?"

Roan's eyes widened. He wasn't sure if Seg was spouting bullshit or if this was the truth.

"Or do you want to open that door and show me what you've been hiding, Roan? Because, yeah, I might be in the closet, I might not be ready to let the world know my personal business, but I'm not the only one who's hiding." Seg's voice lowered even more. "If those two nights meant even half as much to you as they did to me, you'll let me in, Roan."

Son of a bitch.

"I…" Roan knew he needed to argue, but he didn't even have a case.

Those two nights meant more to him than any other night he'd spent with any other man. He wanted Seg in his life, in his bed. Unfortunately, he needed to remain grounded in reality before he got too caught up in the things Seg was saying, because the man honestly didn't know the first thing about him.

"Let me come in, Roan."

It was said more as a demand than a request, and damn it all to hell, Roan found himself stepping back, making room for Seg to move past him.

Twelve

SEG WASN'T SURE his legs were going to carry him across the threshold. He'd honestly believed that Roan was going to send him on his way. Somehow, he managed to put one foot in front of the other. When the door closed behind him, Seg found himself glancing around the room.

It suddenly dawned on him that this was his very first glimpse at Roan's life.

He noticed the bright, open space, the muted beige tones on the walls, the giant television mounted above the fireplace, a huge brown suede sectional set up to separate the small dining area from the living area.

The small house was … homey. It felt like a place you wanted to go to after a long day at work, a place to sit down and relax. Seg wasn't sure if that was because of the niceness or the cleanliness or simply if it was because Roan was there.

Of course, that wasn't *all* he noticed.

His mind whirred as he took in the baby swing sitting at one end of the sofa, a package of diapers on the two-seater dining room table, the blue baby blanket lying over the arm of the couch, and the pacifier sitting on the coffee table.

"I have a son," Roan blurted, coming around to stand beside him. "If that bothers you, I think—"

"But you're not married, right?"

"Uh … no."

"No long-term boyfriend?"

"No."

Yeah, it was safe to say Roan had been hiding something, but the overwhelming relief at knowing it wasn't a husband or significant other nearly brought Seg to his knees.

Seg spun around so fast he nearly knocked Roan over. Instead, he grabbed Roan's head and pressed his lips to the man's. He wasn't rough, but he hoped like fuck Roan felt his relief.

"I thought you were married," he mumbled against Roan's lips before pressing his forehead against Roan's. "I thought you were hiding because you were in a relationship. The idea of you belonging to another man gnawed at my gut, made me crazy."

Roan pulled back, staring into his eyes. "Did you hear me? I have a kid."

Seg smirked. "And that should bother me why?"

"Because…"

Clearly Roan didn't have an answer for that one.

"Because I'm a hockey player? Why in the hell would I want kids? Or because I'm in the closet? Couldn't possibly want kids then either, right?"

Roan's golden eyes widened, and Seg knew the man had been using both of those things as excuses for not being with him. Roan definitely intrigued him, even if he had a way of pissing him off like no one else.

Forcing himself to take a step back, he released Roan. "Is he here? Your son?"

"He's asleep."

"Ahh." Seg purposely lowered his voice. "I'm sorry, I'll try to be quiet. I didn't mean to be so loud."

"Is this really happening?" Roan looked sincerely perplexed.

"You don't think too highly of me, do you?" Seg retorted, ignoring the hurt that consumed him.

Roan's dark eyebrow lifted. "You thought I was married."

"Touché." Seg glanced around the room once more. "How old is he? Your son."

Seg heard Roan release a breath. "Four months. Tomorrow. His name's Liam. He's my sister's son. I'm his legal guardian, now that she's…"

Yeah. Seg didn't need him to finish that statement. He nodded in understanding.

"Can I get you something to drink?" Roan offered, his eyes fixing on anything except for Seg's face.

"Sure. Whatever you've got is fine."

"Baby formula, beer, water, milk, tea…"

"I think I'll pass on the formula this time," he answered with a grin.

When Roan stared at him, he could tell the man was still trying to figure him out.

Rather than let him come up with his own reasoning, Seg took a step forward, then another until he was once again crowding Roan. "I don't know about you, but *right here* is where I want to be *right now*. I'm not here to push or prod my way into your life, but you let me in the door. I think the most we can do is live in the moment, eh?" Seg tilted his head to the side. "I can't deny how much I want you, what I'm willing to risk simply to be here. I'm not asking you to give me more than you can, Roan."

"I'm not good at this." Roan's words were so soft, so tormented.

"I want you. The real you. With all your baggage. I don't expect you to be someone you're not. Let's just take this one step at a time, see where we go?"

It was what felt right to him, and personally, Seg was tired of being someone he wasn't. The fact that Roan let him in the front door was enough for him. Right now.

Unable to resist, Seg leaned down and kissed Roan. He wasn't trying to consume him the way he had every other time. He simply wanted to feel him, to taste him, to explore him. To be with him.

When Roan kissed him back, Seg put his hand on Roan's hip, pulling him closer. Not close enough for their bodies to touch completely, but closer. Enough that he could feel the man's warmth. Seg didn't let the kiss ignite, not wanting to allow Roan to get into his own head for too long.

He pulled back and met Roan's gaze head on. "This," he whispered, "is all I'm asking you for."

Roan nodded. "Beer?"

Seg gave an answering nod. "That's a good start, too."

ROAN FELT STRANGELY comfortable with Seg wandering around his house. He wasn't sure how he expected the evening to go once he'd allowed Seg to sweet-talk his way inside. And sweet-talk he had.

Seg's words were still running through Roan's head. Even now, as they sat at the kitchen table, staring at one another.

"So, tell me more about Liam. He's four months old." Seg grinned. "And forgive me, I'm not up to speed on all things baby."

"Don't feel bad," Roan told him. "I'm not either. He's precious though. No, he doesn't sleep through the night, but he's sleeping for about six hours at a time. I consider myself lucky there."

"I'd like to meet him sometime," Seg said softly, drawing Roan's attention back to him.

He still wasn't sure that this was real. Colton Seguine, star defenseman for the Austin Arrows, a man Roan had slept with twice—well, to be fair, it had been more than twice, but only two nights—was sitting at his kitchen table asking about his son.

"And your sister," Seg prompted. "What happened to her?"

"She overdosed. Not on purpose. She was addicted to drugs."

"Oh, damn. I'm sure that was hard."

"It wasn't easy, no." Roan glanced at his hands once again, holding the beer bottle tightly. "I moved in with her when she was five months pregnant. I guess I was hoping to be her savior, to get her out from under the drugs. It didn't work."

"And the baby's biological father?"

Roan shook his head. "She had no idea who he was. Said it could be one of a dozen." He didn't think she was exaggerating either.

"Probably for the best," Seg noted. "I'm sure Liam's got everything he needs with you."

"I'd like to think so. My parents aren't exactly convinced of that. My stepmother thinks it's not a good idea for him to be raised in a gay household."

Seg leaned back. He looked as though he was considering that.

"My father died five years ago," Seg explained. "My mother and I are close, but not that close. We talk every day, but I keep her in the dark about a lot of things. She's back home in Toronto, so I don't get to see her as much as I'd like. She gets down here every couple of months, and I visit whenever we have games up there. Ever been to Canada?"

Roan shook his head.

"She still lives in the same house I grew up in." Seg grinned. "When I visit, I sleep in the same bed I did when I was a teenager."

"Does she know that you're…" Roan doubted she did, but he wanted to ask anyway.

"I think she has an idea, but no, I've never told her. I've never told anyone."

"That why you date women?"

Surprisingly, Seg nodded. "I didn't think that was the case until… Well, if I'm completely honest, it wasn't until you." He sounded resolute in his explanation, and Roan found he liked his honesty. "I've kept all female contact on the friendship level since … a year and a half ago. I've got a few women who're willing to be on my arm and not expect anything from me. Recently, I did a mental health awareness benefit dinner with a woman who works in the Arrows media department. She asked me. Again, as friends."

"So no sex with women since … me?" Roan still found that hard to believe.

"No sex with *anyone* since you."

Nodding, he looked down again. "I guess it's not too farfetched."

"You think it would be? That because I'm a professional athlete, my dick works differently than yours? I can't control myself?"

Roan felt his defenses shoring up. "I didn't say that."

"You didn't have to."

Sighing, he took a sip of his beer, then met Seg's gaze head on. "I haven't had sex with anyone since you either. So, no, it's not unbelievable. But I don't live my life in the public eye. I don't have anyone prying into my business every time I turn around. It's easier for me." He could admit that much.

"The interest tends to lag when you don't give the public something juicy," Seg stated. "Plus, they've got all they need right now, feeding off the failings of our last two seasons. The speculation over whether or not the team management is capable of bringing us back from the bottom is off the charts."

"Y'all will get through this." Roan was resolute in his belief of that.

"We will," Seg replied, sitting up straight. "So, tell me about your parents. You mentioned your stepmother. What about your mom?"

Roan hated talking about his mother, but he found he liked sitting here with Seg, getting to know him on more than a physical level. Although, he was having a damn hard time keeping his hands to himself. His palms itched with the need to touch him.

Shaking off the thought, he remembered what Seg had asked. "She left when I was a teenager. Actually, she left when I came out to my family. She insisted the devil had inhabited my body and she wasn't about to subject herself to that."

"Ouch."

"Yeah. So, when she left, I vowed never to hide who I truly was to anyone. If people don't like it, they can mind their own fucking business."

Seg glanced down at the table and Roan realized what he'd said. He hadn't meant to be so harsh about it.

Roan sighed again. "I didn't mean that it's wrong of you to keep your secret. I get it, even if I don't like it. I've paid attention. It's not easy for professional athletes to come out."

"No, it's not."

"Hopefully that'll change at some point." Roan wasn't going to hold his breath, but he got it. He really did.

"One day," Seg noted before taking a long pull on his beer.

"And until then...?" Roan had to know. He wasn't about to invest his heart in this man only to have him refuse to go out in public with him. It was one thing not to show affection in public, but Roan wanted what his friends had. He wanted to live his life, proud of the man he was with and vice versa.

"Can we take this one day at a time?" Seg inquired, his eyes imploring Roan.

Knowing he wanted to see where this thing was going, Roan had no choice but to agree. After all, he'd spent the past year and a half thinking about Seg. And the man was right about one thing. Whatever this thing between them was, it didn't happen every day. Hell, he wasn't sure it happened every lifetime.

Roan nodded, but before he could say anything, a familiar wail sounded from the monitor sitting on the bar. He glanced over to see Seg smiling from ear to ear. Seg must've seen his confusion because he got to his feet.

Seg shrugged off his suit coat and laid it over the back of the chair. "I get to meet him, eh?"

Strange how Seg's eagerness went straight to his heart.

Thirteen

AFTER FOLLOWING ROAN down a short hallway off the living room, Seg paused while Roan opened the first door they came to. For whatever reason, Seg's chest felt as though he'd been inflated. Why he was so excited, he had no fucking clue.

The blue-tinged glow from a nightlight allowed him to make out the furnishings in the room. Crib, changing table, rocking chair. When Roan flipped on the light, the colors came to life. On the wall were several black-and-white framed pictures. They were mostly of Liam and Roan, with a couple of a woman Seg assumed was Roan's sister. Looking at them had some unnamed emotion filling Seg's chest.

A baby.

Roan was a dad.

Seg watched as Roan went right to the crib, smiling down at the little boy, who was dressed in blue pajamas and clearly unhappy about something. Truth was, Seg really didn't know the first thing about babies. He was an only child and his parents didn't have any siblings either. Which meant, without any brothers or sisters or cousins, and without any friends who had small children, Seg was completely out of his element. This was new for him.

Exciting.

Like he'd told Roan, he wasn't up to speed on all things baby, but he could use his common sense. The little boy probably needed a clean diaper or food or both.

Sure enough, Roan deftly changed the squirmy baby's diaper, in record time at that, then lifted him into his arms. The ear-splitting cries simmered down to a pathetic little sob that wrenched Seg's heart. He was so consumed by the sight in front of him it took a second for him to realize Roan was staring at him. It took another second to notice the surprise in Roan's eyes.

Seg offered a tentative smile as he reached out and rubbed the baby's downy-soft head. The little boy stared at him, seemingly taking in his facial features. Seg wondered what his first thought was.

"Can I hold him?" Seg asked. "You know, so you can get a bottle or whatever."

That request seemed to stun Roan even more, but he didn't argue. Seg took instruction from Roan on how to hold him. Apparently, at four months old, Liam was capable of squirming out of Seg's arms if he wasn't careful, especially if he threw a tantrum, which, according to Roan, was bound to happen any second now. That scared him a little, so he kept a firm grip on him.

"You're tiny, little guy," Seg whispered to him as he followed Roan out of the bedroom toward the kitchen. "You're gonna have to get some meat on your bones so you can play hockey when you grow up. That or baseball. Maybe your dad likes baseball."

Roan did his thing in the kitchen, putting together a bottle, then turning back to him expectantly.

"I'll feed him," Seg offered, simply because he was enjoying holding the little guy. "You know, if that's okay with you." He certainly didn't want to overstep.

Roan nodded toward the living room, so Seg headed that way, careful to keep Liam close to his body as he sat down. Roan propped a pillow under his arm, and Seg laid Liam down in his lap. Seg was careful to keep his right hand propped on his leg to keep Liam from hitting his finger.

"Keep his head propped up," Roan told him softly.

Seg did as instructed, then took the bottle and, what do you know, Liam's fussiness died instantly as he took the nipple into his mouth.

Part of him had expected Liam to be little more than a bundle of skin and bones. It appeared he already had quite a personality. As Seg fed him, Liam tugged at the bottle with one hand while kicking his left foot repeatedly. They watched each other intently until Liam stopped drinking and grinned. Seg laughed, realizing he was distracting the kid from his task.

"You sure you don't have experience with kids?" Roan asked, sitting down beside him.

"First time to ever hold one," he admitted, still smiling down at Liam.

"I remember the first time I held him," Roan mused, staring down at his hands. "I was terrified that I'd hurt him. He was so tiny when he was born." Roan's gaze lifted. "And sick. He was addicted to drugs like his mother. He was in the hospital for a while, and Cassie didn't want to have much to do with him. So I would go down to the nursery every chance I could. They let me hold him and feed him. Sometimes I would sit there and stare, wondering how in the world anyone could be that small."

Seg could hear the love in Roan's tone. The man was completely in love with the little boy he now called his son. Seg had to admit, he was a little jealous. Of both of them.

It didn't take long for Liam to finish off his late-night snack and fall into dreamland once again.

"What do I do now?" Seg whispered. He hadn't read the baby manual, but he'd watched enough television to know that something came next.

"You need to burp him."

"All right, little guy, don't get mad at me," he said softly, shifting Liam so that he was once again on his shoulder. He patted the little boy's back gently.

"Probably gonna have to add a little more force than that," Roan informed him with a grin. "He's much sturdier than he looks."

Seg patted a little more firmly, not wanting to hurt Liam but taking Roan's instruction as gospel. Within minutes, there was a loud baby belch that made Seg laugh.

"Does he go back to bed now? Until the next time?"

Roan nodded, his eyes wide as he sat there staring at them. Seg liked that he'd surprised Roan. It might be true that Seg didn't know the first thing about Roan, but the opposite could be said as well. A lot of people stereotyped professional athletes, when in truth, most of them were normal guys, seeking normal lives outside of their sport.

Seg was one of those. At one point in his life, he thought he'd have a brood of kids, a wife, a house in Canada. But he knew underneath it all that some of those dreams weren't his, they were what he felt he was supposed to want. Did he want kids? Absolutely. Did he want a wife? No. He'd come to accept the fact that he was gay. Although he couldn't admit it, feared what that news might do to his career, Seg still accepted it.

But that didn't change the fact that he still wanted a family. Kids, a husband, a house to hold them all.

Pushing to his feet, he carried Liam back to his room. Seg passed him over to Roan and watched carefully as he put him back in the crib.

"No blanket?" Seg whispered, noticing the crib was completely empty.

"Nope."

Well, then. Seg had a lot to learn.

Without a word, he led the way back to the living room, but rather than sit down, Seg turned to face Roan. He wanted to strip the man naked and bury himself in his body, but he knew tonight was a turning point for them. He wasn't about to make this about sex and give Roan an excuse to run and hide again. This was going to take some finesse on Seg's part, he knew.

"Thanks for letting me come inside," Seg told him, stepping closer. "I'm serious about this. About us. I know you're probably skeptical, but I want to see where this goes." He offered a smile. "And I'm pretty relentless in my pursuit of what I want. Truth is, I've never wanted anyone or anything as much as I want you."

Roan didn't respond, but Seg didn't expect him to.

Reaching for Roan, Seg leaned in and kissed him. Slowly at first, then more insistently. He pushed his tongue past Roan's smooth, warm lips, wrapping his arms around him and holding him close. When Roan reached for him, Seg released the pent-up breath he'd been holding for the past couple of hours.

"I have to go," Seg whispered, cupping Roan's head in his hand. "But I'll be back. I want to spend time with you. And Liam. If that's all right."

Roan nodded, which nearly had Seg falling to the floor. He could take a tremendous amount of physical assault, but this man relenting to his request was enough to take him out at the knees.

ROAN HAD KNOWN that Seg intended to leave tonight. He didn't want him to, but he knew it was for the best. He needed time to think. To figure out how this was supposed to work. How he was going to open himself up to someone when that was quite possibly the hardest thing he would ever have to do.

Hell, who was he trying to kid? He'd spent too damn much time thinking as it was. He knew what he wanted, just not how it was supposed to play out.

"Stay," he whispered, pulling Seg closer. "Stay tonight."

He could see the concern in Seg's blue eyes. The man was torn, which only made sense. This thing between them was new; it was fragile. Neither of them was in a place for a relationship, certainly not one that was threatening to go full steam ahead without pause.

Roan opted for the truth. "I don't want to be alone."

Seg pressed his forehead to Roan's. "You're gonna be impossible to resist. I can feel it now."

"Then don't. Don't resist."

Seg's head lifted, his hands coming up to cup his neck, and Roan held his breath.

"You understand what I want, right? You're not confusing this thing between us with lust. I'm all for fucking you senseless, Roan, but I want more. One night here and there is not enough for me."

Roan nodded. At this point, his resistance was futile. He didn't want Seg to go. Hell, he didn't care if they even had sex tonight. He simply didn't want to be alone. He needed this man like he needed air. His companionship, his friendship, and yes, his desire.

"Stay," he repeated, hoping Seg understood he was on the same page.

Seg nodded, his hands sliding beneath Roan's shirt. Roan had to take a deep breath, to steel himself for feeling the man's hands on him again. He felt both vulnerable and needy. He wasn't sure he'd ever wanted a man the way he wanted Colton Seguine. And that was such a ridiculous thing to think about. But he couldn't help it. In fact, he'd been thinking about it, along with a million *what ifs,* for months now.

The feel of the bandage on Seg's finger brought him out of his thoughts. "I don't want to hurt you."

Seg frowned.

"Your finger."

"Want to touch," Seg whispered, shrugging him off. "All of you."

Roan kissed him, sealing their mouths together. He got lost in Seg for a minute, enjoying the soft, sensual way his tongue stroked his, the way his hands glided over his skin, touching him absently, as though this was all that mattered.

Roan tilted his head when Seg's mouth drifted down to his neck, Seg's strong hands curling around his ribs, holding him firmly in place. Roan's body heated, warmth infusing his blood, making him light-headed. His dick went from semi-hard to an iron rod in seconds. He attempted to grind his hips against Seg's, but the man held him back.

"Not yet. We'll get there. Eventually."

This man was going to make him lose his mind. He didn't like the wait. No one had ever accused him of being patient. The fact that he had no choice in the matter was new to him also. Until Seg, Roan had always been the one in control. Always. Maybe that was why he felt so vulnerable. He wanted Seg to be in control, to take care of him. It wasn't something he'd ever thought about until he met this man.

Seg's hands slid higher, forcing Roan's shirt up. He got rid of the damn thing because he needed to feel all of Seg against him. His hands, his mouth, his body.

"Aww, God," he groaned when Seg's fingers pinched his nipple.

"Shh. Don't wake the baby."

Roan still couldn't believe that Seg was okay with the fact that he had a kid. When Seg had asked to hold Liam, then offered to feed him, Roan had known the man owned him right then and there.

"Show me your bedroom," Seg insisted, standing to his full height.

Roan swallowed, trying to remember where the damn bedroom was. He was so caught up in the moment, he forgot that they were standing in his living room.

Seg's satisfied smile snapped him out of it, and he turned and led the way down the narrow hall after grabbing the baby monitor. He set the thing on the dresser, then turned to find Seg standing behind him, his shirt unbuttoned. The guy was hotter than fuck. Lean and ripped, and so damn tall. Roan wasn't short by any means, nor was he a small man, but Seg made him feel that way. Six foot four with a body as hard and unyielding as a brick wall, Seg took his breath away.

Roan's mouth watered with the need to touch and taste, to give and take. Except he couldn't seem to make his brain focus enough to do what he wanted to do. Instead, he found himself relying on Seg, waiting to see what happened next. He watched, his eyes roaming every inch of the man as Seg kicked off his shoes, then removed his socks. The shirt went next, leaving Seg standing there with his slacks riding low on his narrow hips. Roan wanted to lean down and run his tongue over the muscles that created a perfect V.

"Come here," Seg insisted.

Roan took a step forward, coming to stand directly in front of Seg.

The man's thumb brushed over his lower lip. "I want to feel your mouth on me. I fucking think about you all the damn time. About how fucking hot you make me, how hard my dick is just from hearing you breathe."

Seg's hand slid into his hair, then urged him down to his knees. Roan reached for the button on Seg's slacks as he lowered himself to the floor, leaning in and kissing the smooth skin directly above Seg's waistband, sliding his tongue along the hard angles of his muscles. He took his time, savoring the taste of his skin as he revealed Seg's thick cock. The man was a force to be reckoned with. While he stroked the velvet-smooth skin covering Seg's shaft, Roan forced Seg's pants down to his ankles before sliding his mouth over the swollen head, wrapping his lips around the crest, teasing with his tongue.

"Damn, I've missed your mouth."

Roan took him to the root, staring up and meeting Seg's eyes. He could see so much desire imprinted on his face. A need that matched what Roan was feeling. He knew they were moving too fast, but he didn't care. Roan knew from experience that one night with Seg wouldn't be enough. Two hadn't come close to dousing the flames that sparked hot and bright inside him. In fact, it only made it more intense, yet Roan didn't care. He wanted to give himself to Seg.

The hand in his hair tightened, shards of pain shooting through his scalp. It made his dick thicken, his body burn hotter. When Seg pulled him toward him, forcing his dick into Roan's mouth, he took all of him again. In. Out. In. Out. Roan let Seg use his mouth, let himself be dominated by the sexy man who had more control over him than anyone ever had.

"So good," Seg growled. "But I'm not done with you yet. Not gonna let you make me come."

Seg's cock slipped from his mouth, and Roan managed to get back to his feet while Seg tugged him up. When he was standing, Seg slammed his body against him, knocking them both to the bed while their mouths united, tongues dueling, teeth clashing. Demanding fingers worked open the button on Roan's jeans, shoving the denim down his hips, all while their tongues explored one another's mouths.

"I'm starting to question whether that finger's really broken or not," Roan teased.

Seg grinned. "The pain is worth it."

Roan moaned as Seg's warmth infused him. He felt him everywhere. On him, in him. It was just as he'd remembered. Intense.

When Seg's hand wrapped around his dick, Roan pulled back, sucking air into his lungs. "Fuck … oh, fuck…"

"You like that? Like when I let you fuck my fist?"

"Oh, God…" Roan's eyes rolled to the back of his head, the feeling overwhelming him. Every damn time the man touched him, Roan thought he would go up in flames. It'd been that way the first time they were together and every other time since. Tonight was no different.

Seg's mouth slid down Roan's chest, then his lips wrapped firmly around the engorged head of his cock, the man's tongue lovingly stroking him. Teasing. Torture.

It was too much, but not enough. Roan wanted everything Seg would give him. Tonight, tomorrow. Forever.

"I don't have the same willpower you do," he warned Seg. "Your fucking mouth drives me crazy."

Roan reached for Seg's head, linking his fingers in the silky blond strands as he held him in place, forcing Seg to take all of him as deep in his mouth as he could.

Of course, Seg overpowered him, letting Roan's dick fall from his lips before draping himself over Roan once more. The weight of him grounded him, his warmth soothing him, calming him.

"Condom," Seg mumbled against his lips.

Roan shifted to the edge of the bed and opened the nightstand drawer, pulling out an unopened box of condoms and a bottle of lube. Until two weeks ago, he hadn't had any on hand, but for some insane reason, he'd bought them the last time he was at the store. Just in case. He hadn't dreamed that Seg would show up at his door, but now he was grateful he'd had the mind to be prepared.

Roan dumped them on the bed, then reached for Seg again, rolling them both until he was on top. He couldn't seem to get enough of Seg, craving his taste, his touch.

Seg's hands roamed over his back, warm and gentle. A shiver raced down his spine; his dick jerked between them. He pulled away long enough to grab a condom from the box, then rolled it down Seg's erection before reaching for the lube, all the while keeping his eyes locked on Seg's face.

He knew in that moment that this thing between them was more than sex, more than pleasure. Roan wanted this to last forever, even though he didn't believe in forever. He wanted to believe, but he didn't. Long ago, he had learned that people would prove whether they were worthy or not over time. Few people in his life had stuck around.

That didn't stop Roan from hoping like hell that Colton Seguine was one of those people who did.

Fourteen

SEG WATCHED AS Roan greased his cock, stroking him roughly, making his breath saw in and out of his lungs. He sensed something in Roan. Something that felt like submission and not merely in the sexual sense.

The first time they'd been together had been crazy hot, but they'd both been chasing the same thing. Then the night that Roan showed up on his doorstep, Seg had taken his time, wanting to savor the moment, needing to find a way to convince Roan that there was something between them. He hadn't succeeded. Not as well as he'd hoped, anyway.

But this… It was different. Roan wasn't combative, didn't seem to be making this solely about chasing his release, driving them both to completion as fast as possible. That gave Seg hope, allowed him to be okay with all the things he wanted from this man. And sex wasn't the only thing on that list.

Although sex was high up on his list of priorities, but only because being with Roan felt right.

At first, he thought Roan was going to take control, to insist on topping him. Seg would've given him anything in that moment, but when Roan sheathed Seg's cock, he felt something inside of him crack open. A deep, possessive desire to own this man consumed him, made his body ache with the need to claim him, to show him just how hot they could burn together.

Roan shifted, scooting forward over him, his knees cradling Seg's hips. Seg watched, not moving, hardly breathing, waiting to see what was in store for him. When Roan guided Seg's cock into his ass, his lungs stopped working. He was engulfed by heat, his dick gripped by the tight confines of Roan's body.

"Fuck, yes," he hissed through clenched teeth. Fuck, this was better than anything he'd ever felt. "Ride me, Roan. Take what you want from me."

Roan nodded, his hands flattening on Seg's chest as he began lifting and lowering, riding Seg slow and easy. Seg gripped Roan's wrists, holding him there while their eyes locked and Roan took him deep into his ass. The temperature in the room spiked as ripples of sensation raced through Seg's body, making his heart pound against his ribs.

Damn. He could do this all fucking night. Watching Roan, his biceps flexing, his pecs rippling with every shift of his body, his abs contracting as he lifted himself off Seg's dick … by far the most fascinating thing he'd seen in his entire life.

"So fucking good," he moaned, urging Roan to continue. "I fucking love being inside you... Oh, fuck... Just like that."

He didn't want Roan to stop doing what he was doing. There was no rush to get to the finish line. Seg could do this forever if Roan would let him. The explosive chemistry between them made it difficult to not touch every part of Roan, but Seg managed. Barely. Content to simply let it be, to take what Roan was offering him.

Finally, he forced himself to sit up, to wrap his arms around Roan's body, to crush their lips together while he took control, pulling Roan onto his dick, driving deeper into the man's ass. They remained locked like that for long minutes, Roan moaning as Seg fucked him with deep, penetrating strokes.

"More," Roan pleaded, biting Seg's lip. "Need more... Need you to fuck me. Hard. Make me come, Colton."

His heart thumped double time. Seg fucking loved that Roan called him by his first name when they were intimate like this. He never called him that any other time—outside of the bedroom—which was probably why it made him feel so damn good. It was a connection he'd never experienced before.

Seg managed to shift again, eventually getting to his knees and pushing Roan to his back without ever dislodging from the man's body. He pumped his hips, slowly at first, then faster, harder. He grabbed Roan's hands and held them above his head while he drove into him. This was a claiming, pure and simple. Seg wanted to own him, to possess him, to have him in every way imaginable.

And yes, he wanted Roan to do the same to him.

Seg stretched his legs out behind him, holding his body above Roan's as he slammed his hips down at an angle, no longer worrying about gentle or easy.

Roan's hips lifted, his knees moving up closer to his chest as Seg continued to put power behind every thrust, fucking Roan harder and harder, deeper, wanting the man to feel him in his entire body.

"Oh, fuck... Right there, Colton. Right fucking there..."

Bending his knees, he put one hand on the back of Roan's thigh, the other wrapping around the heavy length of Roan's cock. Seg penetrated Roan's ass as he stroked him, wanting to push him as far as he could.

"Gonna come like that..." Roan's growl was loud. "Fuck... Don't... Oh, shit..."

Seg's gaze dropped to Roan's shaft, watching as he pulsed in his hand, cum spurting onto his chest, his stomach. It pushed Seg closer to the edge, but he couldn't stop, taking his pleasure from Roan's body until he thought his head might explode.

"Come inside me, Colton," Roan urged, his hands gripping Seg's forearms. "Right fucking now."

Coming on command wasn't an easy thing, but Seg forced himself to let go, his hips slamming against Roan's ass one last time as he came, the room spinning from lack of oxygen to his brain.

He fell forward, brushing his hand through Roan's hair, kissing him gently while his dick softened. He was reluctant to pull out of him, not wanting to break that connection. Seg honestly hadn't come over with the intention of fucking Roan, but now that he had, he wasn't sure he'd be able to stop. He already wanted more, but he knew Roan needed to sleep. He probably didn't sleep all that much anyway with Liam waking up every few hours.

Finally, he forced himself up, then followed Roan into the bathroom, where they both cleaned up. A quick shower made that easy, but not easy enough. Seg willed his dick to chill the fuck out. The promise of sleeping next to Roan was the only thing that really helped.

ROAN WOKE TO the sun shining in through his bedroom window. He stretched, then jolted, sitting up abruptly. No way should he be in bed this late. Liam had to be awake, and Roan didn't know how he wouldn't have heard him. His gaze swung to the dresser, searching for the baby monitor.

Shit. It wasn't there. How had he forgotten it?

"Fuck," he mumbled, grabbing a pair of sweat pants out of the drawer and dragging them up his legs. He took a moment to run to the bathroom, then flung the bedroom door open only to come to an abrupt halt.

There, in his kitchen, was Seg, talking to Liam.

"It's true, little guy," Seg said, his back to Roan. "No experience whatsoever. But I think I did well, eh? I will have to invest in a book though. Get a few pointers on how to put that smile on your face more often. Maybe get an instruction manual on this thing, too. What does this button do?"

Seg pushed a button and a musical note played from the bouncer Liam was reclining in.

"I like it," Seg said, sounding proud of himself.

Roan's heart was in his throat as he listened to Seg talk to Liam.

He cleared his throat.

"There's your daddy now," Seg said, glancing over at him. He must've noticed the sheer fear etched on Roan's face, because Seg stood up straight and stared at him. "I'm sorry. When Liam woke up, you didn't budge, so I thought I'd hang with him for a while and let you sleep. We managed through the diaper change, and it took a minute, but we got the bottle figured out thanks to the directions on the formula can. I fed him, too. I only did what you did last night, so if there's something else he needs..."

"No, that's—" Roan moved closer, glancing down at Liam, who was sitting in his bouncer on the kitchen table. He was smiling as he glanced between the two of them. "I thought I didn't wake up and he was still crying."

"I'm sorry," Seg said softly. "I took the monitor so we wouldn't wake you. I really didn't mean to freak you out."

"No, it's fine." Roan glanced at the stove. "Are you … making breakfast?"

Seg smiled. "Bacon, eggs, and toast. Figured since you had it in your fridge, you probably ate it." He peered back over at Liam. "I hope that's okay. I put him in this thing so he could see me. Thought maybe if I chatted with him, he'd stay chill."

"He likes it," Roan assured him, his head still buzzing from the fact that Colton Seguine was in his kitchen, making breakfast, talking to his son. It felt like a dream. One he hoped he didn't wake up from.

Knowing Seg was worried thanks to Roan's reaction, Roan moved over to him and kissed him quickly. "Thank you. I… I haven't slept like that in a long time."

"I'm glad to do it. Me and Liam … we're tight now. He's been making sure I do everything right. Plus, he puked on me." Seg's grin widened. "I thought maybe that was his way of officially accepting me."

Oddly, the thought of the badass hockey player not freaking out because a baby spit up on him was endearing.

Roan's heart did a slow turn in his chest. The fact that Seg was there, taking care of the baby, making breakfast for the two of them… If Roan wasn't careful, he was going to fall hard for this guy. It wasn't that he was purposely holding himself back either. He was scared. Terrified even. Life simply didn't go that way for him. Sure, he had a job he loved, enough money to do anything he wanted, friends who would be there whenever he needed them, but Roan had never found love. Not the real thing. In fact, not since high school had he even contemplated the idea. He was thirty-four fucking years old.

"Sit," Seg commanded. "Food's done. I have to head over to the rink for practice in a bit."

Roan watched the sexy man in his kitchen. Seg was wearing his slacks, but he was shirtless—probably removed it when Liam spit up on him. There wasn't a single thing that marred his beautiful body. All sleek, smooth skin covering hard, toned muscle. He was a sight for sore eyes, someone Roan never imagined would be making him breakfast. Yes, his thoughts seemed to be on a repetitive loop, but he couldn't help it.

"Let me guess," Seg said as he set the plates on the table. "You didn't think a hockey player could cook either."

Roan grinned. He might've been thinking that, sure.

"My mother insisted that I know how to cook," Seg explained. "I think she knew I'd be a long way from home at some point, and if I didn't know how to cook, I wouldn't eat."

"You could always grab food out."

"And I do. Sometimes. I don't do fast food. Ever. And since that's all I have time for most days, I've learned how to make my own meals. Of course, I cheat. I've got a housekeeper who's sweet as pie and makes me meals that I can pop in the microwave. Quick and easy. Nothing fancy. Although I make some mean brownies."

"Good to know."

Seg sat down in the seat across from Roan. "I have to head out of town tomorrow. We've got away games—two in a row. Sunday, then Tuesday. But then I'll be back for the game here on Thursday. Wondered if maybe the three of us could do something next weekend."

"The three of us?" Roan glanced at Liam, noticing the baby was gnawing on his fist, staring at Seg.

"I know he's not up for miniature golf or anything like that, but surely there's something we can do. That or I'm happy to come over here. Of course, the two of you could come to my place."

Roan swallowed hard. He wanted to do all of those things with Seg. Again, fear inched its way into his veins.

Seg reached over and touched his hand. "If I'm moving too fast, say something, Roan. Don't leave me hanging and don't run. I want this. I want you. Just give me a chance."

"You're willing to go out in public?" Roan asked, picking up his fork.

Seg shrugged. "I'm not going to think too hard on it."

Roan appreciated that Seg was willing to go that far for him, but he didn't want to put the man in that position. "It might be easier for you to come here," he mentioned. "Or we'll come to you."

Seg smiled. "Thank you."

And just like that, Roan found himself wondering if this was what a relationship felt like.

Fifteen

One week later…

SEG'S FOCUS WAS spot on.

He didn't know what it was, but he was driven in a way he'd never been before. Maybe it was because Roan had texted before the game and told him good luck. That had sent a strange sensation soaring through his entire body, one that was still there, still coursing in his veins. It was similar to the feeling he'd gotten when he made his first goal in the NHL.

"How's the finger?" Coach asked when Seg took the bench.

"Fine." He hadn't thought about it once. The trainer had wrapped it before he'd gloved-up, and that probably helped immensely.

"Keep it up, Seg."

He nodded, watching the play on the ice, thankful for short shifts because he wanted to be back out there. His muscles hummed with adrenaline; his need to get to his feet was powerful. But he kept his ass glued to the bench, watching, waiting.

He briefly wondered if Liam was wearing his jersey tonight. He knew that Roan would be watching the game at home because he'd told him he would. So, Seg had gotten online and ordered Liam a jersey—he'd been surprised to find someone who made them that small—and had it rush delivered so Liam would have it tonight. Of course, he hadn't been able to resist ordering one for Roan, wanting the man to be wearing his name, too.

It was surprising how much Seg missed Liam and Roan. He wished the team was playing at home so he'd be able to go see them tonight. He hadn't seen them since last Friday morning and now he wanted to more than anything.

"Kaufman, Benne, Valeri," the assistant coach called from behind him. "Seg and Crosby."

Seg was up on his skates and out on the ice in a flash, trading places with the other defenseman like they'd choreographed it. He managed to get in position in front of Kingston, gearing up to keep Chicago's forwards from getting close enough to get a goal. He loved this shit, had since he was a little boy. His dad used to take him out to the pond to play, ever since he was big enough to put on skates.

He was pretty sure that pond was the reason his parents had bought the house. Since his father played—as a hobby—he imagined it had been a huge draw. Growing up, Seg remembered being out there for hours, having fun, enjoying the time he spent with his father.

His love for the game had started then, and his parents had been supportive. He'd known from the beginning that he wanted to play professionally. At this point in his life, hockey was the only thing he knew.

"Play it," Spencer Kaufman, a.k.a. Optimus, called out to their goalie, Kingston Rush, who had slipped behind the net to grab the puck.

With Chicago's right wing barreling down on him, Seg shot to the corner boards as Mt. Rushmore tapped the puck toward him. A brief scuffle ensued as he tried to get the puck after getting plowed in the back. He caught a glimpse of Optimus, waiting. He got his stick on the biscuit, then shot it right to the captain, shoving the player off of him as he turned.

He put on some speed, chasing his teammates toward the opposite end of the ice. Optimus passed to Benne, who passed to Mattias. Optimus got control, moving down the ice at a blurring speed. While the opposing team's defense was distracted, Seg took the opportunity to move in closer to the goal. Optimus passed to Benne. In a fraction of a second, Seg made eye contact with Benne, who fired the puck toward him.

Seg shifted, turned, shot.

Goal!

Rather than go out to the bar after the game, Seg went straight to his room. He was bunking with Cullen Crosby, as he usually did, which meant he would likely have the room to himself for most of the night. Cullen was known to hang with friends wherever he went. The man didn't usually hook up with puck bunnies, choosing to stay unattached for whatever reason. Seg didn't mind the fact that he would be alone tonight though.

After taking a long shower, Seg pulled on some sweats, then grabbed his cell phone and crawled onto the bed. He propped himself up on pillows as he unlocked his phone.

His heart nearly pounded out of his chest when he noticed a text from Roan. He clicked on the picture of Liam, enlarging it so he could see it better. He laughed, seeing the baby wearing his jersey, all but buried in all that material.

Roan: *He rooted for you the whole time. Thanks for the jersey, by the way. I'm sure he'll grow into it.*

Seg wanted to make the picture his screen saver, but he thought better of it at the last second. As high as he was on life right now, he knew he had to be careful. It would be so easy for him to let his guard down when it came to Roan and Liam. Part of him didn't care if the world figured it out, but he knew that wouldn't be in his best interest. If he wanted something lasting with Roan, he had to do this the right way.

And yes, even as new as this thing was between them, Seg had already considered having a chat with the team's owner, Phoenix Pierce. It wasn't a secret that Phoenix was bisexual and that he was in a permanent relationship with both a man and a woman. In fact, the three of them had even had a wedding, which had been the talk of the sports world at one time.

If Seg intended to come out—which he was still on the fence about—he knew he would have to do it a certain way. Talking to the team's owner was the first step.

Well, technically, there was one other person he had to talk to first. The most important woman in his life deserved to be the first—well, technically third at this point—to know.

Before he could respond to Roan, his cell phone rang, his mother's phone number popping up on the screen.

"Hey, Ma," he greeted, leaning back on the pillows. Sometimes he wondered if they had some sort of psychic link. She always seemed to know when he was thinking of her.

"Seggy! You were amazing!"

He chuckled. Yeah, she always said that. "Thanks."

"Marjorie came over again. You'd think that woman would learn." His mother giggled. "She was not impressed that I wasn't having a bout of insanity all the other times. I think she knows it's permanent, so I really doubt she'll be back to watch another game."

She said that almost every time, too, yet Marjorie came over and watched every single game. It helped that Marjorie lived right next door to his mother.

"Ma, you're going to drive that poor woman to drink."

"Maybe. So, how are you? Are you feeling better than the last time I talked to you?"

"Yeah." It was the truth. He'd been preparing himself for this conversation. "Ma, you mentioned coming down."

"Yes."

"I'd like you to do so. Soon. I need to talk to you about something, and I don't want to do it over the phone."

"Just tell me when, honey. I'll be packed and ready to go. Just make sure I get tickets to the home games while I'm there."

He laughed. That was his mother for you. "Of course."

"But you're really doing okay?"

"I am," he assured her. "Let me look into flights, and I'll let you know."

"Okay, honey. Like I said, whenever you want me there, I'm there."

"Thanks, Ma. I love you."

"Love you, too, Seggy. I need to find my other jersey. The home jersey," she said, but Seg knew she was talking to herself. "I can't wear this one to a home game. Hmm."

"Ma, I'm going to let you go now."

"All right, Seggy. Love you. Talk to you soon."

Seg hung up the phone and pulled up his text message app.

WHEN CAM AND Gannon left, Roan bathed Liam, got him dressed for bed, then offered him a little bit of the infant cereal the doctor recommended they try out. The kid was a healthy eater, that was for sure. However, Roan decided they'd do the bath after dinner in the future since his boy was also a messy eater.

Once he'd cleaned Liam up for a second time, Roan changed him, then put him in his bed. The boy would probably sleep for several hours. He usually did after spending any amount of time with Cam. The guy spent so much time entertaining Liam it was a wonder how neither of them fell asleep where they sat.

Since the day Cam had found out about Liam, and Roan had come out to the rest of his friends, everyone seemed infatuated with the little boy. Not that Roan could blame them. Liam was the cutest kid ever. He liked that Liam would get to grow up with so much love around him. Between Cam and Gannon, Dare and Noah, Hudson and Teague, and Milly and AJ, the kid was set.

Roan's phone buzzed in his pocket and he pulled it out, glancing at the screen.

The smile on his face was instant and automatic.

Hockey boy: *Love the pic. Thank you for that.*

Roan had entered Seg's name initially but changed it to hockey boy for one reason only. To protect Seg. Although he didn't want to live his life hiding, Roan would do what he needed in order to keep Seg's career safe. If the man decided to come out publicly, it would be his choice, not because Roan fucked anything up for him.

Roan: *I wish I could say Liam watched the whole game.*

Hockey boy: The bigger question is, did you watch?

Roan: Of course. Not an easy feat when my friends kept eyeing me every time you came on the screen.

Hockey boy: I take it they've figured us out.

Roan: They won't say anything.

Hockey boy: I'm actually smiling, Roan. I'm not worried. It's not the people close to you that I'm worried about.

Roan: I get it.

Hockey boy: Do you?

Roan: Yeah. I do.

Hockey boy: I've invited my mother to come to Texas. I want to tell her in person. I think it's time to let her know the truth. She knows me too well. She knows something's different.

Even now, a grown man with a child, Roan could admit to a certain insecurity when it came to trusting that people wouldn't react badly. He'd learned long ago that just because someone *claimed* to love you didn't necessarily ring true when it came to certain things.

Roan couldn't deny the fear that trembled beneath his skin. He remembered coming out to his parents. The way his mother blew a gasket, the way his father sat there, staring at him like he couldn't have possibly heard him correctly. Although his mother hated him after that and his father acted indifferent, Roan didn't regret telling them. As a teenager, it had been a weight on his shoulders that threatened to tear him down. He couldn't imagine having lived his entire life in the dark.

Roan: How do you think she'll take it?

Hockey boy: To tell you the truth, I don't know. But my mother's love has always been unconditional. That's why I want to give her the respect she deserves and tell her before she hears it from someone else.

Roan: Someone else? You've told others?

Hockey boy: No. But I'm scared I won't hide it well. I don't want to hide you, Roan. Not from anyone. If it gets out, that's on me. I think I'm going to talk to Phoenix. Get his perspective.

Roan: The owner? The one who's bisexual?

Hockey boy: Yeah. He's not in a position to pass judgment. Doesn't mean he'll think it's a good idea.

Roan: I get it.

He did get it. Roan understood the sports world. He knew there were a few professional athletes who had come out of the closet. Since he never heard much after the fact, he didn't know if that was because they'd disappeared or if they'd managed to go about their normal lives because people were willing to overlook it. Not everyone, of course. Roan wasn't naïve. Although he lived in a fairly sheltered world where being out was okay—his friends were all out—Roan knew it wasn't that easy for everyone.

Hell, it hadn't been easy for him. There were times he hated himself because of what his mother had done. The fact that she packed her shit and abandoned the family, blaming him solely, had hurt more than he was willing to admit. But that was a lifetime ago, and he'd since come to terms with it.

Mostly.

Roan: I'm here, whatever you need.

Hockey boy: I need you, Roan. That's what I need.

Roan felt heat swamp him. He wasn't sure Seg's statement was a sexual one, but that didn't stop his body from coming to life. If he allowed himself to think about it, he knew he missed Seg. He wanted to see him, to spend time with him, to watch him hold Liam and smile the way he had the first time. This was new for him. But he wasn't running from it.

Roan: I'm here. Right where you left me. Waiting for you.

Hockey boy: You're torturing me and you don't even know it.

Roan: I assume you mean that in a good way.

Hockey boy: Having your dick rock hard isn't necessarily a good way to spend the evening when you've got a roommate.

Roan: Well, we'll have to do something about that when you get back.

Hockey boy: You're going to be the death of me, Roan.

Roan: One hell of a way to go.

Hockey boy: You're telling me.

Roan stared at his phone, realizing he was still smiling. A long time ago, Cam had told Roan that one day a man was going to come out of the blue and blindside him. Cam had assured him that he wouldn't know what hit him.

He'd been right.

Sixteen

USUALLY, WHEN SEG got back home, he didn't want to go anywhere at all. He enjoyed being at his house, liked the solitude that it afforded him. Today ... not so much. The instant his feet were back on Texas soil, there'd been a strange push-pull in his body. He wanted to see Roan. He'd go so far as to say he *needed* to see him.

Which was the reason he was pulling up to the marina now. When he'd texted Roan to find out what his plans were for the night, Roan had informed him he was working today. Seg had gone home, packed a bag, and hopped back in his Range Rover.

After parking in the lot, Seg climbed out and looked around. He liked this place, had the first time he'd come here back when the team had scheduled an outing. There was a peacefulness that could be found here, one Seg had enjoyed immensely.

Of course, that inner peace was at war with the rioting lust that consumed him, so today was one of those days he couldn't appreciate it as much. Unlike the last time, he wasn't here for the scenery.

Granted, the day they'd done the team outing, Seg hadn't had the chance to talk to Roan, but he'd gotten a glimpse of the man. At the time, he'd thought it was his overactive imagination playing tricks on him. Of course, Roan had been running back then and he'd left the marina. Seg knew now that was because he'd shown up.

He hoped like hell Roan wasn't going to do any more running anytime soon. The past year and a half had been hell. Wanting something he knew he'd never have again wasn't easy to deal with. And when he'd run into Roan again at the rink, Seg's entire world had been turned upside down. He believed everything happened for a reason, and seeing Roan that day told him that the man was supposed to be in his life.

As for what the future held for them, he didn't have a clue. But he was more than willing to stick around and find out.

"Hey, man," Dare greeted when Seg stepped into the small office. "What brings you to the slums?"

The man's smile was infectious and Seg laughed. "Oh, you know ... carrying around the golden hockey stick gets tiring."

Dare's grin widened. "Well, take a load off. We can certainly put you to work."

"Yeah?"

"No, not really," Dare admitted, leaning his elbows on the counter that separated them. "We're slow right now. Will be for another couple of months. Good for us though. We're all getting to take some time off. Which means..."

Dare disappeared, bending down behind the counter.

When he stood up, he was holding Liam in his arms.

Seg smiled so wide he thought his face might split. "There's the little guy."

It wasn't until the words were out of his mouth that he realized how he sounded. Yes, he and Roan had gotten closer recently, but he wasn't sure whether Roan had let his friends in on that secret or not.

"Your turn," Dare said, lifting Liam up so that Seg could take him.

"Gladly," he stated, reaching to take Liam and turning him so he could look at Liam while Liam's feet pressed against the countertop. Liam's little knees buckled, but then he pushed up, bouncing slightly. Seg laughed. "Ready to start skating already, eh?"

Liam's fist flew out, his hand reaching for Seg's nose, and he smiled, filling Seg's heart instantly. God, he could get used to this.

The back door opened with a squeak, and Seg looked up to see Roan coming inside. The man didn't actually smile—his lips didn't really move—but Seg noticed his change of expression. He seemed happy to see him. Seg would take that as a win.

"Hey," Roan greeted, glancing between Seg and Dare. "Didn't know you were gonna stop by. What time is it?"

"Time for y'all to go do somethin' fun," Dare noted. "I've got this for another hour."

"You sure?" Roan glanced at Dare.

Seg watched the two of them, and it wasn't hard to notice the way Dare urged Roan with his eyes. It was almost laughable how obvious he was being.

"Positive. Now get." Dare leaned down again. "But take this with you."

When he stood, he was holding Liam's car seat. Well, that explained why Liam had been on the floor.

"Don't have to tell me twice," Roan said, grabbing the car seat.

Seg continued to stare at Roan. He'd only been away from the man for a week, yet it felt like an eternity. He wasn't sure why he was this infatuated, but he was. He really was.

"Don't do anything I wouldn't do," Dare called out as they turned for the door.

Seg reached over and took the blanket from the car seat, tossing it over Liam, which made the little boy giggle. The temperatures in Texas weren't anything like up north, but it was chilly.

"Where to?" Seg asked when they reached Roan's truck.

He waited while Roan secured the car seat in the back seat. Once that was done, Seg situated Liam in it and watched while Roan fastened the buckles over him.

"Have you eaten yet?" Roan asked.

"No."

"I can cook dinner. If that's okay with you."

"It's more than okay with me." Seg had the overwhelming urge to kiss this man, right here in the open, but he managed to hold himself back. He was going to have to pay attention to stuff like that, because when it came to Roan, Seg lost all sense of decorum. It had never been an issue for him before.

"Follow me?"

Seg nodded, then touched Roan's hand briefly before turning toward his SUV.

SEEING SEG STANDING in the marina office, holding Liam in his arms…

181

Admittedly, Roan had never in his life felt the sort of emotions that had risen inside him the moment his brain processed what was going on. And to think, he'd spent so long running and hiding because he didn't want to burden anyone, when in reality the people in his life wanted to be there for him.

Of course, he thought about that often. Thought about how he'd pushed everyone away, making assumptions that shouldn't have been made. Yes, he'd been trying to protect his friends, not wanting them to endure the hell Roan had endured with Cassie. He also wondered whether or not things would be different if he'd been open about what was going on. Would Cassie still be alive? Would Seg be in his life?

As for Seg, it wasn't like Roan knew that would be the case though. It was merely a godsend, something Roan found himself giddy about.

Giddy.

Wow.

He knew for a fact he'd never used that word to describe himself or how he was feeling. Not ever. Yet he couldn't deny it now as he pulled into the driveway of his house, Seg's gleaming black SUV pulling in beside him.

Roan took a deep breath, then let it out slowly. He needed to chill. No way was he going to jump headfirst into something that might get him hurt. Or worse, get Liam hurt. The last thing Roan wanted was to get attached to someone who might not stick around. However, he refused to assume the worst. For the first time in what felt like forever—not counting Liam, of course—Roan had something to look forward to. Some*one*. He damn sure wasn't going to project his fears on their relationship.

"One day at a time," he mumbled to himself as he turned off the engine and climbed out of the truck.

Seg was instantly at the back passenger door, opening it for him. Roan released the car seat from the base and hefted Liam out of the truck. It didn't surprise him that the little boy had fallen asleep during the short drive home. He'd spent the better part of the day with Dare. That in itself would tire anyone out.

"Lemme get him changed, and I'll get dinner started," Roan told Seg as he headed toward Liam's bedroom.

"Or I could do one or the other for you," Seg suggested, closing the door behind him.

Roan stopped and turned, took several steps back, closing in on the sexy hockey player. He couldn't help himself. Roan reached for Seg's head, pulling him down for a quick kiss. Of course, quick didn't play into the equation once their lips touched. It felt right, being here with Seg and Liam.

"God, I missed you," Seg whispered, cupping Roan's head.

Roan's insides went haywire at those words. He already knew he was in serious trouble when it came to this man.

Knowing Liam couldn't take care of himself, Roan managed to pull away and headed right for Liam's room. He changed him quickly, which awakened the sleepy baby. Grinning like a fool, Roan lifted him into his arms. It was Liam's dinner time, as well, which meant he'd probably be back asleep in the next fifteen minutes. If Seg wanted to spend time with the baby, he would have to do so now.

When Roan returned to the kitchen, Seg was standing there, staring into the refrigerator. He turned and Roan held Liam out to him. The look on the man's face was pure adoration, and once again, Roan's heart did a flip in his chest.

"Hey, little guy," Seg said softly. "You up for some dinner, too?"

Roan got the bottle ready, then handed it over to Seg. While the two of them went into the living room, he got to work, pulling things out of the fridge.

Half an hour later, Seg had put Liam in his bed, and Roan had chicken Alfredo spooned onto plates.

"So, what's it like being on the road?" Roan probed, curious as to the life of a hockey player.

"It's not glamorous, that's for sure," Seg told him, picking up his fork. "Not when you consider all the gear that has to be taken as well as all of the assistance that's needed to haul it."

Roan smiled. "So, not the lifestyle of the rich and famous travel? No jets with leather seats and cocktail bars?"

Seg chewed before responding. "Unfortunately, no. Lots of sweaty guys who were tired on the last trip and hadn't yet caught up on sleep."

"You mentioned you had a roommate?"

"Yeah." Seg picked up his water glass. "Cullen Crosby. Nice guy. Quiet. Keeps to himself mostly and doesn't spend much time in the room."

"That probably helps."

Seg grinned. "I sleep like the dead, so I never know when he's coming or going."

"Funny, you don't sleep all that much when I'm with you."

Seg's eyes heated. "That's because I've got more important things to do than sleep."

When they were finished, Seg insisted on cleaning up, which again surprised Roan. He didn't argue, simply carried their dishes from the table to the sink while Seg rinsed them and stuck them in the dishwasher. Once all the domestic duties were handled, Roan's nerves began to riot. As though he hadn't been intimate with this man plenty of times already.

Naturally, he didn't get a lot of time to dwell on anything, because Seg was right there, invading his personal space, pulling him in close, and crushing their mouths together.

Roan grabbed Seg's shirt, jerking him closer, giving in to the overwhelming desire that'd been on a slow simmer inside him since he first saw Seg in the marina office. He took them both down to the couch, landing on top of Seg before rolling to the side, keeping one leg over Seg's thigh. Hands were everywhere, touching, holding, trying to get closer, but still it wasn't enough.

Finally, needing to take a breath, Roan lifted his head and stared down at the blond man who looked so damn good laid out beneath him. "I'm glad you're here."

"Me, too." Seg's hand trailed down Roan's face.

It was a gentle move that had Roan's body doing strange things. He liked that Seg was so loving. It wasn't all about domination. About hard and fast and no holds barred. It was as though Seg could see deep into his soul, knew what Roan needed, the assurance he sought.

He couldn't resist kissing him again, but this time, Roan reduced the rapid boil to a slow simmer once again, wanting this to last forever. He'd never been the type to make out on the couch, but he was good with this. Sure, he wanted more. He wanted to strip Seg down to nothing but sleek, warm skin and ravish him from head to toe, but this worked, too.

Or it had. For about ten minutes. At that point, Roan's dick was so fucking hard it hurt. He needed more.

A lot more.

Seventeen

SEG NOTICED THE subtle shift in the air around him. The way Roan went from pliant to hard in an instant. The man was holding back, that was obvious. Seg liked that he could, but yeah, after a solid week of being away from Roan, he was ready to eat him alive.

Somehow—though he wasn't sure exactly how it happened—their clothes finally disappeared, strewn across the floor around them while they remained on the couch, Roan still atop him. Seg didn't want to let him go, didn't want to stop touching, stop kissing. The warmth of his body was a welcoming comfort he hadn't realized he'd needed until now. It was like he could feel for the first time in his life. Well, it was like that every time he was with Roan really. There was tremendous pressure inside him, a need that continued to gain strength with every passing second.

"Don't move," Roan groaned.

Seg released him when Roan pulled away, getting to his feet and padding naked down the hall. He returned a second later with a condom and lube, making Seg smile. Glad it'd been Roan who had to temporarily pull the plug. Had it been Seg, he wouldn't have had the strength to get up.

When Roan was near him again, Seg pulled him down, sliding his hands over Roan's back, his ass, his thighs. He pulled him closer, never getting as close as he wanted though.

He could feel Roan's hand working between them. He didn't pay enough attention but figured Roan was suiting up, ready to get on with the program. Seg was on board with that plan.

When Roan kneed his legs apart, then propped Seg's left leg over his forearm, he knew what was coming. He pulled back enough to watch as Roan guided his cock to Seg's tight entrance.

"Not sure how easy I can be this time." Roan's admittance sounded more like a warning.

Seg nodded, completely entranced by the sight of Roan guiding himself home.

Several minutes later, while their bodies were pressed together, hands still groping, Roan was finally lodged balls deep inside him. The pain warred with pleasure, merging into something potent, something that ripped at Seg's resolve. This was too good.

"Okay?" Roan whispered, nipping Seg's bottom lip.

"Oh, yeah." He was better than okay.

"Relax for me."

Seg nodded, trying his best.

Roan lifted Seg's other leg, propping it on the couch cushion, changing the angle of penetration. Seg was stretched painfully tight, unsure how long he could take Roan not moving inside him. When Roan finally did begin to shift his hips, Seg released the breath he'd been holding, grabbing Roan's hair and pulling his mouth back down to his.

The slow thrust and retreat sent chills through him until, finally, Seg was overcome with sensation. Pure, brutal ecstasy raced beneath his skin. It fired up every nerve, every molecule, until he was trembling from the overwhelming, mind-numbing intensity.

When Roan fucked him, Seg felt more than the physical aspect of it. He was overcome with emotion, driven by a hard need to be one with this man. It'd been that way since the first time, and Seg knew without a doubt he'd never find that with anyone else.

"Gonna fuck you hard now," Roan told him, burying his face in Seg's neck. "But don't wanna hurt you."

"You won't hurt me." Reaching around, Seg gripped Roan's ass, jerking him forward, taking him as deep as he could. Roan groaned, then lifted his head, propping his upper body up with his hands beside Seg's head.

The next few minutes were exquisite torture as Roan pounded him over and over, deeper, faster, harder. Even when they were both coated in a fine sheen of sweat, the man didn't stop. Seg accepted every punishing thrust, his cock throbbing, untouched between them. No way could he stem his release; it barreled down on him, surprising in its intensity.

"Roan..." He groaned, bucking his hips, his cock jerking as he came hard. So hard it stole his breath.

"Son of a bitch," Roan yelled, his hips slamming down one last time. "Fuck, yes. Ahhh!"

Roan's mouth was on his once more. Seg forced his heartbeat to slow, stroking his hands over Roan's back. "That was quite possibly the hardest I've ever come in my life."

"Yeah?" Roan's head was buried in his neck. "I know the feeling. Not sure I can walk."

"That's cool. I'm good. Right where you are."

ROAN WASN'T KIDDING when he said he didn't think he could walk. He was completely wiped after that mind-blowing orgasm. Seriously. Maybe they should work themselves up to sex next time Seg was away for any length of time.

The thought of there being a next time relaxed him. Roan had the ability to get into his own head, to make things more difficult than necessary, but that wasn't the case. He didn't want that with Seg. Whatever it was, he was content with it. With this.

After a few minutes, Roan finally managed to make his way to the bathroom to clean up. He then went to the kitchen while Seg disappeared to do the same. He pulled a box of brownie mix along with the necessary ingredients and pans to make it out of the cabinet and was setting the oven to preheat when Seg returned.

"What are you doing?"

Roan grinned. "I'm not doin' anything, but I specifically recall you mentioning you make mean brownies. I want brownies."

Seg came up behind him, hugging him close to his body. "I'll make you brownies, but only if I get to lick the remaining batter off your body later."

"Well, you drive a hard bargain, but okay." Roan stepped around the small bar and took a seat on a stool, watching Seg work. "So, any news on when your mother's comin' down?"

Seg met his eyes. "She gets here Wednesday, the twenty-fifth. She'll be here until the fourth of February."

Roan nodded. He wasn't sure he could go that long without seeing Seg. However, it seemed incredibly selfish to mention that.

"Why the frown? I haven't made them yet," Seg stated, nodding toward the bowl of batter.

Forcing a smile, Roan lifted his head. "Not frowning."

"Scared to meet my mother?"

Okay, now he really was frowning. "You want me to meet your mother?"

"I would, yes." Seg stared into his eyes, holding his gaze. "Unless you have something against that."

"No," Roan blurted. Surprisingly, he really didn't.

"I'm planning to sit down and talk to her. If all goes well, which I have no reason to believe it won't, I'd like to introduce her to you and Liam."

Now it felt as though they were moving a little too fast. Roan fought the urge to panic.

"Settle down," Seg said, his voice soft. He was standing directly beside Roan, his hand instantly going under his chin, forcing Roan to look up at him. "I'm not asking for more than you can give. If this isn't the right time, say so."

Roan swallowed hard but didn't say anything. He continued to get lost in Seg's steel-blue eyes, in the warmth he saw there. This man was for real, which was quite possibly what scared him most.

"Tell me," Seg insisted.

"No, it's just—" Roan leaned up and kissed Seg, unable to resist. "I'm good. I'd be honored to meet your mother. And if something changes, if you don't want to introduce us, I understand."

Seg kissed him back, cupping his face and swiping his thumb down Roan's cheek. The gentleness in the man's touch was so different than what he'd expected. Here was this formidable badass hockey player who took hits that most men couldn't handle, and he was being so sweet.

"Thank you."

Roan looked up, his confusion obviously showing. "For what?"

"For being at that bar that night, for showing back up out of the blue at the rink, for being on my doorstep when I least expected it, for … for everything."

"You make it damn near impossible to resist you, you know that?" Roan chuckled.

"That's my plan."

"Yeah, well, it's working." Roan had never admitted something quite that truthful in his life. Something that made him feel so vulnerable.

Yet the look on Seg's face didn't reflect an ounce of arrogance.

"You about done with those brownies?" Roan asked, changing the subject. "I'm waiting to get on to the brownie batter portion of tonight's entertainment."

"Oh, we'll get there."

Roan couldn't wait.

Eighteen

Wednesday, January 25th

SEG WAS AT the airport late Wednesday night when his mother's plane arrived. The minute he saw her coming down the escalator toward him, his spirits lifted. The woman would never cease to amaze him. Although he knew it'd been a long day for her, she was still smiling, greeting him with a hug and a kiss before he grabbed her suitcases and walked her to the Range Rover.

"Tell me what you did today, Seggy," his mother prompted as he pulled out of the airport and onto the highway.

"I went shopping," he informed her.

"Grocery shopping?" She grinned.

"That, too."

"Really?"

Seg cast a quick look her way. "Of course. You sent me a list, remember?"

His mother giggled. "What else did you shop for?"

Feeling his face heat, Seg remembered the kind woman at the baby store who had helped him locate all the things he was searching for. This thing with Roan was permanent. Maybe they hadn't quite talked about it completely, but as far as Seg was concerned, Roan and Liam were it for him. Hence the reason he went in search of a car seat, portable crib, and books. Lots of books on all things baby.

Rather than tell his mother that, he grinned. "Just things." Knowing he had piqued her curiosity, he opted to change the subject. "How about Mexican food?"

"Oh, heavens yes. That sounds perfect right about now."

She leaned her head back and closed her eyes for a minute and Seg drove.

The drive back into Austin didn't take long, even after they'd stopped for dinner at a little Tex-Mex place his mother loved to visit when she was in town. Now that they were at his house, Seg's nerves were beginning to unsettle, and he found himself pacing his kitchen while she put her things away.

When she appeared in the doorway, he forced himself to stop moving.

"Okay," she said, her tone serious. "Let's talk. Spit it out, Seggy. I know there's something on your mind, and you're not that great at small talk."

He smiled despite his nerves. The woman knew him too well. And true, he'd probably used up all his small talk during dinner, which admittedly hadn't been much. They could only talk about the weather for so long.

"Wine?" he offered.

"Does anyone ever say no to wine?"

"I do," he admitted.

"You don't count."

Seg poured her a glass of wine, then led the way to the living room, urging her onto the couch. He fought the urge to pace and forced his ass onto a cushion nearby.

"What is it?" It was clear she wasn't going to be happy until he told her what had him so worked up.

"I met someone." That was the easy part of the conversation, he knew.

"I assume it's serious since you meet a lot of *someones* yet you never mention them to me."

"It's serious."

She nodded, watching him closely.

Seg took a deep breath. "I'm not sure how to say this because I'm just getting used to it myself." He wrung his hands in his lap, then lifted his gaze and met hers head on. "I'm gay, Ma."

Debra Seguine didn't move a muscle. She didn't appear shocked or outraged. There was no disgust or disdain etched on her aging face. And yes, he looked. He was searching for any nuance that would give away her initial thoughts. Somehow, she masked her expression perfectly. That or she wasn't at all surprised. In fact, his mother looked the same as she always did when he told her anything important. She was processing the information, likely coming up with a dozen questions.

"I assume this isn't something you recently figured out."

"Not really, no. I've had my suspicions."

"You and me both," she said, a smile curling the corner of her mouth.

Seg lifted an eyebrow.

"Oh, come on. You've dated supermodels, honey. And not one of them has ever managed to truly catch your eye. It's not a total shocker."

It was to him. Kind of. "Do you have any questions?"

His mother smiled. "Who's the lucky man who brought my boy out of the darkness and into the light?"

Funny that her words were actually how he felt. He'd spent his life pretending to be someone he wasn't, hiding from everyone, including himself. Now that he was out with himself, he felt free. "His name's Roan."

She nodded again.

"He's got a son," Seg explained. "Liam. He's four and a half months old. He was Roan's sister's son, but she died a couple of months ago. Drug overdose." He frowned, hating to think of the pain Roan had gone through.

"Tell me about them," she prompted. "The baby. He's okay?"

Seg nodded. "Liam's the cutest thing I've ever seen, Ma. He's growing like a weed. Roan said the doctor is impressed with his progress."

"And Roan? How old is he? Has he ever been married?"

"Never married," Seg told her. "And he's great. He's thirty-four, owns a marina with three of his friends."

"A marina? Like boats?"

"Yes. Boats. Coincidentally, the team went there about a year ago."

"Is that where you met him?"

Seg felt the blush creep up his face. "No."

This time her smile lit up her entire face. "Oh, Seggy. I'm so happy for you."

"Really? You're not freaked out? Disappointed?"

Her eyebrows darted downward. "Not once in your life have I ever been disappointed in you. Why would I be now? We're talking about love here, Colton. Not winning or losing a hockey game. You're a smart man, always have been. I don't think you've ever done anything lightly, and I know that if you're having this conversation with me, this is real for you. I love you. *You.* Not the image of you I want to project, not a fictitious version of what someone believes a son should be. From the moment you came screaming into this world, you have been my heart. And I'm truly happy for you."

His mother always knew just what to say to set his world right again.

Seg swallowed hard. "Thank you. That means ... a lot. And I love you, too."

"Now for the harder question." Her smile slipped away. "Are you planning to come out publicly?" She held up her hand to stop him. "Now, wait before you answer that. I want you to know that I don't feel strongly one way or the other. I'm simply asking. So I can support you regardless. But you and I both know that not everyone is supportive. However, I know that Mr. Pierce is married to a man and a woman." She waved her hand. "In theory or whatever."

"He is. And I'm planning to talk to him. Right now, I'm taking this slowly. Roan knows how I feel. Knows that I can't come out right now. Maybe not ever."

Seg continued to watch her.

"But Ma, I don't want to hide him. That's my problem, I think. I don't want to hide what this is. I've never felt anything like this before. He'll think it's too soon, but Ma, I want to ask the man to marry me. I want to spend my life with him. And no, we haven't been seeing each other for long. Not like this. I've known him for a year and a half and I think ... I think I fell for him the very first day I met him. Yes, even as I say it, I know it sounds ridiculous."

"No, it doesn't, Seggy. Who puts a time limit on love? Who ever said that you have to be with someone for a week, a year, a decade before you know that person's it for you? I knew your father for a month when I realized I wanted to spend my life with him. I was sixteen years old, Seggy. The timing isn't important." She placed her hand over her heart and tapped her fingers against her chest. "This is."

The relief he felt was staggering. She understood him. Then again, Seg had known that she would. His mother had always been his rock.

"So, when do I get to meet Roan and Liam?"

Of all the questions she could've asked, Seg should've known that would be the most important one. For her, at least.

"WHY ARE YOU pacing the floor? Sit down, for chrissakes," Cam grumbled as Roan made another pass through the dining room. "Your daddy's gonna make me crazy, Liam."

Roan stopped mid-stride, watching Cam as he gently bounced Liam on his knee, smiling down at the boy. Roan had come over to Cam and Gannon's in an effort to keep his mind off the fact that Seg's mother was coming into town tonight. It hadn't helped in the least.

"Where's your man at tonight?" Gannon asked, making his way back to the kitchen.

"He's not my man," Roan argued without thinking.

"I'd beg to differ," Cam stated, his intent to argue evident in his tone. "I've never seen you quite this neurotic. I can only assume that's because he's your guy."

Roan knew there was no point in disputing Cam's accusation. They'd figure it out soon enough. No way could Roan keep up the charade that things weren't serious with him and Seg. But shit, it was still hard to believe that *things were serious*. Hell, he hadn't known Seg all that long, so how was it even possible that serious was something he thought about?

"His mother's coming into town tonight," he explained, wiping his sweaty palms on his jeans.

Cam's eyes widened. "Oh, shit."

"Yeah. My sentiment exactly."

"Lemme guess," Gannon said. "She doesn't know he's gay either."

Roan shook his head. "She might now. He was going to tell her."

"Maybe he should ease into that conversation," Gannon mumbled beneath his breath. "It's not something you blurt out over spaghetti and meatballs."

Roan knew that Gannon didn't have a high opinion of coming out of the closet. He hadn't been one of the lucky ones either. Like Roan, Gannon's parents hadn't embraced the news.

"Are they close?" Cam asked.

"According to him they are."

"Then I'm sure it'll be fine. Is he gonna call you?"

Roan shrugged. They talked nearly every day. If not on the phone, then by text. He figured for sure Seg would tell him what was going on, but if things went bad…

"Quit worrying about it," Gannon stated firmly. "There's nothing you can do to change the outcome. It is what it is. Think positive."

Positive. Right.

Roan's cell phone buzzed in his pocket, and he damn near went through the roof. He yanked it out and stared at the screen while Cam laughed.

Hockey boy: *Gonna call you in half an hour. Cool?*

Roan responded with: *Yeah.*

"You've gotta go." Cam pasted on his puppy dog eyes. "And you're taking this sweet boy away from me, aren't you?"

"I am."

"Fine." Cam got to his feet and headed for Liam's diaper bag. He tossed in the few things they'd pulled out, then held the bag out for Roan. "If you need to talk ... about anything..."

Roan nodded. "I know."

"So I assume you're gonna meet Mama Seg during this visit?"

That wasn't something Roan wanted to think about right now. He'd been dreading the outcome of Seg's conversation almost as much as the idea of meeting Seg's mother. Seriously. Not once in his life had he ever been introduced to the parents.

Cam chuckled. "You need to relax."

Roan hefted Liam's diaper bag onto his shoulder, then took Liam into his arms. "Easier said than done."

"The Arrows are at home this weekend," Cam noted as they headed for the door. "You wanna catch at least one game? Milly's been beggin' me to ask you if she can babysit."

"I'm sure we can work out somethin'."

Half an hour later, Roan was sitting on the couch while Liam sat in his swing, staring at anything and everything he could. It didn't fail to amaze Roan how quickly the little boy was growing. It seemed every day Liam developed a little more. He was gurgling nonsense frequently, pushing up his upper body when he was lying on the floor, smiling more and more, and grasping on to things with a surprisingly strong grip, including the little toys Roan gave him.

When Roan's phone rang, he tried to play it cool. He even let it ring twice, though he was terrified he'd miss the call. *Pathetic, much?*

"Hey."

"Hey."

Roan tried his best to decipher from the tone of that one word what Seg's mood was. It didn't work.

"How'd it go?" Roan asked, leaning back into the cushion of the couch.

"Good. My mom's … good."

Roan released a breath, and his shoulders instantly relaxed.

"Roan?"

"Hmm?"

"I want to see you."

Oh, God. "I wanna see you, too," he answered softly. This was all new and strange for him. He hadn't had a… What was Seg to him? His boyfriend? Lover? Roan didn't even know.

"Can you talk to me for a bit?" Seg asked, his voice warm. "I just want to hear your voice."

Yeah, this man was impossible to resist. Roan wasn't sure where things were going or how they'd end up, but he knew for a fact that he was already falling for this sexy hockey player.

And he was falling hard.

"So, how'd it go?" Roan probed, hoping Seg would feel comfortable enough to share the details. "What did she say?"

"She said she loved me," Seg admitted. "But I never doubted that for a second."

Roan was genuinely happy that it worked out for Seg. Unfortunately, that wasn't always the case, as Roan knew firsthand. "I came out of the closet when I was a teenager," he told Seg. "Fourteen, maybe. I can't remember. Anyway, I thought I was in love. Figured there was no way I could hide that from my parents. Hell, I didn't want to. I was happy. I think more so because I came to terms with the fact that I was gay. Looking back on it now, I wish I'd known then what I know now."

"Aww, babe," Seg groaned. "I'm so fucking sorry."

"It happens. My mother packed up and left, took her suitcase and everything. Said she couldn't live in a house with the devil. Thankfully, Cam's parents were cool."

"And your dad?"

"He never said anything, but I know he blamed me for my mother leaving. Truth is, I think they were headed for divorce anyway. They didn't even bother trying to hide their arguments. Of course, my sisters both blamed me, and they were very verbal about how they felt."

There was silence for a few seconds before Seg said, "I really want you to meet my mother. I told her about you and Liam. She's … happy."

Roan didn't know what to say to that. He wasn't sure how he felt about meeting Seg's mother. In theory, it was fine. But once he did that, it meant he accepted that this relationship was going full steam ahead. As much as he wanted that, Roan was still scared to make that commitment.

"I won't push you, Roan," Seg added, his voice low.

Closing his eyes, Roan sighed. "I know."

"I'll let you go. I've got practice early. We've got a game on Friday and Saturday. I was hoping you'd come to one or both."

"I'd like that," Roan admitted.

"Good. And I'll see you at some point this weekend. I'm not sure I can stay away for too long. Good night."

"Good night."

Roan disconnected the call and opened his eyes to see Liam snoozing in his swing. He wished Seg was there now so he could avoid the cold, lonely bed. Just a short time with the man and Roan was already looking forward to having him there.

He only hoped like hell he wasn't jumping the gun on this one.

For Liam's sake.

And Seg's.

Nineteen

Thursday, January 26th

"IF YOU KEEP pacing the floor, you're going to drive me insane," his mother claimed when Seg walked through the kitchen and then back out.

He had no idea what he was doing, where he was going, or even what he wanted. Well, that wasn't entirely true. He wanted to see Roan, but he was doing his best not to push the man too far, too fast.

"Why don't you invite Roan over," Deb suggested.

Seg stopped moving. "Really?"

His mother's smile brightened. "Why not? It's obvious you want to see him."

He did. More than anything. Seg had hoped he'd be able to make it until Friday before he made the suggestion. He figured his best chance to see Roan was after the game.

Deb went to the refrigerator and pulled out the chicken breast she'd had him buy—one of the half dozen things on her list. "I'll make dinner. Nothing fancy."

Seg continued to stare at her, wanting to believe this was real, but still hesitant.

She shot him a grin over her shoulder. "Of course, I could always call him for you."

"No. Not necessary." He could only imagine how that conversation would go. Probably something like: *Hi, Roan. This is Seg's mom. He told me all about you, including how he's head over heels in love and wants to make you his husband. Feel like coming over for dinner tonight? We're having chicken.*

Seg choked on a laugh.

"What's funny?"

"Nothing." Nothing at all.

"Go. Call him. Tell him dinner will be ready at five."

Seg nodded, then headed for his bedroom. He pulled his cell phone from his pocket and stared at it. He was working up the nerve to call when his phone vibrated in his hand. He stared down at the screen to see a text from Roan.

Roan: *I give up. I'm trying to be patient, but it isn't working.*

Seg grinned. Rather than type a response, he hit the button to call Roan.

"Hey," Roan answered.

"Come over," Seg said by way of greeting. "My mother insists."

Roan chuckled. "It's that easy, huh?"

"That easy," Seg confirmed. "As long as you're that easy, that is."

"Oh, I'm easy, all right."

Seg laughed. That was so far from the truth, but Seg appreciated Roan's attempt to make him laugh.

"So, is that a yes?"

"Yeah. Do I ... uh ... need to bring anything?"

"Nope. Just you and Liam. We've got the rest covered." God, he missed this man.

"Okay then. I need to get Liam changed, but then we'll be heading that way."

"Perfect. And Roan?"

"Hmm?"

"I fully intend to make out with you while you're here."

A soft growl was Roan's only response before the man started mumbling to Liam.

Seg lowered himself to the edge of his bed as he listened to Roan's voice. He couldn't remember ever feeling this off-balance over the fact that someone was coming over. He'd always figured he simply hadn't met the right woman, but now he knew what it really was. Seg had been waiting for a man.

This man.

"See you in a bit."

"We'll be here."

An hour and a half later, Seg was sitting on the couch, flipping through the channels on the television. It was that or pace the floor. He knew he'd get shit from his mother if he did the latter, so he settled for glancing over at the front door every few seconds. Thankfully, she was still in the kitchen working her culinary magic while he slowly went out of his mind.

They'd spent the first thirty minutes getting the portable crib set up and going through the baby books he'd purchased. She'd gone a little nuts when she found the blankets and sheets but no laundry detergent to wash them. Apparently, babies had a special detergent, and the next thing Seg knew, he'd been on a grocery store run to get the detergent. When he returned, he found that his mother had opened all the packages and had the washing machine loaded and ready to go.

When the knock sounded, Seg's heart slammed into his sternum and he inhaled sharply. He knew he shouldn't be nervous about seeing Roan, but he couldn't help it. Taking a deep breath, he pushed up off the couch and went to the door.

He brushed his hand down over his shirt, smoothing it out before gripping the knob and pulling it open. The instant he saw Roan, his heart skipped another beat.

Yeah, it was safe to say he was in over his head with this one. Way over his head.

Roan lifted an eyebrow and smiled. A strange warmth filled Seg's insides.

"Invite me in," Roan whispered, still grinning.

"Right." Seg stepped out of the way, allowing room for Roan to pass, taking the diaper bag from his arm as he did.

When Roan set the car seat down, Seg instantly leaned over to greet Liam, unbuckling the straps.

"Can I pick him up?" Seg whispered, peering up at Roan.

Roan nodded.

The little boy was snoozing, but Seg gently took him out of the carrier, then settled Liam into his arm and took a moment to drink in the sight of him. Yeah, he'd missed the little boy, too. He wasn't sure he'd ever really envisioned himself having children—he'd wanted them, yes, but had never gotten to the point of thinking it could really happen— but with Liam, there was an instant connection. He even imagined teaching the little guy how to play hockey one day.

"I'm nervous," Roan said, pulling Seg's attention away from Liam.

"Don't be. She's harmless," he told him. "Really."

"I think you've used that term to describe yourself, too." Roan smiled. "I'm not sure you know the meaning of it."

Seg laughed, then motioned with his head for Roan to follow him.

It was clear that his mother was doing her best not to race over to them when Seg entered the kitchen. Deb was making every effort to play it cool, but that was one thing his mother had never mastered. She turned, her eyes taking in Roan first, then dropping to the baby Seg held in his arms.

"Ma, this is Roan." Seg tilted his head toward Roan. "And this is Roan's son, Liam. Roan, this is my mother, Debra Seguine."

It was interesting to watch the way her smile slowly spread across her face. Her eyes brightened, and Seg was almost certain she was going to cry, but then Deb spoke.

"It's great to meet you, Roan." She moved closer, then lowered her voice as she pulled back the blanket that was covering Liam. "And you, too, Liam." Her eyes lifted to Seg's and another smile tilted her lips.

Seg cleared his throat, not sure what to say. Except for the one girl he'd dated in high school, this was the first time Seg had ever introduced his mother to anyone.

"Dinner will be ready in about half an hour. Why don't you boys go in the living room."

Seg nodded.

Deb glanced over at Roan. "But you let me know the minute Liam's awake."

"Yes, ma'am."

"Oh, poo. Call me Deb."

Roan laughed. "Yes, ma'am."

Deb chuckled, then turned around to go back to what she was doing.

And that's when it sank in.

Seg had officially introduced his mother to … the man he loved.

ROAN FELT LIKE he was in the principal's office waiting to have a conversation about something he'd done.

No, he had no reason to fear Seg's mother, but still. He couldn't seem to relax, no matter how hard he tried. From his spot on the couch, he could hear her moving around the kitchen, and he waited on pins and needles for her to pop her head out and ask him something. It would likely be a question he wouldn't know the answer to. That's the way it worked for him. Then again, she could ask him how old he was and Roan wasn't sure he could come up with the answer. His nerves had successfully fried his brain cells.

"Relax," Seg whispered, reaching over and touching Roan's hand.

The warmth infused him and Roan suddenly wished they were alone. Hell, he hadn't even been able to kiss Seg yet, and he'd been looking forward to it since the last time he'd kissed the man.

"I'm trying."

"No, you're not." Seg chuckled.

"Fine, I'm not."

"Are you nervous?"

Roan shook his head. "No, I'm terrified."

Seg laughed again and the sound eased some of the tension in Roan's shoulders.

"She doesn't bite."

Roan peered over at Seg. "So, you've done this before?"

"Done what?"

"Introduced your mom to…" Roan didn't even know what this was.

"To my boyfriend?" Seg's eyes glittered with amusement. "Can't say that I have, no. In fact, I've only ever introduced her to one person, and that was the girl I dated in the tenth grade. Needless to say, it wasn't serious."

Roan was still hung up on the word. Boyfriend. He liked the sound of it. Especially when Seg said it. It was strange, yet it filled him with a weird sense of … hope.

"Boys! Dinner's ready!"

And just like that, the hope disappeared and terror surged through Roan's veins. Thankfully, Liam chose that exact moment to stir from his spot on the couch between him and Seg. Roan turned his full attention to the baby, trying to regulate his breathing. It would suck if he passed out right about now.

"I hear that baby."

Roan glanced up as Deb was heading toward them, her eyes locked on Liam. She instantly started talking to him, cooing and smiling. Roan shot a quick look at Seg, noticing the man was still watching him.

"You boys go on in there and get some food. I'll be along in a minute."

Forcing himself to his feet, Roan prayed he wouldn't fall over.

"Does he have a diaper bag?" Deb asked.

Before Roan could head over to get it, Seg held him back with a gentle hand on his shoulder. "Kitchen."

Okay, so clearly Seg could see Roan's distress. He hated that he couldn't hide it better, but the truth of the matter was he had no idea how to react in a situation like this. Being in a committed relationship was so far outside his realm of experience Roan wasn't even sure how to act.

Once in the kitchen, Roan took a deep breath and planted his palms on the counter to steady himself. He was attempting to rein himself in when he felt warm hands on his back. He turned, coming face-to-face with Seg.

"I've waited long enough."

Roan was processing Seg's words when the man leaned in and kissed him. It wasn't a quick, chaste kiss either. This one sparked a flame inside Roan's gut, and he grabbed Seg, jerking him closer. This was more like it. For whatever reason, he could easily get lost in Seg's kiss.

"Ahem."

Seg smiled against Roan's mouth before pulling away. Roan's face flamed with heat as he did his best to make eye contact with Seg's mother. It wasn't easy. Didn't matter that she was smiling either.

Half an hour later, the three of them were still sitting at the table. Deb was holding Liam in her lap, bouncing him gently while she regaled Roan with stories of Seg as a child.

"No matter what we did, we could not convince him that sleeping with his hockey stick would not improve his game."

"It worked, didn't it?" Seg asked, taking a sip of his water. "I might've never made it into the NHL if I hadn't done that."

Deb grinned. "I doubt that's true, but we will never know." She turned her attention to Roan. "Do your parents live close?"

Roan swallowed. "My dad and stepmother do."

Her eyebrows lifted as though waiting for him to provide more information.

"I ... uh..." Roan glanced at Seg briefly before turning his attention back to Deb. "I haven't seen my mother since I was a teenager. She left and never came back. Not even to visit."

"Well, that's a shame," Deb stated. "Whatever her reason, she's the one who missed out."

Roan appreciated the fact that he didn't have to go into detail. It wasn't easy talking about his mother. Sure, he shrugged it off and pretended it didn't bother him that she'd left, but deep down, he still felt the pain from it.

"Did Seg tell you about the time he shot a puck in the house and broke his grandmother's lamp?"

Roan smiled, enjoying the fact that Deb seemed in tune with his discomfort. She never made it apparent that she was probing into his life. "He didn't, no." Roan glanced over to see Seg rolling his eyes.

"He was eight. His father and I heard the noise and we instantly knew what it was. However, like any creative eight-year-old, when we asked Seg what happened, he insisted that he'd been watching TV and the lamp just shattered."

"It was magic," Seg said, deadpan.

"Never mind the fact that his hockey stick was lying on the floor in front of him or that the puck was still protruding from the metal frame that surrounded the bulb."

Seg grinned cheekily.

Deb laughed, then peered down at Liam, who was smiling up at her. "I was thinking that Liam and I would go into the living room," Deb said, her gaze darting between Roan and Seg. "Then after the two of you do the dishes, maybe you could spend some time together."

Heat infused Roan instantly. He knew he shouldn't be embarrassed, yet he was.

"Thanks, Ma. If you need anything, let us know."

"When does he take a bottle?" she asked Roan directly.

Roan glanced at his watch. "Anytime now."

Deb nodded. "Good. If you want to make that for me after the dishes are done, I'll be happy to feed him."

Deb got to her feet, grinning down at Liam as she walked out of the kitchen. Roan didn't move from his seat.

"You all right?" Seg asked.

Roan shook his head, but he said, "I will be." And he would. It would take a little time to get used to this.

"Let's get the dishes done." Seg leaned in closer. "Then we'll go make out in my bedroom."

If this man wasn't careful, Roan was going to spontaneously combust.

HARMLESS

Talk about embarrassing.

Twenty

SEG FELT LIKE a teenager.

More so than he'd ever felt like one before. Even back when he was in high school. Because hockey had taken over his life at an early age—by his choice—Seg hadn't spent much time doing simple, adolescent things such as making out with someone he liked. Sure, he'd had girls flock to him because he played sports, but he'd spent his time perfecting his game, his desire to make it into the NHL a driving force he hadn't been able to shove to the side.

Perhaps his lack of interest stemmed from the fact that he was gay, even if he hadn't realized it at that point. It was true, he hadn't experienced any stop-the-press type feelings for any one particular girl. Or guy, for that matter. Thinking back on it now, maybe he'd been trying to figure it out, and focusing on hockey was just easier.

So this … making out with Roan made him feel like he was fifteen years old. Although, he wasn't sure a fifteen-year-old should be doing what they were doing.

Seriously. Roan was half naked, lying on Seg's bed, his shirt on the floor, his jeans around his ankles, and Seg had two fingers buried in his ass, fucking him slow and easy.

"Seg…" Roan breathed out roughly, his rough groan muted against Seg's neck.

"Do you like that?" Seg whispered. "Like when I finger fuck your ass?"

"More than you know." Roan's hands clutched at Seg's T-shirt, his body tense.

"Good. Because I'm enjoying the hell out of it."

Roan groaned when Seg shifted his finger, seeking that one spot he'd recently learned of that would blow Roan's mind.

"Oh, fuck … oh, fuck…" Roan buried his face deeper into Seg's neck, his words muffled by Seg's shoulder.

The man was clutching him tighter, his breathing coming as fast as his heartrate. Seg briefly wondered if he could get off on this. Simply by watching the overwhelming pleasure consume Roan.

"Seg…" Roan groaned softly. "More. Please."

"I'll get you there, I promise," Seg assured him as he continued to penetrate Roan's ass. "Promise."

Hell, he could've gotten Roan off twice already, but Seg wasn't ready for that yet. He enjoyed the fuck out of teasing the man. Not to mention, God only knew when he'd get to see him again, and Seg wasn't ready to be done.

He shifted his position so that his mouth was inches from Roan's dick. Strong fingers latched into his hair, and Seg chuckled. Apparently Roan was hanging by a thread.

"Finish me," Roan commanded, his voice nothing more than a gruff whisper. "Right now."

Seg opened his mouth and took Roan's thick cock to the root. He sucked roughly, bobbing his head up and down slowly, then faster, his fingers still fucking Roan's ass, matching the pace of his mouth. Roan managed to control the pace by tightening his grip on Seg's hair. Seg had no choice but to give in, to allow Roan to fuck his face.

Suddenly, Roan jerked his hair, causing Roan's dick to fall from his mouth. Seg moved again, this time leaning down to brush his lips against Roan's, inhaling the man's choppy, rough breaths. The guy was so fucking sexy like this.

He had absolutely no idea how many minutes passed because he was so caught up in listening to Roan's rough growls and spine-tingling moans. If he was right, Roan was lost to the sensation, focused solely on getting to the finish line.

"Oh, fuck … oh, fuck … oh…"

Yeah, just like that. Seg's fingers moved faster, pushed deeper as Roan's body tensed. The man was…

Right there.

When Roan reached for his cock, Seg stopped him with a firm, "No."

Roan's eyes snapped open.

"Only I get to touch you."

Knowing he'd been tormenting Roan for long enough, Seg shifted so that his mouth was in line with Roan's cock again. While he continued to thrust his fingers into Roan's ass, he sucked the swollen head into his mouth, applying suction.

"Son. Of. A…" Roan's fingers clutched Seg's hair and he yanked at the same time he erupted.

Hell yeah.

Roan came roughly and Seg swallowed him down, licking and laving gently before pulling his fingers from inside him, then shifting on the bed, crawling over Roan as he did.

"Damn, that was hot," he whispered against Roan's lips.

"My turn," Roan insisted.

Seg shook his head. "Not tonight."

The sheer disappointment in Roan's golden gaze both made him laugh and stole his heart. He would never get enough of this man. Not if they lived to be two hundred years old.

"We need to get back downstairs," Seg told him.

"Oh, shit." Roan tried to sit up abruptly, but Seg held him in place with his body.

"Relax. I'm sure my mom's having fun with Liam. She's probably completely in love with him and ready to plan our wedding."

Roan's eyes went wide, and Seg suddenly regretted throwing that out there. He hadn't meant anything by it. Or had he?

"I ... uh..." Seg pushed off the bed and got to his feet. "Why don't you go downstairs and I'll meet you there in a sec."

Before he could make it to the adjoining bathroom, strong fingers clasped on to his bicep, successfully spinning him around. He was face-to-face with Roan.

"Don't you run from me, Colton Seguine," Roan demanded, his eyes bright. "I heard what you said. I also know it was innocent, so don't freak out."

Funny. Usually Seg was the one saying that. Roan was the one prone to freaking out, not Seg.

He forced air into his lungs and tried to relax. In fact, Seg was so focused on breathing he didn't even notice as Roan unbuttoned his jeans and lowered his zipper. It wasn't until Roan's fist was wrapped around his dick that reality sank in.

"My turn," Roan repeated, grinning.

Seg choked out a laugh as Roan tugged him toward the bed, his hand still gripping Seg's dick. He was about to question him when Roan pulled open the nightstand drawer and retrieved a bottle of lube. Seg's dick twitched in Roan's hand.

"Oh, shit…" Seg sighed as Roan slicked his hand and began stroking Seg's dick. Slowly at first, then faster, his fingers tight around his shaft.

"Like that?"

"Fuck yes." Damn, it felt good. Too good.

Seg tried to hold on as he watched his cock tunnel in and out of Roan's slippery hand. The sight had his balls drawing up tight, his cock pulsing. He was going to come. No two ways about it.

"Roan… God, yes…" Seg threw his head back and came violently, his entire body shuddering as his cock spurted in Roan's fist. He wasn't sure what the appeal was about Roan stroking his dick, but it did it for him. In a big way.

"*Now* we should really go back downstairs," Roan said.

Seg peered at Roan, noticing the man's wicked grin. Unable to help himself, he grabbed Roan's hips and yanked him closer, crushing their lips together. He kissed him roughly, his fingers digging into his skin. He didn't want to let him go. Not now. Not ever.

"I want you to stay the night."

Roan pulled back, staring into Seg's eyes. The man didn't have to say a word for Seg to realize that wouldn't be happening.

"I want that, too," Roan admitted. "But you know that's not a good idea. Not tonight."

Seg nodded. He did know. "But you're coming to the game on Saturday?"

"I wouldn't miss it."

Well, he'd settle for that then.

For now.

217

BY THE TIME Roan got Liam into his own bed two hours later, he was wishing he'd agreed to stay at Seg's. He'd started missing him about the time he stepped out of the house.

Maybe it made him a pussy to want to spend time with the man, but he couldn't help himself. Hell, he wanted to spend every waking minute with Seg. Even after tonight. After meeting Seg's mother. Not that it was a bad experience. Quite the opposite actually. She was probably one of the few people in the world who had openly accepted Roan right from the beginning. She made him feel as though he was important to her and that surprised him.

Thanks to his own experiences, Roan was prone to remaining on the defensive when it came to people. Sure, he'd had a few people in his life who'd accepted him. Cam's father was the first one off the top of his head. However, Roan had never come to expect people to look at him with anything other than confusion or disgust. It was a flaw in his design, he supposed, but that didn't mean he was going to change.

His phone buzzed in his pocket.

Hockey boy: When you get Liam in bed, call me.

Roan smiled to himself as he made his way to his bedroom after shutting off all the lights and making sure the doors were locked. He quickly stripped off his clothes, grabbed his cell phone and climbed into bed. The room was dark, except for the small nightlight in the hall that provided a dim glow. Roan had figured he needed it after he'd run into the door at least three times when getting up with Liam in the middle of the night.

Roan dialed the phone.

"Hey." Seg's rough whisper greeted him on the other end of the phone.

"Hey."

"Liam asleep?"

"Yeah." Roan smiled. "I think your mom wore him out."

"They did play forever." Seg chuckled. "And she talked about him nonstop for about an hour after you left."

"Yeah?"

"Oh, yeah. She adores him. Then again, most people do."

Roan felt warmth in his chest. He knew that Seg adored Liam, too. He could see it in the way the man looked at him, held him, spoke to him. And to think, Roan had been terrified of introducing the little boy to anyone. If he'd only realized it sooner...

Hindsight being twenty-twenty and all that shit.

"What are you wearing?" Seg asked, his tone dropping an octave.

"Nothing." Roan pushed the sheet off, his dick thickening from the sound of Seg's voice alone.

"Hmm. I like you in nothing."

"Do you?"

"Fuck yeah." Seg's breathing sounded rough, choppy.

Roan reached down and palmed his dick. "I wish you were here."

"Me, too. So fucking bad."

The warmth in his gut bloomed outward, filling his entire body. It had been far too long since Roan had felt like this. Hell, maybe he hadn't ever felt like this. Whatever it was, he liked it. A lot.

There was the sound of something rustling. Roan figured Seg was getting comfortable.

"Are you in bed?" Roan questioned.

"I am. Right here in my bed wishing you were here."

"What would you do to me if I was?" Roan asked. He knew where this was going and he wasn't about to pass up the opportunity. Tonight had been a mere tease when he'd been with Seg. Not that this would be much more than that, but still.

"First, I would kiss you," Seg replied. "And from there, I'd trail my mouth all over your body. I want to feast on you for hours. I want to map your body with my tongue."

"Mmm." Roan liked the sound of that. His dick did, too.

"Can you imagine that, Roan? My tongue sliding all over you?"

"Mmm-hmm."

"I want to feel your mouth on me," Seg whispered. "And I'm not talking about on my dick."

"No?" Roan grinned, his hand tightening on his dick.

"I want your mouth everywhere." Seg's voice deepened, his tone raspier.

"You want to feel my tongue on your ass, don't you?" He knew Seg loved that.

A strangled groan was the only response he received. It was enough to spur Roan on.

"I'd put you on your knees," Roan explained. "Your chest flat on the bed. I'd be kneeling behind you, running my hands over your back while I licked your ass, fucking you with my tongue, getting you ready to take my cock."

"Fuck..."

"You'd like that, wouldn't you?"

"Yes."

"You want me to make you come that way? Tongue-fucking your ass?"

Seg grunted.

"I could eat your ass for hours, Colton. Make you beg me to fuck you. But I wouldn't give in."

Another grunt.

"Are you jacking off?"

"Yeah," Seg groaned. "Keep talking."

"That's what I'm gonna do next time I see you," Roan told him. "I'm gonna bend you over and lick you until you can't take anymore. Then I'm gonna ram my dick in your ass and fuck you. Hard."

Roan was stroking himself roughly, the image he painted in his own head more than he could stand. He wanted Seg more than he wanted air. He needed to feel the warmth of the man's body strangling his dick.

"Roan ... damn..."

"Come for me, Colton. Come while you're thinking about me fucking your ass. Taking you. Claiming you..." Roan jacked himself faster. "Owning you."

"Fuck!"

A rough growl followed and Roan knew Seg was coming. Unable to hold back, he came, too, his eyes closed, the sound of Seg's mumbled groans echoing in his ear.

The only thing that could've been better would've been to hold Seg in his arms while they drifted off to sleep. However, he wasn't going to dwell on that right now.

One day.

One day real soon, he got the feeling things were going to end up exactly the way they were meant to.

Twenty-One

"WHAT'S ON THE agenda this afternoon?" his mother asked when Seg walked into the kitchen early the next morning.

He shrugged. "Completely up to you. I've got morning skate, but then I thought I'd take you to lunch. Maybe head over to the Oasis since it's supposed to be nice." The restaurant that overlooked Lake Travis was one of his mother's favorites in town. Since Seg didn't do much eating out, he tended to go to places he knew she enjoyed when she was here.

"That sounds perfect." Deb sipped her coffee. "I like Roan."

Well, that was random. Seg pulled his head from the refrigerator and peered over at her. "I'm glad."

"Y'all are cute together."

Seg choked on a laugh. "We're not cute together," he argued.

"But you are." Her grin widened. "But neither one of you is as cute as Liam."

"I won't argue with you there."

She turned to face him. "Did you ever plan to have kids?"

He was shocked by the question, but he knew he shouldn't be. His mother often asked random questions, but this quite possibly could've been the most off-the-wall.

"I hadn't given it much thought. I mean, sure, I wanted them. One day."

"Is that because you thought you were gay?"

Pouring milk into his coffee, Seg cast a quick look at his mother. "No." He put the milk back in the refrigerator and shut the door. "I'm serious when I say that hockey has been the most important thing in my life. Even above relationships."

"Until Roan." Her smile softened.

"Yes." Seg felt a blush creep up his neck. "Until Roan."

"They say when you know, you know."

Whoever "they" were ... they were right. Seg had known right from that first look.

"Where did you meet Roan anyway?"

"I told you. At a bar."

His mother's curiosity had increased, it was evident by the way she crossed her legs and rested her arm on the table. "You did mention it." Her grin said she was happy his answer hadn't changed. "Did he approach you? Or vice versa?"

Seg sipped his coffee. "I approached him."

"That makes sense."

Seg's eyebrows furrowed in confusion. "How do you figure?"

"When the two of you are together..." She smiled again. "It's obvious you've got a good handle on the situation. Although I can tell Roan's into you, I can see a little hesitancy there. Like he's waiting for the other shoe to drop."

Looking away, Seg pretended that didn't hit too close to home. How his mother could get that from Roan in the short time they'd spent together, he didn't know. But it was true. Seg got the sense that Roan always had one foot out the door, ready to throw up those protective walls if necessary. Seg only prayed he never gave Roan a reason to run from him, because the guy's running shoes didn't have much tread left.

"Well, I'm going to shower and then call Marjorie while you go to practice. Then we'll meet back here around one?"

"That's the plan."

Deb got to her feet and walked over to him. Seg watched her, then leaned down when she went on her toes to kiss his cheek. She patted his other and smiled warmly.

"I'm happy for you, honey. I knew one day you'd find what you were looking for."

When she walked out of the room, Seg stared into the empty space behind her, smiling to himself. He had found what he was looking for.

Even if he hadn't known he'd been seeking it.

"HE ROLLED OVER!" Milly squealed. "Oh, my goodness. Did you see it?" Her eyes widened as she shot Roan a shocked look over her shoulder.

"I saw it."

Her expression sobered. "Has he done that before?"

It was clear Milly wasn't happy that she wasn't the first one to see the milestone, which was kind of amusing. "Only once."

Milly's lip protruded in a pout. "You have to tell me these things from now on."

Laughing, Roan said, "I'll be sure to do that."

Milly's small hand covered her rounded belly and smiled over at AJ. "One of these days, we'll have a little one rolling over, too."

"We will," AJ agreed, smiling at Milly.

Roan had come over to Cam's at his request. Milly had driven out to their house so she could go to the event at the children's home with Gannon, but when she got there, she admitted she wasn't feeling well. Since Gannon needed someone to assist, Cam had offered his services, and Roan had agreed to come chill with Milly. Not long after he and Liam arrived, so did AJ, as well as AJ's brother, Hudson. Teague hadn't been far behind. So, the six of them were having a regular old party right there and the homeowners weren't even present to stop them.

"I assume the pizza will be here soon," Milly grumbled. "I'm starving."

"Ten minutes or so," Roan added.

"So, how's the hot hockey player working out?" Milly inquired, shifting around to face Roan more fully while still being able to keep an eye on Liam.

Roan knew there was no such thing as a safe topic with Milly. He also knew that she'd been chomping at the bit since he arrived to ask about Seg.

"He's good."

"And I heard you met Mom, too."

Great. Nothing was sacred anymore. He knew he shouldn't have mentioned it to Cam. "I did."

"That go okay?" Milly's expression was one of true concern.

"It was fine."

"Either she liked you or she didn't," Teague mused. "Which was it?"

"I'm sure she liked me just fine." Roan didn't know for sure, but he had no reason to believe otherwise.

Milly held out her hand, and AJ got up to help her to her feet. "Does this mean things are serious?"

Roan cocked an eyebrow. "Define serious." He glanced down at her belly. "If you're asking whether we're gonna have kids together…"

"Smartass." Milly giggled. "You know that's not what I meant."

He gave Milly and AJ a pointed look. "Are things serious between you two?" Roan countered, wanting to get off this subject. He was quite content with how things were going between him and Seg right now. He didn't want to jinx it by talking about it too much.

"Define serious," she mocked, rolling her eyes.

Roan glanced at AJ, who was smiling at Milly, a slight shake of his head. The guy had been around her long enough at this point he probably wasn't surprised by anything she said or did. The rest of them had long ago gotten used to it.

It was obvious AJ and Milly were getting along well. For two people who'd had a quick fling on a cruise ship, things had turned out different than they'd anticipated. Considering they were having a baby in a couple of months, Roan figured it was drastically different.

"When are you two gonna have kids?" Milly asked, her question directed at Teague and Hudson.

Hudson grinned and Teague paled, making the rest of them laugh.

"Leave the poor guy alone," AJ told Milly. "They'll have kids when they're ready."

Or not, based on the wide-eyed look Teague was giving Hudson.

Roan glanced at AJ, then over to Hudson. He figured they were thinking the same thing he was: there was only one way to shut this woman up these days and that was to feed her.

God, where the hell was that pizza?

Twenty-Two

Saturday night, January 28th

THANKS TO ROAN calling to ask if he could pick Seg's mother up and bring her to the game, Seg had been able to focus completely on getting in the right mindset for tonight. That had paid off big-time. Not only did the Arrows win but they managed a shutout on top of that. Although Kingston Rush, their goalie, had been having an off month, it looked as though he was back. At least for now.

Seg would take it. Well, that and the two assists he'd received tonight. Certainly not a bad way to end the day.

And now as he rushed to get showered and dressed after spending twenty minutes on the bike, he couldn't stop thinking about spending the rest of the night with Roan. No, he hadn't talked to Roan about it yet, but he fully intended to just as soon as he saw him.

It was a fucking wonder Seg could concentrate on anything at all, actually. No matter what he did, he thought of Roan. He thought about the past, present, and future. His brain insisted on pulling up mental images of how they'd met, the things they'd done to one another that night. Of course, the year of pain and misery between then and seeing Roan again was all a distant thought, shoved to the back of his mind where it belonged.

Admittedly, he spent more time dwelling on how to convince Roan to spend more time with him. Not to mention, how to make that happen with the season underway. They still had two more months unless the Arrows made it to the playoffs, then it would be more. For the first time in his life, Seg was torn over whether or not he wanted to make it to the playoffs.

No, that was only partially true. He definitely wanted to make it to the playoffs. This was what he lived for.

Or it had been until he'd met Roan.

As for the future, Seg had never been the type to think about what might happen tomorrow. With Roan in his life, he had plenty of those thoughts.

But honestly, he needed to focus on the next few minutes of his future if he expected to see Roan at all.

Twenty minutes later, Seg strolled out of the locker room to find the hallways nearly empty. Most of the players had jetted already, only a few still lingering to chat about the game and what their plans were after they left the arena.

"Hey, Seg! You wanna meet us over at the Penalty Box?" Kaufman asked.

"I'll have to see what my mother wants to do," he told him.

Spencer grinned and Seg rolled his eyes. So what if his captain wanted to give him a hard time about his mother. Right now, nothing could bring him down.

"Cool," Spencer stated. "We'll see you if we see you."

With a half-ass wave, Seg continued toward the players' parking lot. He had no intention of going out tonight. The only thing he wanted to do was go home and spend the rest of the evening with Roan, Liam, and his mother. He smiled to himself. He was thinking like a regular old family guy.

"Hey, Seg! Can you answer a question?"

Seg turned at the unfamiliar voice. He spotted a young guy moving toward him with a purpose. The guy wore jeans and an Austin Arrows jersey. The ball cap on his head was also Arrows. Seg didn't recognize him, but he stopped anyway. If he was a fan, Seg would offer a quick autograph and be on his way.

"What's up?" Seg replied, quirking a brow in question, waiting for the man to state the reason for chasing him down.

"I saw your mom at the game tonight."

The hair on the back of Seg's neck stood on end. He had no idea who this guy was, but anyone who started out a conversation like that was questionable. For one, Seg made sure to keep his mother out of the spotlight. And two, Seg didn't know this guy from Adam.

"She was here with a guy."

Definitely creepy.

The guy grinned, as though he was Seg's best friend. "They looked to be having a good time. Laughing. Joking."

Seg had no idea where this guy was going with this.

"Is it true that you're in a serious relationship?"

Seg tried to play it cool, pretend he wasn't sweating, because he had the sudden suspicion that this asshole wasn't a fan. He was a reporter and he was fishing for some information. As for how he'd become privy to something like that, Seg had no idea.

The guy grinned and this time he looked like a shark. "And your new ... how do you put it? Boyfriend? He was here at the game tonight?"

Seg grimaced. "What the fuck are you talking about?" He didn't bother waiting for a response before turning and heading toward his Range Rover.

"Come on, Seg. It's cool if you cross swords in your spare time. No one's gonna judge you, bro."

Seg didn't respond, and it took everything in him not to turn around and punch the dickhead in the face.

He reached his SUV and hit the button to unlock the door.

"So, I take that as a yes. You won't mind if I make it public record, will you?"

Unable to refrain, Seg spun around and grabbed the guy by the front of the jersey. Clearly the asshole hadn't been expecting it. His eyes widened and he sucked in air.

"Leave me and my personal life alone," Seg growled.

The bastard smirked.

"Hey, Seg? You have a problem?"

Shit.

Kaufman strolled toward them and Seg was forced to release the asshole. The last thing he needed was to be brought up on assault charges. This dickweed wasn't worth it.

"No problem," the guy said cheerily. "Seg and I were just chatting, Optimus. Talking about good times. New relationships. Did you know Seg was dating a dude?"

Kaufman stopped beside Seg, glaring down at the asshole. Seg could only assume he was a reporter. Fans didn't usually take to harassing him.

"Fuck off," Kaufman growled, his voice low. "What Seg does in his off time is none of your goddamn business."

Son of a bitch.

Seg understood that Kaufman thought he was standing up for him, but the way he worded that gave the little fucker all the ammunition he needed.

"That's what I thought." The guy brushed off his jersey and turned to walk away. "Thanks for the confirmation, Optimus. I'll make sure you're quoted in the article."

"Fuck." Seg's hands fisted at his sides and his teeth clamped together so hard he thought he might crack a molar.

"What the hell was that about?"

Seg glared at Kaufman, but he didn't answer. Instead, he shook his head and opened his door. No way could he trust any damn thing that came out of his mouth right now.

"I THINK YOU'RE the first person who hasn't freaked out when I get so excited during a game that I dump half my popcorn," Deb stated as Roan sat on the couch across from her.

He smiled. She did get quite animated during a game.

"In case you didn't figure it out, I'm quite the hockey fan."

Oh, that was obvious.

"Even before Seg started playing when he was little. His father had played some in high school. Never wanted to go pro, but he sure looked good out there playing. Granted, when Seggy took it up, it only fueled my passion for the sport. His father used to make fun of me."

Roan didn't know what to say to that.

"So, how's Liam? Have you checked on him?"

Roan nodded. He'd already called Cam twice tonight. Once during the first period and again after the game. Based on what Cam told him, Milly had come over to help watch him so there was absolutely nothing for Roan to worry about. Not that Roan was worried. He knew his son was in good hands. Didn't stop him from missing the little boy though.

"Have you taken him to a game yet?" Deb inquired.

"Not yet."

"That's probably for the best. Wait until he's a little older. It's cold in there."

Roan smiled, refusing to check his watch. It wasn't that he minded spending time with Deb, but he was hoping to spend a little time with Seg tonight. He was torn between running home to see Liam or sticking around for a while. The selfish side of him won out. He could easily go home later or even first thing in the morning.

It wasn't lost on him that he'd started doing the exact opposite of what he'd set out to do. Originally, he'd intended to put his love life on the back burner, dedicate every waking moment to raising Liam. Then Seg came along and he'd gotten some of his priorities mixed up.

Well, that wasn't entirely true. Roan knew what his priorities were. Liam, first and foremost. But he was trying to compromise because this thing with him and Seg was going somewhere. He could feel it. And the last thing he wanted to do at this point was miss out on what could possibly be something real and true.

"I thought Seg would be here by now," Deb said. "Do you want something to drink?"

"No, I'm good. Thank you though."

"Suit yourself." Deb yawned again. She'd been doing it for the past half hour.

Roan grinned. "You don't have to stay up for my benefit."

Deb chuckled. "Oh, thank heavens, because I'm pooped. I didn't want to seem rude."

"Not at all." Roan leaned back into the cushion of the couch. "I'll just wait for Seg."

Deb got to her feet. "Okay, then. I'll see you in the morning?"

Roan swallowed as heat engulfed his face. Once again, Debra Seguine had managed to embarrass him.

She clearly knew that she did because she giggled as she passed by. "Tell Seg I thought he was fantastic tonight."

"Will do."

"Good night, Roan. And thank you for taking me to the game and for putting up with me."

"It was my pleasure." And that was the truth. He'd had a good time with Deb tonight. The woman knew her hockey.

When Deb disappeared at the top of the stairs, Roan glanced down at his watch. He'd figured Seg would be home by now, too. A trickle of unease skated down his spine and Roan reached for his phone. He dialed Seg's number, but the call went straight to voice mail. Made sense. Seg probably turned his phone off during a game. Maybe he forgot to turn it back on.

Figuring Seg would be home shortly, Roan turned on the television and got comfortable.

Two hours later, Roan woke up in the same spot he'd been in. He glanced around to see Seg's house looked exactly the same. And no Seg anywhere in sight.

He got to his feet and yawned, stretching his back muscles. Sleeping on the couch sucked ass, especially doing it sitting up.

Roan made a quick trip to the bathroom, then peeked into Seg's room to make sure the man hadn't simply gone right to bed. The bed was still made.

He tried Seg's phone again.

"What?"

Roan's eyebrows shot upward at the rough sound of Seg's voice.

"Hey. You okay?"

"Fine."

Roan glanced around the house, confused. "Are you … uh … coming home?"

"Nope."

Roan frowned. *What the fuck?* "No?"

"You heard me. I'm not coming home."

"Where are you?"

"Does it fucking matter?"

Roan dropped onto the couch, phone clutched to his ear. "Actually, yeah. It does matter."

"Well, too bad. No, not you, sweetheart. You just keep that sweet little ass right here in my lap."

"What the fuck?" Roan shot to his feet, a furious growl escaping when he did.

"Sorry, man. This is the way shit goes sometimes. I stopped to grab a beer with the guys, and this cute little puck bunny found her way right into my lap. Yep, I'm talking about you, doll."

Roan couldn't help but notice Seg's words were slurring. "Did something happen, Seg?"

"Not yet. But give me another couple of beers and this cutie'll be bouncing up and down on my dick."

Roan felt sick to his stomach. The thought of Seg and someone else…

Nope. He wasn't going there.

Rather than listen to any more, Roan cut the call and raced to the bathroom. His stomach erupted violently, his chest so tight he thought for sure he was having a heart attack. It took a few minutes for his body to settle, and when it did, he washed out his mouth and went in search of his keys. Within minutes he was in his truck on his way home.

He was tempted to stop and pick up Liam because he didn't want to be alone, but he knew he couldn't do that. Liam was fine where he was. Roan would go home, get some sleep, and start over again tomorrow.

Maybe then some of this would make sense.

Twenty-Three

"FUCKING HELL," SEG groaned when he rolled over. His head was spinning, the blood pounding behind his eyes. He fought to keep them open, to look around.

He recognized his room. His alarm clock. His bed.

Well, the good news was that he'd somehow managed to make it home, but he must've face-planted on the mattress, because the damn thing was still made, but his pillows were on the floor.

"Thank Christ," he grumbled.

He got the feeling that was all the good he'd get for today. Maybe forever.

Rolling over onto his back, he closed his eyes again, trying to remember what the fuck happened last night.

It all came back to him in a blinding rush and his stomach lurched.

The game. The reporter. The Penalty Box.

"Ah, damn."

He recalled the puck bunny, but he didn't remember her name. Not that it mattered.

Kaufman.

"Seg, what the hell are you doing, man?"

Looking up, Seg noticed the concerned gaze of his team's captain. "Wassup, Optimus?"

"Man, no more for you." Kaufman's tone left no room for argument.

"No worries," Seg explained. *"I was just about to leave. Going home with…"* He glanced at the woman sitting on his lap. For the life of him, he couldn't fucking remember her name.

"Hey, sweetheart," Kaufman said to the woman. *"He's had more than his fair share tonight. Why don't you write down your number and I'll make sure he gets it."*

Seg didn't want her fucking number. He didn't want her.

With Kaufman's help, the woman got off Seg's lap, her blue eyes twinkling as she smiled down at him. Seg tried to smile. He wasn't sure if he succeeded or not because he was numb. Head to toe. And he had the alcohol to thank for that. The shots had worked nicely.

"I need to go home," he muttered to himself, trying to push up out of his seat.

"I've got a cab coming for you," Kaufman told him.

Seg nodded. He might be the world's biggest dumb ass—proven by his actions tonight—but he damn sure knew he was in no shape to drive.

As the memory faded, Seg's head pounded at the base of his skull.

Shit.

Had it not been for Kaufman interfering, who knew what Seg might've done last night.

He forced his eyes open.

Yes, Kaufman had both driven the nail into the coffin of his career and saved him from doing something stupid. The guy had convinced Seg to dump the puck bunny and go home. He'd even called Seg a cab.

Forcing himself to sit up, Seg dropped his feet over the edge of the bed and waited while his brain stabilized. He stared at the floor as the conversation with Roan replayed in his head.

Damn it.

He'd fucked shit up in a bad way last night.

For that, he deserved the hangover.

And then some.

After taking a shower, Seg managed to make his way to the kitchen. His mother was sitting at the small kitchen table, playing on her iPad.

"Good afternoon, sunshine," she greeted, though her tone wasn't as cheerful as she probably thought.

"Afternoon," he grumbled back, making his way to the refrigerator.

"Long night?"

"Yeah."

"What time did Roan leave?"

Seg didn't look at his mother. No way could he answer that without her realizing what a total fuckup he was. He had no idea what time Roan left, but he assumed it was shortly after Roan called him and Seg pretty much blew him off by telling him he was going to let the puck bunny ride his dick.

Aw, damn. He was going to be sick. He headed for the sink, leaned over, and planted his hands on the counter.

"Seggy?"

"Hmm."

"Want to talk about it?"

"Nothing to talk about."

"No?"

He glanced over to see his mother holding up her iPad.

"I'd beg to differ."

Seg squinted at the screen to see a picture of Roan and Deb smiling and laughing. It was taken during the hockey game last night. Seg didn't have to be a rocket scientist to know what the article was about.

He stood up straight, took a deep breath, and exhaled through his nose. The nausea subsided. "I need to call Roan."

"Seggy, sit down."

Seg turned toward his mother. Her expression was serious, her tone reflecting her worry.

"I don't need a lecture, Ma."

"Sit. Down."

When Debra Seguine took that tone of voice, Seg knew not to argue. He grabbed a bottle of water from the fridge and took the chair across from her.

"I want you to think back to before last night."

He continued to watch her.

"You were happy."

It wasn't a question.

"More so than I've ever seen you, in fact."

He couldn't argue with that.

"You finally figured out who you are, no?"

Seg nodded, staring down at the water bottle.

"And Roan makes you happy."

He offered another nod.

"Then I have to ask you something."

Lifting his gaze to meet hers, he waited.

"Why are you letting this reporter win?" She waved her hand toward her iPad. "He's turned something good into something foul. Is that how you see yourself? This thing between you and Roan? Is it a bad thing?"

"Of course not."

His mother pursed her lips, her doubt evident on her face. "Could've fooled me."

She brought the iPad to life and scrolled down the screen. There in vivid color was the picture of Seg with the puck bunny. His stomach lurched, and he once again fought the urge to puke.

"When you told me you were gay, Seggy, I wasn't surprised. Nor was I disappointed. Like I said, I love you for you. You have nothing to be ashamed of. Yet last night ... whatever happened ... it was clear you were ashamed."

"I wasn't," he countered, though he didn't buy it himself.

Her expression told him she didn't believe him.

"And I have to say, as soon as I saw the picture, I was disappointed. My first thought was of Roan and how much pain he would be in after seeing this."

Seg closed his eyes. As much as he wanted the picture to disappear, he knew there was no way Roan hadn't seen it.

"Seggy?"

Forcing his eyes open, Seg looked at his mother.

"I understand the need to keep your private life private. I even understand the world of professional sports being somewhat conservative in the matter of gay athletes. But honestly..."

Seg waited, knowing she wasn't finished.

Deb leaned back and rested her hands on the table. "You've got these football players taking a knee during the national anthem." Her face scrunched in disgust. "Now, I'm not from the States, but I can tell you that I stand proudly for the national anthem—mine and theirs—my hand over my heart. This country has given my son the ability to do what he loves to do. And the men and women who have fought for their country deserve the respect of me being on my feet. It's the absolute least I can do. So, if the National Football League can sit back and state that those men have the right to express their disdain for their own country, then by God, you have the right to love who you want to love, and the National Hockey League is going to stand behind you."

As heartfelt as he knew that speech was, his mother was wrong. "It's not the league I worry about, Ma."

"No? It's the other players? In the locker room? What? Do they think you'll be in there ogling them? These are men who've played hockey with you for years. They respect you and your abilities. I don't think you give them enough credit."

"So you're saying I should come out?" He felt his anger rising.

She sighed. "That's not what I'm saying. However, I'm saying that you're letting one little twiddle fart screw up your entire life, just when you've found yourself. So what if he publicly states that you've got a boyfriend. You do, don't you?"

No. He'd *had* a boyfriend. After last night, Seg seriously doubted Roan would ever speak to him again, and he couldn't blame him.

His mother reached over and took his hand. "Seggy, what I'm telling you is that if you try to hide who you truly are, you're going to be miserable. I can't tell you that you can live out and proud while playing hockey, but you don't have to hide in the dark anymore either."

He nodded.

"Did you talk to Phoenix? What does he think about all this?"

Seg hadn't had the chance.

No, amend that. He hadn't even tried to talk to Phoenix.

"I didn't think so," Deb stated, reaching over and patting his hand. "I want you to go talk to him. For one, you owe him an explanation since I'm sure he's had the displeasure of seeing this article. Then, once you've done that, you can call Roan, get down on your knees, and beg him for another chance. That man doesn't deserve what you did to him."

Seg felt tears prick the backs of his eyes. He hated himself for what he'd done.

"Think of it this way," his mother continued, "if Liam was old enough to read this…"

Oh, holy fuck.

His stomach churned and Seg shot to his feet and bolted to his bathroom. The mere thought of hurting Roan was bad enough, but Liam…

Seg suddenly wasn't sure he even deserved them anymore.

Cheater or bisexual? Or is there a difference?

Let's talk hockey, shall we?

Or rather, let's talk about what's in the water back in the locker room.

No, I'm not referring to lead or anything like that. I'm talking specifically about the water the Austin Arrows organization is passing out. It appears to be tainted.

If you're familiar with the Arrows, you know that their owner, Phoenix Pierce, came out a couple of years ago spouting some nonsense about being in a relationship with a man and a woman. Initially, I thought this was his way of guarding his secret, passing off being gay as some sort of party trick. Seriously. A man and a woman.

However, I can no longer question them because Phoenix has officially—albeit not legally—tied the knot with both Mia and Tarik. It appears Phoenix is bisexual.

Now, don't get me wrong. I still think this is a fad. If you go to the local high school, chances are you'll find a handful of bisexual students. Or so they claim. More likely, they're bi-curious, and since they're just now getting a glimpse at the hormones wreaking havoc on their lives, it makes sense. But for a grown man to publicly claim he's in love with both a man and a woman... I call bullshit.

But here's what gets me.

Last night, while at the game against Los Angeles, I caught a glimpse at a family member for one of the Arrows players. You probably know him. First line defenseman Colton Seguine. I thought it would be interesting to try to get a bit of information from dear old mom since Seguine's been having a great year. It was good to see his family support.

So, I moved closer.

That's when the night got really interesting.

Turns out, you can pick up some rather juicy details while you're watching a hockey game. Details such as the fact that the gentleman sitting beside Seguine's mother happens to be Seg's...

Boyfriend.

Yes, you heard it here first. Colton Seguine is gay.

When I confronted Seguine, trying to get my facts straight, I was told by none other than the Arrows captain, Spencer "Optimus" Kaufman, that "what Seg does in his off time is none of your goddamn business." That's a direct quote, folks. It appears Seguine has support from his teammates on this matter.

Another interesting fact came when I found Seguine at the Penalty Box—a local hangout for the Arrows players owned by none other than Kaufman's kid sister, Ellie. During my time at the sports bar, I found Seguine dabbling in a little female companionship.

Does it sound to you like he has a boyfriend?

And that brings me back to my original question. What's in the water in the locker room? It appears that whatever it is, it's possibly spreading through the Arrows organization like wild fire. So, does this mean that Colton Seguine is gay? Or bisexual? Or is he merely a cheater?

We'll have to wait and see, I think. I'm sure he'll let it slip out sooner or later.

"WANT TO TALK about it now?" Cam asked as he lifted his gaze from his phone, where he'd been reading that absurd article for the second time. Maybe third.

Roan wanted to incinerate his best friend with his eyes.

Cam had brought Liam home three hours ago, yet he was still there, still sitting on Roan's couch, still pestering him to talk about last night.

Roan didn't want to talk about it. Not now, not ever.

"You know I'm not gonna quit, right?" Cam stared at the television, but Roan knew he was talking to him. "I can sit right here all damn day if I have to."

Well, then he'd keep on sitting there, now wouldn't he? Roan wasn't going to talk about Seg. He wasn't going to talk about the fact that he'd been a fool and fallen in love with a man who would never come out of the closet. Not willingly, anyway.

Yes, Roan had held out hope. He'd even understood, but last night's fiasco was proof that Seg had no intention of ever being truly happy.

Roan had seen the article. And he'd dry heaved for about ten minutes after he'd read it. The mere idea of Seg with that girl… His stomach gurgled again.

"Maybe it's not what you think," Cam stated.

"Eternal optimism is bullshit," Roan grumbled.

"You haven't talked to him. How do you know?" Cam's eyes reflected both sympathy and curiosity.

"Because he told me. And I can see with my own two eyes."

Cam waved him off. "You know better than to believe everything you read."

Roan shot to his feet and stomped into the kitchen. The more he thought about Seg, the angrier he got. How could he have been so fucking stupid? He'd spent his entire life guarding his heart, and the one time he let someone in…

That would teach him.

"You know what your problem is?"

Roan spun around to find Cam standing directly behind him.

"You think too damn much."

"Fuck you." There was no heat in his words, but Roan could feel his anger simmering.

"No, it's true. You think you don't deserve to be happy, and you spend so much time dwelling on it."

"What the fuck are you talking about?"

"Trust me," Cam continued, "you're not the only one. I've done it. Dare's done it. Teague... Well, we won't even get into that."

Roan didn't know where Cam was going with this.

"You spend so much time as the martyr, Roan. You've given up your whole life for others. Namely your sister. Why? Because you felt there was some truth to her saying your mother wouldn't have left if you weren't gay." Cam rolled his eyes. "That's bullshit and you know it. She was looking for a way out from day fucking one. I remember all those days and nights I hung out at your house. They fucking fought like mad. I'm tempted to say your mother hated your father. You were her scapegoat."

"Are you trying to piss me off?"

Cam's smile was sad. "Not at all. But I am trying to get you to see that you deserve to be happy, too."

"I am happy. I've got Liam. He's all I need."

"Yeah? So you haven't been walking around with your head in the clouds since you met Seg? Secretly wishing you could see him again? Don't even try to deny it. I know you better than that."

"I'm not gonna spend my life hiding for him," Roan countered, taking a deep breath.

"And you shouldn't. But don't lie to yourself. You considered it. You were happy enough with him to compromise." Cam took a step closer. "That's what love is."

"Well, love isn't having some bitch perched on your lap to prove to the world that you're not gay," Roan snapped.

"No, it's not. But did you happen to think of what he was going through at the time? If that reporter threatened to out him and Seg thought for a second he was going to lose everything he's worked so damn hard for..."

"Fuck that. He could've talked to me."

"So you've never gone off half-cocked and said or done something you regret?" Cam's eyes flashed.

Roan looked away. He knew Cam was referring to the time Roan blurted out that he was in love with his best friend. It hadn't been true, but he'd been desperate at the time.

Roan sighed. "You know, I really hate it when you're rational."

Cam chuckled. "I know, right? You're lucky it doesn't happen often."

"So what do I do?"

"You give it some time, but you don't write Seg off just yet."

Roan wasn't even sure why he was worrying about it. It wasn't like he'd heard from Seg anyway. He doubted he would. With all the shit he was probably having to deal with, Roan figured he was the last thing on Seg's mind.

"Can you at least promise me that? You won't kick him out of your life just yet?"

Roan shrugged. He didn't know what he was going to do. He needed time to think this over, to figure out what it was he even wanted. Seg had violated his trust in a big way by pulling that stunt last night. And if Seg spent the night with that woman...

That would be unforgiveable.

No way was Roan going to be second to anyone. Ever.

Twenty-Four

Monday, February 6th

SEG BOTH ANTICIPATED and feared having this conversation with Phoenix, but it was long overdue. For one, it had been a week since that article was printed. The one that had directly drawn Phoenix into the spotlight for something that Seg had done.

Well, technically, Seg hadn't done anything to garner the attention of the reporter, but everyone knew they were like sharks when they smelled blood. And that article had spawned a half dozen more by other news outlets. Up to this point, Seg had declined all comments and refused to speak about the situation.

Phoenix, on the other hand, was fielding the questions and being much more politically correct about it. That was probably the very reason the man was a business mogul, running a multimillion-dollar (perhaps billion, Seg wasn't sure) real estate empire along with owning an NHL team.

"Mr. Pierce will see you now," the receptionist informed him, motioning him toward Phoenix's office.

Getting to his feet, he forced his legs to move to the door.

"Come on in," Phoenix called from his spot behind his desk.

Swiping his hand over his suit jacket, Seg tried to smooth out the nonexistent wrinkles. He wasn't sure why he'd dressed up for this meeting, but that was how it worked. When you were directly summoned to Phoenix Pierce's office, you painted on your professional face.

Seg stepped into the plush office, bracing himself for the ass reaming he deserved.

"Can I get you anything? Water? I hear it's got some magical powers or some shit."

Seg laughed, shaking his head. The guy was joking about this?

"No? Suit yourself. How are you doing?" Phoenix asked when Seg took a seat in the leather chair directly across from Phoenix.

"Great."

A slow grin formed on Phoenix's face. "Yeah? Well, you look like shit."

The breath he'd been holding released in a rush. "I feel like shit," he admitted.

"And you should. Your world's been turned upside down in the past week." Phoenix smiled. "But it hasn't affected your game, so I give you props for that."

Seg barked a dry laugh. "Thanks?"

"Anytime. So, tell me what's going on."

"You want the personal details? Or the facts?" Seg questioned drily.

Phoenix cocked an eyebrow, his smile disappearing.

Seg leaned back and crossed one ankle over his knee. He wiped the imaginary lint off his pants leg, then looked up at Phoenix. "I'm sorry you got dragged into my personal bullshit."

Another smile formed on Phoenix's mouth. "Oh. Is that why the press is all over me about being bisexual? Thank Christ. I mean, I thought for sure it was old news by now and the reporters were done with me." Phoenix rolled his eyes, then leaned forward and rested his forearms on his desk. "Look. I'm not going to pretend to know what's going on with you. It's not my business either. Not unless you want to talk about it. However, I'll tell you one thing. The media has had a field day with me. This isn't the first time and it damn sure won't be the last. And I'm okay with that."

Seg snorted. Okay with it? How the fuck could this man be okay with the media being so fucking curious as to what Phoenix did behind closed doors.

"Don't get me wrong. I wasn't okay with it in the beginning," Phoenix continued. "But what do you do? I'm happy. My husband and wife are happy. My mother's happy. My father's probably in heaven laughing his ass off because the reporters think they're hurting me every time they bring my name up. What's the saying? No publicity is bad publicity?"

Seg stared at Phoenix, letting it all sink in. He seemed seriously okay with this.

"The bottom line is, my family is doing well. That's all I care about. As long as they aren't being harassed, I'm golden."

Shit. Seg didn't even think about the fact that Roan might be dealing with this bullshit, too.

"Talk to me, Seg. Because you've done a drastic one-eighty and closed yourself off completely this past week, I'm going to have to assume the rumors are true."

Seg didn't respond. He didn't want to admit it. He didn't want to be ousted from the league.

"No comment. Okay, then. I'm moving along with the assumption that, yes, you are gay." Phoenix leaned back and rested his hands on his stomach. "Now for the hard part."

Seg waited, his breath locking up his lungs. He felt light-headed.

"No, wait. That was the hard part." Phoenix grinned. "Actually, the hardest part was probably coming to terms with yourself, huh?" He shook his head. "No, I'm not a shrink, but I can tell you that I've been down the road you're on. It's not an easy one. But the one thing I learned a long damn time ago… If you want to be happy, be happy. If you want to sit around and drive yourself and everyone else insane, pretend that it didn't happen. That always goes over well."

Seg's heart was pounding a mile a minute.

He'd always liked Phoenix. The owner of the Arrows was an all-around cool guy. He was quick to laugh and joke with the players, always making sure he was available for them. He considered the team as much his family as he did his actual family.

"How's Roan doing with all of this?" Phoenix asked. "That's his name, right? It's what I read on the Internet, which means it must be true."

Seg couldn't help but laugh. And relax. A little. "Yeah. His name is Roan." Seg dropped his foot to the floor and leaned forward, resting his elbows on his knees. "I don't know how he's doing. I haven't talked to him."

"Understandable." Phoenix cocked an eyebrow. "Considering you were pictured with a woman, I guess it's safe to say there's some tension between the two of you."

Shit.

Seg nodded. No sense denying it.

"Kaufman came to me," Phoenix admitted. "He said he was there the night the reporter approached. Given he was mentioned by name in the article, I'd already come to that conclusion. Want to know what he said?"

Seg wasn't sure he did, but he nodded anyway.

"He said it's all bullshit."

"It's not," Seg admitted. "I am gay."

Phoenix's smile was slow and knowing. "That's not what he meant."

"Oh."

"He thinks the attention you're getting is bullshit. He doesn't see you any differently than anyone else. No one's crawling up his ass asking for details of his relationship, now are they?"

Seg didn't know.

"If you don't mind me asking, is Roan out? Or rather, was he before this?"

"Yeah."

"Well, that probably helps. At least the press won't harp on him for it. They'll be more interested in how he managed to turn you gay. Because that's what happened, right? You were straight as an arrow before." Phoenix chuckled. "Bad pun. I know."

"I hadn't come to terms with it," Seg told him, holding his stare. "Not until I met Roan."

"And suddenly you knew."

Seg nodded.

"I get it. Nothing to be ashamed of there."

"How do I deal with my teammates?" Seg blurted.

Phoenix didn't seem taken aback by the question. "Well, that's easy. You walk around acting weird and shit. Pretending that nothing's going on. That's the way they prefer it."

Seg drew in a deep breath. Clearly Phoenix was going to put him in his place by not actually putting him in his place. "So they're cool with it?"

"Well…" Phoenix appeared to be considering this. "When we all sat around having coffee this morning, chirping like old ladies, they didn't seem bothered by it."

Seg laughed. "Okay, I get it."

"Do you?" Phoenix's tone turned serious.

Seg met and held his gaze.

"Is your hockey career over, Seg?"

Frowning, Seg tried to process the question.

"Because from where I stand, you've got a lot of years in front of you. It's all about what you make of it. Are all your teammates going to be okay with the fact that you're gay? No, probably not. But are you okay with the fact that Benne's a self-proclaimed womanizer? Or that Rush has something going on with Kaufman's sister? Or that Evans is still dating the same girl he dated in high school, but he hasn't been faithful? Or how about the fact that Coach Moen has five dogs?"

"This is more serious than that."

"Is it?" Phoenix didn't look convinced. "Did you think about how Coach Putnam feels about Benne? Putnam has a daughter in college and Benne met her. He's probably more worried about whether his nineteen-year-old daughter is going to get played by Benne. Or how about Kaufman? His ex-girlfriend works in media relations. Amber North? Know her? It's all relative, Seg."

Seg shook his head. The guy was a veritable gossip rag all on his own.

"They only give a shit if you give them reason to, Seg. They knew you before that article came out. Will someone come to me because they're uncomfortable that you're in the locker room at the same time they are? Probably." Phoenix sighed. "And I'm gonna tell them to grow some balls and get over it. It'll only be uncomfortable for them if you let it be."

It all sounded good, but Seg knew better. Phoenix was trying to talk him off the ledge. Granted, he was doing a decent job, but that didn't mean that Seg could ignore all the press he was getting. His name was everywhere. Reporters wanted his story. Hell, they'd started harassing his mother for exclusive information. So much so that Seg had put her on a plane and sent her home with the instruction to keep it to herself.

"Look. I can't make this easier for you. Not entirely. But I can tell you that your position within *my* team is stable. You're here for the duration. We just renewed you and your contract's not up for another seven years, Seg. Unless you decide to do something different, you're still playing hockey."

Seg nodded. That was all he cared about.

Well, that wasn't entirely true. He cared about Roan, but he knew without a doubt that he'd fucked that up beyond repair.

And nothing Phoenix could say or do would change that.

"IT'S TOO DAMN cold to be here," Dare groused, standing at the counter of the marina office. "Only a dumb ass would be here today."

Roan cocked an eyebrow.

"You know what I mean."

"Noah at work?" Cam questioned.

The three of them, along with Liam, were sitting in the marina office shooting the shit. Well, technically Liam wasn't contributing a whole lot. Then again, neither was Dare despite his mouth constantly flapping, but that wasn't anything new.

"Yeah. My man's out saving the world, one floor heater at a time." Dare hefted himself up onto the counter. "Have you talked to Milly lately? How's she doing?"

Cam grinned. "Same old Milly. Driving Gannon absolutely batshit crazy."

"How far along is she now? Seven months? Eight? I don't keep track of that shit."

"She could pop at any minute," Cam stated. "According to her anyway."

"She's thirty-seven weeks, right?" Roan asked.

All eyes turned on him.

"What?"

"I thought they went by months," Dare noted. "Not weeks."

"Nope." Cam grinned. "Apparently it's all tracked in weeks." He glanced at Roan. "And yes, she's thirty-seven weeks. She's going to the doctor once a week. They think she'll go early."

Dare glanced between the two of them. "And AJ?"

Roan laughed. He'd spent some time with Milly over the past week, and it seemed that where Milly went, AJ went. She acted like it drove her insane to have him underfoot, but her baby's daddy was quite adamant that he wasn't going to let her go into labor without him there.

Although the two of them weren't technically in a relationship, one wouldn't know that by looking at them. Roan was pretty sure Milly was still on the fence about how to make it work, insisting that an accidental pregnancy was no reason for them to fake it. From Roan's point of view, there wasn't anything fake about it. Those two liked each other. A lot. They were both simply clueless about how to make it all work.

"He's excited," Cam told Dare.

"That's an understatement," Roan added.

"So, they gonna get married or what?"

Roan and Cam shrugged at the same time.

"Well, they're running out of time to make it happen before Baby Balcomb gets here."

"Says the man who's living in sin," Cam added. "Wait. They're naming their kid Balcomb?"

Dare smirked. "Ballard and Holcomb."

Cam rolled his eyes.

"And hey. We're getting married," Dare insisted. "We just haven't set a date yet."

"That's not what I heard." Roan leaned back in his chair. "I heard that every time Noah comes up with a date, you shoot it down."

"He wanted to get married on Christmas," Dare grumbled. "I'm not getting married on Christmas. I mean, who would be there to officiate anyway?"

"I would," Cam said. "I got ordained just for this glorious occasion, remember?"

Roan laughed. He remembered when Cam had been harassing Dare about it in the beginning. That quickly took Dare's rebuttal off the table. Now he was down to bitching about the weather patterns of the months that Noah suggested. Too hot. Too cold. Too rainy.

"Do you not want to get married?" Cam questioned.

"Of course I do." Dare glanced down at his hands. "In fact, I wish it had already happened. I'm just not keen on the idea of going through the motions. I don't want a wedding."

"Then don't have one," Roan noted. "Do what Hudson and Teague did."

Dare sighed. "Milly's making a big deal out of it."

Considering Milly was Noah's stepsister, it made sense. She wanted to make a big production out of everything. They'd even caught her in cahoots with Dare's grandmother, trying to plan it all out.

"How's Seg?" Dare asked, clearly changing the subject.

Roan sat up straight and turned toward the computer screen. The last person he wanted to talk about was Seg.

"Have you called him?" Cam inquired.

Leave it to Cam to interrogate him in front of Dare. Since the guy wasn't getting the answers he wanted one-on-one, it seemed the logical route. Didn't mean Roan was going to answer him.

"I heard he's doing a press conference."

Roan spun around to stare at Dare. "What?"

"Yeah. Same reaction I had. Looks like he's gonna come out officially."

This was the first Roan was hearing of it. "Why would he do that?"

"Sounds to me like he's got the support of the team's owner. They just announced it. I was checking the schedule for their next game and it's a side note on their website."

"Interesting." Cam pinched his chin with his finger and thumb. "Sounds to me like you've run out of excuses, too."

Roan glared at Cam, then looked at Dare. "So, the wedding's when again?"

Two could play that game.

The minute he pulled down his street nearly three hours later, Roan knew there was a problem. A big one. There were vans lining both sides of the street in front of his house and these weren't just any vans. They were news vans.

"Looks like we're gonna take a detour, little buddy," he told Liam as he drove right on past their house.

He seriously doubted that it was a coincidence when his phone rang a minute later. The screen read: *Hockey Boy.*

Yeah.

Not answering that.

The dry ember of anger in his gut sparked to life from the mere thought of Seg calling him. Really. It'd already been a fucking week, and the asshole hadn't had the balls to call him yet. Why was he doing it now?

When the call went to voice mail, Roan dialed Cam's number.

"Hey."

"You mind if Liam stays the night tonight?"

"Not at all. Why? Something wrong?"

"Looks as though the news crews want a piece of me now that Seg has come out of the closet."

"Oh, shit."

"Yeah. They're stalking my house."

"Why don't you stay here, too?"

"You're too good to me," Roan told him.

"That's what friends do."

"We're on our way. And Cam?"

"Yeah."

"Thanks."

"Not a problem. You know we'd do anything for you."

Yeah. Roan did know that. Took him a long damn time to finally admit it to himself, but he knew.

He also knew that he had to do something to make this stop.

Unfortunately, in order for that to happen, Roan had to cut Seg loose forever.

It was the only way he could protect Liam.

Not to mention, his heart.

Twenty-Five

SEG ABSOLUTELY DETESTED being in front of cameras. Sure, he had to do these things from time to time, but those were vastly different. He could talk about the game all night long. But this... All these reporters standing there watching him, waiting to hear the juicy dirt that was his personal life. Yeah. No fucking thank you.

"You'll do fine," Phoenix said softly, his hand landing firmly on Seg's shoulder. "Only tell them as much as you want to share."

Seg managed a nod, then moved to the long table where the microphone had been set up. In front of him was a glass of water. He eyed it, hesitant to look at the people ready to pummel him with questions.

Finally, he took a breath and made eye contact at the same time Phoenix took the seat beside him.

"We're ready," Phoenix informed the media. "But I want you to understand, if I don't like your line of questioning, I'll call a halt to it. Keep it professional, keep it clean. And by all means, remember that Colton Seguine is a human being, just like you. He doesn't have to be here at all, so consider yourselves warned."

Someone cleared their throat, and then the first question came like a shot out of a cannon.

"Seg, can you tell us when you realized you were gay?"

Frowning, Seg swallowed hard. He thought about his past briefly, about the couple of encounters he'd had with men, about how meaningless they'd been. Then he thought about Roan.

"It's something I realized recently," he informed the woman watching him.

"And what about the man you're seeing?" someone else questioned. "Who is he? How long have you known him?"

Seg reached for the water. He took a sip, trying to formulate a response. Phoenix's words replayed in his head: *Only tell them as much as you want to share.*

"Look," he stated firmly. "I'm not interested in answering questions, so I'll give you a summary. Yes, I'm gay. And the man that I've been with ... he's my soul mate. I knew it the very second that I met him."

"What about the woman?"

Taking a deep breath, Seg opted for the truth. "I panicked because someone was digging into my personal life. I don't care much to share my life off the ice. That's not the important thing. I'm here to play a game and I do that. But in an effort to quell your curiosity, I'll tell you that the man I've been seeing is the only man I've ever had any feelings for. Are they real? Absolutely. Will he ever forgive me for what I did? Probably not. And I doubt I deserve it either. But that's the way it is. I was scared. I freaked out, and I hurt the one and only person I've ever cared about. So now, if it's possible, I'd like to move on with my life. I'd like to get back to playing hockey."

Seg glanced over at Phoenix.

"Thanks for coming, folks. We appreciate it." With that, Phoenix ended the press conference, and Seg made a valiant effort not to run from the room.

Had Phoenix not been the one guiding him out, he probably wouldn't have succeeded.

Two hours later, Seg was in his Range Rover.

Showing up at Roan's house unannounced wasn't the brightest idea he'd come up with lately. Not only because it was clear Roan wasn't home, but also because it had brought the news crews right to Roan's doorstep.

Seg should've known that the press conference he'd held earlier at Phoenix's suggestion would have the reporters chomping at the bit. It seemed they were no longer questioning his sexuality since he'd come out and said yes, he was gay. No, now they wanted to know who'd snagged his attention. And if he'd thought his dating life had been under scrutiny before, he was now learning what that really meant.

Rather than wait for Roan, Seg hoped to string the reporters along with him. There was no way for them to know whose house this was. Well, unless they pulled the tax records.

Shit.

No doubt they'd already thought of that. Which meant they had all the information they needed on Roan.

Too bad Roan wasn't answering his phone so Seg could warn him.

Not knowing where to go, Seg opted to drive around. He ended up in the marina parking lot only to find the place shut down tight.

"Shit."

He dialed Roan's number again. When it didn't go right to voice mail, he held his breath and waited.

One ring.

Two.

"What?"

His heart slammed into his sternum at the sound of Roan's voice.

"Hey."

No response.

"Roan?"

"What?"

"We need to talk."

A strangled laugh erupted on the other end of the phone. "Yeah, I'm thinking we're beyond that at this point."

Seg needed to talk to Roan. He needed to make this right. "Please. Let me explain myself."

"I think you've made yourself pretty clear already."

"Roan…" Seg wasn't beyond begging.

A defeated sigh was the only thing he heard. Seg waited. He wasn't going to give up. Not yet. This man was far too important to him for Seg to allow Roan to walk away without a fight. Yes, he needed to do some groveling, but he was prepared to. In fact, Seg was prepared to do any damn thing he had to in order to keep Roan in his life.

"I want to talk. To explain. At least let me do that."

"Fine," Roan groaned.

"Can I meet you at your place?" Seg asked.

"There're reporters there."

"We'll ignore them."

"It's only going to give them more shit to write about."

Seg shrugged. "I don't care. The only thing that matters is setting things right with you."

He prayed that was even a possibility.

"Fine." The sound of muffled voices followed before Roan returned to the phone. "I'll head home in about fifteen minutes. You can stop by after that."

Relief swamped him. "Okay. I'm in the parking lot of the marina, so I'll be there in a few."

"Why are you at the marina?"

"I was looking for you."

No response.

"Roan?"

"What?"

"Thanks for hearing me out."

"Yeah." Pause. "It's kind of inevitable if I want to get my life back in order."

Seg wasn't sure exactly what Roan meant by that, but unfortunately, he didn't think it meant something good for him. If he wanted Roan back, he was clearly going to have to work for it.

Considering Roan was the only thing in the world he did want, Seg was going to make every effort.

Half an hour later, Seg was following Roan up his front steps while a half dozen reporters shouted at them from the street. Of course, the circus taking place in the front yard was drawing the neighbors out of their houses. Seg hated that he'd brought this shit down on Roan, but for the life of him, he didn't know how to change it.

Part of him didn't want to change it.

Oh, sure, he would've preferred not to have the news media camping out in Roan's front lawn simply to get dirt on their relationship—if they even had a relationship at this point.

He didn't even want to contemplate this being over. Not yet.

While Roan unlocked the front door, Seg turned to the reporters. Their eyes grew wide as though he was about to make a big announcement.

"I'm going to tell you this one time. This is private property. You do not have permission to be here. We will press charges." He didn't bother to listen to their rebuttals, choosing to turn and follow Roan in the house.

Once inside, Roan flipped on the lights and Seg closed and locked the door.

"We should probably close all the blinds," Seg told him, his gut churning.

Roan pinned him with a glare, then headed for the front windows. Seg took on the task of closing the ones at the back. The tension in the air thickened as they blocked out the view from the outside. Seg's heart was beating faster than when they did drills on the ice. His mouth had long ago gone dry. He knew he had to make the first move, try to calm the waters between them. Not that he thought Roan was going to give him a second chance, but Seg had to hope.

It was all he had left.

"I'm sorry you were dragged into this."

Roan spun around, his face a mask of anger. "*This?* Is that what you're calling ... whatever this thing is between us?"

"No. God, no." Shit, Seg was fucking this up already. "I meant the reporters."

Roan's eyes narrowed.

"Look, Roan..."

"No." Roan stood straight. "I don't want to hear it. I let you come over here so you could see that I'm through. My tolerance for bullshit is so low I can't ... no, I don't *want to* deal with this shit."

Well.

That wasn't how Seg had hoped this would go.

Neither of them said anything for several tense seconds. A million things ran through Seg's mind. But only one thing made sense.

"I love you."

Roan's snort of derision echoed in the living room. "You've got a fucking funny way of showing it. Fucking puck bunnies? Is that how you profess your love, Seg? No fucking wonder you're single."

Ouch.

Seg's heart constricted and he held Roan's gaze. "I don't want to be single," he said softly. The tortured tone of his voice should've made him wince, but it was truly how he felt. He loved this man. "I know I fucked up, but I swear to God, I didn't do anything with that woman. I was…"

"What? You were what? Pissed? Hurt? Scared?" Roan shook his head, his gaze dropping to the floor. "And you think flaunting a chick is going to make you straight?"

Fuck. Seg took a step closer. Then another. His muscles were coiled tight, his body gearing up for a fight. He got the feeling this was going to be the fight of his life.

Roan's head snapped up, his golden eyes locking with Seg's as Seg closed the distance between them.

"I'm not straight," Seg admitted. "And yes, I had a moment of panic. I freaked out. I was fucking terrified."

"So much so that your new girlfriend helped ease your pain?"

Seg thrust his hands in his hair. "Nothing happened with her. I went home alone."

"You shouldn't've been with her in the first fucking place, Seg."

"I know." He tugged on his hair until pain shot through his scalp. "Trust me. I fucking know."

Staring into Roan's eyes, he prayed that Roan had an ounce of sympathy for him. Something to tie them together, because the thought of losing Roan forever…

That was worse than the idea of never being able to play hockey again.

Too bad he hadn't realized that *before* he'd gone and fucked shit up.

HARMLESS

ROAN FELT AS though he were suffocating. The pain wasn't confined to his chest either. It radiated outward, through his entire body.

It took everything in him, but he met and held Seg's gaze, needing this to be over because he couldn't take any more. He wanted nothing more than to crawl into bed and sleep until Seg didn't matter. Until everything they'd been through these past few months was merely a fuzzy memory. Eventually that day would come. It would probably take years, but Roan would endure. After all, he had no other choice.

"I love you, Roan," Seg whispered, dropping his hands to his sides as he took another step closer.

Roan knew he should step back. Hell, he should probably turn and run, because he felt his resolve crumbling from the tormented look on Seg's face.

He didn't want Seg's love. He wanted...

Fuck. Who was he kidding? He wanted Seg's love more than he wanted anything, but he wasn't about to let Seg know that.

"You should've thought about that before." Renewed anger sparked in his gut. "I fucking waited for you, Seg. I sat at your house and waited for you after the game. I was there. If you'd simply come home that night, I could've helped you through it," he snapped. "Instead, you ran off to the bar, sat some ... woman... God. A fucking woman, Seg. You were so hard up to convince the world, and probably yourself—"

"No!" Seg moved so quickly Roan didn't have time to put space between them. Seg's hands cupped Roan's face, holding him in place, their gazes slamming together. "I wasn't trying to convince myself. I know what I want. *Who* I want. I've known it since the first night I took you back to my place." Seg's voice lowered as he continued. "I've known it since then, Roan. I spent an entire year thinking about you. Only you. I had one night with you, yet you consumed my every thought. I was desperate to see you again."

Roan swallowed hard.

"And then there you were," Seg whispered. "At the arena. And I tried to tell myself that I couldn't make it obvious, that there were people around who would see my interest, but I couldn't help it. I had to talk to you. I couldn't let you walk away again. I knew *then*."

Fuck. Roan wanted to believe him. Every word. He wanted it all to be true. Everything he'd felt these past months... He needed it to be real.

But he couldn't ignore the fact that Seg had hurt him.

"I can't do this," Roan confessed, his words laced with the gravel that seemed to be clogging his throat. "I can't wonder whether or not you're gonna run into the arms of a woman when you're scared. That's not how it works."

Seg leaned in, his forehead resting against Roan's. "I know. I fucked up. And I know it doesn't make it right, but I swear nothing happened. I didn't so much as kiss her."

Roan jerked back. "But you touched her, Seg. I saw the fucking picture. She was sitting on your lap smiling at you. It was what you wanted."

"No!" Seg once again grabbed Roan, jerking him closer, his hand clasping the back of his neck, his fingers massaging the tense muscles. "God no. The only thing I want is you. In that moment, I knew it was wrong because it *felt* wrong. But I won't lie. I was scared. I thought my world was crumbling down and I panicked." He swallowed. "But my heart belongs to you, Roan. Only you. Now and forever."

Roan's defenses were weakening with every tortured word that came out of Seg's mouth. It pained him to see him hurting, although he deserved it. Seg deserved to feel the same gut-wrenching agony Roan had felt when he'd heard Seg on the phone that night. But shit, Roan didn't want Seg to be in pain. He didn't want him to hurt. He didn't want him to be scared. Roan wanted to take all of that away because...

Because he loved Seg. He loved him and wanted to protect him from the world. He hated himself for it because he knew Seg had the power to break him. To shatter his heart.

Yet it was the truth.

"Do you love me, Roan?" Seg asked, tilting Roan's head just enough to force him to meet Seg's gaze. "Tell me you love me. Tell me there's a chance that I didn't ruin everything. I need to hear it."

Roan didn't want to admit it. If he kept that to himself, his heart stood a better chance of repairing the damage this one man had done.

"Please tell me," Seg pleaded, his eyes glistening.

And that was what broke him. Seeing this man so close to the breaking point was more than Roan could bear.

"Yes," he choked out. "I love you." He narrowed his eyes. "God help me, I don't want to, but I do."

Seg didn't move, their eyes still locked together. He could sense that Seg was searching for something. A second chance, maybe?

Roan knew he shouldn't give him one. He shouldn't.

But he would because he fucking loved him. He didn't want to live without him. He wanted everything Seg had offered before that stupid fucking reporter had stuck his nose where it didn't belong.

"I want to be with you, Roan," Seg whispered, as though realizing the battle waging inside Roan's head.

Roan swallowed hard.

Seg continued, "I want to be with you and Liam. I don't care who knows. Hell, I don't care if I get ousted from the league. None of that matters anymore because I know that the only thing that's important is how I feel when I'm with you."

He was so fucking weak.

Not Seg. Roan.

Roan wasn't strong enough to resist this man. He did love him, no matter how painful it was to accept it. Would Seg pull this stunt again? Roan didn't know. He would never know.

"I'm not sure I can trust you," Roan admitted. "I want to, but…"

Seg nodded, but he didn't leap into a million platitudes aimed at convincing Roan otherwise. Did that mean it was a possibility? Would Seg have another freak-out moment and end up in some woman's bed because he needed to feel better about himself?

If only Roan could predict the future.

Then again, if he could've done that, he would've done it when he was fourteen years old and he'd come out to his parents. He would've kept his secret to himself in order to keep his family together.

Or would he?

Knowing what he knew now, would it have made a difference? Would his entire life be different?

Would he own a marina with his best friends?

Would they have met Teague? Or Hudson?

Would Noah and Dare be together now?

Would Cam have even met Gannon?

Would Cassie still be alive?

Would Liam even be here?

Would Roan have been in that bar at the same time as Seg at that one moment in time?

It could all be different.

Did he really want that?

No. He didn't.

Seg leaned in again, slower this time. When his forehead rested against Roan's, Roan closed his eyes. The warmth of Seg's hands on his neck offered him comfort he hadn't known before. He felt whole when he was with Seg.

Even now.

Even after all this.

"I can't tell you that it won't happen again, but I can show you. I can prove to you that you are it for me."

"You came out to the world today, Seg," Roan stated.

"I did." He pulled back. "Did you watch?"

Roan forced his eyes open and nodded.

"I came out because I'm tired of hiding. I want to be happy. This … you and me … this is my happy. You and Liam are all I want in this world, and I'm prepared to prove that to you."

"It won't be easy," Roan told him.

"Probably not. But that's okay. I'm not looking for the easy way out. As long as you'll give me another chance, I'll endure whatever I have to in order to make this right with you."

Roan's defenses were crumbling. The pep talk he'd given himself on the drive over had been pointless. He was going to give in.

After all, he was in love with this man, and when he thought about spending the rest of his life without Seg in it…

Yeah.

He wasn't sure he was strong enough to do that.

Even if it was the best thing for him.

Then again, he wasn't even sure that was true anymore.

Twenty-Six

A SECOND CHANCE with Roan?

Seg hadn't thought it would be possible, yet he could see the indecision in Roan's eyes. He wanted this as much as Seg did.

Sure, Roan had good reason not to give in, but Seg wasn't going to give up. He'd screwed up in a big way, but he could make this right. He could prove to Roan that he was worthy of his love. He had to.

"What do we do about these reporters?" Roan questioned, taking a step back.

Seg allowed him to move away, not wanting to make any assumptions just yet. Although Roan was acting as though he could forgive Seg, that didn't mean it was so. "It's not what you want to hear, but they will go away eventually. There's no story here."

"Not anymore," Roan added, his tone still rough with disappointment.

"Right. Not anymore." Because Seg had announced to the world—and all of his teammates—that he was gay.

He still didn't know how things were going to go at practice tomorrow. Hell, he might end up boycotted from the arena by the same guys he'd considered family for all these years. Seg wasn't sure which he was more scared of. Them ousting him … or them accepting him.

He'd spent so long pretending to be someone he wasn't in order to appease everyone else. The idea that all this hiding could potentially be behind him filled him with as much fear as elation. No one knew how this would play out.

Locking eyes with Roan, he held the man's stare.

He now had someone to live for. Someone who didn't deserve to be in the dark with him. He wanted the world to know that he was in love with Roan.

"So, you talked to Phoenix?"

Seg nodded, holding Roan's gaze. "I did. He was dragged into this mess because of my stupidity. Plus, I'd intended to talk to him before this happened." Seg knew that if he'd done that, they probably wouldn't be in this position.

Looking back on it now, it was easy to say that he'd been an idiot for not trusting Phoenix in the first place. He should've done what he'd originally intended and he could've bypassed all this pain. For himself and everyone around him.

"And your mom?" Roan's eyebrows lifted in question. "Is she doing okay?"

Seg liked that Roan was concerned about his mother. He was close to her, and knowing that Roan would be the type of man who would worry about her the same way he did gave him a sense of peace. It was another reason he loved this man.

"I sent her home. I didn't want her getting mixed up in all of this."

It wasn't as simple as sending her back to the house he'd grown up in, but Seg knew that having her here wouldn't help matters any. Mostly because she wouldn't be able to hold her tongue. With reporters practically camped out on his porch, she would've eventually lost her cool, and Seg didn't want her to go off on a tangent. Not that she wouldn't have put them in their place, because that would've been one hell of a dressing down, but still.

"You need to know that she's disappointed in what I did," Seg told Roan. "She's already come to care about you and Liam. I've spent my entire life working to put a smile on her face, and she's never openly admitted her disappointment. So, not only did I let you down, I let her down too."

Seg needed to man up and own this, and by admitting as much, he felt as though he was. He didn't need his mother's protection. Seg had to show the world—and himself—that this was how things were going to be. It was the only way he'd be happy.

"What do we do now, Seg?" Roan leaned against the counter and crossed his arms over his chest. "Do we start over? From the beginning?"

Seg couldn't stop the memories from flooding his brain. Those from the very first night they were together. The smile took over before he could stop it.

"That's not what I meant," Roan noted, but there was a small smile forming on his succulent lips.

Before Seg could close the distance between them, Roan's phone rang.

Seg watched as Roan pulled out his phone and glanced at the screen.

"It's my dad." Roan's eyes were wide.

Seg nodded, knowing Roan needed to answer the call. He turned and walked into the kitchen, offering Roan a small amount of privacy.

"Dad?"

Unable to help himself, he watched Roan. The expressions that moved across his face were a mixture of fear and concern. The conversation seemed mostly one-sided since Roan's responses were all single words.

But then Roan sighed dramatically, followed by, "Yes, Liam's fine." His brows lowered. "No, we're good. No issues."

The conversation continued with Roan frowning more and more. Seg had no idea what was being said, but he could see Roan's irritation level rising.

Finally, Roan ended the call with an abrupt good-bye and then turned to Seg.

"Everything all right?"

Roan shrugged. "With him, I'm not sure anything's ever all right. But yeah. It's fine."

Seg heard the silent *for now* but he didn't push for more details. There was evidently something wrong, but Roan wasn't going to share. Since they had other things to deal with, Seg steered the conversation.

"Where's Liam?"

"With Cam and Gannon." Roan sighed. "And I really should get back to him."

Seg nodded. "I don't suppose I could talk you into bringing him back to my place. The two of you stay the night with me."

Roan immediately shook his head. "It's late. I have to work tomorrow. You've probably got practice."

It was clear he was losing this war, even if he'd won part of the battle.

Seg didn't want to let Roan go. If the man had time to think, he'd probably come up with a plan to sever all ties with Seg. Roan was nothing if not a thinker.

Rather than argue, Seg moved closer, coming to a stop directly in front of Roan. He tilted Roan's head back so he could look directly into his eyes.

"I was serious when I said I love you. I've never said that to anyone before. And I honestly don't care who knows, Roan. I'm done hiding, done being scared of what this all means. I've lived my whole life trying to hide who I really am. Scared, in fact, of who I am. Not anymore."

Roan didn't respond.

"I want to spend my life with you." Seg put a finger over Roan's lips when he started to speak. "I'm not finished."

Roan's golden eyes widened slightly, but he clamped his lips shut.

"It's going to take effort, but I will prove to you that I'm worthy of your love. That I'm not the asshole you think I am. I accept that I fucked up, and I fully intend to make it up to you. I'm not sure how yet."

Seg noticed the way Roan's Adam's apple bobbed in his throat, his eyes dropping to Seg's lips.

Damn it. He came over here with the intention of talking, of working things out so they could move forward. That wasn't easy to do with Roan eyeing him like he was dessert.

"When you look at me like that…"

Fuck it.

Seg leaned in closer and pressed his mouth to Roan's. He kissed him slowly at first, but the heat between them caught fire, and the next thing Seg knew, he had Roan pinned against the counter, his tongue thrusting deep into Roan's mouth.

When Roan's hands wrapped around him, jerking him even closer, Seg lost all sense of decorum. His body took over, his need for this man far too great to ignore. His practical side warned him that this was the wrong thing to do, but the other side, the one that was terrified he might never have the chance to hold Roan again, was winning.

"Seg…"

"I need you, Roan," he whispered against Roan's lips. "So much it fucking hurts. Let me touch you. Just for a little while."

He fully expected Roan to push him away. It was what he deserved after the stunt he'd pulled. Instead, Roan yanked him close again, their mouths crashing together. Hands fumbled with clothing as they began moving. Seg wasn't sure who was leading whom, but they finally made it to Roan's bedroom, a trail of discarded clothing behind them.

He hadn't meant for it to go this far, but now that they were there, Seg wasn't even remotely close to wanting to let this end.

ROAN REALIZED LONG ago that he was losing control of this situation. And when Seg kissed him, for half a second, Roan forgot what they'd been arguing about in the first place. The only thing he wanted was for Seg to touch him, to kiss him, to make all this shit disappear.

And clearly Seg was capable of doing that, because somehow they made their way through the house and onto Roan's bed before he even realized it. Their clothes had even miraculously disappeared during one of those drugging kisses.

"Let me make love to you," Seg pleaded. "I want to feel you. All of you."

Roan hadn't intended for this to happen, but now that they were on his bed, skin to skin, he couldn't stop it. He was starving for this man's taste, his touch. The past week had been hell, and Roan wanted a little reminder of what was good between them.

The way Seg made him feel… It set his world to rights.

Roan must've given Seg the green light, because the next thing he knew, Seg was retrieving a condom from the nightstand drawer.

When Roan attempted to turn over, Seg stopped him with a hand in the center of his chest.

"I want you to look at me," Seg stated, his tone gruff, his eyes wild. "Look me in the eye when I make love to you."

Roan swallowed past the lump in his throat. Sex with Seg was always intense, to the point Roan lost a little of himself every time. This would be no different, he knew. It wasn't ideal, because Roan knew he couldn't protect his heart when he was this close to Seg, but he wanted him with every labored breath he took.

Once Seg rolled on the condom and lubed his cock, Roan pulled him down to him, fusing their lips together. He let the kiss consume him, the feel of Seg's warm body adding a level of security that had Roan desperate for more.

Seg positioned Roan's leg over his forearm and stroked his cock against Roan's ass. A desperate moan ripped up from Roan's throat as he gripped Seg's neck, kissing him with every ounce of desire that raced through his bloodstream.

When Seg's cock breached his ass, Roan sucked in air, stilling as the pleasure-pain seared him. He relaxed, allowing the pleasure to win out.

"Oh, fuck," Seg groaned. "You feel so fucking good. God. I could stay just like this for the rest of my life."

Roan knew the feeling well. Every time he was with Seg, he never wanted it to end. And he hadn't admitted it, but he'd been hooked from the very first time. Granted, he'd been strong enough to resist at that point, but only because the rest of his world had been crumbling down around him. Had he been in a better place at that point...

"Love me, Roan," Seg whispered, his breath fanning Roan's lips. "That's all I want." His voice dropped an octave, his tone full of emotion. "For you to love me."

"I do," he admitted, his chest expanding from his heart overflowing with the feelings behind the words.

There was a flash of something Roan couldn't put his finger on in the smoky blue depths of Seg's eyes. It was as though he'd given Seg the world, and that brought more emotion churning through him.

Seg's thrusts were deep and slow, his breathing ragged. Roan could feel Seg's pulse pounding in his neck, mirroring the same jackhammer effect his own heart was having.

Roan wrapped his arm around Seg's back, pulling him closer although they were as close as two people could get. He wanted to feel every inch of him against him.

Seg's hips flexed, shifting forward, pushing him deeper into Roan's ass. He retreated slowly, inch by inch, then surged in again. The pleasure was overwhelming, driving Roan dangerously close to the pinnacle of a release that was likely going to blow the top of his head off.

"Let me look at you," Seg groaned.

Roan released his hold, and Seg shifted up onto his knees. His eyes trailed from Roan's face down to where their bodies were joined. Roan watched the expressions wash over Seg's features as he pumped his hips, fucking Roan so painfully slow he wanted to scream.

But then their eyes met again and Seg began fucking him. Deep. Hard.

And it was too much. Seeing the emotions glittering in Seg's eyes was more than Roan could handle. He was drawn too tight, hanging by a fragile thread that was going to snap at any second.

"Come for me, Roan. I want to watch."

"Fuck. Me," he gritted out between clenched teeth, his release hovering just out of reach.

When Seg pounded into him over and over, deeper, harder, faster, that was all it took. His entire body flew apart in a climax that rivaled anything he'd ever felt. He briefly wondered if he'd ever be whole again, because this was too much. Not only the pleasure but the emotion ... it coalesced into something akin to pure ecstasy.

"Fuck, yes. Just ... like... Oh, God, Roan!" Seg's hips slammed into him one last time as he pulsed and shook, his body coming down over Roan's.

Feeling incredibly vulnerable, Roan grabbed Seg, pulling his mouth down and kissing him for all he was worth. It was that or lose the threadbare grip he had on his sanity.

Considering that was the only thing he had left, Roan knew he couldn't let go completely.

That would come in due time.

And for some reason, he had a feeling that time would be soon.

Very, very soon.

Twenty-Seven

ROAN WOKE UP in an unfamiliar bed. It took him a moment to realize he was at Cam's. His brain instantly brought forth images of last night with Seg. He'd hated leaving the man, but the call from his father had freaked him out enough that he knew he needed to be near Liam.

Speaking of…

He listened closely but didn't hear a sound coming from the other room. Considering the sun was up, he knew there was no way Liam was still asleep, which meant Cam and Gannon were likely taking care of him.

No way was Roan winning father of the year this morning. His best friends had not only kept Liam last night so Roan could spend time with Seg but were also taking care of him this morning.

Shit. For some reason, that made Roan feel like a failure.

That could've been due to the way his own father had spoken to him last night. As though Roan had no idea how to care for a child appropriately. He hadn't explained his reason for calling out of the blue, but Roan knew he had one. The man didn't do anything simply because he cared. Deep down, Roan figured his father blamed him for Roan's mother leaving, although the man had never come out and said it.

Forcing his feet to the floor, Roan summoned up the energy to get out of bed. He went straight for the shower. Fifteen minutes later, he walked into the kitchen to see Cam and Gannon talking quietly while Liam relaxed in his swing beside the kitchen table.

The second Cam looked his way, Roan knew something was wrong.

"Mornin'," Gannon greeted, pushing up from his chair. "Coffee?"

"Yeah. Thanks." Roan didn't look away from Cam.

"Sit."

Roan sat.

"I got a call from Lydia this morning."

Roan could see the concern in Cam's eyes. It was obvious there had been nothing normal about this phone call from Roan's stepmother. Then again, when Roan's stepmother called Cam, it couldn't possibly be simply to shoot the shit. For whatever reason, Lydia had never been Cam's biggest fan.

"And...?"

"And she wanted to know the situation with you and Seg. Apparently they've had some visitors." Cam glanced down at his coffee cup. "Reporters. She's concerned."

"About...?"

Cam gave him the look that said, *seriously, you are not that dense*. Roan pretended not to notice.

Before Cam could elaborate, Roan's cell phone rang. He prayed it was Seg, but even before he pulled his phone from his pocket, he knew he wouldn't get that lucky.

It wasn't Seg. It was his father.

Twice in such a short time meant something bad was lurking. Roan could feel it in his gut.

Cam got to his feet. "Go ahead and answer it, then we'll figure this out."

Roan grimaced. He didn't like the sound of that.

After hitting the button to answer the call, his gaze traveled to Liam. His son was grinning, and Roan's heart instantly swelled.

"Dad? What's up?"

"Roan, what's going on?"

Roan glanced at Cam. "What do you mean?"

His father's voice held a hint of frustration. "What I mean is I've got reporters camped out in my front yard asking to talk to me about my son and his … famous lover. When I called you last night, I thought I'd give you the benefit of the doubt. See if you'd share with me, ask for help. But you didn't. You went on as though nothing was wrong."

"Nothing *is* wrong," he assured him.

"Now you're lying to me again."

Son of a bitch.

"Dad—"

"Roan, I don't know what the hell you're up to, but I honestly think you need to consider what this could do to Liam. Your face is all over the news and they're talking about..."

"About…?" Roan wanted to hear his father finish that sentence.

"Your … uh … *love* life."

So fucking what? There wasn't a damn thing Roan could do to change that, so what was his father all up in arms about? Or was this his way of interfering? Of trying to make Roan the bad guy?

Probably.

Then again, this sounded like something Lydia would say. Not Daniel. Was his father the bearer of bad news these days? Did they really believe Roan would do anything to harm Liam? Or put him in a harmful situation?

It was bullshit, and they both knew it. Maybe the sports stations were airing the details, but this wasn't big enough to hit national news.

He let his father continue anyway.

"Lydia wanted me to call you. She ... uh ... *we* think you should bring Liam to us. That boy has been through hell already. He doesn't need to be subjected to anymore trauma."

A sudden chill filled him, ice forming in his veins. "*What?*"

"It's apparent that your love life is more important than raising Liam. You promised us you weren't seeing anyone. And we believed you. You need to think about what's in his best interest, son."

What the hell did that have to do with anything?

Roan couldn't speak. A million rebuttals were on the tip of his tongue, but he couldn't put voice to any of them. Shit. His father didn't know the first thing about what was going on in Roan's life. Or Liam's, for that matter. The man never bothered to call. In fact, neither his stepmother nor his father had made an attempt to see Liam in the past month. What in the hell gave them the impression that Roan wasn't raising Liam right? Why would Roan even consider allowing *them* to raise him?

"Look, Roan. Lydia said if you'll bring Liam to us, allow us to take care of him, that she won't make this into a big production. You can sign guardianship over—"

Roan caught the "she" in that statement. *She won't make this into a big production.*

Blood roared in his ears and Roan's body tightened, preparing for a fight. "What the fuck?" he growled.

"You know that's not a good situation to put Liam in, Roan," his father said, his tone one of complete authority. "He shouldn't be dealing with this. It was bad enough he had a drug addict for a mother, now this."

"Are you saying that being gay is in any way related to being a drug addict?" The man was off his fucking rocker.

"What I'm saying is that Liam would be better off in our care."

"Not. Gonna. Happen."

"Don't make this difficult, Roan. It's what's best, and you know it. Cassie's probably rolling over in her grave knowing that her son's being raised by…"

"By what, *Dad*? By a gay man?"

His father didn't respond.

"And actually, Cassie's the one who insisted I raise Liam should she not be able to. We discussed it at length back when I was the one taking care of my sister because you and everybody else had abandoned her." Roan tried to keep his voice level, but it was getting more difficult as the rage shifted and grew inside him.

"You and I both know Cassie wouldn't want this for Liam."

That was his father's retort? Seriously.

Roan didn't know anything of the sort. Not to mention, his father didn't know the first fucking thing about what Cassie had wanted. He hadn't bothered to be there for her.

Not that any of that mattered anymore. Roan was raising Liam, and no one could do a damn thing to change that. He wouldn't allow it to happen.

Roan found Cam and Gannon staring back at him, concern glittering in their eyes.

"I have to go."

Without waiting for more nonsense to spew from his father's mouth, Roan hung up the phone.

"What did he say?" Cam questioned, his eyes soft.

Roan took a deep breath. "Thanks to all this bullshit, it looks as though he wants to fight me for custody of Liam." Even as the words came out of his mouth, a red haze filled Roan's vision. "And this is all Seg's fucking fault!"

Cam moved toward him quickly. "Relax. You can't take this all out on him."

"No?" Roan snapped his mouth shut when the word came out as a roar and scared Liam.

The little boy's chin quivered, and Roan was instantly lifting him out of his swing. "I'm sorry, little man," he whispered, hugging Liam tightly to him. "It's all good."

And it would be. No way would he let his father win this battle. Roan would give up everything in this world for Liam. Everything.

Including the only man he'd ever actually loved.

IT TOOK SOME time to get going the following morning.

Seg had been hard-pressed to get out of bed, not wanting to let go of the dream he'd had. It had been about Roan and Liam. The three of them had lived happily ever after.

Or as happily ever after as they could, considering all the shit going on around them. In his dream, Roan had forgiven him completely, agreed to marry him, then allowed him to adopt Liam. They'd moved into Seg's house, his mother had come down for the wedding, and they were gearing up for the honeymoon.

Seg wished like hell it hadn't been a dream.

Because he knew life didn't stop for wishes, Seg had forced himself out of bed and stumbled to the shower, life coming front and center. Life being that he had to face his teammates this morning while being completely uncertain how they were going to react to the shit storm Seg had created.

After he took a shower and downed a protein bar, Seg went to practice like he always did. He kept a smile plastered on his face despite the nervous tension coursing through his body. He was damn glad he and Roan had managed to somewhat fix things last night, because having to worry about that along with how his teammates would react to him would've been too much.

"What's up, Seg?" Rush smacked him on the back when they passed in the locker room. "You ready to kick some serious ass tonight?"

Seg offered a chin nod and a smirk. He was ready, all right.

"Yo! Seg!"

He turned to see Patrick Benne staring over at him from where he was lacing up his skates.

"You ready to dish out a little payback? We owe these guys an ass whoopin' tonight."

Well, there you go.

No one seemed to give two shits about the fact that Seg had announced to the world that he was gay. That or they were pretending it hadn't happened. Surely they weren't oblivious to the fact that there'd been a handful of news crews in the parking lot. If he had to guess, they'd been asking his teammates what they thought of the gay man they had to work with day in and day out.

Either way, Seg would take it. He didn't want things to be weird. He was ready to move forward, to put the past behind him and find a way to pave the road for his future. His future being playing hockey and working things out with Roan. Those were the only two things on his mind right now.

Taking a seat on the bench near his locker, Seg toed off his shoes. He looked up to see Mattias Valeri watching him closely. He cocked an eyebrow in question, but Mattias turned away, grabbed his bag, and disappeared.

Okay, so not everyone could be happy about the news.

Seg glanced around the room.

Kaufman was standing in the corner talking to Evans, the rookie defenseman. Rush was sharing a couple of pointers with Locke, who was likely going to be in goal tonight. Benne was chatting on the phone, grinning like a fool. Coach was chatting it up with Cullen Crosby, the defenseman Seg was currently paired with.

No one was paying any attention to him.

Taking a deep breath, Seg decided to go forward as though nothing had happened. In truth, nothing had happened, other than his secret was now out. But that didn't make him a different man. He was the same guy who'd come into this locker room hundreds of times before. He needed to focus on morning skate and get his mind in the right place for tonight's game. He didn't have time to second-guess himself, or anyone else, for that matter.

An hour before the game, Seg took a minute to call Roan. He hadn't heard from him all day, and he'd tried to call twice. Once after morning skate and once before he headed back to the arena. There was a weird tingling sensation on the back of his neck, and he got the feeling something was wrong.

Roan didn't answer, so Seg left a message. "Hey. Wanted to see how you are. Check on Liam. The game starts in a bit, but I'll call you after. I'd like to see you tonight if that's possible. We head out on the road tomorrow and I won't be back until Sunday. That's too long to go without seeing you." He took a deep breath. "All right. Well, I guess I'll talk to you in a bit."

Seg hung up the phone, staring down at the screen for a couple of minutes. His mind drifted back to last night. He tried to recall whether he'd missed something. He and Roan had made love. Twice. The only reason Seg had willingly gone home was because Roan had needed to get back to Liam. He didn't remember anything being wrong.

Well, nothing more than all the shit they'd been dealing with. But he could've sworn Roan had forgiven him. Or at least was beginning to.

Shit.

"All right, guys," Kaufman called out. "Let's have a chat before we head out there and kick some ass."

The other guys standing around roared their agreement while Seg tossed his phone into his bag. He'd have to worry about Roan later, because right now, he had a job to do. And no way was he going to let these guys down. He damn sure didn't need to give them a reason to be pissed at him.

After all, he'd given everyone enough reason already.

Twenty-Eight

A KNOCK SOUNDED on the glass door of the office.

Sitting in his chair behind the counter, Roan lifted his head to peer over. The room was completely dark because he hadn't bothered to turn on the lights. Since it was a few minutes shy of midnight and the office was closed, he hadn't wanted to alert anyone that he was there.

Cam and Gannon were the only people who knew where Roan was. He'd spent the better part of the day dodging reporters, trying to pretend life was normal for him. It wasn't. Not by a long shot.

What normal person had reporters camped out to get dirt about his relationship? What normal person's father and stepmother wanted to destroy his life because of said relationship? What normal person was worried that the man they loved was scared shitless about who he was and resolved that fear by perching a woman on his lap?

"What a fucking mess," he murmured into the darkness.

Whoever was at the door could turn around and go the other way.

The only reason Roan was here was because he needed a little time to himself. It was the very reason he'd borrowed Gannon's car in an effort to throw off the reporters and headed straight for the marina after feeding Liam and putting him down for the night. He'd been grateful that Cam had offered to come over to Roan's house. As far as he was concerned, it was where Liam needed to be. At home in his own bed. Should he wake up, Cam and Gannon would be there.

He forced himself to be content with that for a little while. The buzzing in his head wouldn't stop, and he simply needed a few minutes to think.

By not going out in public, Roan avoided the hassle of the news crews, plus reduced the risk of seeing Seg. He'd received the man's voice mails, both before tonight's game and then after. When Seg insisted on coming by to talk, Roan had known he needed to find a place to go so Seg couldn't find him.

Maybe Hudson or Teague had heard him come in and they were coming to check.

Another knock sounded.

Shit.

Either Hudson or Teague forgot their key upstairs or it wasn't either of them.

Roan prayed they'd forgotten the key because the alternative...

Knock. Knock. Knock.

"Fuck."

Getting to his feet, Roan ambled over to the silhouette of a man standing on the other side of the glass door. He twisted the deadbolt and pushed it open.

It damn sure wasn't Hudson or Teague standing there.

Son of a bitch.

Anger and sorrow twisted his gut. His first instinct was to rail at Seg, to make him go away, leave him in peace.

"Hey," Seg greeted.

"I don't want you here," Roan told him, meeting his gaze at the same time a lump of emotion formed in his throat.

"Please don't make me leave," Seg said softly, halting Roan's protest.

For whatever reason, seeing Seg, all the emotions moving over his attractive features, was more than Roan could handle. All the feelings—anger, sadness, hurt, love—warring inside him blended into a storm of epic proportions.

"Why are you here?" he choked out, trying to hold himself together. He'd managed all damn day; he couldn't afford to fall apart now.

"Because I'm not going to let you push me away. Not this time." The determination in his tone belied the concern etched on his face.

Roan stared at Seg, taking in the dark shadows on his face, trying to peer into his eyes, to find the comfort he needed, because he was quickly falling apart.

"Roan..."

The next thing he knew, Roan was sobbing, Seg's arms coming around him and holding him tight.

This was all too much. Every damn bit of it.

Liam.

Seg.

His father.

The stupid fucking reporters.

Roan didn't want to fight his parents for custody, and he shouldn't have to. If Seg hadn't pulled his stunt, none of this would be happening. But damn it all to hell, Roan would do what needed to be done in order to protect his son. He wanted Liam in his life, wanted to raise him. So what if he was fucking gay; it didn't mean he didn't love that boy with all that he was.

Seg's hand cradled the back of Roan's head, warm, strong, comforting. He didn't ask questions, didn't offer any meaningless words of comfort. He merely held him, and Roan needed that right then. He needed the physical security, something to hold him together while he let it all out.

Several minutes passed before he managed to compose himself. Pushing away from the warm man offering him solace, Roan looked up at Seg's face, backlit by the light from the parking lot.

"Cam called you." It wasn't a question.

Seg touched his forehead, then brushed one blond eyebrow down with his fingers. That was a tell of his, Roan had noticed. It didn't necessarily mean he was lying, but it did mean he was uncomfortable about something. Which likely meant that Cam had called him and he'd also asked Seg not to say anything about it.

He would have to have a conversation with Cam later.

"How're you holding up?"

Roan wasn't sure how to answer that question, so he shrugged. He wanted to ask Seg why he was there, but his answer really didn't matter. Roan wasn't sure how he felt about it yet, but he'd been an asshole long enough. Right now, he simply needed to process what was going on in his life and not focus on the shit that didn't matter.

Not that Seg didn't matter. He was a … Roan was going to say friend, but that was bullshit. Seg was everything. He'd long ago fallen in love with the guy even if he was too stupid to accept it. No matter how hard he tried, Roan couldn't completely write him out of his life, but right now, he didn't know what to do with the giant blond staring back at him. He wanted to ask Seg to hold him some more, to turn back time and erase everything that had taken place in the last couple of weeks.

But no matter what, Seg couldn't hold him because Roan needed time to himself, time to process what his next steps were. He knew Seg wanted to work things out, and maybe that was a possibility, but Roan wouldn't know that for sure until he could wrap his head around all the shit going on.

"Knock, knock."

Roan peered around Seg to see Teague peeking in the small gap in the door where he held it open.

"Shit," Roan grumbled. "Did I wake you up?"

"No. I'm not an old fucker like you. I don't have dinner and fall asleep after," Teague assured him with a smirk as he stepped inside. His expression sobered. "Hudson and I were watching TV. I heard the door chime a second time and wanted to check on you." Teague glanced over at Seg. "Looks like that's already being taken care of."

"Yeah." Roan didn't look at Seg. "Thanks. I'm just gonna hang here for a while. Cam and Gannon are watching Liam."

Teague frowned. "I heard about your stepmother, man. I'm really sorry she's pulling this shit. If you ask me, he's better off with you anyway. He's happy. That's what matters."

Roan nodded. He briefly wondered how Teague had heard, but he didn't ask. It didn't matter anymore. "Thanks. That means a lot."

Teague rolled his eyes. "Whatever, man. You might not believe me, but it's true. I'm not blowin' smoke up your ass. But anyway. You do what you gotta do." Teague cast a quick look at Seg. "You stay with him. Keep him from thinkin' too much."

Before Roan could protest, Seg's hand came down on his shoulder, giving him a gentle squeeze. It was a silent reassurance that doing what Teague said was the right thing to do.

"Thanks, Teague ... for everything."

"Anytime. Let us know if you need anything."

Roan hoped he wouldn't have to ask for help. He wasn't big on leaning on other people or relying on them. However, he was starting to think it might be time to. If nothing else, he needed to know he had people behind him, people who believed in him.

Because no matter what, Roan wasn't letting anyone take Liam from him. He would give up everything else before he allowed that to happen.

JUST WHEN HE thought things were starting to look up...

Seg had realized after the game that Roan was ignoring him. Rather than blowing up the man's phone, Seg had hopped in the Range Rover and headed right for Roan's house only to find no one was home. He'd remembered Roan telling him that Cam and Gannon lived somewhere close to the marina, so he'd headed that direction while searching for Cam's phone number.

He hadn't been driving long when his phone rang. At first he'd thought it was Roan, but he'd been shocked as shit when Cam introduced himself on the other end of the line.

"Hey, man," Cam greeted, his tone low, serious. *"I'm probably breaking some sort of bro code by calling you, but I wanted you to know."*

"Know what?" Seg didn't like where this was headed already.

"Roan's ... well, the most accurate way to describe it is falling apart. He had a fight with his father earlier and he's out of sorts. He just left with Liam, heading back to his place. Gannon and I are gonna go watch the baby so Roan can get out of the house for a bit."

"Where's he going?" Seg would track him down one way or the other.

"The marina. He does that sometimes. Goes there to think."

"Thanks."

"Give him a bit, and do me a favor, man?"

"Anything."

"Don't tell him I called. He doesn't like when I get all up in his shit, but ... as much as he's hurting right now, he needs you. And the two of you need to work this out." Cam chuckled roughly. "Damn, now I sound like a fucking shrink."

Half an hour later, Seg was en route to the marina. And here he was.

Seg moved back as Roan shut and locked the door behind the guy who'd come by. He hadn't met the guy other than the one time at the arena so long ago, and he'd heard enough from Roan to know he was one of the business partners who lived above the marina. Seg wasn't great at memorizing faces and names, so he'd only caught on when Roan said his name.

Not that it mattered.

"You really shouldn't be here," Roan said when he turned to face him.

Seg knew he needed to defuse this situation and fast. Cam had given him some of the details of what happened today. The guy had filled him in on how Roan's father and stepmother were up in arms about the shit going on with Seg and they'd found the leverage they needed to fight for custody of Liam.

Or so they thought.

No way were they going to get away with it. For one, Seg had more than enough money to fight these people. And he'd do it for Roan. He'd do anything for Roan and Liam.

"We need to talk," Seg said, halting Roan from sending him on his way.

"There's nothing to talk about, Seg. I've got too much shit on my plate to deal with this right now." Roan ran his hand over his face. "I need time to myself. Time to think. I can't do that with you around."

"Shit." Seg turned and stalked across the room. He'd known this was coming, but he wasn't about to let Roan shove him right back out the door.

They'd come too far for this.

"You need to go, Seg," Roan said softly. "I don't think now's a good time for us to do this. A relationship is the last thing I need."

Seg spun around to face him, his stomach twisting into a knot. He wanted to talk, not end this. "What? *No.* Don't do this, Roan."

"It's the only way I know to—"

The sound of the door opening was the only thing that stopped Roan from launching into his spiel, Seg knew. The overhead lights flickered on, and suddenly, Seg and Roan weren't the only two people in the room. Near the door stood...

Seg had to count.

There were six men standing there, all looking at Roan intently.

"Son of a bitch," Roan mumbled. "Don't you people know how to leave someone alone?"

"We've done that before," the biggest one said. "Look where that got us." The guy looked over at Seg. "Not sure if you remember us by our faces, but I'm Cam." He turned and started pointing. "This is my husband, Gannon. Then Teague and his husband, Hudson. Hudson's mute—doesn't speak but he can hear. And that's Dare, I think you've met him here at the office."

"We've met," Seg agreed.

"And this is Dare's fiancé, Noah."

"Where's Liam?" Roan inquired.

"With Milly. She and AJ are at your house."

Cam glanced between Roan and Seg, then turned his attention to Roan. "Now why don't you fill everyone in on what's going on so we can move on to the solving-the-problem part."

Roan huffed, but he didn't move. "My stepmother wants custody of my son. She doesn't believe that Liam should be raised by a gay man. And this"—Roan motioned between him and Seg—"only adds fuel to her fire."

The anger radiating from Roan was palpable, and to be fair, Seg couldn't blame him. If Seg hadn't had a full-blown meltdown when that reporter approached him, none of this shit would be happening. He wouldn't be trying to solidify his place in Roan's world because their relationship wouldn't even be in question.

And now this.

With or without the audience, Seg fully intended to keep the conversation with Roan going. He appreciated the fact that Roan's friends had Roan's back, but Seg wasn't done here. "Have you talked to a lawyer?"

Roan pivoted to face Seg, his eyebrows lifted as though the thought hadn't occurred to him.

"You have legal guardianship, right?"

"Yes, but that won't stop the court from siding with my father and deciding Liam would be better off with them."

"Why?" Seg didn't get it. Roan was a fantastic father. "Why would you even think that?"

Roan glared at him.

Seg continued, "Would he? Would he be better off with your father?"

"Fuck no."

"Then you need to get a lawyer."

"I will," Roan stated, his eyes locking on Seg's face. "But first, I need to get my life in order. And to do that, I need the reporters to go away. Which means…"

Seg needed to go away.

"Roan—"

Roan took a jerky step closer. "No. You don't get it, Seg. Liam is the most important person in my world. Nothing or no one compares to him."

"I *do* get it," Seg snapped. "Because that's how *I* feel about the two of you. You and Liam are the most important people in *my* world."

"Then you understand why I'll give up everyone and everything before I give him up."

"Who said you had to?" Now it was Cam's turn to get pissed. "Why the fuck do you think you have to go about this alone? You took on taking care of Cassie by yourself. You pushed all of us away. We didn't even *know* about Liam."

Roan spun to face Cam. "I apologized to you for that."

"I don't want your apologies, Roan," Cam hissed. "I want to know why the fuck you think you need to shut us all out."

"I wanted to protect you from Cassie's bullshit." Roan thrust his hand through his hair. "So I did what I had to do. This time I'm protecting Liam."

Seg stepped in. "Are you? By shutting out everyone who could help you?"

"You can't help me," Roan growled, pinning Seg with a disgusted look.

"The hell I can't," Seg snapped, moving closer. "I love you, Roan. Don't you fucking get that? I want to spend the rest of my life with you and Liam. I'll move heaven and earth to keep that boy safe, the same way you will. But you have to stop thinking that you're the only person who can handle this. Your parents can do whatever the hell they want, but do you really think they'll go up against an army to get Liam? Hell, in the months we've been together, I've never even met your parents." He didn't add that he'd never seen the guys standing behind him either. Nothing more than when he'd met them at the arena all those months ago. "I've never even heard you mention that they'd come by to see Liam."

"Because they haven't," Roan noted, his face expressionless.

"But your friends have. They've helped when you needed help—"

"I don't *need* help," Roan yelled. "I can take care of him on my own. I don't want some judge thinking I'm incompetent."

Seg's mouth fell open as he stared at Roan, but Cam was the one to speak. "Is that what you think? That by relying on the people who care about you, you're incompetent? Damn. That's the stupidest fucking thing I've ever heard."

Roan looked at his friend, seemingly speechless. Seg could see the hurt look on Cam's face.

"So what?" Gannon asked, stepping forward and placing his hand on Cam's back, probably to soothe him. His eyes were laser focused on Roan. "There's an invisible bubble that you can wrap around yourself to protect you and your charge? First it was Cassie. Now Liam."

"It doesn't work that way," Dare stated, moving closer to Roan.

Seg watched the dynamics between these men. It was clear they were family. They'd come together in the middle of the night in an effort to show Roan that he wasn't alone.

If that in itself didn't make Roan see he didn't have to do this by himself, Seg figured nothing would.

Meanwhile, back at Roan's house...

MILLY WAS ANTSY.

She wasn't sure if that was because AJ was so close and because he smelled so good or if there was something else at play. She enjoyed being with AJ, and she liked that he'd come over to help her babysit. Although babysit was probably a stretch for what she was doing. Considering Roan had put Liam to bed before he left and Cam and Gannon had agreed to watch him, Milly was pretty much guarding the house and that was it.

"Wanna watch a movie?" AJ asked, glancing over at her.

She wondered if he could feel the tension, too. It was there every time they were together. Ever since she'd told him she was pregnant, they'd become friends.

Not more than friends.

Not friends with benefits even.

Just plain old boring friends.

Sometimes she wished for more.

That was probably her hormones talking though.

"I don't care," she told him.

Before he could flip through the channels to find something to watch, there was a knock on the front door.

Milly's gaze slammed into AJ's. It was midnight, for goodness sake. Who in the world was showing up at Roan's house in the middle of the night?

"Probably Cam," AJ said, getting to his feet. "He jetted out of here so fast, probably forgot his key."

Milly nodded, watching AJ as he walked to the door.

Damn, the guy had a nice butt.

Like, really nice.

Again, hormones talking.

AJ frowned after peering through the security hole. "It's Roan's dad."

It took more than a little effort, but Milly managed to get to her feet. Being a million months pregnant was a pain in the butt.

"Want me to open it?" he whispered, his gaze imploring her.

"Yeah." Milly had a few things she wanted to say to this man. She'd heard all about the crap he was pulling with Roan, and she didn't much care for it.

AJ opened the door and Milly joined him, staring at the newcomers. Not only was Roan's dad standing on the porch but Roan's stepmonster—the nickname Milly had lovingly given the woman—was there, too.

"Roan's not here right now," Milly informed them. "Is everything all right?"

Daniel looked a little put out to be standing there when he should've been sleeping, but Milly didn't miss the nudge Lydia gave him.

"We wanted to check on Liam," Daniel said with a sigh.

"He's asleep."

"Where's Roan?" Lydia questioned. "It's the middle of the night. He should be home with Liam."

"He ran an errand," Milly lied effortlessly. "He should be back any minute now."

"Then we'll wait," Lydia stated, pushing her way into the house.

No, Milly wasn't fond of this woman. She'd met her on the day of Cassie's funeral, and something about the woman had put her off then.

AJ placed his hand on her shoulder and gently guided Milly out of the way.

"I … uh…" Milly did not want to sit here with these people. "Why don't I tell Roan that you stopped by."

Lydia's gaze dropped to Milly's left hand, then her belly, then up to AJ.

No way could Milly resist rolling her eyes.

"Lydia," Daniel said softly, his eyes searching the room. "I think she's right. We should go home."

"I need to know that Liam's safe in this house."

Okay, so maybe her hormones were a little out of whack from the pregnancy, but Milly did not miss the accusation in the woman's tone.

"Liam's perfectly safe," Milly told her.

"I'll check for myself."

"Uh, no." Milly was not going to let this woman come into Roan's house while he wasn't here. "He's asleep and I don't want him woken up."

Lydia paused, once again glancing down at Milly's belly.

"As a soon-to-be mother," Lydia began, "I would think you would understand my concern."

Milly lifted an eyebrow. "Actually, no. I don't."

"Is that man Roan's dating going to come back here with him?" Lydia inquired.

"Uh…" Milly glanced over at AJ, then back to Lydia. "I'm not sure. Not that it's any of your business. Or mine, for that matter."

"It is if you're at all worried about Liam."

Okay, enough was enough. Milly was tired and she wanted to sit down. Motioning toward the door, she forced a smile. "Well, I'm happy to say that Liam's perfectly fine. And he's more than safe with Roan and his boyfriend."

And yes, she added that part just to piss the woman off.

Lydia's gaze moved to Daniel, a line forming between her eyebrows.

"If you don't mind," Daniel said with a huff. "We'd like to take Liam back to our house tonight. We need to talk to Roan about a few things, and we can do that when he comes to pick him up."

Milly's back straightened and her anger exploded.

"No. First of all, I'm babysitting for Roan. He didn't mention you coming over at all, so I think it would be best that you leave." She turned her attention to Daniel. "If he chooses to come talk to you and he wants to bring Liam along, he can do that tomorrow."

"Young lady," Daniel snarled, his hand lifting as he pointed toward the back of the house. "That is my grandson in there and I have every right to—"

"Actually, you don't," Milly snapped. "Go. Now."

AJ's warm hand curled around her waist and Milly appreciated the comfort. She could tell he was on edge, but he was doing his best to stay out of it. With him there, she felt safe. Then again, with him there, she felt a lot of things.

Lydia started to the bedroom and Milly stepped directly in front of her.

"I don't think so."

"I will call the police if I need to," Lydia stated softly.

"Well, you need to," Milly countered. "Because I am damn sure not letting you leave this house with Liam. And if you try, I'll call the police myself. That's kidnapping."

The woman's eyes grew wide. She probably wasn't used to anyone standing up to her, but Milly wasn't a pushover. There were a million things she wanted to say to Lydia Gregory, and she'd managed to keep her mouth shut so far. She was playing nice.

That wasn't going to last much longer.

Twenty-Nine

FIRST OF ALL, Roan did not appreciate his friends ganging up on him like this.

Secondly, he did not like the fact that they were right. That only added insult to injury, and Roan was far beyond feeling tattered and broken.

It pained him to acknowledge that he couldn't take care of Liam on his own. Oh, sure, he could physically do whatever the boy needed, but Roan knew he did need these people in his life. They were his friends. Hell, they were his family.

"We'll forgive you for being a jackass once," Cam stated.

"*Once?*" Dare looked confused. "You think he's only been a jackass once? You mean once an hour, right?"

A rumble of laughter eased some of the tension.

"We're going to get through this together," Cam added. "Look at who you've got in your corner, Roan. We're not a bunch of lightweights here."

Roan glanced at all the faces before him.

Gannon's phone buzzed, and Cam instantly turned toward him.

"It's Milly. I have to get this."

Roan waited, his heart in his throat as Gannon answered the phone. He was silent for what felt like ever, but finally nodded.

"Yeah. Okay. Thanks for calling, AJ. We'll meet you at the hospital."

Roan's eyes widened, panic setting in.

Hospital?

Oh, shit. Was Liam okay? *Please, God, let Liam be okay.*

Gannon ended the call and glanced at Cam first, his tone a little flustered when he said, "Milly's in labor." He peered over at Roan. "Looks like your dad stopped by your house. Milly confronted him. She got a little riled up."

Oh, shit.

Gannon's smile was that of a man who was proud to call Milly a friend. "The woman can't leave well enough alone."

"Is she all right?"

"Yep. Although she is in labor and that baby's not gonna wait for us."

A rush of relief nearly sent Roan to the floor. That was when Roan realized Seg was standing directly beside him, there to catch him if he fell.

"We'll follow you," Dare told Gannon.

"We're … uh … leaving right now," Teague stated as Hudson turned and bolted for the door.

Roan swallowed hard when Cam turned toward him.

"We're right behind you," Seg stated, reaching down and taking Roan's hand as though that was the most natural thing in the world. "I'll drive."

Gannon nodded but then turned and walked right out of the building with Cam directly behind him. It was clear he was in a hurry.

"My father made Milly go into labor," Roan mumbled as he allowed Seg to lead him to his Range Rover.

"Is she not due yet?"

Roan shook his head. "Not for a couple of weeks." Roan felt the tension in Seg's fingers. "Not that it's a bad thing. The doctor told her she could have the baby any time now."

Seg's hand relaxed as he opened Roan's door.

Climbing inside, Roan realized this was the first time he'd been in this man's vehicle. He peered into the back seat and noticed... No way. The guy had a car seat identical to the one Roan had for Liam.

His heart leapt into his throat.

It was then Roan also realized they'd never been on a real date. Then it dawned on him that they'd bypassed all of that dating bullshit and jumped right in the deep end. Without a life jacket.

Roan's gaze tracked Seg as he crossed in front of the SUV. Roan's eyes were still following him when Seg climbed behind the wheel. The man looked calm and cool, not to mention sexy. Far beyond how Roan felt at the moment.

Without saying a word, Seg started the SUV, then pulled out of the parking lot and followed the caravan on the way to the hospital.

When Seg reached for his hand, Roan almost pulled back. Now that his brain had come back online, he was still contemplating his next steps. He didn't pull away, however. Having Seg here with him...

Roan glanced over. "I'm not sure I deserve you."

Seg cut his eyes over, frowning. "Funny," he said, without even an ounce of humor. "I was thinking the same thing. I definitely don't deserve you."

Roan wouldn't go that far. Despite both their faults, they did have amazing chemistry.

"We're quite the pair, huh?"

"Maybe that's why we work," Seg replied evenly.

"Do we?" Roan glanced out the window. "Work?"

"I'd like to think we do." Seg sighed. "That doesn't mean it'll always be easy."

"Nothing ever is."

"Or that I won't fuck it up," Seg mumbled.

Roan squeezed Seg's hand. "It was a knee-jerk reaction."

"That's no excuse. I take responsibility for my actions, Roan. I'm not looking to make excuses."

The fact that Seg didn't jump at the opportunity to brush what he did under the rug made Roan love him more. As much as he wanted to guard his heart, protect himself from pain, he knew he couldn't. Not completely. That was the very reason he'd been alone before Seg. It all boiled down to the fact that Roan was scared to take a chance.

"I want this to work," Roan told him pointedly.

"Me, too." Seg's eyes left the road briefly to glance his way again. "But the only way to make that happen is to be in it together. We're both guilty of doing things our own way."

Roan knew that was true.

He also knew that he was in desperate need of having someone at his side. Sure, he had friends to see him through this, but he knew there was only one way he'd come out the other side in one piece.

And that was to have Liam *and* Seg with him.

After all, that was the only way he'd be truly happy.

STRESSFUL SITUATIONS TENDED to make people overreact. Then again, sometimes they did the complete opposite and came to their senses.

Seg wasn't sure which could be said for Roan's sudden one-eighty.

Now that they were at the hospital and they'd been informed by AJ—who, based on the quick rundown he'd received from Dare, was Milly's baby's father as well as Hudson's brother—that Milly's labor was going smoothly, things had calmed down somewhat.

Mostly.

Gannon seemed to be a mess, which was rather amusing, since it was obvious the guy was trying to pretend to hold it all together. The slight twitch in his left eye gave him away. Seg probably wouldn't have noticed except Gannon continued to push his glasses up on his nose, which drew attention to it.

That and the animated conversation about Roan's dad sending Milly into early labor—Dare was overly dramatic—was the reason Seg had taken Liam for a walk down the hall. Technically, Seg was doing the walking, but Liam didn't seem to mind. The little boy was doing quite well to be up so late past his bedtime. Then again, he'd slept for several hours, so maybe he simply thought it was morning.

"What's up, little guy? You ready for a … uh…" Seg didn't know what Milly's baby would be to him. Considering how close everyone was, he figured something more than a friend of the family. "We'll call it your cousin. *It* because we don't know the sex yet. But we will." Seg glanced at his watch. "She's been in there for hours."

Seg stopped and sat in one of the vacant chairs on the far side of the waiting room. He propped Liam on his knee so the little boy could face him.

"Do you think you'll be happy if it's a girl?" Seg teased. "She'll probably want you to play with girl toys." Seg twitched his eyebrow. "Then again, she might want to play with your cars, eh?"

Liam grinned, then reached for Seg's mouth. Seg kissed his knuckles.

"Okay, good. Cars are high up on the list of things you have to have."

"Boats, too."

Seg looked up to see Teague had joined him, his dog at his side, service animal vest and all.

"Boats are good," Seg agreed.

"Hudson wants him to be a mechanic."

"Ahh." Seg glanced at Liam. "So, maybe have a hobby? Hockey player by trade though. Boat mechanic in your spare time."

Teague barked a laugh that sounded a little rusty. "Don't let Hudson hear you say that. Or Noah. They're in competition to see who can recruit the kid first."

Seg didn't take his eyes off Liam. "You're a lucky kid."

"He is," Teague noted.

"So, what's with the dog?" Seg asked when Liam leaned over to grab a handful of the animal's hair.

"Service dog." Teague appeared sheepish. "Let's just say I've got abandonment issues. Hudson got him for me. He keeps me company."

Well, there was no shame in that. Seg knew better than to ask for details. It wasn't his business.

"What's his name?" Seg scratched the dog's wide head.

"Charger."

Seg took Liam's hand and showed him how to rub the dog's head.

"So what're your intentions here, hockey man?"

Smirking, Seg peered up at Teague. He figured the guy couldn't be much younger than he was. But he was definitely younger, which made the topic of conversation entertaining. He looked like a surfer just in off the water, not a care in the world. Teague was wearing baggy cargo shorts in the middle of February. His shaggy hair was long, his clothes wrinkled. The look that said he'd rather be at home, but someone had insisted he tag along. Yet he sounded like Seg's father.

"What should my intentions be?" he tossed back, trying to throw Teague off.

Teague took a seat next to Seg. "I'd say they shouldn't be fuc—" Teague snapped his mouth shut as he glanced at Liam, then took a deep breath. "Messing around with some chick."

"I agree." Seg wasn't going to argue that point. He deserved to have to face the music. He'd fucked up. It was only fair that Roan's friends had a chance to tell him how they really felt. Perhaps this wasn't exactly the appropriate place, but whatever.

"Despite your obvious lack of sense at times, I think you're good for Roan."

That surprised Seg. "Do you?"

Teague waved him off. "Oh, don't go gettin' all gooey on me. I'm probably the most screwed up here, so take my thoughts with a grain of salt. My husband does."

Seg noticed Teague grinning as he glanced across the room at said husband.

"And I like that you tell him like it is," Teague noted, peering sideways at Seg as he leaned forward to rest his elbows on his knees. "He needs that. Roan's the quiet type, always lost in his head. He's proven he knows best for himself. Or thinks he does, anyway. I haven't known many people to change his mind either."

"You know quite a bit about him." It wasn't a question. What Seg was wondering, though, was why Teague was sharing all this.

"I don't, actually. I've been a partner for years, but I've managed to keep my distance. Personal shit and all that." Teague caught his slip, his eyes darting to Liam in apology for the curse word.

Sitting up straight, Teague smacked his hands on his thighs, then pushed to his feet. "Well, that's all the words of wisdom I have for today, children. I'm off to irritate my man." He grinned. "It's what I do."

When Teague walked away, Seg turned his attention back to Liam. "I can only assume that's the first of many talks I'll have in the near future."

Liam grinned as though he knew what Seg was talking about.

"You got my back though, right?"

Liam swatted at his mouth.

"Good deal. With you on my side, I can handle anything."

In fact, with Liam and Roan on his side, Seg had the key to his happiness.

"It's true, you know?"

Seg looked up to see Cam walking his way. "What's true?"

"That little boy makes you feel like you can conquer the world." Cam took a seat in the chair Teague had vacated. "You're good with him. You got experience with kids?"

"Not a lick," Seg admitted.

"Wouldn't know it by looking at you with him."

Was he supposed to say something to that?

Cam sighed. "I wanted to get in my two cents."

"Get in line," Seg told him, keeping his voice low.

"Teague's harmless. He means well."

"He does."

"And so do the rest of us. Roan's like a brother to me," Cam told him, his eyes watching the men on the other side of the room. "He's got his faults." Cam peered over at Seg, grinning. "But don't we all?"

Seg nodded, glancing back at Liam.

"Don't worry. I'm not here to read you the riot act. I like you. I like that you're fighting for Roan. He needs that in his life."

"He makes it difficult," Seg admitted softly.

Cam laughed on an exhale. "Ain't that the truth." His face sobered. "Just keep in mind that he's trying. Why he thought he had to take this all on himself, I don't know. I think I'm partially to blame. We were closer before Gannon and I got together."

Seg knew how that was. He'd spent years hanging out with teammates. Women came and went in their lives, but every now and then, one stuck. And when that happened, the guy got snagged in her web faded away from the pack, spending time with the person who meant most to him. It made sense.

"You mentioned earlier that you didn't know about Liam," Seg prompted, bouncing Liam on his knee.

"Not until the night Roan's sister died. He kept it a secret, which again falls back on me. We grew up together. Shared everything."

Until Gannon. Seg got it.

Cam's voice lowered as he looked directly at Seg. "Don't give up on him. He's the one who usually gives up. Until Cassie, I'd never seen him fight for much of anything. Then Liam came along…"

Seg understood. However, he also knew he couldn't be the only one fighting for this relationship. If Roan didn't want it, Seg had no recourse. As much as it would kill him to do so, he would have no choice but to walk away.

Peering down at Liam, Seg's heart squeezed in his chest. He'd only been part of their world for such a short time, but he felt like he'd been there forever. He didn't want to walk away, but he couldn't do all the work either.

"He cares about you," Cam said. "I know he does."

Seg nodded, never looking away from Liam. He didn't want to see the sympathy in Cam's eyes. He could hear it in his voice.

"He needs you in his life, Seg. You're good for him."

That was exactly what Seg had thought. It'd been his reason for coming to Roan tonight.

Only now, as he glanced over at Roan, he wondered whether or not the opposite was true. If he wasn't in Roan's life, they wouldn't be here. Milly probably wouldn't be having the baby early. Roan wouldn't be dealing with his father's shit.

Ultimately, Roan would likely be happy.

Which meant only one thing.

Seg had to make a choice.

His happiness.

Or Roan's.

He wished like hell that wasn't a no-brainer.

Thirty

MIRANDA LYNN BALLARD was born at 3:07 a.m.

The precious little girl came screaming into this world with a head full of dark hair, weighing in at a whopping eight pounds, six ounces, with a set of lungs that could rival an opera singer.

At least according to her father.

Roan had been right there with the rest of them when the proud dad joined them in the waiting room to give them the good news. Possibly for the very first time, they witnessed Gannon break down in tears.

Of course, Hudson, the proud uncle, informed them all—via sign language—that he had dibs on teaching Miranda to fix a boat. AJ didn't protest, but Roan was fairly certain AJ was hanging on by a thin thread himself. Had Gannon not been the one to fall apart, AJ would have.

"Time to call it a night," Cam informed them all, putting a strong hand on Gannon's back. "Momma and baby are in good hands with AJ, so we'll be back bright and early to visit."

Roan wasn't about to argue. He was dead on his feet and it was time to get Liam in his bed. As it was, Liam had fallen asleep on Seg's shoulder more than an hour ago, and the man refused to let the kid go.

"You about ready?" Roan asked Seg when the others started filtering out into the hallway.

"I am." Seg met his gaze, held it briefly. "Do you want me to take you and Liam home? Or back to the marina to get your truck?"

The man was giving him an out, Roan knew.

"I didn't take my truck," Roan told him. "I drove Gannon's. So yes, you can take us to my house."

"Okay."

The guy wasn't much for talking, obviously. "It's late. You want to stay?"

Seg didn't answer, and Roan didn't push. He would wait until they got back to the house before he broached the subject again.

The drive from the hospital to Roan's house was quiet. Liam snoozed in his car seat while Seg focused on the road. Roan had no choice but to stare out the window, which he did when he wasn't sneaking glances at Seg.

He wasn't sure whether they'd made any progress tonight or not. He'd run to the marina with the intention of thinking, and that seemed to be the last thing he'd done. Not about what he'd set out to think about anyway. While at the hospital, Roan had spent more time watching Seg with Liam than anything else.

"Looks like the reporters called it a night," Seg noted when he pulled into Roan's driveway.

"They'll learn soon enough that I'm not a hot topic," Roan said, turning to look at Seg, who hadn't turned off the SUV. "What are you thinking about?"

Seg shrugged, his attention on the garage door in front of them. "I don't know how this plays out, Roan."

The man sounded tortured and it slashed at Roan's heart. "I don't either."

"The last thing I want is to be a burden on you. You've got your hands full with Liam and now dealing with your father. The only thing I've wanted since the very first day I met you was to have a little bit of your time. Then I got it and I wanted a little more. Now I want everything. And I'm not sure that's fair to you."

Roan's chest constricted. It sure sounded as though Seg was going to walk away. As much as Roan had pretended to want that, he didn't. Not at all.

Reaching over, Roan turned Seg's face so he was forced to look at him. "Don't give up on me yet."

Seg's eyes were sad. "I could never give up on you. But I'm not above walking away if it makes things easier for you."

"That won't make it easier," Roan said, searching Seg's eyes, needing him to know that this was what he wanted. Sure, he was confused and he had a ton of shit to work out, but he wanted Seg in his life.

Not that he'd been good at expressing that. His constant flip-flopping was probably making Seg dizzy.

"Are you sure?"

Swallowing hard, Roan leaned closer. "I've never been more sure about anything in my life. I just need time to work it out in my head."

Seg nodded, as though that was all he needed to hear. "Stay the night with me. We can go back to the hospital in the morning to see the baby."

Seg shook his head, and Roan's stomach plummeted. "We're heading out on the road in a few hours."

Roan glanced at the clock. It was already 5:45 a.m. It looked like the day was already underway. He looked at Seg. "For how long?"

"I'll be back on Sunday."

This was something that Roan understood. Seg was a hockey player. They were on the road a lot. He didn't like that he couldn't have the man all to himself, but he got it.

"Then stay. It's almost six. Sleep for a couple of hours and then you can drive home."

Seg peered into the back seat at Liam, then turned his gaze back to meet Roan's, and Roan instantly knew that the answer he was going to get was not the one he wanted.

"I need to get home."

Roan's knee-jerk reaction was to get his feelings hurt, but before he could turn to get out of the SUV, Seg reached for him, holding him in place.

Seg pressed his forehead to Roan's. "I want whatever the next steps are, Roan. Whether that's dating or more than that. But I want you to have the time you need to think on it. I can't be left in the lurch, not knowing."

Damn it. "Fine."

"No, not fine," Seg countered, pulling back. "Why do you do that? Why do you get angry when I'm giving you what you asked for?"

Roan swallowed back the retort, hating that Seg was right. He managed to take a deep breath.

Their eyes locked together as Seg held the back of Roan's neck, not allowing Roan to move.

"I love you," Seg whispered. "I don't say that lightly. And yes, I've got my own sins to atone for, but I gave it some thought tonight at the hospital. I'm going to give you the space you need to think, to work it out in your head. And when I come back from this trip, I need an answer. You have choices. You can keep me in your life and we move forward and fight for our family. You, me, and Liam. We confront your father together—you and me—or you move forward and fight him on your own. Either way, I know you'll win. Liam is lucky to have you. But I want to be in your life because you want me there. I've gotten too attached. To both of you."

Roan could hear the emotion in Seg's voice, see the way he swallowed hard to hold it back. He wanted to tell him that he already knew what he wanted, but he understood where Seg was coming from. This way, Roan got the time he'd said he needed, and he could prove to Seg that this wasn't one-sided.

"Okay."

Seg's gaze dropped to Roan's mouth briefly, and the next thing he knew, Seg was kissing him. Gently, softly.

Roan was caught up in the emotion, his chest constricting, his heart ready to burst at the seams. He loved this man, there was no doubt about that.

But Seg was right. Roan needed some time to think. Some time to process what his father was doing. Hell, he needed to have a rational conversation with the man without having to deal with any of the other shit.

When the kiss ended and Seg pulled back, Roan reached for him, cupping his face. "Call me the minute you get back?"

Seg nodded.

As Roan climbed out of the SUV, as he unbuckled Liam and pulled the sleeping boy from the car seat, as he walked to his front door, a million thoughts were running through his head.

And not a one of them good.

Why was it he felt as though his world was ending right here and now? The eerie feeling that he'd never see Seg again shredded his composure, threatening to take him out at the knees.

He didn't know why he felt this way. Seg was merely giving him time.

Right?

Whatever the reason, he couldn't shake it.

And that scared him more than anything ever had.

SEG DIDN'T GET a chance to sleep after leaving Roan's, but he figured he could easily grab a nap on the plane to Boston.

That had been his thinking right up until he arrived to find everyone talking about Mattias leaving the team. No, it wasn't official, but it did sound as though the guy had an issue. Seg could only guess what that issue was. Surely it wasn't a coincidence that Mattias had given him the stink eye in the locker room last week.

"Hey, man," Kaufman said, leaning down near Seg's ear from where he was standing in the aisle, arm landing over the back of Seg's seat.

Seg turned his head slightly to hear what his captain had to say.

"Phoenix wants to talk to you when we get to Boston. He said not to freak out. It's nothing bad."

Seg smirked. The guy obviously knew that Seg was still on pins and needles regarding all the shit that had gone down.

"Cool."

Kaufman touched his shoulder, then headed back to his seat. Seg leaned his chair back and closed his eyes. He had a feeling he knew what Phoenix wanted to talk about. And since he had no desire to dwell on that right now, he figured he might as well get some sleep.

Three and a half hours later, Seg was sitting across from Phoenix at the coffee shop in their hotel. He'd checked in with him as soon as the plane landed, and Phoenix had informed him he would be about an hour behind. That had given Seg enough time to dump his stuff in his room, grab a quick shower, and make it back downstairs.

And now here they were, small talk out of the way. Seg anxiously awaited Phoenix's news, his hands practically vibrating from the tension coiling tight throughout his body.

"I wanted to talk to you first. Give you a heads-up on what's going on. I'm sure you've heard some talk."

Seg nodded, encouraging Phoenix to continue.

"Valeri is looking to be traded. His contract is not up yet, but when his agent came to me about the request, I didn't put up a fight. He'll be snatched up pretty quick, I'm sure. But it'll probably cost him."

Seg knew Phoenix meant in regards to a new contract. When a player decided to leave a team for personal reasons, the potential new team usually did some digging. No doubt about it, there would be some team out there with compassion for Mattias's issue, whatever that might be. However, it'd likely include less money than he would've received if he'd been a free agent.

"Because of me." Seg dropped his gaze to the table as it all made sense.

"He claims to have an issue, but Seg ... look at me."

Seg looked up.

"He's the only one who's come forward with a problem. Do you realize what that means?"

No, he didn't.

"You need to relax. Not everyone in the world is going to be happy with the decisions we make for ourselves. But those who don't like it have options. You can be who you are and they can be who they are." Phoenix leaned back, his position casual. "He's handling this well, in my opinion. He hasn't come out publicly, and he doesn't intend to."

That was a relief. Seg had suspected Mattias had a problem with him, but he wasn't about to stir shit up for no reason.

Phoenix leaned back. "Plus, I've got a bead on a great winger who'd be perfect for the team."

That caught Seg's interest. For one, he hadn't expected Phoenix to share any more details than he had to.

"Heath Rush."

Well, that was a name that everyone knew. Kingston Rush's brother played for Colorado, and he was one of the best damn forwards in the league right now. Not that Valeri was a lightweight.

"If all works out, we'll have Heath in place for next year, and Mattias will be leading the line for someone else." Phoenix's eyes softened. "How are you doing otherwise? Any issues?"

Other than the fact that he'd practically given Roan a reason to walk away? "No. No issues."

"Good." Phoenix sat up, took a deep breath. "Well, I'll let you get back to it. Good luck tonight."

"Yeah. Thanks."

When Phoenix disappeared, Seg remained where he was, staring at the coffee cup in his hand while he processed everything that was going on. He reached for his cell phone as his mind whirred with so much chaos. He pulled up his contacts and hit the button.

"Seggy?" his mother greeted. "Are you okay?"

"I am." He hadn't talked to her but briefly in the past week. Ever since he put her on a plane home, he'd kept from burdening her with his issues. He knew she worried, which was why he was calling her now.

"Are you in Boston?"

"Yeah. Got here a couple of hours ago."

"How are things back home?"

Seg went on to explain about Roan's father, about Milly having the baby a little early, and also about his decision to walk away should Roan feel that was the right thing for him.

"You've always been good at that," Deb said when Seg finished.

"At what?"

"Putting everyone above yourself."

Seg didn't think that was true, but he knew that arguing with his mother would get him nowhere.

"I'm so proud of you," she continued. "You are one of the finest men I've ever known. And I'm not just saying that because you're my son either. I want you to be happy, Colton. And I think you understand what that means now. I hate what Roan is going through. It's not easy being a parent in general, and to have to deal with his own turning on him… I hope he makes the right decision."

Seg chuckled, although he found little humor in it. "The right decision *for him*."

"The right decision for him is to stand up for the ones he loves. To never give up. To give you the same love and devotion that you give him. But I think he knows that."

Seg wanted to have his mother's optimistic viewpoint, but he just couldn't. He knew that walking away from Roan, not insisting that this thing between them was right could potentially backfire in his face. However, he'd been the one pushing since day one, and he'd come to a point last night when he needed to know that he mattered to Roan.

Roan easily said he would push everyone else away to do what was best for Liam. He understood that to a degree, but Seg had no desire to find out one day he was on the back burner again. He needed to be a partner in this relationship, not a liability.

Seg had been as clear as he could be in his feelings for Roan. He'd told him repeatedly that he wanted to be with him, to stand behind him, to love him. Now he needed Roan to do the same.

Because no matter what, Seg had tackled the biggest obstacle of his life. He'd come out. Risked his career even. He was finally free and that mattered to him. He wasn't going to settle for second place for anyone. Not when it mattered most.

"I want you to go out on that ice tonight and play like you always do. Play to win, Seggy. That's what you do. In every aspect of your life."

Wanting to break the melancholy mood, Seg forced a smile and sat up. "I will, Ma. Is Marjorie coming over to watch the game?"

Deb giggled. "She is. Which means I've got to come up with a way to freak her out again. So, maybe you could score a goal or something. That should send me right over the edge."

Seg chuckled. "I'll do my best."

"You always do. Oh, and Seggy?"

"Hmm?"

"I love you."

"I love you, too, Ma."

Thirty-One

Sunday, February 12th

"YOU'RE SURE Y'ALL don't mind watching him?" Roan asked Cam, observing his best friend closely.

It'd been a hell of a week for Cam and Gannon. Ever since Milly brought the baby home, she'd been in rare form. From what Roan had been told, she called them with a million questions. Mostly about work and her fear that Gannon would not be able to survive without her. Of course, Gannon had assured her that he would barely scrape by, but he would manage.

"We're sure," Cam assured him. "We're just hanging out tonight, so you're good. Go."

Roan nodded, then headed over to Liam. He kissed his son, told him he'd see him first thing tomorrow morning, and made his way to the door. He hated leaving Liam right now, but with Seg coming home, Roan needed to fix things between them. Only then could they move on with the rest of their lives.

"Thanks," Roan called out as he opened the door. "And call me if you need anything."

"We won't. We're pros at this now."

That wasn't far from the truth. Cam and Gannon had helped more than Roan ever expected them to, and he was beyond grateful.

Roan made a beeline for his truck. Five minutes later he was on the way to Austin. He wasn't exactly sure what time Seg would be home, but he'd waited as long as he could. He had purposely not called or texted—however, Seg hadn't either—for the last few days. Roan had focused solely on trying to figure out what he wanted.

It hadn't been difficult. He knew what he wanted; he merely didn't know how to go about getting it. Did he want what Cam and Gannon had? Or Noah and Dare? Hudson and Teague?

Of course he did. Would he be able to sustain a relationship with little effort the way those guys did? Doubtful. Roan wasn't perfect. He'd proven that already.

However, he didn't think he'd gone so far as to kill this thing between him and Seg. It was clear he'd pushed too far, not giving Seg a chance. That was on him. And tonight he intended to lay it all out for Seg. Tell him how he felt and just what Seg meant to him. He'd spent hours thinking about how he would deliver that message, but he'd never come up with the perfect plan, so he intended to wing it.

Along with thinking about Seg these past few days, Roan had also had to deal with his father. They'd talked, but not at length. His father had invited him and Liam to dinner tomorrow night. Roan had tentatively accepted but had every intention of inviting Seg to go with him. That would likely shock the shit out of his old man, but it was the way it was going to be.

If all went well tonight, Roan would be moving on to the rest of his life.

He only prayed Seg was on board for that wild ride.

Forty-five minutes later, Roan pulled up to Seg's house. It took him a few minutes to get the nerve to get out of his truck, but he finally got some starch in his legs and managed to make it to the front door.

He knocked.

There was no sound from the other side. He prayed that meant Seg wasn't home and not that he was ignoring him. There was no way Roan could accomplish his goal if Seg didn't give him a few minutes at least.

Still, he stood there, staring at the door, willing it to open.

"Come on, Seg," he whispered.

A tap on his shoulder had Roan spinning around so fast he nearly toppled them both off the front porch.

"Damn it," Roan grumbled. "You scared the shit out of me."

With his hands securing Roan's upper body, Seg glanced over his shoulder to where he'd parked his Range Rover. "I thought for sure you heard me."

Roan shook his head. "No. I was too busy pleading with a higher power to open the door."

Seg grinned and the move caught Roan's breath. He hadn't seen Seg smile like that in a while.

"Would you like me to unlock the door?" Seg asked.

It took a second to process Seg's words, but when he did, he grinned shyly and stepped out of the way. Seg got the door open, then allowed Roan to precede him into the house. Once inside, Roan peered around while Seg disengaged the alarm. It looked the same as it did every other time he'd been there.

"Can I get you something to drink? Beer?"

Roan turned to face Seg, the memory of the first night he was there coming back in a dizzying rush.

"I don't want anything to drink," he stated, his eyes raking over Seg's handsome face.

Living without this man wasn't an option. When he wasn't with him, he wanted to be. And when he was with him, Roan never wanted to be anywhere else.

FROM THE SECOND Seg saw Roan standing on his front porch, his heart had relocated to his throat. And now, as they stood in his foyer, he found that breathing was becoming difficult.

He hadn't expected this, but he'd secretly prayed for it.

Now that he had Roan inside his house, he was at a loss for words. He had so many things he wanted to say, but Seg knew now was not the time to share his thoughts. He'd forged through the past few days, giving Roan the distance he'd asked for. It was Roan's turn.

However, he felt a familiar sense of déjà vu, Roan turning down the offered drink while standing right here in this very spot.

"No drink? So, what *do* you want?" Seg waited patiently, trying to regulate his breathing.

"You."

One word. That's all Roan said, and Seg felt as though he'd shared a million of them.

"I've been doing some thinking," Roan continued. "And believe it or not, you plagued every single one of my thoughts."

"That's a bad thing?"

A small smile curled the corners of Roan's lips. "No. Not unexpected either."

Good to know.

"How's Liam?"

Roan's smile grew wider. "He's good. He's with Cam and Gannon tonight."

"All night?"

Roan nodded.

Seg still didn't move. He couldn't. Roan was here to make a point. Seg needed him to get on with it or he risked losing every ounce of his patience in the next few seconds.

"I didn't know if you'd be home or not, but I came prepared to sit outside all night if I had to."

"I'm home."

"You are." Roan took a step closer. "And I don't want to sit outside."

"No?"

Roan shook his head. "I want to spend the night with you."

"I'm sure that can be arranged."

Roan reached up, cupping the side of Seg's neck. The warmth of his touch had Seg's heart kicking in his chest. Still, he managed not to move.

Roan's thumb grazed his jaw. "I love you."

It was a wonder that Seg's knees didn't give out. Somehow he found the strength to stand right where he was, watching this man, waiting.

Roan didn't speak.

"I'm running out of patience, Roan," Seg warned, encouraging him to continue.

"I need to say more?" he teased.

"Well, we could move on to the naked portion of our evening, but that might take some time. So, if there's something on your mind…"

Roan grinned, closing the distance between them completely as he backed Seg against the door. "I want to spend the night."

"You mentioned that."

"Tonight." Roan pressed his lips to Seg's.

"That's probably a given," Seg mumbled, Roan's intoxicating scent going straight to his head.

"And every night."

Seg pulled back slightly, studying Roan's eyes, trying to find the hidden meaning.

Roan's nod was nearly imperceptible.

But Seg got it.

Damn, did he.

That did it. Seg's thin grip on his self-control snapped, and he flipped their positions, shoving Roan against the door, crushing their lips together. When Roan's hands gripped him roughly, jerking him closer, his fingers digging into his back, Seg groaned.

This was pure heaven. He was right where he wanted to be. Now and forever. Secretly, he'd wondered if he'd seen the last of Roan. Finding the man waiting for him… Seg's world had been righted.

He tore at Roan's clothes in his haste to get the man naked. He needed to feel him, to hold him, to touch, taste. He needed Roan more than he needed the life-giving oxygen that flooded his lungs.

And he couldn't wait long enough to get to the bedroom.

"You don't have anything to say to that?" Roan said against Seg's lips.

"Oh, I'm saying it all right. Just without words."

"Got it." Roan's mouth slid to Seg's neck. "Maybe we should move this to the bedroom."

"Don't want to wait."

"Gonna need some stuff in your nightstand," Roan muttered.

Right.

Turning, Seg grabbed Roan's hand and jerked him toward his bedroom. Roan stumbled along behind him, laughing. It made Seg's heart swell, his body lighter than he'd been in months.

When they reached his bed, Seg fully intended to take control, but Roan clearly had other ideas. Seg wound up on his back, Roan straddling his hips, their jeans still on.

"I need to taste you," Roan informed him. "All of you."

Seg nodded. Like he was going to say no?

Roan grinned, then backed his way off the bed. Within seconds, Seg discarded his shoes, then his jeans, socks following close behind. He propped his hands behind his head, watching as Roan stripped down to beautiful bare skin.

Lube and condoms appeared beside them, but Seg was so caught up in the way Roan's mouth engulfed his dick that he hardly noticed. A desperate groan escaped him as he grabbed for Roan's hair, pulling him onto his cock.

"Fuck," he hissed. "So damn good, Roan. Your mouth…"

Seg's head fell back, his body tense as the pleasure consumed him from his scalp to his toes.

When Roan's mouth descended lower, drawing Seg's balls into his mouth, his abs contracted painfully.

"If you're not careful, I'm going to come from your mouth alone."

Roan chuckled, but he didn't stop the sensual assault. In fact, he took it a step further, pushing Seg's legs up and back, his knees close to his chest.

"Son of a…" Seg growled when Roan's tongue pierced his anus.

He'd never in his life felt anything as good as that. He had no idea why it felt so fucking good, but shit… Seg was lost, his body floating on the sensations ripping through him.

Roan's tongue was replaced by one finger, then another.

"Want more," Seg panted. "Need more." He lifted his head to make eye contact with Roan. When those golden eyes met his, he added, "Now."

"Turn over," Roan insisted, reaching for the lube and condoms.

Seg twisted his body, turning over onto his stomach.

"On your knees," Roan instructed.

Seg did as he was told.

A minute later, Roan pushed inside him. The initial pain quickly dissipated, long forgotten when Roan's hands curled over Seg's shoulders, pulling him back as he slammed into him.

"I need you, Colton," Roan said on a tortured groan.

"You have me."

"All of you," he added, pumping his hips, filling Seg completely.

Roan jerked him backward, his hips slamming into him. Seconds turned to minutes as the pleasure stole his thoughts, his words. Seg gave himself over to Roan, allowing the man to fuck him hard. He could sense the need in Roan. This was different than any other time. For the first time, Seg realized he didn't need sweet and gentle to feel all that Roan was feeling. He liked that he drove the man to lose control.

"Fuck … Colton … I can't get enough."

Seg pushed back against the intrusion, adding to the intense friction, driving Roan deeper.

"I'll never get enough."

Roan's teeth sank into his shoulder and Seg lost it. All control disappeared as he came in a rush, taken completely off guard by the intensity.

"Fuck … fuck … fu-u-uck," he roared as he came.

His release must have triggered Roan's, because the next thing Seg knew, he was flat on his stomach, Roan's body covering his. Roan's fingers linked with his and they remained just like that for...

Seg didn't even know.

And he honestly didn't care.

Thirty-Two

"MY DAD INVITED me to dinner tomorrow night," Roan whispered in the dark.

After their intense bout of sex earlier, they'd followed it with a long, relaxing shower where Seg had driven Roan clean out of his mind with his fingers, after he'd gone full-throttle with his tongue. Yes, Roan had enjoyed the hell out of that, and he'd made sure Seg knew it. Roan liked that Seg figured out Roan's weaknesses all on his own. And the man was getting damn good at stroking his prostate just the right way to make him lose it.

Once Seg had brought him to the pinnacle of release for the second time, Seg had fucked him slow and easy, right there against the slick tile.

At that point, Roan could hardly walk, so it was a wonder he'd even made it to the bed. But here they were, practically wrapped around one another, lying together in the dark.

"How's that situation going?" Seg inquired. "With your dad?"

Roan shrugged, his shoulder bumping Seg's because Roan was lying with his head in the crook of Seg's arm. "We haven't talked much. I told him I was disappointed that he'd come over and expected to take Liam while I wasn't there."

When Milly had informed Roan about the conversation she'd had with Daniel and Lydia, Roan had nearly lost his mind. He had no idea what was going through their heads or why they were hell-bent on interfering with a good thing.

"How do you think it'll go at dinner?"

"I don't know." Roan lifted his head, peering at Seg in the dark. "I'd like you to go with us."

"Us?"

"Me and Liam."

"Of course I'll go."

The fact that Seg agreed without any thought eased some of the tension where Roan's father was concerned.

"He's not a hockey fan," Roan noted, his attempt at lightening the mood.

"Not a problem. I have other charms."

"Do you? Like those that you've used on me?"

"Which ones do you prefer?" Seg shifted so that Roan was flat on his back, Seg hovering over him.

"All of them," he admitted, his voice choked by emotion. "Every single one."

"Well, I have to say, those particular charms are for you and you only." Seg's hand slid down his cheek and Roan leaned into the touch.

"You won't hear me complaining."

Roan could feel the intensity of Seg's stare.

"Did you mean what you said earlier? About wanting to spend every night with me?"

"Yeah."

Seg's kiss was soft, soothing. "Good."

"How do you propose we make that happen?" Roan hadn't thought that far ahead, so he was hoping Seg had.

"It doesn't have to happen immediately, you know. We can take things slowly."

"I'm thinking that a year and a half of this has been relatively slow, huh?"

Seg chuckled. "We did manage to make up for some serious lost time, eh?"

"Hmm. I'm not sure we made up for all of it."

"I can fix that," Seg told him.

Roan took the opportunity to kiss Seg. Just kiss him. He ran his hands over the smooth skin of Seg's back, feeling the flex of his muscles as he moved closer. This was what he'd wanted for so long. Something real, steady. A promise of years to come.

It was what all his friends had recently found, what Roan thought would never be available to him. Who would've thought that a one-night stand all those months ago would've resulted in this?

Love.

"Which one of us is gonna have to commute to work?" Roan asked when they broke for air.

"Me," Seg said instantly. "Liam needs to be close to your friends so they can help when we need it. I have friends who would help out in a pinch, but they're not as close as you are with your friends. Plus, I can manage the daily drive."

"What if we bought a house somewhere in the middle? Share the drive. It would allow me to be close enough to the marina, to Cam and everyone, but also limit the amount of time you have to spend driving."

Seg lifted his head and smiled. "I'd like that. The idea of buying a house that's ours..."

Roan liked the idea, too.

Then again, if it involved sharing a life with Seg, he more than liked it.

"NOW THAT WE'VE got that settled," Seg prompted as he eased onto his back and pulled Roan closer, "tell me all I need to know for tomorrow night."

"Like?"

Seg turned his head to look at Roan. "You haven't exactly been forthcoming with details about your family. What does your dad do? Your stepmom? How long have they been married?"

"My dad works as an electrician. He's semi-retired though. My stepmother works at a bank. They got married when I was twenty-two, so ... twelve years."

"Does she have kids of her own?"

"No. I'm not sure why that is either. Maybe she can't have them. I've never asked."

"Semi-retired and your dad wants to take on the task of raising another child? Sounds backwards to me."

"It is." Roan shifted. "I honestly don't think my dad wants to raise Liam. However, Lydia can be pretty persuasive."

"And her issue with you being gay?"

Roan sighed. "She always claimed it wasn't an issue. Not until Cassie died. Then she voiced her opinion of a child being raised in a gay household."

"You think maybe it's just a knee-jerk reaction? If they didn't know about Liam, maybe she's disappointed Cassie never came to them?"

"No. I mean, sure, I get that they could be upset, but you have to understand the relationship they have with my sisters. Cassie was a wild child from about thirteen. She acted out in school, and she ran with the wrong crowd. They dealt with her drinking when she was in high school, but my dad pretty much washed his hands of her when she left home. Cassie didn't like Lydia for whatever reason."

Based on what Seg knew of Lydia, that didn't surprise him. He didn't even know the woman and he wasn't a fan.

"Do you think they would've wanted guardianship?" Seg asked.

"I'm not sure. Maybe. It sure seems that way, but I don't think they're in it for the right reasons."

"If you don't mind me asking, how did you end up getting guardianship?"

Roan sighed again. "When Cassie was in the hospital, after she had Liam, Child Protective Services paid her a visit."

"Oh, shit."

"Yeah. They had a file on her, a note to keep track of the baby if she made it to term. She knew she had a problem, and no, she didn't make much effort to fix it. But she did know what was right for her child. When they were handling the birth certificate, they asked about the father. She had no clue who the guy was, and honestly, I don't think she cared.

"I think CPS put the fear of God into her, telling her in no uncertain terms that they would be keeping an eye on her. After that meeting, Cassie and I had a heart-to-heart. First one ever, I think. She told me she wanted me to be Liam's guardian. She said she knew she wouldn't be a good mom, but she wanted to give it a shot. She wanted to try. Unfortunately, Cassie never was good at following through on anything."

Seg was grateful that Roan had been there to pick up the pieces. That Cassie had been smart enough to know she needed her brother.

"As for Lydia..." Seg shifted closer. "She has experience with that gay household thing? Two moms? Or two dads?"

Roan chuckled, just as Seg had hoped he would. "No, she's merely judgmental."

"Well, if we don't make headway tomorrow night, we'll let my mom get ahold of her," Seg joked. Only he wasn't completely joking.

"It turns my stomach to think about fighting with them on this."

"There's no need to fight," Seg told him, turning so he could get more comfortable. "You're the best thing that's happened to Liam. They'll see that if they just open their eyes."

Roan yawned.

"Get some sleep. We'll talk more in the morning."

"Mmm-hmm."

As Roan drifted to sleep in his arms, Seg held on to him. He didn't want to close his eyes although it would be so easy to do. He wanted to call his mother, to ask her what she thought about Seg going to dinner with Roan's parents tomorrow.

Then again, he knew what she'd say. She'd tell him to fight to win because that was what he was good at.

It was true. He didn't usually give up on what he wanted. Not with hockey, anyway. That had been his dream when he was a kid. He still remembered his first NHL game. He'd been a nervous wreck, but he'd made it through the game without any mishaps.

Surely he could do the same tomorrow.

Pretend dinner with Roan's father and stepmother was just like any other game. He'd go in with a plan.

To win.

And if they didn't like it?

Well, he'd deal with that when they came to it.

Because Seg hadn't been kidding when he said Roan's parents wouldn't want to go up against an army. And Seg would make sure they paid heavily for doing this to Roan and Liam. He had the money to fight them for as long as necessary.

However, he knew it would be best to resolve this amicably. No reason to cause Roan any undue stress.

Seg hugged Roan tighter, brushing his lips over his forehead, then closed his eyes.

And for the first time in at least a week, Seg fell into a dreamless sleep.

Thirty-Three

EVEN AS THEY walked up the path to his father's front door, Roan wished he were anywhere but here. He'd tried to back out of this dinner a half dozen times today, but Seg had assured him that it would be fine.

Clearly Seg hadn't met Roan's stepmother.

It wasn't that she was a bad person. Lydia Gregory had a good heart beneath her overabundance of prejudice. Although no one was as prejudiced as his own mother, Lydia certainly wasn't a member of PFLAG.

Thankfully, Roan had been out of the house by the time his father and Lydia made the decision to get married. Cassie had still been at home, but that hadn't lasted long. Cassie and Lydia had butted heads. But Cassie had butted heads with everyone at that point in her life.

Taking a deep breath, Roan glanced over his shoulder. Seg was standing directly behind him, carrying Liam. Their eyes met and Roan knew Seg was letting him take his own sweet time.

"Okay, let's get this over with." Roan knocked, then took a step back, keeping Seg at his side.

When the door opened, Roan's father stared back at him, his face a little more weathered than he'd remembered. The man looked tired.

What was he thinking wanting to raise an infant? Even if it was Lydia's grand scheme, surely the guy knew he was getting too old to be starting over.

"Roan." Daniel's dark brown gaze drifted over to Seg.

"Dad, this is Colton Seguine. Colton, this is my father, Daniel Gregory."

"Nice to meet you, sir," Seg said instantly, holding out his hand. "You can call me Seg."

Roan's father nodded, shaking Seg's hand and then stepping out of the way. The man had never been much of a conversationalist.

"Lydia's in the kitchen," Daniel informed them.

"I'm right here," she said, stepping into the small living room. Her eyes darted from Roan to Seg, then back. "I didn't know you were bringing ... a friend."

"Nice to meet you, Mrs. Gregory," Seg said, greeting Lydia with the same smile he'd greeted Daniel with. "And I'm a little more than a friend."

Roan nearly choked, shocked to the roots of his hair that Seg was so upfront during their introduction.

"This is Colton. He goes by Seg," Daniel informed Lydia, his tone dry.

Seg grinned, then glanced over at Liam. "Look who it is, Liam."

"Hi, sweet boy," Lydia greeted, stepping closer but not quite close enough to touch Liam. "You're getting so big."

That tended to happen after four months of not seeing a baby, but Roan didn't say as much. He'd promised himself he'd be on his best behavior. At this point, he was going to take a page from Seg's book because the guy had managed to break the ice within the first thirty seconds of being in the house.

"Have a seat," Daniel stated gruffly, waving toward the couch.

"Thank you," Seg responded.

Roan fought the urge to grin. The man was on his absolute best behavior. It was kind of hot.

"You have a lovely home, Mrs. Gregory."

Lydia's eyes swept from Daniel to Roan, then over to Seg. "You can call me Lydia. Please."

Seg nodded, then gave the air a little sniff. He grinned sheepishly. "Would you possibly have somewhere I could change Liam?"

Lydia's eyes widened while Daniel nearly choked on a laugh.

"Yes. Uh … you can use the guest room."

"Perfect. If you'll lead the way…" Seg got to his feet, still holding Liam. He shot Roan a quick grin before snatching the diaper bag and following Lydia down the hall toward the back bedrooms.

"You're serious about this one?" Daniel asked, his deep voice little more than a whisper.

"What gave it away? The fact that I introduced him to you?" Since Roan had yet to introduce his father to anyone he was interested in, he got it. He also got the fact that his father noticed.

Daniel didn't respond to Roan's retort, just slid his bored gaze over Roan's face. "He the reason reporters were camped out in front of my house and yours?"

"He is."

"You're okay with that stunt he pulled? Can he be trusted?"

Roan was surprised that his father knew what had happened, but he hid his initial reaction. "I am, and yes, he can."

Daniel nodded as though processing that information. He met Roan's gaze. "How's Liam doing?"

"Great. Strong, healthy, growing like a weed."

"And this guy likes Liam?"

Roan narrowed his eyes. *This guy* was changing Liam's diaper. He figured it was safe to assume Seg was more than a late-night visitor to Roan's bed.

"He loves him."

"And he's still got a job? After that fiasco with the woman?"

Roan sighed. "It wasn't the fiasco with the woman. The heat is coming from the fact that he's gay. But yes, he does still have a job. And that's behind us. He hadn't come out to anyone, Dad. He's a professional athlete. It was bound to make news. But it's out there now and he's dealt with it."

Seg returned to the living room, carrying Liam, with Lydia right at their side. She was laughing at something Seg said. Seg must've felt the tension because his eyes traveled between Roan and his father, then back. He quirked a brow in a silent question. Roan nodded slightly, forcing a smile.

"Lydia said dinner's about ready. You hungry?" Seg asked, his question directed at Roan.

Thankfully Roan's father got to his feet and followed his wife into the kitchen.

Roan peered around Seg to ensure no one could hear him. "You seriously did not make her laugh within five minutes of being here."

"I told you. I've got charm." Seg winked.

"There's no way this is over. That's too anticlimactic."

Seg grinned, then leaned in and kissed Roan lightly. "Always looking for the drama, eh?"

Roan huffed out a laugh, a real smile forming this time.

Seg was obviously proud of himself, because he winked. "It's not over, trust me. But the night's young. Give it a chance."

Roan didn't like the sound of that. In order to give it a chance, he was going to have to listen to a lecture from his stepmother.

And if that wasn't enough to kill his appetite, the dirty diaper Seg passed over certainly was.

FROM THE INSTANT Seg walked in the door, he understood the dynamic of Roan's parents. His father was clearly the strong, silent type. He didn't seem to care about much of anything except his television and dinner. Lydia, on the other hand, wanted to be the center of attention. More so than Liam, even. Which was odd, but whatever.

Dinner had been a relatively tense ordeal. Thankfully, they had Liam to help calm the waters. Everyone spent most of their time watching him chow down on applesauce and make a complete mess of himself despite the fact he never touched the spoon.

Luckily for everyone, small talk was minimal. They'd talked about the fact that Seg was from Toronto. Being that none of them had been to Canada, Seg noticed they didn't know much about geography. He explained that he'd gone to college in the States. Again, Roan's father and stepmother didn't seem all that interested that Seg had gone to the University of Minnesota; however, they did happen to call out that he pronounced a few words differently such as house and mouse. (Although he never said mouse.)

"How long have you been playing hockey?" Daniel asked from his spot on the sofa, clearly trying to ignore the discomfort of the situation and make conversation.

Seg had to respect the guy for trying. Then again, Seg got the feeling he was attempting to keep Lydia from saying too much.

"Since I was a kid. Played pond hockey with my old man when I was three, I think. Haven't stopped since."

"What're your plans after?"

"After?" Seg raised a questioning brow. "You mean when I retire from the NHL?"

"Or get hurt. Or…"

Seg leaned back, resting his arm on the couch behind Roan. He was making an effort to show these people that he wasn't scared of who he was. "Or…?"

Daniel had the decency to blush, but Lydia was the one who spoke up.

"What Daniel is trying to say," she explained with a slightly haughty tone, "is what will you do when you get fired from the league?"

"That is *not* what I was asking," Daniel corrected, a glare directed at his wife. "I meant when he was too old to play."

Seg was interested in the obvious offense Daniel took to Lydia's accusation. He set it aside for a second and decided to answer Daniel's initial question.

"I've got a degree in sports management," Seg confessed.

"Really?" Daniel seemed content with that revelation. "Same as Cam."

"It's a good thing you thought ahead," Lydia added. "I hate to play devil's advocate, but I feel your career playing hockey is limited. Once they have the right to speak up, they will."

"They? Who's they?" Seg asked pointedly, keeping his eyes on Lydia. He damn sure wasn't going to make this easy on her. It was clear she was trying to make a point, and Seg was going to let her. But she was going to have to come out with it.

"The fans, the other players, owners."

Seg pretended to misunderstand. "Last I checked, they didn't have a say in my performance evaluation. Not the fans or my teammates, anyway."

Lydia's face darkened. "Mr. Seguine—"

"Please, call me Seg. My friends and family do."

Lydia cleared her throat. "Seg. There's a reason you didn't come out before now. You know that it's frowned upon to have homosexual players in sports."

Seg cocked his head to the side. Again, he acted oblivious to her line of questioning. "Frowned upon? As in it makes people sad?"

Roan cleared his throat and shifted, but Seg put one hand on his shoulder, giving him a gentle squeeze. This woman wasn't going to push him back into the closet, that was for damn sure. And Seg was more than ready to school her on a few things.

Reaching for her drink, Lydia glanced over at her husband. Seg figured she was looking for some support, but Daniel did what he'd been doing all night. He pretended not to notice.

"Being gay is a phase, Seg," she said.

Surprisingly, the woman had the balls to look Seg in the eye when she said that.

"A phase?" Seg leaned forward, resting his elbows on his knees as though processing that information. "Shit. If I'd known that, I would've kept my mouth shut." He lifted his head and pinned Lydia in place with a glare. "So what you're telling me is that Roan's been going through this *phase*"—he used air quotes for emphasis—"for twenty years now? It must burn your ass that you haven't been able to redirect his attention to women."

Lydia looked appalled. For half a second, Seg thought Daniel was going to speak up, but he kept his mouth shut. Smart guy.

As for Roan, Seg felt his eyes on him. But Seg came here with an objective tonight. After meeting Lydia, he got the impression that Daniel backed down from her whenever conflict arose. As for Roan, it was obvious the man didn't have much to do with his father or his stepmother. Probably for this very reason.

"He's rebellious," Lydia said with a wave of her hand.

Seg choked out a laugh. "Is that what you call it?" He sat up straight. "I call it something else entirely."

"I just don't think that this is what your mother would want for you," Lydia told Seg directly. "As you've probably heard, Roan's claim to be homosexual is the reason his mother left."

Wow. This woman was certifiable. But based on her calm, cool demeanor, she honestly believed the bullshit coming out of her mouth. Luckily, Seg had honed his patience before he walked in the door, because he definitely needed it now.

"First, let me tell you something about my mother," Seg began, elbows on his knees, hands hanging between them, giving his full attention to Lydia. "She's been my biggest supporter my entire life. No matter what I attempted to do, she stood behind me. And when I came out and informed her that I was in love with a man, she didn't bat an eyelash. That's why she's a mother. There's this thing called unconditional love, and she was blessed with it. Unfortunately, the same can't be said for Roan's mother. If she'd possessed it, you and I probably wouldn't be here."

Lydia bristled.

Seg continued, "Because Daniel would still be married to his first wife, and Roan would've long ago found happiness rather than avoiding it in an effort to deal with the bigotry that comes from his family."

"I don't think that's the case at all," Lydia countered.

347

"Let me ask you something, Lydia." Seg added a hint of frustration when he said her name. "When you and Daniel have sex, is it always missionary?"

"I don't think that's any of your business," she said with a gasp, her face turning a shade lighter than the maroon curtains hanging over the windows.

"No? Then why is my sex life any of your business? Or the media's? Or my teammates', for that matter? Is it not enough that we can look at each other and see that we're happy in our respective relationships? Because I'll be the first one here to tell you that I'm in love with Roan. I fully intend to marry him. And I intend to help him raise Liam."

Seg hadn't wanted to be the one to mention the elephant in the room, but he knew someone had to or this would possibly last all night long. And quite frankly, he was damn tired of this conversation already.

Lydia once again glanced at Daniel, but the man had disappeared in plain sight. He clearly had nothing to contribute to the conversation.

"We think it would be best if Liam is raised by…" Lydia trailed off, her eyes searching the room but never able to land on anyone or anything in particular.

When she finally met Seg's gaze again—evidently she was only having this conversation with him—she didn't say anything.

With a questioning look, Seg waited.

And waited.

When Roan shifted, Seg put his hand on Roan's leg, wanting him to wait. It seemed Lydia and Daniel could talk the talk when it came to harassing Roan over the phone, but they were having a hard time in person.

"From what I've seen, Roan is a great father," Lydia finally stated.

"But…?" Seg interjected.

"I simply don't think it's wise to raise a child in a gay household."

"What's different about a gay household from yours?" Seg asked. "I'd really like to understand. There are two people, they both love the child, both have jobs, stability. Plus, Roan has plenty of friends he considers family. They've been there for Liam when it was necessary. In fact, it isn't much different than the house I grew up in. So, please, Lydia, help me understand."

"I just don't think Liam needs to be subjected to that."

"That?"

"Two men being intimate."

"Ahh," Seg said, sitting back, his eyes wide with mock understanding. "I think I see where the confusion is."

"Where's that?"

"See, if that's the way you did things here"—he leaned forward and lowered his voice to a whisper—"being intimate in front of the children … I can understand why you'd be worried. But be assured, that's not the way it's done in our house." He masked his expression with concern.

Roan's eyes cut to him and Seg could feel the weight of his stare. Yes, he'd said "our house." And he'd meant it. Because that was where they were headed, and Seg wanted Roan to know, without a doubt, that he was on his side.

Now and forever.

Thirty-Four

SEG HAD A way with words. No way could anyone dispute that.

While Roan would've gone on the defensive, Seg had played the role perfectly, urging Lydia to explain her reasoning for wanting to raise Liam. So far, Seg had managed to shoot down her every excuse.

And it was kind of amusing. At one point, Roan was pretty sure his dad's lips had twitched, but he'd managed to hold back his smile.

Although nothing had been officially settled, Roan had come to the conclusion that his father played no part in this, other than being the one to deliver the message. For some reason, that made him feel better. Daniel Gregory was a lot of things, but a homophobe he was not.

"And quite frankly, Lydia," Seg continued, "I'm not sure that'd be good for Liam. You know, if you were to raise him. The being intimate in front of him might be more than he can handle."

Lydia's face turned an interesting shade of purple. "That's not what I meant."

"No?" Seg's tone remained even. "That's what it sounded like. You made the assumption that's what takes place at our house. Why shouldn't I think that's what happens at yours?"

Roan's father cleared his throat and all eyes drifted to him.

"This is going nowhere," Daniel said in that same flat, gruff tone.

Sitting up, Roan decided it was time to bring this to a close. "Look. We get that you're concerned about Liam. We get that you want to spend time with him, and we want that, too. But you have to realize that we have and will put his best interest before anything else." Roan forced himself to look at Lydia. "Seg's made a good point. Gay, straight, or whatever, my house is no different than yours." Roan held up a hand before Lydia could interrupt. "And this is what Cassie wanted. She signed over guardianship of Liam from day one. She knew she had issues, and she knew I would put him first. I loved my sister, in spite of all her flaws. She screwed up her life, but she made the conscious decision not to screw up Liam's."

Seg reached over and brushed his pinky against Roan's leg. It was a silent show of support that Roan appreciated. "So, I'm gonna put an end to this right now. I am going to raise Liam. And when the day comes that Seg and I get married, he will adopt him if that's what he wants."

"I do," Seg leaned over and whispered softly.

Roan couldn't help but laugh. Yeah. He'd already known that. Which was why he'd brought it up.

"And when you want to spend time with Liam, you get to do that. As his grandparents. You get to enjoy that time without having the strain of raising another child." Roan looked at his father. "Do you really want that, Dad? To start all over?"

"No," Daniel said sharply. "I don't. I want what's best for Liam."

Roan glanced between the two of them. "Can you honestly say that I don't have his best interest at heart?"

Daniel shook his head, and Lydia glanced away.

At that moment, Liam decided he'd had enough and erupted into a loud cry from his spot on Roan's knee, where he'd been chewing on a teething toy and watching everything in the room. Roan was instantly shifting him so Liam could stand, while Seg gave him his full attention.

"What's up, little dude? Is it past your bedtime?"

Roan continued to watch his parents while Seg spoke to Liam. Lydia didn't seem as convinced as Roan's father.

"I do want you both to know that I don't want any animosity between us." Roan waited until they both looked at him again. "But I am prepared to fight for Liam. I'm not handing him over." He didn't want to be a dickhead, but he knew he needed to make his point very clear. "So, if you decide to push this issue and take me to court"—Roan pinned Lydia in place with his eyes because he knew this was her issue—"I will spend every penny I have, and I'll ensure you're broke by the time it's over."

A flash of anger brightened Lydia's eyes, but she didn't say anything.

"And I'll put my money behind him," Seg noted, his tone hard for the first time since he walked into the house. "Let's just say that I'm a very frugal man and I make a shit ton of money. That degree I have … I'll only have to use it if I choose to."

Roan swallowed a laugh that erupted in his gut. He loved that Seg was willing to go to bat for him and Liam. In fact, he loved Seg period.

"You ready, little guy?" Seg lifted Liam into his arms and turned him to face Lydia and Daniel. "Say good night to Granny and Pop Pop."

This time Roan couldn't hold back his laugh.

He seriously doubted Lydia wanted to be called Granny.

"Roan," Lydia said, ignoring Seg completely. "I think we need to talk about this some more."

To Roan's shock, his father interjected. "I think we've done enough talking, Lyd."

"*Daniel?*"

"No," he stated harshly. "I've sat back long enough. I see no issue with the way Roan lives his life. I never have. And I never will. I dealt with this homophobic shit from one wife…" He held Lydia's stare. "I won't do it again. Enough is enough."

Roan's heart pounded like a bass drum as his father took up for him. For the first time in his life, the man was standing up for him.

"You don't mean that."

"I do. Roan's a good man. He's a good father. Plus, this is what my daughter wanted."

"Your daughter was a drug addict," Lydia countered hotly.

"Yes," Daniel acknowledged. "But she was also my daughter. I'm done having this conversation. Today and forever. If and when Roan needs help, he can come to us. Otherwise, we'll visit our grandson. And enjoy the time we have with him."

"Daniel—"

"No." Roan's father got to his feet. "I'm putting my foot down this time. I'm tired of fighting for no reason."

Roan was beyond shocked by his father's words. He'd never thought his dad had an issue with him being gay. At least not when he'd been growing up. Daniel had never shown any animosity toward him either.

But Lydia…

"Good night, Liam," Daniel said, walking right up to Seg and Liam, hooking Liam's hand with his finger and giving it a little shake. He turned toward Roan. "I'd like to spend some time with him. When you're ready for that to happen."

Roan nodded. "Of course, Dad."

Of course.

ON THE DRIVE back to Roan's, Seg had managed to remain quiet. Not because he didn't have anything to say but because he could feel the relief coursing through Roan.

He'd known that Roan's father had put some undue stress on Roan. It had been evident simply by looking at the guy. And tonight…

Truth was, Seg was shocked as shit when Daniel finally stood up and stated how he really felt. Of course, Lydia wasn't at all happy about that, but shit happened. We don't always get what we want.

"Please tell me you're staying the night," Roan said when they pulled into the driveway.

"I don't want to be anywhere else," he admitted.

Roan smiled. "Good. That's … good."

Clearly Roan was at a loss for words.

To help him out, Seg got Liam out of the truck, carried him into the house, then proceeded to get him ready for bed. All on his own.

Oh, sure, Roan had been watching from the sidelines, but Seg suspected that was more because he had nothing else to do.

Half an hour and one finished bottle later, Liam was down for the night, and Seg found Roan standing in the kitchen, staring out the back window. When Seg approached, Roan turned to face him.

"I love you," Roan stated, his tone chock full of emotion.

The words weren't exactly a surprise; however, he'd expected Roan to start with something else. This would work though.

"I love you, too."

"I didn't know how tonight would go when I asked you to go with me. The only thing I knew was that I would be able to handle it better simply by having you there. In fact, I feel that way now. I don't know what the next road bump is gonna be, but I know that I'll handle it better because you're in my life."

Seg didn't say a word. He didn't move. Hardly breathed.

"We've had a wild ride so far," Roan continued. "But it's a ride I want to continue. With you." Roan took a step closer, but they were still separated by the kitchen island. "I was serious when I said I wanted to spend every night with you. Starting tonight, Seg."

Seg wasn't sure his lungs were working at this point.

Roan sidestepped the island, coming to stop directly in front of Seg.

If he hadn't been watching closely, Seg wouldn't have noticed when Roan reached into his pocket.

"And I want you to marry me."

Okay, now he knew for a fact his lungs weren't working.

Roan went to one knee in front of him.

Seg grinned. "I never took you for the traditional type."

Roan's eyes were serious. "Marry me, Colton. Marry me and spend every night for the rest of our lives with me." Roan grinned. "You know, except for the nights you're on the road."

It was Seg's turn to speak, so he reached for Roan's hand and helped him to his feet.

"I thought for sure I'd be the one to propose to you." Seg dug into his own pocket, pulling out a ring. He grinned, then reached for Roan's hand. "Marry me, Roan. I want you to be my husband and Liam to be my son. I want you both to take my name." Seg smiled.

Roan's eyebrows rose. "I've never considered taking someone else's name."

"Are you against it? We could do the hyphenated thing. Maybe they'll call me ... Segory." Seg frowned. "Aw, damn. That's worse than Seggy. Please don't make me hyphenate my name."

Roan closed the distance between them, placing his ring in Seg's hand. "You don't have to hyphenate your name."

"No?"

"No. Liam and I would be honored to take your name."

Unable to stop himself, Seg pulled Roan into him, pressing their lips together and showing this man exactly how much he loved him.

Needless to say, he wasn't about to stop with just a kiss.

Or just one night.

Epilogue

Wednesday, April 12th

"ARE YOU NERVOUS?" Gannon asked Seg as they stood on the back porch of the house Roan and Seg had just moved into.

The spacious two-story was in a quiet, gated community that offered them a little more privacy than either of their houses before had. With four bedrooms, they had plenty of room to expand and had a room always ready for when Seg's mother came to visit.

Seg glanced over at the man. "I wasn't nervous. Until you asked me that."

The horrified expression on Gannon's face was amusing.

Cam laughed, putting his arm around Gannon's shoulder. "Leave the poor guy alone. It's just the playoffs. No biggie. Just another game."

Seg snorted. "Exactly. No biggie."

"Really?" Gannon appeared confused.

"Of course it's a biggie," Seg's mother called from where she sat at the patio table, Liam in his high chair beside her. "It's the playoffs, you goofs. The Arrows are going all the way this year!"

Grinning, Seg scanned the people standing around. They'd all come over for dinner as a way to celebrate the fact that tomorrow was the first game of the playoffs for the Arrows. Everyone was there. Cam and Gannon, Noah and Dare, Hudson and Teague, Daniel and Lydia, Milly, AJ, and Miranda, as well as Seg's mother, who had flown in yesterday so she could attend the game. Kaufman had stopped by for a few minutes earlier, and Phoenix had promised to stop by before the night was over.

Of course, Seg's mother had claimed she'd only come to town to see Liam. And he knew that was high on her priority list, but he also knew his mother was vibrating with excitement that they were in the playoffs.

"Hey," Roan greeted, coming to stand beside Seg.

He turned to face his husband, grinning. He still couldn't believe they'd tied the knot and he officially got to refer to this man as his husband. March fourth. Their anniversary.

It had been a small but perfect ceremony with only their closest friends and family in attendance. Cam had officiated and the day had been perfect. They'd intended to keep it small and personal, but to Seg's surprise, Cam had reached out to Phoenix, and several of Seg's teammates had come to crash the after party. Seg imagined that day felt a whole lot like what it would feel like to win the Stanley Cup.

"Need anything?" Roan asked, his eyes locked with Seg's.

"You," Seg whispered, leaning in so his mouth hovered by Roan's ear. He lowered his voice even more. "Naked. With your dick in my mouth."

Roan shuddered, pulling back to look at him. "Say the word and I'll send them all on their way."

"My mother's here," Seg reminded him.

Roan frowned.

"We could always sneak inside while everyone's outside," he proposed.

When Roan didn't argue, Seg took his hand, setting his beer on the table. Without saying a word, he pulled him into the house, then led the way down the hall to their bedroom. With a quick flick of his wrist, Seg had the door locked. He wasted no time at all, crushing his mouth to Roan's while he started pulling articles of clothing off. Roan wasn't a wallflower, by any means, and the next thing he knew, they were both naked.

And yes, Seg instantly dropped to his knees, sucking Roan into his mouth as he looked up the length of his body.

"I've been waiting for this all week," Roan groaned.

Seg hated being away from Roan and Liam when he was on the road, but he'd learned that when he came home, Roan usually made it up to him. Since Seg's mother had shown up yesterday, they hadn't had time to play catch-up from the few days Seg was gone.

"Fuck, yes," Roan hissed, his fingers tugging Seg's hair, jerking his head closer. "Fucking suck me."

Seg deep-throated him, his fingers digging into Roan's thighs as he held on to him.

"Can I come in your mouth?"

Seg gave a slight nod, then increased the friction and the movement of his mouth. His one goal was to drive Roan right over the edge.

"Later, I'm going to fuck you in the shower. I'm going to drive my dick deep into your ass... Oh, fuck, Colton. I'm gonna come... Ahh..."

Seg swallowed Roan down as he came on a strangled moan, then quickly got to his feet.

"I think that might've been a record," he told Roan, turning him so that he was facing the bed. "Bend over."

Roan bent over while Seg retrieved the lube from the nightstand. Within seconds he was balls deep in Roan's ass, gripping his hips as he ground his pelvis against Roan.

"Fuck me," Roan insisted. "God, I've missed you."

Seg couldn't speak, his body strung tight as he fucked Roan roughly, pounding into him, his hips jerky, completely out of control. He wasn't going to last, but that was the point of a quickie, so he had no intention of apologizing for it.

Seg heard the back screen door slam shut.

"Better hurry," Roan urged, rocking into Seg.

Seg picked up speed, pounding into Roan, focusing solely on the sexy man in front of him. Seconds later, he soared right over the edge into a blissful climax.

And not a moment too soon.

The doorknob jiggled across the room.

"Seg? Roan? Dare said you better get your asses outside," Teague hollered from the other side of the door.

Seg retreated to the bathroom at the same time Roan replied with, "Why?"

There was no answer.

Within minutes, they were both cleaned up and dressed.

"They know what we were doing," Roan told him, his cheeks flushed.

"I'm sure they do." Seg wasn't sure whether he should be embarrassed or not, so he put on his game face as they headed down the hall toward the kitchen.

Everyone was still outside, which was a plus. Perhaps they didn't know.

"They're on the way," Teague announced as Roan pushed on the screen. "I'm pretty sure they were sneaking in a quickie."

Okay, *now* he was embarrassed. Then again, he should've known. Roan had already warned him about Teague. The guy had come out of his shell in recent months, and somewhere along the way, he'd seemingly lost the filter from his brain to his mouth.

"*Teague!*" Three voices said in unison, all eyes going to Seg's mother as Roan and Seg stepped outside.

Deb giggled but turned her attention to Liam. "Your daddies are silly, you know that?"

Yeah. It was clear she knew what they'd been doing.

"There they are," Teague informed everyone unnecessarily.

"What's goin' on?" Roan asked, looking around.

Dare stepped onto the bottom step of the deck, his gaze floating from face to face, a smile forming on his lips as he did.

"The suspense is killing us," Gannon informed him.

"We're getting married," Dare announced.

"Uh…" Roan's forehead creased. "That's not news, Dare."

"What I meant to say is"—his grin widened—"we're getting married *right now.*"

"What?" Milly squealed, getting to her feet. "What do you mean right now? You can't get married right now." Her head snapped over to her stepbrother. "Why didn't I know about this?"

"Because we didn't want a big production," Noah said, taking Dare's hand.

Both men looked at Cam expectantly.

Cam retrieved an iPad and headed over to the couple.

"Wait!" Milly shrieked. "You can't be serious. We need a best man."

Roan stepped forward, moving to stand beside Dare.

"That's only one," Milly said, frowning.

Hudson got up from his spot at the table beside Deb.

"What about your mom?" Milly asked Noah. "And my dad?"

"We'll call them afterward," Noah told her.

"No, seriously," Milly countered.

"We're serious," Noah told her. "I've been asking this man time and time again to give me a date. If he wants to get married today, then I'm going to marry him."

"What about a marriage license? Did you think of that?"

Cam reached into his back pocket and retrieved what Seg could only assume was a marriage license.

"This is not funny," Milly groused.

"We'll let you put together a party," Dare told his future stepsister-in-law.

"Really?"

Seg was shocked at how that seemed to appease the woman. In the short time he'd known her, he'd learned that Milly Holcomb was the female equivalent of the Tasmanian devil. Sure, she'd been a little subdued when she was pregnant, but Seg had seen a different side of her since then.

"Are we ready now?" Cam asked, glancing around. "I assume no one is going to interrupt this ceremony or insist that these two should not be married."

All eyes went to Milly.

Her fingers went to her mouth and she zipped the imaginary zipper before moving closer to AJ, who was holding their sleeping daughter.

When Cam spoke again, Seg moved closer to his mother, his eyes on the life-changing event taking place in front of him. Although he was happy for the couple, he couldn't take his eyes off Roan.

His husband.

It was amazing how much his life had changed from a year ago. He'd come out of the closet to the world and married the man of his dreams. They had a son, a house … a life.

And to think, it all started with a little harmless one-night stand.

Seg grinned.

Yeah.

It was safe to say there was absolutely nothing harmless about that night.

And if he could go back and do it all again, he damn sure wouldn't change a single thing.

Oh, except maybe a little more than one night in the beginning.

Then again, he had a lifetime to make up for all the time they'd lost that first year.

♥□□□□♥□□□□♥

I hope you enjoyed Roan and Seg's story. Harmless is the fourth and final book in the Pier 70 series. And if you didn't know, Seg is from my Austin Arrows series. You can read more about the sexy guys in charge of the marina or the smoking hot Austin Arrows hockey players by checking them out on my website.

Personally, I wish the Pier 70 series could go on forever. I absolutely adore all the men. Not to mention, Milly. And yes, for those of you who have asked, Milly will have a story. It will likely be a novella, but at this time, I don't know when it will be written.

Want to see some fun stuff related to the Pier 70 series, you can find extras on my website. Or how about what's coming next? Find more at: www.NicoleEdwardsAuthor.com

If you're interested in keeping up to date on the Pier 70 crew as well as receiving updates on all that I'm working on, you can sign up for my monthly newsletter.

Want a simple, *fast* way to get updates on new releases? You can also sign up for text messaging. If you are in the U.S. simply text NICOLE to 64600 or sign up on my website. I promise not to spam your phone. This is just my way of letting you know what's happening because I know you're busy, but if you're anything like me, you always have your phone on you.

And last but certainly not least, if you want to see what's going on with me each week, sign up for my weekly Hot Sheet! It's a short, entertaining weekly update of things going on in my life and that of the team that supports me. We're a little crazy at times and this is a firsthand account of our antics.

Acknowledgments

There were times when I wondered whether this book was actually going to be written. Throughout the first three books, I knew something was going on with Roan, but I wasn't sure what. I knew something was going to happen to his sister, but it wasn't until I was writing it that it all made sense.

Okay, now on to the acknowledgments. I know that I will likely leave out someone important, but here goes.

First of all, I have to say thank you to my amazing husband who puts up with me every single day. If it wasn't for him and his belief that I could do this, I wouldn't be writing this today. He has been my backbone.

Chancy Powley ... Chancy, Chancy, Chancy. All those hours spent on the phone is what motivated me through this book. I love our brain storming sessions and I hope we have many, many more.

I have to thank my beta readers – Denise Sprung, Amber Willis, Allison Holzapfel, and Karen DiGaetano. Ladies, I look forward to what the future has in store for us. Thank you for coming along for the ride.

Wander Aguiar...where do I begin? A HUGE thank you to you and Andrey for making my characters come to life on the new covers. They are better than I ever could've imagined and I can't wait to work on another project with you!

Thank you to my proofreaders. Jenna Underwood, Annette Elens, Theresa Martin, and Sara Gross. It's your attention to detail that has allowed this book to be the best that it can be.

I also have to thank my street team – Naughty (and nice) Girls – Your unwavering support is something I will never take for granted. So, thank you Traci Hyland, Maureen Ames, Cindy Rockey-Bocz, Erin Lewis, Jackie Wright, Chris Geier, Kara Hildebrand, Shannon Thompson, Tracy Barbour, Nadine Hunter, Toni Thompson, and Rachelle Newham.

I can't forget my copyeditor, Amy at Blue Otter Editing. Thank goodness I've got you to catch all my punctuation, grammar, and tense errors.

Nicole Nation 2.0 for the constant support and love. You've been there for me from almost the beginning. This group of ladies has kept me going for so long, I'm not sure I'd know what to do without them.

And, of course, YOU, the reader. Your emails, messages, posts, comments, tweets... they mean more to me than you can imagine. I thrive on hearing from you, knowing that my characters and my stories have touched you in some way keeps me going. I've been known to shed a tear or two when reading an email because you simply bring so much joy to my life with your support. I thank you for that.

About Nicole Edwards

New York Times and *USA Today* bestselling author Nicole Edwards lives in Austin, Texas with her husband, their three kids, and four rambunctious dogs. When she's not writing about sexy alpha males, Nicole can often be found with her Kindle in hand or making an attempt to keep the dogs happy. You can find her hanging out on Facebook and interacting with her readers - even when she's supposed to be writing.

Nicole also writes contemporary/new adult romance as Timberlyn Scott.

Website: www.NicoleEdwardsAuthor.com
Facebook: www.facebook.com/Author.Nicole.Edwards
Twitter: @NicoleEAuthor

By Nicole Edwards

The Alluring Indulgence Series
Kaleb
Zane
Travis
Holidays with the Walker Brothers
Ethan
Braydon
Sawyer
Brendon

The Austin Arrows Series
Rush
Kaufman

The Bad Boys of Sports Series
Bad Reputation
Bad Business

The Caine Cousins Series
Hard to Hold
Hard to Handle

The Club Destiny Series
Conviction
Temptation
Addicted
Seduction
Infatuation
Captivated
Devotion
Perception
Entrusted
Adored
Distraction

The Coyote Ridge Series
Curtis
Jared

The Dead Heat Ranch Series
Boots Optional
Betting on Grace
Overnight Love

By Nicole Edwards (cont.)

The Devil's Bend Series

Chasing Dreams
Vanishing Dreams

The Devil's Playground Series

Without Regret
Without Restraint

The Office Intrigue Series

Office Intrigue
Intrigued Out of the Office
Their Rebellious Submissive

The Pier 70 Series

Reckless
Fearless
Speechless
Harmless

The Sniper 1 Security Series

Wait for Morning
Never Say Never
Tomorrow's Too Late

The Southern Boy Mafia Series

Beautifully Brutal
Beautifully Loyal

Standalone Novels

A Million Tiny Pieces
Inked on Paper

Writing as Timberlyn Scott

Unhinged
Unraveling
Chaos

Naughty Holiday Editions

2015
2016

BECAUSE NAUGHTY CAN BE OH SO NICE.®

NE LTD